DAVE vs.
THE
MONSTERS
ASCENDANCE

JOHN BIRMINGHAM

DAVE vs. THE MONSTERS

ASCENDANCE

TITAN BOOKS

Dave vs. the Monsters: Ascendance
Print edition ISBN: 9781781166253
E-book edition ISBN: 9781781166260

Published by Titan Books
A division of Titan Publishing Group Ltd
144 Southwark Street, London SE1 0UP

First edition: June 2015
2 4 6 8 10 9 7 5 3 1

A CIP catalogue record for this title is available from the British Library.

Printed and bound by CPI Group (UK) Ltd, Croydon, CR0 4YY

For my mum, who always checked my spelling.

PROLOGUE

LOS ANGELES

Wasn't no mystery to it.

Jellybean knew where all the customers got to. 'Cept for the neediest fiends, they was all hunkered down in the hovels as evening fell, watching cable news and hiding from monsters.

Jellybean shot a dark, Pepsi-flavoured stream of spit through the gap between his front teeth. A thin tendril of sticky-sweet drool dropped onto his Lakers singlet, staining it. Right now, looking over the empty car lot in front of the Retread Warehouse, the only souls he could see were the ones Stross owned, looking bored with business. Moping around in front of the 'done clinic. And that was some telling shit right there. The corner with the methadone clinic was always busiest. There were a couple of packs of runners here and there, little kids, not running anywhere right now, on account of having no fiends to step and fetch it to.

'Monsters,' said Jellybean, shaking his head.

At first they'd been great for business. Dope fiends spilling out on the streets to party, everyone talking a big game about N'Orleans. And when the army and that dumb cracker kicked ass outside of Omaha? Man, that was like Christmas and Thanksgiving got high and had themselves an orgy with the Fourth of July's hot sister. Fiends were kickin' it. Not just fiends though. Everyone, the whole city. You could hear music all over and there was fireworks and everyone was out on the street, and then that Super Dave asshole turned up in LA to party in person?

Damn. They banked some foldable currency that day, Jose. Not much since though.

And not today, that was for damn sure.

Couldn't hear no music now either, but you could see fireworks in the gathering gloom, if tracer rounds counted. You could hear the crackle and hammer of automatic weapons all over LA. Sometimes, like just now, long ropy streams of fire, all orange and yellow, flew up from the earth, racing away into the sky. You heard sirens, of course. But they weren't always racing toward the gunfire. Fat Skin told Jellybean the cops weren't even busting motherfuckers for open carry. Not even hassling, bro! They just pointing, saying, monsters-be-that-a-way-son. Go git.

And that was terrifying, because Jellybean Johnson might not go to church these days, but those nuns they beat the fear of God in deep. And flip over the fear of God you gots your fear of the Devil and all his works.

Devil's work was what happened down N'Orleans. And the Devil's fiends be those sabre-tooth orc motherfuckers with Godzilla's own cojones. Them and the dragons and the fuckin' zombies they got shambling around the ass-end of Nebraska now.

Jellybean searched for the gun at his hip, even though he could feel the weight of it there. He just needed to touch the grip, to reassure himself.

Thing was, the mayor? He'd lost his shit. Weren't one damn monster anywhere inside LA. They all out in the desert getting smoked by the air force. But whitey already freaked the fuck out. Open carry was proof of that.

That's what scared Jellybean. White money was the most powerful gang in the city. It didn't just rule, it was an absolute fucking monarch.

Didn't need demons coming in here to tear this city down. It was gonna tear itself apart because the king gone mad.

Jellybean could feel it coming.

Wait.

No.

He could hear it.

Screaming.

Not just the random screaming of some bitch gettin' schooled by her old man, or someone gone crazy on bath salts or something.

A lot of screaming by a lot of people.

They could hear it down on the corners too, he could see that.

Dog-10 and the King were already weapons out, hard up against cover. Knees bent, Dog-10 leaned into the corner of the 7-Eleven and bobbed his head around, gun first.

Jellybean heard the flat crack of the pistol, slightly muted by distance.

Two shots, a pause, then three.

Then all at once everything broke open down on the streets. The corner crews blasting away at nothing Jellybean could see yet. The runners fleeing, adding their tiny high-pitched cries to the swelling crowd noise that rolled toward them like a big surf.

He fumbled his own weapon free, looking for something to shoot. Jellybean saw movement a few blocks away. Hundreds of people, maybe thousands. All running and screaming, all coming straight at him. The roar of the crowd swelled and swallowed the gunfire. First Tonik broke and then Fingaz, and then all of Mr Stross's soldiers be running.

Jellybean found himself doing a stupid dance, a little two-step. One step toward the rusted ladder that would carry him to the ground. One step back toward the AK leaned up against the roofline.

No way would Officer fuckin' Friendly be letting Jellybean Johnson step out with a Kalashnikov. But that sort of artillery was precisely what a captain needed to own this area of operations.

That's what Stross always called the hood. The area of operations. Didn't matter which hood. It was always the area of operations to Mr Stross.

Jellybean stood, dancing from toe to toe, at the broken, grimy parapet of the Retread Warehouse, with his mouth hanging open as a human tide washed over Stross's area of operations. You could see those peeps were running from something. So many of them screaming, looking back over they shoulders, sometimes stumbling and tripping when they turned. Getting ploughed under, trampled by the madness of the herd.

Well, fuck Stross and fuck his operations, Jellybean decided. He turned and ran as fast as his stumpy, overstuffed sausage legs would carry him toward the creaky ladder that would deliver him to the ground. He had time, just enough time he was sure, to jump into his ride and lay down some tyre smoke headed for anywhere but here.

He had no idea what the crowd was running from, but it had to be something as bad as N'Orleans. Had to be monsters for reals this time.

His hand drifted to the gun at his hip as he made the ladder and put his foot on the first rung. But of course he couldn't climb down while he was holding a big-ass .45.

And then he understood that he couldn't climb down at all. Because he was too late. The monster was already here.

Standing – no, floating! – actually floating like a magic motherfucker directly below him in the dark, shaded lee of the Retread Warehouse.

Jellybean didn't stop to take in the show. He got a quick impression of some long thin streak of evil misery, somehow drifting a foot or so above the ground, and his balls crawled up into his body and kept on going. They crawled so high, so fast, they might have choked him if he hadn't reacted with the quick wit and immoral ruthlessness that had allowed him to rise so high in the esteem and organisation of Mr AOR Stross.

Without thinking on consequence, Jellybean Johnson aimed the silver-plated big-ass Colt and unloaded half the clip directly into the melon of that spooky floating motherfucker directly beneath his feet.

01

Dave's gun dropped to the floor with a loud, metallic clatter. He flinched, expecting it to go off, but it didn't. He had carefully removed the magazine and thumbed the safety on before warping out of the underground garage to infiltrate the Russian consulate. If by infiltrate, you meant put a wrecking ball through the place.

'What the hell!' Trinder yelped. The dark-suited spook flinched too, although whether at the sound of the gun landing on the concrete, or at the sight of Dave disappearing and then reappearing in the literal blink of an eye, he could not say. The agents flanking Trinder reflexively dropped into a shooter's stance, each reaching for their weapon. Dave knew them from Las Vegas. Comeau and the woman called Madigan. They both realised what had happened at the same time, and he saw the uncertainty in their eyes. They had seen him do this before. The man, Comeau, was the first to lower his gun. Madigan followed only when Trinder gave her permission to stand down.

'Sorry,' said Dave, nodding toward the pistol he'd dropped on the floor. 'Told you I'm not great with guns. An uncle tried to teach me, when he was sober, which wasn't often. He did show me how to turn it off though and take the bullets out.'

Trinder, not really hiding his disgust, was about to speak when the rumble and crash from the half-destroyed consulate building rolled over them. Probably a supporting wall or another part of the second floor collapsing. The sound of smashing glass arrived as a tinkling counterpoint to the deep bass notes of his demolition work. Trinder looked more shocked than he had when Dave performed his little magic trick of popping into and out of the world. A cell phone buzzed, and Trinder took a BlackBerry from his pocket. He looked at the screen, not really paying attention. He turned it off. His eyes, bloodshot and a little jaundiced now that Dave looked, darted up toward the street.

'What the hell did you do out there?' he asked. He sounded almost fearful.

'Yeah, about that,' Dave said. 'The whole sneaking into the embassy thing didn't go so well.'

Agent Comeau took a few tentative steps toward the garage ramp, his knees bent and his shoulders bowed as though he expected this building to fall in on top of them too.

'I think the Russians are going to need another consulate,' Comeau said when he was able to see something of what had happened up on E91st Street.

Trinder looked as though he had been poleaxed, and Dave even felt a little sorry for him. He himself was still coming to terms with everything that had happened, and he'd at least had some time to get used to the idea. Enough time to sneak into the consulate, explore the building, track down Karen Warat and destroy a couple of rooms – the better part of a whole floor really – fighting her at warp speed. Enough time to all but get his ass handed to him before Lucille saved that same worthless ass. And how she'd managed that, he still couldn't say. Time enough to get beaten to a broken and bloody pulp, to recover, to fight to a dishonourable draw and then to cut a deal with Warat, or Varatchevsky, or whatever her name was, and to return here to the garage under the Office of Special Clearances and Records. Or under a building these guys leased, at any rate. He doubted this was Trinder's actual Death Star.

Dave had done all that in the space between two of Agent Trinder's heartbeats. But for Hooper it had taken nearly three-quarters of an hour.

Nothing had changed in the basement garage. Trinder and his goons hadn't moved, except for a step or two backward in surprise at Dave's magic act. The same cars, mostly black SUVs, were still parked in the same slots. The elevator doors were closed, the car still up on the fourth floor where OSCAR had offices. But outside on the street all was violent disorder. Screams, honking horns, the muted thunder of the Russian consulate imploding. It had to be messing with Trinder's head. Had to be messing with all of them.

'You might want to run up there and grab your mole,' Dave said. 'That little girl you had holding the door open for me, if that's what she was doing. I put her out on the street. She's probably freaking out. It looked like one of the embassy guards had figured out she was up to no good and, you know, since I just demolished half the building they're probably going to want to beat her with rubber hoses or something while they ask her about it.'

'Agent Madigan,' said Trinder, rubbing his eyes. 'If you would.'

The woman in the black pants suit said, 'Yes, sir,' and

hurried up the ramp, holstering her weapon as she went.

'Anything else I need to know, like what the fuck happened?' Trinder said.

Dave shrugged and pushed gently at the gun on the ground with the toe of his boot, carefully turning the muzzle away from Comeau.

'Had no trouble getting in,' he said. 'That little cutie you had on the inside just held the door open for me. I wandered in, had a look around. Didn't see anything on the ground floor, just a bunch of office workers. There were a couple of gorillas guarding a staircase down a hallway, so I checked it out. Poked around upstairs, found your spy, or you know, she found me. There was no warping around her. She hadn't slowed down at all. Matter of fact, I'd have said she was chock full of 'roids and amphetamines, she moved that quick and hit that hard.'

Agent Comeau, a wiry-looking Mediterranean type, rejoined them from the foot of the ramp where he'd been trying to keep an eye on the street. He looked Dave up and down. A very sceptical look.

'But you're okay now? And you don't have her with you. So what happened up there?' Trinder jerked his thumb toward the street.

'She pretty much kicked my ass, damn near killed me, in fact,' Dave said, hefting the splitting maul up into the palm of his hand. 'Lucille here is the only reason I'm still alive.'

'Oh, this is not good,' said Trinder, mostly to himself. He was looking at the ground, his eyes sweeping back and forth as though he might find something there to help him.

'Nah, it's okay,' said Dave. 'I got better.'

'That's not what I meant,' Trinder snapped. 'I understand

it's the case, Mr Hooper, that you weren't particularly good at listening to Captain Heath. But you're not even listening to yourself. You just told us that one of the most dangerous hostile agents ever set loose in this country had no trouble defeating you in close combat. *You*, the superhero.'

The way Trinder said 'superhero', it sounded as though he didn't really believe it. Dave got that a lot.

'Well I wouldn't say she *defeated* me,' he said. 'She just kicked my ass is all. And look, I gave her plenty to be gettin' on with. So in the end we called it a draw.'

'Where is she now?' asked Trinder, sounding very tired.

'I dunno,' muttered Dave, reminding himself of one of his sons. When neither of the OSCAR men looked happy with the answer he followed on. 'I think she was going to go talk to her boss.'

Comeau's eyes went wide and Trinder stared at him.

'She what?' The senior agent's voice sounded small and cracked.

Dave held up his hand, forestalling the ass-chewing he sensed was coming.

'Look, she knew all about you guys. It's not like I gave away any secrets or anything. She obviously knew about you because she escaped when you tried to arrest her. Remember that? When you fucked everything up?'

Trinder did not look as though he appreciated being reminded of the bungled raid at the art gallery opening a week or so earlier. On the day the monsters crawled out from the UnderRealms.

'Yeah, she's got your number, buddy,' Dave said, grinning at him. 'But I don't think you have to worry. We had a talk. All she wants to do is go home and kill monsters for mother

Russia. Thresh. And Morphum, and Krevish and Djinn. She doesn't like you much, Trinder, but she doesn't think you're a monster. Just an asshole.'

Trinder was about to say something when his eye was drawn to the ramp, which Madigan now hurried a young woman down. The pretty little secretary Dave had removed from the consulate before he and Warat had torn the place down. So, it looked like he got at least one thing right today. Trinder waved Madigan and her young charge past and they hurried toward the elevator, which pinged open just as they arrived. Another woman stepped out, dressed in the dark suit Dave was coming to think of as a uniform for these guys. He recognised her instantly from Las Vegas. He knew his notoriously sketchy memory had received an upgrade from his recent embiggening, but there'd have been no forgetting this chick. A smoking hot Asian, with half her face covered in some sort of tattoo. Dave had to adjust his grip on Lucille, moving her slightly to conceal the sudden, unseemly bulge in his black combat coveralls. His memory wasn't the only part of him that'd got a tune up.

'Anyway,' he said, trying not to think about the tattooed hottie, 'there's no way you can stop her from getting home.'

Unless a sniper puts a bullet in her head, I suppose.

'If you could live with 50,000 nuclear warheads pointed at you for so long, I reckon you'll cope with a treacherous blonde and her samurai sword. She's going to tell her bosses the same thing about me, which you may not care about, but I do.'

Both Trinder and Comeau turned their attention fully back to Dave.

'You didn't think I'd thought it through, did you? Because if you have a hard-on for taking Varatchevsky out of the game, it has to be a lay-down certainty that your opposite number back in the USSR feels the same way about me. Right?'

'It's not the USSR anymore,' said Trinder.

'Beatles reference,' said Dave as the exotic young woman hurried up to them. 'Anyway, my super friend and I have agreed we won't be doing any more UFC cage matches. In fact, we're going to catch up in an hour or so, after she's talked her guys off the ledge, and we're going to swap information. The thing she killed, this big-ass Thresh daemon, it's not like Urgon. It knows different things, which seems to mean that she knows different things. It'd be cool if she and I could compare notes and –'

'Absolutely not,' Trinder barked. He spoke so abruptly, so loudly, that the young woman who was jogging toward them flinched. It was a more obvious reaction than the slight flush Dave had seen on her caramel-coloured features, the widening of her eyes, when she'd got a whiff of ol' Super Dave's secret sauce. 'You can't share intelligence with an enemy agent.'

And then Trinder froze. His teeth, yellowed by nicotine, bit off the end of the last thing he had said. His nostrils flared and his eyes slitted, giving him a dangerous canine appearance.

'What the hell?' said Dave, and then realised someone other than him had hit the pause button. Comeau was frowning, hands on hips. The Asian chick had been caught mid-stride and was actually floating, suspended a few inches off the concrete floor. Dave could see now that she wasn't Vietnamese as he had thought, but some mix of races which had passed through Southeast Asia at some point, with a good pinch of African-American stirred into the melting pot. The doors on the elevator from which she had emerged were starting to close, and he could see Madigan and the shoulder of the young Russian woman through the gap. He looked back toward the ramp, surprised, yet not at all surprised, to find Colonel Varatchevsky, still rocking her spanky black motorcycle leathers, striding down from the street. A sword hilt poked up over one shoulder.

Dave's first thought was that she had come, or been sent, to retrieve the traitor, the secretary he had rescued.

'I thought we were gonna be cool,' he said. It sounded like a protest, a weak one. He didn't see how he could stop her taking the girl back without an explosion of cartoon violence that would bring this building down around their ears just like the Russian one.

'I heard what Agent Trinder said. You can't share with the enemy.' Karen smiled.

She took her foot off the accelerator – it had to be her; Dave had done nothing – and they dropped out of warp.

'Yes he can,' she said, raising her voice, addressing Trinder directly.

The tattooed female agent gave a little squeal of surprise as she landed and found the enemy in their midst. Trinder cursed and Comeau drew his weapon again but Dave put a hand on his arm. Comeau's draw seemed inhumanly fast, until you understood what 'inhuman' really meant.

'Don't, man,' said Dave, easing the agent's gun arm back down. 'She'll kill you before you can even squeeze off a shot.'

'I will,' said Karen, a statement of fact, not a threat.

'Stop her, Hooper. Put her down,' Trinder demanded.

'Stop her doing what?' Dave asked. 'If she was going to do anything, it'd be all over by now.'

'Mr Trinder, sir?' It was the Asian girl. Trinder seemed even more unhappy at being interrupted than he was at finding

Karen Warat in his basement. Probably, Dave thought, because he knew he could safely shift his ire on to his underling.

'What?' he snapped.

'It's Washington, sir,' said the young woman. And then she faltered in her already nervous delivery, her eyes flicking toward the Russian spy, before being drawn to Dave. Always to Dave.

Colonel Varatchevsky spoke before Trinder's agent could continue. 'She came down to tell you what I came to tell you, Hooper,' she said. 'The monsters are back. They're here. In the city.'

02

'Boston has been trying to reach you, sir,' the agent confirmed. 'And the Pentagon. And Homeland.'

'I turned my phone off, Agent Nguyen,' snapped Trinder. 'With good reason.'

'Yeah, because it's a BlackBerry.' Dave smirked.

He thought he saw Agent Comeau suppress a grin. Karen Warat was eating protein bars, peeling the wrappers and inhaling the contents as though she were loading bullets into a gun. Dave wasn't feeling all that hungry, yet, but he knew he'd burned through a lot of his reserves fighting her, and then repairing the damage from that fight. He patted down the pockets of his coveralls looking for something to eat.

'What does Boston want?' asked Trinder, with the air of a man who didn't care for the answer.

Nguyen tried to keep her face blank, but failed. Even the boss-looking tattoo couldn't hide her grimace. She really didn't want to be the messenger.

'You've been ordered to detach Mr Hooper back to OSTP for temporary –'

She didn't finish. All of the colour which had previously

leached away from Trinder's features came flooding back in a hot, red flush.

'The hell I will,' he said, loud enough that it echoed around the garage.

'Sir, if you would just turn on your phone . . .' Agent Nguyen said, or tried to. Her cute little mouth froze in a perfect 'O'.

Dave was ready for it this time.

'Will you stop doing that!' he said, turning to Warat, the only other human being who was still in motion. She had frozen the others, or warped with Hooper, or whatever the fuck it was they were doing when they did this. He was beginning to understand how annoying it must be when he did it to other people.

'We don't have time for their bullshit,' said Warat, tossing him an energy gel. 'I just orbed out of the consul-general's office while I was explaining why I had to cut the third secretary into sushi chunks. We have monsters to fight. So eat up, Super Dave.'

He caught the packet and frowned.

'You know, you really shouldn't call me that unless you mean it,' he said, emptying the gel with one squeeze. He didn't mind blowing off Trinder. The guy was turning out to be even more of a pain than Heath; although, admittedly, not nearly as much as Compton had been. And since Karen hadn't said or done anything about that little Russian woman he'd rescued, the smart money was on getting her out of Trinder's building before she noticed Agent Madigan spiriting the girl away. He'd explain it to Trinder later. Couldn't let big bad Colonel Varatchevsky catch them in the act.

'Okay. Let's go,' he said. 'Where are these critters at?'

Dave hefted Lucille across one shoulder. She was humming their special tune again.

'Forty-second Street,' Warat said as they jogged up the ramp.

East 91st Street looked even worse than it had before. Traffic had been piling up outside the ruins of the consulate, smoke and people pouring from the wreckage, when Karen hit warp. Dave could hear a long, unnatural wail which had to be sirens, and one police car, its flashers caught turning, threw a crazy blue glow up the side of the buildings. The cops had driven their patrol car right up onto the sidewalk and been busy trying to direct consulate workers away from the burning building, while ordering rubber neckers to get the hell back across the street. To get the hell out of the street altogether. The frozen tableau looked like some sort of cinematic special effect to Hooper, and he realised he had never really seen so many people caught in his . . . what? His warp field?

'You did this, right?' he asked, waving a hand at the unmoving chaos.

'You helped,' said Karen.

'No, I don't mean the demolition job. I mean the pause button, the warp field, whatever you call it. I didn't do it, you did, right?'

She strode on down the sidewalk, weaving her way around the living human statuary.

'Yeah, come on,' she said. 'I want to try something.'

Dave found himself wondering if Karen had caught a whiff of his super-powered pheromones. She hadn't given the slightest hint that she was affected by them. He'd seen the flush colouring Madigan's cheeks, and the sexy Asian chick with the tattoos on her face as well. They got within about twenty yards of him and he could tell they just had to . . .

'Knock it off, you fucking idiot. I wouldn't suck your dick if it blew espresso martinis.'

Dave almost tripped over his own feet he stopped so suddenly. Karen rolled her eyes.

'The Threshrend are empath daemons. All the sects use them. When I get close enough, I can tell what they're thinking, and, God help me, you're even easier to read than they are.'

'You can read my mind?' asked Dave, alarmed at the idea.

'Don't worry,' she said. 'You're more Dr Seuss than Tolstoy. Now get on. I want to try this.'

She swung a leg over a motorcycle, a big-ass rice-burning Jap number.

'You ever try this?'

Dave looked dubious.

'You mean riding? While, you know . . .' He twirled a finger to take in the stalled world around them. 'No,' he admitted. Probably because he'd presumed it wouldn't work. Or if it did, that any machinery would just run stupidly slow.

Warat seemed to have none of his reservations. She had a key for the motorcycle, perhaps explaining the leathers she wore. One long leg scissored over the bike, she seated herself, turned the key, flicked a succession of switches and thumbed the ignition. The bike roared into life.

'Get on,' she said, indicating the pillion passenger space behind her.

'I don't normally need to be asked twice to climb on for a lady,' said Dave. 'But what about helmets and Lucille and your nasty little friend there?' He indicated her sword. 'Last guy who touched that thing, I heard his arms fell off.'

Warat regarded him with a look verging on contempt. She slid the scabbard off her shoulder, examined the sword and tossed it at him without warning.

'Catch!'

'Fuck!' squawked Dave, but he couldn't help himself, plucking the sheathed weapon out of midair. No body parts fell off him.

'I don't think it will be a problem.' Warat smiled. 'That guy you heard about didn't even touch the blade, just the scabbard. Get on. It'll be quicker and we'll save energy.'

He passed her sword back, frowning. 'You know, for a traitorous bitch, you're quite an asshole.'

She passed one arm through the old leather strap of the katana's sheath and seated it comfortably on her back again.

'I'm not a traitor,' she said. 'I'm a patriot. Just not for your country.'

Dave was still trying to get his head around the idea. Her voice, her looks, her energy, everything about her was so American. He carefully climbed on the bike, a Honda, gripping Lucille up near the business end, and slipping his other arm around Varatchevsky's waist.

'Nice abs. You work out, right?'

'Just because the sword didn't cut you doesn't mean the sword wouldn't cut you. Now shut the fuck up and hold on.'

Warat leaned forward slightly and Dave felt one arm flex as she fed power into the bike. They leaped away from the sidewalk and threaded through the chess pieces of all those motionless bystanders and consular workers. He felt awkward, riding behind her, as though he might spill off at any moment, but Warat seemed entirely comfortable. Her body flowed with the bike as it leaned one way then the other. Immobile figures blurred past on both sides as she accelerated away from the weird, 3D still of the burning building. He adjusted quickly, finding his balance in a way he knew would not have been possible a week earlier.

By the time she leaned into the turn onto 5th Avenue, Dave was seated as comfortably on the speeding Honda as she was. He'd only ridden a motorcycle once in his life. A disastrous misadventure at a county fair as a teenager. He'd put the little dirt bike straight through a fence and come out of hospital with twelve stitches and a promise never to ride again. Now he felt as though he could take the wheel of this thing and give the Russian a run for her money. Just as soon as she showed him which buttons to push to turn it on and off.

Sadness caught him by surprise. Marty Grbac would have loved to race this bike.

They roared down the avenue, heading toward 42nd Street. Dave found it easier to keep his gaze forward, over her shoulder, watching her anticipate the moves needed to plot a course through thousands of motionless, or nearly motionless, vehicles. He knew the stasis wasn't total, that the world was still moving, but that they were moving through it on some hyper-accelerated fast track. He also knew that even using the motorcycle, they were still burning energy, running down their reserves, to hold the warp field in place.

Or maybe he was wrong.

Maybe they hadn't hit pause on the whole world. Maybe they were in something like a bubble, bending space and time around them, and only them. Urgon knew nothing of this ability and Dave was no better informed. He didn't know how he'd even begin figuring it out. Whenever he was in warp anybody who might help him, a friendly Nobel-winning physicist for instance, was frozen out of the effect.

The Honda screamed past a line of yellow cabs which were

crawling slowly – very fucking slowly now – past Saks. He wondered how the drivers and passengers would experience the motorcycle's passage. As an inexplicable blur of light and sound? A small sonic boom?

Dave held tightly to Lucille, who was humming louder as they moved downtown. Could Warat hear it too, the murder song? He supposed not, since he couldn't hear any backing vocals from her magical sword.

And then his stomach clenched.

Hunger.

A second pang, stronger and lasting twice as long quickly followed.

'Stop,' he yelled in her ear. 'Pull over.'

He was pushed into her back as she applied the brakes and brought them to a fast stop near the intersection of 5th and E49th Street.

The bubble didn't burst. Everything and everyone but them remained suspended.

'What?' Karen asked, exasperated.

'Sorry. You gotta gimme a second. Honest, it's important.'

'It had better be,' she warned.

He dismounted the Honda. Light blazed from storefronts and above them from office windows climbing away into the sky. Turning a quick circle he estimated he could see thousands of people, hundreds of vehicles. And beyond them? The whole city, a stopped watch. All of existence, frozen.

His stomach cramped again and hot flushes followed cold chills through his body. There was no way they could be doing this to the whole world. He'd been turned into some sort of mystical freak, but he was still an engineer and he knew that the energies needed to affect all of existence like this – even mystical energies – were so vast as to be impossible. Whatever effect he and Warat had generated, and were maintaining, it had to be limited to them. They couldn't, for instance, be dragging the planet out of its orbital track. But even limited to some temporal bubble around the two of them alone, there was a cost. Just as there had been a cost for all of the energy he'd spent fighting her.

Karen was starting to look annoyed.

'We don't have time for you to scratch your balls and ponder the mysteries of magical physics,' she said, obviously reading him.

'Just give me a minute,' he said testily. 'They're not going anywhere.' He waved his hand at the tableau around them.

'No, Hooper. We're the ones not going anywhere.'

Dave let her protests fall behind him as he found what he wanted a short way down 49th. A steakhouse.

'One minute. Promise,' he called back to Warat as he started toward the restaurant. Another racking gut cramp doubled him over, almost tripped him as he mounted the sidewalk at the corner. He was careful not to bump into anyone as he passed. He could probably impart enough energy with a tap to send them flying when his time stream synced with theirs again. Best not to take the chance.

He recognised the steakhouse as part of a chain operation, but a boutique chain. Smith and Wollensky. There was one in Houston that was popular with the carpet walkers at Baron's. Dave left Lucille by the door and carefully picked his way through the suits at the entrance and into the main dining room. His mouth flooded with saliva as he smelled chargrilled meat and melted cheese and the salty goodness of deep-fried carbs.

'Sorry, darlin',' he said to a waitress as he ghosted past her.

'I only got time for a dine and dash.'

Two bizoids in dark suits and hundred dollar haircuts were already tucking into their mains at a nearby table. Without ceremony or apology he scooped up the long-boned rib eye of the older, portlier gent and, grimacing, the steak tartare of his companion. The loose pile of nearly raw meat started to come apart in his hands, forcing Hooper to stuff the lot into his mouth. He had memories of hating this dish, but when the uncooked flesh hit his taste buds it arrived as a revelation.

'Fark,' he gargled, surprised at how much he blissed out to the taste and mouth-feel. If they got through this latest orc attack he was definitely coming back for more. He'd even pay for it. Or get Trinder to. He hurried back out, licking his fingers and stuffing a couple of baked potatoes into his pockets. He grabbed up the enchanted splitting maul and tore huge bites from the rib eye as he trotted back to Warat through the unmoving crowds and traffic.

'You want some?' he asked, around a mouthful of half-chewed meat.

Her face curled into a disgusted expression, but she took the proffered bone and bit off at least half the remaining flesh. She chewed and swallowed quickly, as if not wanting to be caught at it.

'You really know how to show a girl a good time, don't you?' she said, wiping blood from her chin.

'They had fries. Smelled good too. I could grab some?'

'No. Hurry up and finish.'

He did as he was told, throwing the bone into the gutter. Seated securely behind her again, he leaned forward slightly as they accelerated away. His cheek touched the hilt of her sword; the same sword which had cut down the agent who'd tried to grab it during Trinder's raid on her art gallery. It wasn't even giving Dave a close shave. He wondered if Varatchevsky would be able to pick up Lucille. Only he had, so far.

The early evening traffic along 5th Avenue whipped past them in a neon blur. The roar of the big bike drowned out the weird background rumble and hiss of the city he'd been aware of since they'd entered warp. Warat weaved through the river of light and steel with fluid grace. A slight shift of her hips to one side, a faint lean to the other and the speeding motorcycle threaded this way and that with Dave doing his best to flow with it. He bet she'd never crashed a dirt bike through a fence because she panicked and forgot the difference between the throttle and the brake. She slowed down appreciably as they hit the intersections, but only to about half speed, and only long enough to pick a course through the cross-traffic. On the far side of the barrier they roared away.

Dave recognised the lions in front of the New York Public Library from about a block away, at the same time as he felt Lucille grow warm and light in his right hand. Her song started to fill his head, as it had every time they raced into a fight with the Horde. The traffic seemed thicker at 5th and 42nd, in a way it hadn't been at the previous cross street. Warat slowed and approached the intersection with greater caution, taking them through the dense, frozen parade at something approaching a reasonable speed, maybe thirty or forty miles per hour.

As they rounded the corner and sped up again he noted the first signs of a change. Far ahead of them the street was jammed with pedestrians and vehicles. He could see people caught sprinting away from something. Some looking back over their shoulders. Some with their heads down and their arms pumping like they were in the last few seconds of a dash for the hundred metre Olympic gold. All of them immobile, trapped by the magic spell that allowed Dave and Varatchevsky to warp from E91st to 42nd Street in less time than it would take those sprinters to move a few inches through space. Karen laid them on a fast track down the centreline of 42nd, and the Honda shrieked as she cranked the throttle. Buildings blurred past, the greenery of Bryant Park a verdant smear on his left. They were moving too quickly for Dave to make out the features or even the outlines of any individual pedestrians, but by the time they were a block down from the library he could tell that the crowd was a mob in full, terrified flight. Lucille felt as light as bamboo in his clenched fist, her battle hymn something he felt as well as heard, the chorus of unseen angels. It filled him with her needs. Her hungers. He felt himself press into Karen Warat's leathers, into the scabbard and hilt of her sword as she slammed on the brakes.

'Jump,' she said.

And then she was gone and he was airborne as the bike impacted with the side panel of a yellow cab.

03

He was aware of time stuttering back into motion just before they struck the vehicle. Warat was there and then she wasn't. Her body tensing, muscles contracting before she seemed to fly directly up, as though launched from an ejector seat. Dave, who wasn't ready and who didn't jump, saw the yellow cab move suddenly. Not toward him, but across his field of vision as they dropped out of warp and the world transitioned from stasis to movement without the slightest lurch of inertia. He heard screams, and the honking of horns. He heard the crunch of metal on metal, and had time enough to realise it wasn't the bike hitting the taxi. And then the bike hit the taxi anyway and he was thrown into the sky and over the roof.

Everything slowed again, but not with the strange temporal distortion of whatever magic powered his ability to warp time. It was that purely subjective, deeply human experience of his senses coming fully alive. The same way perfectly normal people recalled time slowing down in a car crash, or some other non-mystical catastrophe. The simple biological quickening of a nervous system flooded with neurotransmitters.

Dave hit the accelerator, thinking to stop his flight, but of course that merely stopped the world around him and he flew on just as quickly as before. He grunted in agony as his vision pixelated and his brain seemed to press painfully against the inside of his skull.

What the fuck?

He dropped out of warp, the pixelation and the pain receding immediately. He saw the cab shunted sideways by the force of the Honda striking it, but the larger vehicle did not shear in two or fly apart, as he'd half expected. The windows exploded outwards in a shower of safety glass and he heard more screams.

At least he wasn't spinning, tumbling end over end, but his flight was uncontrolled, and he could see he was going to hit the asphalt and skittle half a dozen people. Even though Warat was spinning and tumbling, she looked like a gymnast executing a routine. She spun once, twice and landed on the road, boots thudding down, knees flexing as she dropped into a shoulder roll and came up with her sword drawn.

And Trinder expected me to kick her ass?

Dave shook off the thought as his own landing fast approached, undignified and dangerous. Without any of the Russian's skills or native grace he simply tucked himself around Lucille in a ball, and swore as he hit the road surface and felt his shoulder break. Again. The pain was huge but dull, as it always was now, and washed away almost immediately in the bathing warmth of endorphins and whatever magical fucking fairy-bots coursed through his bloodstream to make good broken bones and torn flesh. He felt the muted impact of those unfortunate enough to be caught in his path as he landed among them. He tried to close his mind to the muffled cries and startled shouts, and one sickly snapping sound, which had to be somebody's leg breaking. There was nothing to be done for them. Not yet. He knew, from Lucille's battle hymn filling all his secret places, that the Horde were upon them.

But where was Warat?

Dave climbed to his feet, muttering apologies and cringing at the sight of the seven – no, eight – people he'd just knocked down. One of them, an old woman in a bloodied head scarf, wailed and clutched at her leg that was bent all wrong at the knee. He struggled to reconcile the banal with the bizarre. A Gap Kids store, the Walgreens on the opposite corner, neon lights and giant posters for Stephen Colbert's *Late Show* and Amazon's *Man in the High Castle,* gunshots cracking out ahead of him, muted only slightly by the roar of the fleeing mob, a dead Fangr, cleanly decapitated, midnight dark daemon ichor pulsing from its neck stump.

More shots, fired rapidly, but singly. Not the automatic weapons fire he'd grown used to, or thought he had, in Omaha and New Orleans. Probably cops and probably only two of them.

He was about to punch the accelerator when somebody else did. Warat, of course.

The crowd stopped. The screams and honking horns and general chaos died away to that familiar distant rumble and hiss. But his vision fell apart in broken pixels again. The pain, the iron fist squeezing his head from the inside was back, and his hunger . . .

The bubble popped and all around him chaos and human madness surged back into motion. The uproar of thousands of voices hammered and clawed at his ears. Frantic, horrified, unbelieving. Dave was buffeted and knocked off balance, almost losing his footing in the surging tide of the terror-struck mob.

He tried one last time to pause the world, and failed. The

pain and blinding disorientation was too great. He pushed through the crowd, trying to exercise some care, but keen to break free. To find Warat. He moved about ten yards, when his stomach cramped and his head swam. He almost stumbled to his knees, but he was clear, or relatively clear, of the worst of the crush and he could see the Russian spy again.

She stood in a clear space at the meeting of Broadway and 42nd, a rough circle surrounded by nine daemons. Three Hunn. Five leashed Fangr. And one of a type he had only seen once before, on a screen in New Orleans, but which he, or rather Urgon, recognised as thresh.

No.

Not as thresh, but *Threshrend*. A fully mature adult. Battle scarred and grown into its power.

A daemon superiorae.

A boss motherfucker.

Two cops, both looking freaked out, stood a short distance behind Warat, pointing their guns at the monsters. The showdown had locked up the better part of the intersection. From the crushed and burning vehicles Dave could only assume the Hunn and their thralls had just jumped in and started laying about them with heavy war hammers and battle-axes.

The daemons looked wary, even fearful, of the naked flames from burning cars and the firewall kept them from rampaging up toward Times Square or further down into the theatre district. Traffic was piling up behind the obstacle, and getting worse as people abandoned their vehicles and fled.

The only thing stopping the tiny monster war band from forcing their way out of the intersection and charging down the terrified masses was Colonel Karin Varatchevsky, and two of New York's finest, looking very much like two of New York's most freaked out.

Bodies lay everywhere, extravagantly mutilated. But human corpses were not the only lifeless remains at Broadway and 42nd Street. Dave counted two Hunn and three Fangr down. Two of the Fangr looked like they'd been shot but a third, like the dead Fangr he had seen a few seconds ago, had obviously been carved up by Karen and her blade, which was dripping darkly. The surviving daemonum snapped and snarled at her, hunkering down on their powerfully muscled haunches, which twitched and spasmed as they either restrained themselves or tried to work up the courage for another rush.

None of the Hunn had Warat's full attention, however. That she reserved for the final member of their war party. The Threshrend daemon. As best Dave knew, they were empaths who amplified the feelings and, to a lesser extent, the thoughts of friend and foe alike. Urgon regarded them as little more than meat trumpets for blowing before battle.

Warat held the gore-streaked katana toward the warrior beasts as a warding totem, but to the toad-like monstrosity with the forest of wandering eyestalks, the Threshrend, she held out her free hand, like a traffic cop. Dave supposed she had to know what she was doing.

Whenever a Hunn would inch forward she turned her body a few inches to meet the possible attack, but her gaze was focused on the ugly, wart-covered empath daemon.

Unsurprisingly, the crowd was thin around them. No sane person wanted to put themselves into that killing field. But that didn't mean it was entirely free of nutjob bystanders. Dozens of witnesses remained, either too shocked and frightened to flee, lest that movement draw attention to them. Or because they were just dumbfucks with camera phones.

Dave carefully approached the cops, hefting Lucille into a two-handed grip. His head seemed fuzzier the closer he drew to them, and his hunger increased. Not ravenous yet, but already uncomfortable in spite of the nearly raw meat he had only just consumed.

'Coming up behind you,' he said, loud enough to be heard over the crowd noise.

'Get back, you idiot,' one of the police officers barked, never taking his eyes off the Hunn. Or rather, off their nut sacks which, as always, were swinging low beneath coarse chain mail and Drakon-hide armour. Dave had to admit, Hunn junk was a horribly mesmerising sight.

'He's with me,' Karen said over her shoulder, still not taking her eyes off the empath.

The cop risked a glance back at Dave. His name tag read Chadderton. It took a moment but Dave saw the recognition light up the man's eyes.

'You. Oh thank Christ.'

'Hey,' Karen said sharply. 'Who got here first and saved your asses?'

'Sorry, ma'am,' said the other cop. A woman. Dave couldn't see her name tag.

The snarls and grunts of the Horde, the musky scent of them, recalled visits to the zoo with his kids. Happy days. Or happier than this at any rate. The moment seemed finely, if not perfectly, balanced, with Karen unable to do any more for some reason, undoubtedly related to her psychic face-off with the Threshrend, and the Hunn unwilling to take a chance that she'd carve them up the same way she had their nest mates.

Dave thought about breaking the stand-off by taking one of the cops' guns and shooting the biggest Hunn in the balls, if only to teach them the wisdom of wearing pants. But he wasn't sure he could pull off the feat – walking up, smoothly taking the gun and making the shot.

He'd look like a bit of a dick if he couldn't, and there were all those cameras on them, so maybe not.

'What's the problem?' he asked, 'You know. Besides monsters.'

'Having a battle of wits here, Hooper,' said Karen, nodding tightly at the Threshrend. He noticed for the first time just how strained her voice was.

'Is this daemon bothering you, ma'am?' he asked. But he could see from the way veins were starting to stand out on her neck that it was. The air seemed to crackle between Warat and the beast, the atmosphere so charged that he could feel the hairs on the back of his arms standing up. The terrible pressure inside his own temples had to be connected to whatever was going down between them, and he wondered if it was also affecting the Hunn and their leash.

Dave rolled his shoulder again – it felt good now – and he hoisted Lucille, smacking the hardwood handle into his palm. Crazy bitch was fairly whistling her happy tune, and he suspected it might even be soothing the sharp pain in his head and behind his eyes. He had the very strong impression that were it not for the enchanted splitting maul, he'd probably be as paralysed as those Hunn appeared to be.

Carefully sliding up beside Chadderton he said, out of the corner of his mouth.

'Hey, my name's Dave. Who are you?'

'Chadderton,' the man answered, his voice steady but

tense with the effort of keeping it so. 'Ted,' he added, and shook his head as if surprised by something he'd said. 'And this is Officer Delillo.'

'Cool,' said Dave. The woman didn't reply or add anything to her partner's introduction. Her eyes remained fixed on the largest Hunn. Dave could see she was aiming at its centre mass, which would do no good at all.

'So. Ted. Officer Delillo. You guys got enough ammo left to put down that ugly ass hell toad over there. The one with all the eyestalks and the warts?'

'I got three rounds left,' said Chadderton.

'Two,' his partner offered.

'Think you can shoot out the base of those stalks?' Dave asked. 'Its thick skull is a lot thinner there.'

'Can try,' said Delillo, her eyes flicking to Dave and widening a little. She had some trouble focusing on the Threshrend again. Dave held back his sigh. She dug his magic Old Spice. But she wasn't hot, and this wasn't the time.

'That's all we can ever do,' he said. 'Karen? *Karin*?' he added as quietly as he could while still being heard. 'You good to go?'

The Russian, who looked about a thousand miles from being good to go, jerked her head up and down and Dave continued his slow sidestepping shuffle toward her, leaving the cops behind, but making sure not to get between them and the Threshrend. Even ducking low at one point to give them the shot.

'Don't. Try. Orb.' Warat grunted each word separately, and for a moment he wasn't sure what she meant. And then he recalled her saying she'd 'orbed' out of the consulate to get him. Some Russian word for 'warp' maybe.

'Yeah, already figured that. Old daemon Kermit there is fucking with us, right?'

'Right,' she said, almost a gasp. She was sweating and tremors ran through her upper body, causing the blade she still held to waver a little. One of the Hunn stepped forward uncertainly, but stopped as Dave turned on him. The beast's nasal slits flared, as though he smelled something he really didn't like.

Dave addressed them as a group, speaking in the Olde Tongue.

'So, you boys aren't from round here, are you?'

He expected the Threshrend, which he suspected was the *superiorae* of this small group, to answer, perhaps giving him a chance to try warping over there while it was distracted. Instead one of the Hunn spoke. The one with the biggest balls, of course.

'You are the champion of this village?' it growled, its deep, guttural voice noticeably slurred.

'Dude,' laughed Dave. 'Are you drunk?' But his smile faltered when he realised that yes, it was, and why it was so shit-faced.

Bloodwine.

'You are the Dave,' growled the Hunn, which had no leashed Fangr, either because Karen had slain them all, or because it was a free-roaming thrall-boss. The growl sounded garbled and indistinct. The creature's face was crimson with fresh blood and dead meat hung in grotesque strips and chunks from its jagged fangs. 'I have heard tell of your prowess in combat but it does not impress me, for I am Jägur and I shall have my battle name from you this night.'

'Dude, really, you're embarrassing yourself,' said Dave.

'You don't even have a battle name yet? Bet your little weenie blade doesn't have a name either.'

He was moving slowly as he trash-talked the daemon, moving away from Karen who was still locked into her Thunderdome duel with the enormous psychic toad.

'Am I right? Or am I right, Jerker. Was that your nest name? Jerker of the Hunn. And that mighty blade you're packing, what are you gonna call that, urmin-tickler or something?'

The Hunn swayed from side to side, unsteady on its giant haunches. Its yellowed eyes squinted at Dave, or maybe just against the light of the burning cars. In a lower voice, and speaking directly to the Hunn now, Dave grinned nastily and channelled his inner python.

'No chance, nest-wetting urmin-type. I burst my pustules at you and call your battle name a silly thing. You are but a tiny-balled wiper of this Threshrend's bottom.'

He didn't have any pustules of course, but the insult did its work. In what passed for etiquette among the Hunn, to purposely rupture a pustule into the face of an opponent was akin to issuing a challenge to a duel by way of flinging a freshly squeezed turd squarely between the eyes.

Dave saw the remaining onlookers flinch back as the young Hunn roared with ungovernable rage and leaped out of the crouch in which it had been standing. The howling bellow all but drowned out the flat, cracking reports of two handguns unloading five rounds into the head of the Threshrend daemon, and the war cries and snarls of the other two Hunn and their leashed Fangr.

Dave felt the pressure that had been building in his head suddenly fall away and, as he dodged to one side to avoid the first clumsy swing of Jägur's cutlass-style blade, he was surprised to find the world suspended again.

Warat.

There was no time to check on her. Lucille sang her high keening tune as he jumped under the arc of the cutlass swing and drove the axehead of the splitting maul up into the Hunn's breastplate, aiming for the vulnerable area just beneath its shield-wise arm, where the smaller of the creature's two hearts lay close to the surface. The steel head bit through boiled leather and shattered hundreds of chain-mail links. Daemon-hide split, bones disintegrated and gore erupted from the wound in a slow geyser.

Dave whipped the hammer head back as the Hunn – moving slowly, but still appreciably faster than the human beings frozen outside Dave's warp bubble – folded in on itself around the fatal wound. Fatal, but not quite fast enough for Dave's liking. He spun Lucille in his hands and swung, bringing the flat, crushing surface of the hammer to bear on the creature's head as it dropped toward the ground. Twelve pounds of forged and magical American steel punched through the thick, nobbled bone of Jägur's skull. Twelve pounds which felt light in Dave's hands, but which he wielded with all his power. The Hunn's skull blew apart in an explosion of daemon ichor, grey-green brain jelly and shards of broken bone.

Lucille came free of the obscene wound with one fierce tug and a sucking sound that made Dave wince. Still half expecting to be forced out of the warp bubble at any moment, he braced himself for the rest of the war band, but it was too late. Warat had all but cut them down.

He shook his head in surprise at the sight of the Fangr, which were markedly swifter in attack than their lumbering

Hunn masters, dying in profligate blood sprays on the edge of her hissing sword blade. She moved in a blur of fluid power, inhumanly fast with the speed and surety of long practice and elemental grace. Karin Varatchevsky – he had no doubt he was seeing the woman reduced to her essences now, without the layers of pretense and assumed identity in which she had cloaked herself for years – Colonel Karin Varatchevsky danced between the hulking, slow-moving carcasses of the Horde. Her blade flashed and hummed and described great, blurred arcs of lethal intent, and wherever she danced, Hunn and Fangr died. They came apart in big raw pieces and Dave was sure that he could discern the unnaturally drawn-out, grating shrieks of their deaths somewhere beneath the rumbling sibilance of the city's elongated soundtrack.

The Threshrend, clutching at the gunshot wounds, which had further disfigured its ugly face, was dropping toward the road surface like a redwood felled by the axeman. Steaming loops and bags of internal organs, purple and green and yellow, spilled from a long diagonal slash which had opened its belly before Karin had turned her attention to the rest of the war band. But with the warrior daemonum now all slaughtered she spun back toward the slain empath, perversely reminding Dave of a ballerina in her leathers and heavy black boots. Her knees flexed as she crouched and leaped a good couple of yards toward the collapsing Threshrend. The sword twirled like a baton major's party trick, raised on high at the last moment, and . . .

The bubble popped.

She brought the blade down in real time with terrible swiftness and resolution, neatly severing the creature's eyestalks at the already ruined base. The sound of screaming all around them redoubled and changed in tenor, as people now cried out more in shock than fear. Warat stood without moving for a few seconds, and then she reached down to pluck a Subway sandwich wrapper from where it had become stuck to one boot. She used it to clean the worst of the gore from her sword. Dave, like the cops, was stunned into silence and stillness. His eyes fell to Lucille, recalling how she had come to life during the fight in the Russian consulate. He was convinced that if she hadn't, Warat would have carved him up as easily as she had the war band.

'Gonna have to ask you to put that away, ma'am,' said Officer Chadderton. He was pointing his gun Karen's way, his eyes flitting anxiously over to the chunks and slabs of cooling monster meat that lay all about them. 'Somebody might get hurt.'

04

Lord Guyuk ur Grymm could admit to himself, if to none other, that the scale of this human settlement, the brute size and weight of it, conspired to crush all *gurikh* from him. To extinguish his warrior spirit, to draw his claws and dull his fangs. It was just too . . . too much. Too vast and wrong to be endured. He tried to shield his thoughts, lest Compt'n ur Threshrend discern his weakness, but everywhere he turned, evidence of profound human dominion confronted him. Even worse, it seemed not to bother the Threshrend at all. But then, why would it? The creature was part human, at least in its thinkings.

'Awesome, right?' said the empath daemon, as if it knew exactly the blasphemy that had soiled Guyuk's mind.

But, no, that could not be. Even Threshrend Superiorae were not given to the subtle reading of individual minds as strong and shielded as Guyuk's. The Lord Commander of all Her Majesty's Regiments Grymm dragged his gaze away from the towering palaces beyond the edge of these woods, a reserve of sorts according to the Threshrend.

'Dude, I love it when a plan comes together, and my plans always do, because they're not just awesome. They're like the internationally recognised benchmark for awesome,' boasted Compt'n ur Threshrend.

So. He had not been attending to Guyuk at all, or taunting him in the leastways, and the lord commander relaxed. Instead, Compt'n ur Threshrend had been partaking in his most favoured indulgence: congratulating himself.

The forested reserve in which they hid – no, in which they *lurked*, Guyuk reminded himself. Warriors Grymm did not hide. They *lurked* with dark intent. The reserve seemed to be surrounded on all sides by the towering palaces of the human elite, or what Compt'n assured him were the elite. The calfling royalty, as he put it, seemingly amused by the very idea. The way Compt'n spoke of them, there appeared to be a whole city full of royalty, bound not by ties of blood but by the simple coincidence of their power. It was absurd, irrational, and even worse there were more human cities like this than there were rival palaces in all the realms.

Much as the greenery set his fangs on edge, Guyuk was grateful for the concealing foliage in which they lurked. The portal was nearby and secured by a half Talon of Grymm. He himself was guarded by a detachment of lieutenants trained especially in the art of close-quarter protection. And, as Compt'n ur Threshrend had just boasted, their plan did indeed appear to be working. The Threshrend Superiorae relayed details from his thralls as they spread across the city, sowing terror and havoc in their wake. The empath assured Guyuk that the humans were reacting not as they had before – checking Scaroth and the Djinn with unexpected violence, expertly applied – but rather with fear and disorder. Guyuk looked forward to leaving the forest and examining the seer stones of the Diwan when they were ready to tell the full story of what he and the Threshrend had wrought. He might not deign to call the execution of Compt'n ur Threshrend's scheme 'awesome', but there was no shame in admitting it was quite impressive.

'How much longer must we remain here?' Guyuk asked.

'Dude, seriously,' said Compt'n in the odd vernacular of the first human whose mind he had consumed. 'You're harshing my mellow here. I gots to have my quiet if you wants me to . . .'

Compt'n ur Threshrend broke off and seemed to sniff the air. 'Okaaay, time to go,' he said suddenly.

'What! What is happening? Why must we retreat?' Guyuk demanded, but the recently ennobled Superiorae dar Threshrendum ur Grymm ignored him, hopping down from the stone table on which he had been standing, sniffing at the air, seeking out the thinkings of his thrall.

'Super Dave is happening. And he brought a friend. Looks like *Kill Bill*'s samurai bitch.'

'The Dave is here? In this settlement?'

Guyuk did not need to be an empath daemon to sense the tension which ran through his bodyguards. The Captain of the Guard stepped forth, drawing his blade.

'My Lord?'

'Seriously, how fucking dumb are you?' Compt'n ur Threshrend whined, sounding very much like one of the calfling prisoners begging for mercy in the cells. 'It's Super Dave and he brought a big can of whoop-ass with him. Plenty to share round. The plan is good. The plan is working, but having the Dave and his bitch go to town on ol' Threshy? Not part of the plan, man. Totally not part of the plan. So let's bounce!'

'We must bounce?'

And Compt'n ur Threshrend was off, across the darkened greensward in the strange, half-hobbling hop-gallop of his kind. Bouncing indeed. Lieutenants Grymm closed in around Lord Guyuk, but without orders, or any immediate and obvious threat, they were uncertain about what they should do next. Not wanting to indict himself as a coward like dar Threshrend, the lord commander made a show of ignoring the perverse display. He took the time instead to examine their surroundings. The bodies of the humans they had surprised upon emerging from the portal lay stacked in a large pile, securely bound with wulfin-hide netting for easier transport to the UnderRealms. The bizarre, unnatural sounds of this metropolis of cattle grew neither louder nor quieter. The popping of their weapons. The strange noise of the beastless chariots. The alien miasma of smells. It was all so outlandish as to be incomprehensible.

Still, until a moment ago the empath had been very pleased with himself. Only the arrival of the human champion –nowhere nearby that Guyuk could see – had interrupted dar Threshrend's constant babble about the brilliance of his scheme, and how well it was working.

'My Lord?' the Captain of the Guard asked again.

'Gather as much of the plunder as we can take,' said Guyuk, turning from the cold light of the human towers and walking deeper into the darkness of the woods. 'Dar Threshrend has apparently seen enough and we are to withdraw.'

'As you will it, my Lord, so shall it be.'

Guyuk saw the Captain Grymm check himself, inclining his head and going down on one knee instead of smashing a full salute into his armoured chest with a mailed fist; another order from Compt'n ur Threshrend, who insisted that stealth be their watchword in the human realm. The half Talon of Lieutenants and Sergeants Grymm gathered up the catch in the nets, suspended it between long poles and carried it back to the portal. The calflings were all dead, an unfortunate necessity given how noisy they tended to be when captured. The flesh would not now be as sweet and toothsome, and of course the bloodwine had already cooled and spoiled in the vein. But Lord Guyuk ur Grymm snorted at his own fussiness in even thinking of such things. It was not so long ago, just a few turnings of night and accursed day here in the Above, that the very idea of dining on man-meat, fresh or otherwise, would have been ridiculous. He would not bother the palace kitchens with anything but the freshest kill. Nonetheless the regimental mess would make good use of all they took back.

Surrounded by his guard, he threaded through the forest, avoiding the stone paths and cleared fields where they might be seen by human eyes. The idea of hiding from the calflings would also once have been ridiculous. More than that. It was heresy. Anathema. And he knew that even his Marshals Regimental were troubled by the idea. But the Threshrend insisted, and so Guyuk ordered, and because he was the lord commander, the most successful of Her Majesty's Lords Commander in a good long eon, the marshals complied. Or agreed to, anyway. Neither they nor their main formations were even deployed. The chaos he thought he could discern in the city, the noises to which Compt'n ur Threshrend had bade him attend, testified to the success of their plan which, for now, did not rely on main-force Grymm or even Hunn elements.

No, this city was tonight taken under siege by mostly untried, untested, *unnamed* Hunn. Hundreds of them, nearly half a legion in all, seemingly scattered at random across the city's boroughs. Lord Guyuk had been sceptical, Marshals Guyur, Sepcis and Khutr positively outraged. But Compt'n ur Threshrend had explained his plan in such a way as to convince them all. He had done so in the infuriating argot of his polyglot minds, but eating the cranial meats of the human Scolari Compton, and the elite warriors captured with him, had blessed the Threshrend with an unusual clarity for tactical and even strategic reasoning.

Even if it was expressed in the bizarre tongue of the calfling known as Trev'r ur Candly.

If and when we repeat this experiment of harvesting individuals from the human Horde for their thinkings, Guyuk thought as they pushed through the thin forest, we will take much greater care with the minds we have our empaths consume, especially as the first one taken imprints itself so profoundly.

'Hurry up, motherfuckers!' came a shout from ahead. 'Threshy wants out of here.'

The empath daemon once known only as thresh, as were all thresh, and now elevated to the high rank of Superiorae dar Threshrendum ur Grymm, Pro-Consul to the Lord Commander, bounced from one horned foot to another, his escape through the portal prevented by a pair of hulking Lieutenants Grymm. Armed with pikes and short swords they barred any escape, crashing the shafts of their principal weapons together to form a giant cross as Threshy charged them at a gallop. He paid them no heed. They were so tall, the point at which the big iron polearms met so far above his eyestalks, all he needed to do was put his head down and boogie on through to deliverance, perhaps even biting one of them on the ass as he shot past. Teach these ugly fucks to show some respect.

Oof!

Threshy flew backward, in exactly the opposite direction to that in which he had intended to keep moving at high speed. Sparks flared across his vision, standing out brightly against the darkness which bloomed in his head. He rolled through leaf litter and dirt, the little copse in the woods of Central Park spinning around him until he came to a stop thanks to a kick from another of the Lieutenants Grymm. A second kick, really, the first one having sent him flying backward. But who was counting?

The security detail, a half Talon of Lieutenants and Sergeants Grymm, ringed the entrance to the portal, a region of darkness a few steps into a stormwater drain, noticeably denser and deeper than the surrounding night. Mail and armour clinked and creaked in the darkness. They cut off his passage as effectively as a high castle wall.

'Step to me, would you, motherfucker?' grunted Compt'n ur Threshrend, but not too loudly, in case they heard him. The little empath daemon had a moment of recall that was both profoundly familiar and alien; the memory, not from its own experience in the nest, but from one of the minds it had consumed. It could not tell which, but knew the reminiscence to be from either the calfling called Trev'r or the Scolari Compt'n. A human nestling very young, very frightened, and ashamed, surrounded by its nest mates – no, its schoolmates, Compt'n corrected – kicked and mocked and spat on and . . .

The tiny unnamed, unlamented thresh, which endured somewhere under all of the layers of memory and understanding it had recently consumed, struggled to understand. But Threshy, the strange, protean personality it had become, remembered well and understood implicitly.

Motherfuckers were pelting him with their filthy jockstraps after gym class.

The daemon shuddered in recall of a humiliation which was not, in truth, its own. Compt'n ur Threshrend glared at the lieutenants from across the vast unfathomable gulf which separated them, anticipating sneers and taunts. Expecting a mouthful of moist jockstrap. But it did not come.

The Lieutenants Grymm merely returned to standing watch.

'Yeah,' said Threshy, very quietly. 'Didn't think you'd fuckin' cowboy up for a second round. Bitches.'

He could hear the approach of Guyuk and his escorts. They didn't crash through the little forest, but there was no way a score of eight and nine foot tall warrior daemonum could move with complete silence.

At least they weren't Hunn, he thought.

Those dumbasses would've charged up Broadway the second they heard the Dave was there. Unable to do the smart thing – get the fuck out of Dodge – Compt'n ur Threshrend used the time left in this realm to reach out for his thrall.

Yeah. That's right.

He had thrall now.

Dozens of Threshrendum. Minorae, majorae and even a couple of motherfucking superiorae. He shut himself off to his immediate surrounds, to the shadows and smells of Central Park, so strangely familiar and alien all at once. Compt'n ur Threshrend reached out across the city with his thinkings, gathering up the sights and senses of all his thrall. Knowing as they knew. He stood atop high towers looking down on scenes of slaughter. He leaped from the roof of a flower delivery van as it spun out of control. He raced through a mall behind a small war band of unnamed Hunn, thrilling with them at the blood and horror. But he did not see the Dave or the terrifying female who seemed to have attached herself to his cause.

That sucked.

Everything had been going so well. He'd brought Fallujah to Manhattan. He'd unleashed scores of small, uncoordinated attacks on soft targets well away from any place the humans were able to concentrate firepower. He'd watched with mounting excitement and delight as the city lost its shit. Totally, completely, to the fucking max. He'd known it was going to work. Had seen the way the entire island seized up. He'd tasted the panic and madness of the calfling masses for himself, not even needing his thralls for that. Their fear was thick in the air, even here, hidden in the forest at the centre of the metropolis.

It was all going so well. Even Guyuk, the stale old fart, was impressed by how much they'd achieved with a comparatively small cohort of untried Hunn, driven to frenzy by the need to prove themselves where proven warriors had failed.

And then the fucking Dave turned up.

'Compt'n, attend! You ordered this withdrawal, now you lag behind.'

It was old Guyuk, storming and stomping toward the portal.

Threshy shook off his troubles and laid aside his resentment at being knocked on his ass by the two Lieutenants Grymm. He scowled and made a special effort to remember their ugly faces and stupid tattoos. He'd settle with them later.

'Coming, my Lord!'

The guard withdrew through the gateway to the

UnderRealms in perfect order, Guyuk and Threshy surrounded by the giant warriors. Their mailed and armoured forms towered over the tiny empath and their disciplined minds were all but closed to him. The transition from Above to below was the same as before, even though this time the rift between the realms was held open by a Master of the Ways, one of the few Scolari Grymm adept in the arcane study of the paths between the realms. Their party proceeded into the darkened cutting, the artificial light of the city dying in the gloom. The natural darkness of night in the Above gave way to the deeper and more profound darkness of the UnderRealms at some point after they passed between the worlds.

Threshy knew exactly when they left the world of men behind because he lost the connection to his thralls. The portals weren't like a Stargate. You couldn't send signals through. Only flesh and metal. There was much he did not yet understand about the portals, or the discipline of those too few masters still able to navigate them. Were they wormholes, some sort of quantum string tying alternate worlds together? How did the Masters of the Ways manipulate them to open a gate to the Above in just the right spot?

Be a hell of a lot simpler if Guyuk would just let him chow down on a few Scolari brains so he could get up on this shit. He'd be a double-plus awesome Threshrend if he knew how to teleport between the realms, but of course, they wouldn't let him do that. Masters of the Ways, who were so recently about as useless a Scolari as you could imagine, were now more precious than Bulgari Edition Apple Watches.

He skinned his fang tracks back at the sweet and sulphurous familiarity of the Horde's one true realm. They were home, the guard drawn up in the large cavern beneath the regimental training fields from where they had ventured Above. Armour clinked and edged metal rasped as the Grymm divested themselves of their fighting gear under the supervision of their captain.

'Best you attend me in my chamber, Superiorae, and we will discuss what just happened.'

'What just happened, boss, is that we didn't get our scaly asses handed to us by the fucking Dave, that's what. But one of my Threshrendum did. A really gnarly old superiorae too.'

'You saw the Dave through your thrall?'

'Yep. The Dave and his sexy lieutenant. Had eyestalks on them right up until the crazy ninja lady chopped them off. And sorry, *el jefe*, but they were close. Too close to you, and to old Threshy too. No point having a cunning plan that's like totally fucking with the enemy if you're not around to enjoy all the fuckin' because the Dave stomped you to monster jelly, is it?'

Lord Guyuk seemed to weigh up the equation, and perhaps Compt'n ur Threshrend's usefulness and life expectancy with it. But then he grunted.

'No. It is not.'

The old prick surprised him once again. Scaroth would have roared some bullshit about his honour and his code and stupid *gurikh* or something. Probably would have charged back up top and got himself killed by Hooper all over again. But Guyuk was smarter than that. Even if it cost him his honour and his code and his stupid *gurikh*.

Or something.

None of them were concepts Compt'n ur Threshrend understood down in his meat and ichor. He wondered, and not for the first time, whether throwing in with the lord commander was the smartest thing he'd ever done, or the dumbest.

05

After killing the monsters, they had cheesesteak. And they talked. The cheesesteak guy, a large-bellied Turk, comped them the food and kept mugs of thick Turkish coffee coming while Dave and Karen fuelled up. It wasn't a leisurely meal. They ate quickly, filling the tank.

The cheesesteak guy babbled at them in his native tongue, and a teenage boy, presumably a son or a nephew, translated his thanks for all the monster killing. The fast food joint was strangely empty, given the mad crush out on the street. But their privacy was guaranteed by a couple of huge bodybuilders, also related to the cheesesteak guy in some abstract way. They stood vigil at the door, holding back the crowd which had piled up out there. The kid wore a Cubs jersey and spoke without a trace of any foreign accent. He took selfies with both Karen and Dave, but he seemed most proud of the one with Karen. That one went to Reddit. Dave only rated Flickr. He tried not to feel a little put out about that. Tried and failed.

The cheesesteak joint was only half a block from Broadway and 42nd, and Dave promised the cop, Chadderton, they wouldn't just disappear without letting him know. Mobs still thronged the streets outside. Some milled around, as if unwilling to leave the uncertain safety of the area where they knew, or had heard, that Super Dave was kicking ass. Some of them were pressed up against the window, watching him eat, and he worried about the glass shattering under their weight. Others surged past in huge pulses of foot traffic, some heading uptown, some headed down, all of them just wanting to get the hell away.

'Excuse me, do you have tea?' Karen asked the owner, a question translated by his young relative, who then answered without waiting for the reply.

'Yes. You like your tea black, lady?'

Karen told him black tea with lots of sugar would be fine as she picked the meat from another platter of cheesesteak rolls. The older man started babbling his own questions from the hot grill, perhaps worried that she did not like his food, but she spoke a few words to him in his own language, or so Dave assumed, and he calmed down.

'You speak Turkish?' he asked, although he supposed he shouldn't be surprised with this chick.

'He's Armenian,' Karen said, not really answering him. 'The protein,' she added, removing another greasy slab of meat from a soft, gravy-sodden roll. 'Just eat the protein, Hooper. It has much higher energy density than the sugary carbs in the bread. And we're on the clock here.'

Dave did love him a steak sandwich, and these were pretty damn good, especially for freebies, but he did as she suggested and started to dismantle the meal. He set the bread aside as they sat under faded posters of Turkish beaches, or maybe Armenian, while the street heaved with frightened crowds and throbbed with the flashing lights of first responders. Lucille was leaned up against the booth where they sat, humming somewhere deep inside his head, wanting to be gone, wanting to be about her business.

'We have to go as soon as we're ready. There are more of them, all over the city,' she said.

'LA too,' the kid put in. 'See?'

He pointed at an old TV, suspended from the yellowed ceiling tiles in a rear corner of the shop. Dave had to turn all the way around in the booth to check out the boxy antique. The screen was a distorted wash of faded blues and greens. The sound was down and it was hard to make out what was happening, but the news ticker scrolling across the bottom was legible. 'Zombies in LA,' it screamed.

Dave frowned. He'd just come in from the west coast this morning, although it felt like days ago. There'd been no monsters out there when he left. Just Boylan, his lawyer. Now it looked like they had a Tümorum infection. Or maybe just a Revenant Master working his mojo – if they were lucky. Dave shook his head, and went back to wolfing down fistfuls of hot meat and melted cheese. Nothing he could do about it from here. He'd told Heath and the army guys how to handle that shit.

'You have cheese on your chin,' said Karen, handing him a napkin. 'Wipe it off.'

'Yes, Mom,' he said, but did as she told him anyway.

He'd already washed his hands in the little sink behind the counter, but his black coveralls were stiff with daemon gore. It didn't bother him as much as it should. And not as much as his cheesy dribbles seemed to gross her out.

'I know where some of them are,' she said between rapidly chewing and swallowing. 'The war bands. I saw them when I was hooked up to the Threshrend. We can't fight them all. We should take the really bad ones the cops can't handle.'

'I don't reckon they can handle any of them,' said Dave, still hurrying through his meal. 'Not until they get some heavy backup. Chadderton and his partner. Delillo. They strike you as having that shit locked down before?'

Karen's tea, poured from a samovar, arrived in a tall, ornate glass. She took care to keep her sword well away from the teenage Turk, or Armenian, or whatever he was. Wouldn't do to have the boy touch the thing and come apart on them.

Dave stood, draining a mug of thick, black, sweetened coffee. He gathered up another handful of fried meat. Felt the need to be moving.

'That big toad-looking freak,' he said. 'The thresh.'

'Threshrend,' she corrected him, drinking her tea, but not rushing to follow him. 'Thresh are just nestlings. Threshrend are fully grown, come into their power.'

'Yeah. The psychic ones. That's how you know where the others are?'

'Something like that,' she said, sipping at the tea again, making no move to leave or even stand. 'It's good,' she said, raising the glass and smiling sweetly at the older Turk as he fired up more meat for them. For a moment Dave could see just how deeply she'd inhabited the character she played. Karen Warat. All-American girl. Not a treacherous Russian spy or human killing machine.

'We should get moving,' he said.

'Almost. I need to hydrate properly. You should too. It's important and we need to think about how we take these things down. The most powerful Threshrend, they can get into our heads. That why we couldn't orb before. That thing was stopping us.'

'By orb, you mean warp, right? Be the Flash?'

'Yeah, if you want. Anyway, just so you know, we won't always be able to run rings around them at . . . warp speed. Not if they have a Threshrend to run signals interference on us.'

Karen stood then, and they gathered their weapons. He started to ask her about the empath daemons but she was already talking to the Armenian again. The man beamed at her, his eyes lighting up. They exchanged something that felt like a formal greeting or ritual of some sort, tossing the word 'Inshallah' between them a few times. The boy gave them a plastic container, filled to the brim with cheesesteak, the lid held on with thick rubber bands.

'Thanks,' said Dave. 'And, er, inch . . . allah, or you know, whatevs.'

The kid grinned.

'Yeah. Whatevs.'

The two steroid giants by the door pushed a path through the crush of onlookers and out into the street. Karen tapped the accelerator to let them weave through the press without anyone coming into contact with her sword.

'We need to hurry. Come on.'

They stepped it up through the inert mass of the crowd.

'Should've done this while we were eating,' said Dave. 'Would've saved some time.'

'We can't save everyone,' said Warat, which wasn't exactly relevant to his point, but he sort of got it.

'So how many war bands?' asked Dave.

'Across the city? A hundred or so. Maybe a thousand-plus Hunn. Call it half a legion's worth. A lot of them with Threshrendum. But not all on Manhattan. They're across the rivers too.'

Karen stopped in the middle of the road, frowning. Dave was struck by the strangeness of the utterly static diorama in which they stood. Like they'd been caught in some sort of giant art installation recalling the atrocities of 9/11. New Yorkers frozen in flight from something they didn't understand, but knew well enough to flee. One obvious difference though; this close to Times Square there were fewer suits, more children. Tourists.

'They're not hitting counter-force targets,' said Karen. 'Just counter value.'

'Counter what?' said Dave.

She carefully threaded a path through a knot of young women. Swedish backpackers, Dave would have bet. They had that Nordic look about them, underneath the terrified bafflement.

'They're not going after hard targets,' Karen explained. 'Military assets, that sort of thing. They're hitting hardest on the soft tissue. Going for maximum shock and awe. Civil disruption, not military.'

She favoured him with a cruel smile.

'What's that feel like? Being attacked by a hostile imperial power.'

'Fuck off,' Dave said. 'You up for this or not?'

'Oh, I'm up for it. But there's something else,' she said as she set off again, running into clear space now, dodging through a part of the crowd where the crush wasn't as heavy, forcing him to run to stay in contact. The crowds were as bad as anything he'd experienced, like New Year's Eve with a terrorist strike thrown in. He carried Lucille gripped just below the heavy steel head. There were half a dozen police cars at the intersection where they'd cut down the war band.

Or where Karen had cut them down. Dave hadn't done that much, really.

'What else,' he said, catching up with her in a relatively clear patch of road around a headless Fangr corpse. He'd just picked Chadderton and Delillo out of the confusion when Karen took them out of warp and they 'popped' into the world of real time again. The roar and chaos of a city in convulsion hit him like a storm surge. Way louder and more shocking than he'd expected. He was certain things had gone south while they'd been filling their faces.

Chadderton jumped in surprise. His partner let go a little squeal. In a moment of perfect incongruity Dave was certain he could hear a big band playing 'Mack the Knife' somewhere nearby. The strobing lights of the squad cars and ambulances laid a stuttering filter of primary colours over the scene. The slaughtered daemonum lay where they'd been cut down. The human casualties had been cleared away. Some assholes were still shooting the scene on smart phones. Even bigger assholes were using iPads.

'There was something about that empath daemon,' Karen said, raising her voice to be heard over the roar as they hurried up to the cops. 'Something unusual. I don't know what yet.'

'Mr Hooper! Ma'am,' Chadderton called out, looking relieved to see them, even if he was a little freaked out by the way they'd materialised in front of him again. 'This is Lieutenant Trenoweth,' he said, introducing a plain clothes detective, a tall rangy man with iron grey hair. Trenoweth put his hand out to shake and Dave took care not to crush his fingers by gripping too hard. Karen bobbed him a quick nod.

'First,' said Trenoweth, 'thanks for this.' A half-turn and a hand gesture took in the crime scene. They'd actually run up crime scene tape. Dave couldn't help but shake his head at that. 'Officer Chadderton said you guys really helped out here.'

'They cleaned house, Lieutenant,' the patrolman said with great enthusiasm.

'Yeah, anyways. I'm supposed to tell you, Mr Hooper, your bosses need you to get in contact right the fuck now.'

Dave shrugged.

'Which bosses?'

'Good question,' said Trenoweth, looking like he wanted to spit somewhere. 'My captain's taking heat from the commissioner and the mayor who are getting it in the ass from the Pentágon, the navy, all sorts-a fucking spooks. Whoever your fucking boss is, Hooper. Call him. Or her,' he added, with a nod to Karen. 'And you,' he said. 'If you're the Russian, I'm supposed to escort you to your consulate. Or arrest you and hold you until some FBI jerk gets here. Neither of which I'm gonna do,' he said. A slow pan around the carnage at the taped-off intersection was explanation enough for why he wouldn't be doing that.

'The jerk's not FBI,' said Karen over the background roar. 'And Hooper has better things to do than check in at the office.'

At that moment Hooper was eating another cheesesteak, the last one, from the plastic take-out container, but he nodded his agreement.

'Any heavy weapons teams you can put on the streets, you'll need them,' said Karen. 'NYPD Swat. Feebs. National Guard. Army. The 10th Mountain out of Fort Drum if you can get them down here. The 2-25th Marines up at Garden City. You need them all, Lieutenant.'

Dave enjoyed the expression of utter confusion on Trenoweth's face as he tried to process the advice from the attractive blonde art dealer in the bloodied motorcycle leathers who he'd been told to assist as a Russian diplomat, or to arrest as a Russian spy.

'Do you have a map of the city, Lieutenant?' she asked, cutting across the police officer's uncertainty. 'With the incidents flagged? The attacks?'

'Not a map, no,' said Trenoweth, putting aside whatever thoughts he had about Colonel Karin Varatchevsky. 'Everything's moving too fast. These fucking things are all over the place. Got them surfacing in New Jersey now too.'

'Give us the worst one nearby,' said Karen. 'We can take that for you at least.'

'If we split up, we could do twice as many,' said Dave, who had finished his take-out. He was about to throw the container away but thought better of it with so many cops around. Weird to be worried about a fine for littering, with burning cars, screaming idiots and tons of butchered monster meat lying around, but he couldn't help it. Cops always made him feel guilty about something, because he usually had something to feel guilty about. Karen shot down the suggestion anyway.

'I told you, Hooper, that Threshrend was messing with us. You can't count on being the Flash. And I can't guarantee the next one won't be able to paralyse you just by thinking about it.'

'So, what?' said Dave. 'I need you riding psychic shotgun on me from now on?'

'I hope not,' she said. 'But for now, we need each other.'

06

'We're gonna need some more Threshrendum. Or a Sith Lord. Dude, that'd be awesome rocking a Sith Lord in our thrall. But even some thresh'd be cool.'

'To what end, Superiorae Compt'n?'

Guyuk and Threshy had returned to the lord commander's crib. The snacks and finger food had all been cleared away by Guyuk's attendants, which was a bummer, but Threshy was confident there'd be a whole heap of fresh, hot man-meat coming down from the Above long before he starved to death. Besides, having escaped the mortal danger of close proximity to the Dave – anywhere within 100 miles of that motherfucker was too close for Threshy – he was excited. Even busted out a little dance move that would have totes impressed Britney. The early, hot Britney, natch. Not the hot mess of late-stage Britney. Threshy was full to brimming over with powerfully charged memories, that were not exactly memories, of the calfling Trevor Candly coupling with the hot Britney.

Now that he had safely removed himself from the unexpected threat of the Dave, Compt'n ur Threshrend had a clearer idea about what had just happened topside. A Threshrend daemon, a powerful elder, had somehow constrained Hooper and his crazy ninja bitch by reaching into their minds and . . . doing something.

It was frustrating as hell that Threshy couldn't figure out exactly what his thrall had done, but whatever it was, that bastard Hooper had been crippled by it. Or at least hobbled. Threshy had been able to feel that through the connection to his slain underling. And that was exciting. That was worth a little victory dance.

'By the suppurating sun, Threshrend, what are you doing?' Guyuk demanded as Threshy shook his fucking tail feather.

Then he stopped.

He didn't have a tail feather, just a stump.

'Sorry, boss. Just had to bust a move, you know. 'Cause this Dave douche bag, I think we got his number, my man. Or, you know, man-eater.'

And to acknowledge the moment, he indulged himself in a few seconds of celebratory twerking.

'Oh yeeeaah.'

Guyuk furrowed the scarred and leathery folds of his brow, bringing Threshy's victory dance to a halt.

'This is good, Superiorae, because it did not feel as though we had the measure of the human champion when we fled from him.' He paused and corrected himself, 'No, when we fled from the mere spectre of him, like cowards.'

'Pfft. We didn't flee, we just withdrew. We were like in tactical withdrawal and shit. Like in *Aliens* 2, with the fucking space marines shootin' and scootin' . . .'

He stopped for a moment, considering the metaphor.

'Except, I guess, we're the monsters.' Compt'n ur Threshrend heaved a very human shrug. 'Meh.'

The lord commander did not appear convinced. His

furious glower was enough to tell Threshy to get on with it.

'Okay. Okay. So I'm up there, you know, in the Above, working my mojo. I gots my loyal thrall on the job. A full Talon of big throbbing brainiac motherfuckers feeding me like daemon CNN. And they're totally fucking winning it, not just with the live coverage but also with the terror, amping that sweet shit up to eleven.'

Guyuk, still clad in his field armour and mail, took a seat on his favoured rock. The old prick would never admit it, but you could tell he was feeling his eons.

'Continue. I think I follow your babbling so far. From the Threshrendum you had the knowing of all the actions in which they were engaged.'

'Fuck yeah. And it's cool. They're all doing that thing they do, latching onto the fear and shit that peeps naturally gets when they meet a monster, even a baby Hunn without a battle name. And they be cranking on the fear like Stephen fucking King. Turn the volume up! Am I right? Gimme a booyah!'

Guyuk nodded warily, 'The . . . booyah is given. But such is the role of the Threshrendum, minor as it might be.'

'Hey, don't harsh my mellow here, big guy. My Threshrendum, they be fucking kicking it up there. So I'm like, in the park, with you and my homes, watching my monster YouTube channels on the psychic interwebs. Are you still with me?'

'Barely.'

'Awesome. And we're good, right? We got our soldiers all up in their grill for a change. Bringing the awesome, putting the fear on motherfuckers. Next thing I know, some crazy ho is stepping to one of my boys, some gnarly old Threshrend with a big throbbing head full of mad powers and she's like BOOM! Have some of that back in yo face.'

'A calfling female? Protecting its young?' said Guyuk, recalling the pathetic attempts of full-grown human nest mates in the dungeons to guard each other and their offspring.

'Nope. Not even,' said Threshy. 'This bitch be like Agent Romanoff or something. And she's got the Dave with her.'

Guyuk frowned again.

'The Dave follows this one? In her thrall?'

Threshy made an equivocating gesture with his fore-claws.

'Meh, not so much I don't think.' He sucked air in through his fang tracks. 'I think she might be another champion.'

He let that sink in for a moment. The lord commander glowered at the revelation, but not at his Superiorae.

'So this city we have invested, it also boasts a champion? And she is in league with the Dave?'

Threshy threw up his claws. 'Like I fucking know. Thing is, she's not like the Dave. She's like . . . me. And my guy she put down. She got like the mind bullets, bro. And she and my Threshrend they're like, I dunno. You ever watch Harry Potter, when the wizards are in the Octagon? No, scratch that. Dumb question. Anyway, the take-away. My guy, his radar somehow picks up the Dave and Romanoff when they get close and he does . . . I dunno . . . he does something to them, gets inside their heads somehow, and it totally fucks them up. Well, not totally, but it does fuck them up. Stops the Dave from doing that thing he did to Scaroth and those Djinn bitches, you know?'

Guyuk obviously did not know.

'Look, he's super fast,' Threshy tried to explain. 'Too fast for us. But it's not a Jackie Chan thing, you know. The Dave didn't train himself to be that fast, he just sort of thinks himself into it. And my guy, because he's got his awesome psychic mojo, he could mess with that. Or, you know, he could mess with it until Romanoff cut his head off.'

The lord commander took a moment to consider everything Compt'n ur Threshrend had just said.

'There is much we do not know of these champions,' he said at last, unable to mask his aggravation. 'And we must take this female as a champion. Another one,' he grunted, not at all happy with the idea. 'This is vexing. Bad enough that our cattle have risen to the level of warrior sect. Now we must contend with a female Dave. What if they should breed a whole race of Daves?'

The very idea was too horrible to contemplate. The part of Compt'n ur Threshrend which was Compton above all else was especially offended.

'Yeah, that'd be just like fucking Hooper. Always falling ass backwards into the pussy pool.'

Guyuk ignored the remark.

'But if what you say is true,' he continued, 'and a Threshrend has discovered a weakness in these champions, we must move to exploit it. So yes, Superiorae, you are correct. We will need to deploy more empaths. But first,' he said, 'we cannot hide from our enemy. Your plan is in effect at this moment, Compt'n ur Threshrend, and we must forge on.'

'Yep, yep, totally with you on the forging,' said Threshy, 'but, hear me out. My plan doesn't involve me climbing into a cage fight with Super Dave. That asshole wanted to kill me in Vegas. Probably best we don't give him a chance to now.'

Lord Guyuk frowned at him.

'The Dave did not wish to kill you, Superiorae. As I understood it, his antipathy was for the human Scolari whose soul you took up. Compton. The one from whom you have taken your sect name.'

Threshy paused for a moment too, his jaws agape.

'Yeah,' he admitted. 'That was weird.'

He knew who he was. And that wasn't some pissant professor. He was the Superiorae dar Threshrendum ur Grymm. He was the motherfucking eater of souls. And that Compton asshole was just a snack. Threshy shuddered and tried to throw off the moment of dissonance. Hurrying on, still dancing around the lord commander's chamber, but mostly just skipping, he returned to his plans.

'The plan is good, the plan is working, and even though we didn't plan for the Dave or his lady friend to roll on us, we can deal. I can deal. We just need to figure out where this asshole is, and then not be there when we go back up. Let him be the fucking hero and we'll . . . hell yeah, I got it, we'll force him to be the hero, and while he's all tied up doing that, we clobber him with the plan. Just like we planned? You cool with that?'

Guyuk shifted on his sitting rock. His armour and chain mail rasped and clinked on the granite.

'I might indeed be cool, had I any idea of what you speak. Please explain yourself, Superiorae. And assume that unlike you I am no empath, just a battle-scarred and increasingly impatient Lord Commander of Her Majesty's Most Terrible Legions Grymm. Imagine I have a very large sword that might cleave you asunder were my impatience to get the better of me. Should it help focus your explanation I could show you this sword.'

'No need, bro. I can tell you 'zactly what we need to do. But I'm gonna need to get one of my Threshrendum back down here. Just to give me a sense of where this asshole's hanging now.'

* * *

The Threshrend who attended them was a veteran of the majorae ranks, an elder of its clan, long pledged in fealty to the Grymm. It hunkered in the chamber, eyestalks down, deferring to Compt'n ur Threshrend as was only proper, he being the lord commander's pro-consul. Guyuk did not need to be an empath, however, to understand that the much larger and more battle-scarred creature was not much impressed with its little master.

M'randm ur Threshrend had first served the Grymm Legions with distinction at the Battle of Nahin Chasm, in the thirteenth war under the capstone, the fourth campaign against the Morphum, at least in the modern era. That made him nearly as old as Guyuk. M'randm ur Threshrend had battle scars older than the human city from which he'd just returned. The scars hidden beneath those wounds were older than any human city.

'My Lord Guyuk,' he said, before adding just slowly enough for the pause to be noticeable, 'Superiorae. I serve at your will.'

'Fuckin' A you do, Mandy,' said Compt'n ur Threshrend. 'So what's with the 'tude? Am I your overlord or what?'

'Superiorae,' warned Guyuk. 'You are not long come to your high station and having taken such an unusual path there you might yet be unaware of the great and valuable services rendered to Her Majesty's Regiments Grymm by the majorae these eons past.'

Guyuk bore down on the words 'eons'.

'Yeah, yeah. Threshy digs it. Mandy is a valuable member of the team. Employee of the month or the millennium or whatevs. I'm sensing some 'tude, that's all.'

'What is this 'tude of which you speak?' asked Guyuk.

'I bring no 'tude,' M'randm ur Threshrend assured them, 'only those reports from the Above which you have requested of me.'

'Perhaps we might hear them,' Guyuk said, with another warning glance at the Superiorae.

'Fine,' said Compt'n ur Threshrend, throwing up its tiny fore-claws. 'Don't bother with me, I'm just pro-consul to the –'

'Excellent. Threshrend Majorae, bother yourself no longer with the pro-consul and report. How stands the human city and its champions?'

'I could suck his brains out and tell you myself,' Compt'n ur Threshrend muttered.

'And I would need another Superiorae when they dragged your carcass out of here and down to the rendering vats in the kitchens,' said Guyuk. 'Majorae?'

The veteran empath bowed deeply.

'My Lord, the calfling island of Manhatt'n stands besieged as my Superiorae directed it be, from within, by the least of our Horde. Unnamed Hunn with soulless blades run amok with no tactical discipline. They are watched by my clan and by the Diwan's scouts, but no attempt do we make to control them. They sow great fear and much uncertainty among the foe.'

'And the Dave. Where he be at?' Compt'n ur Threshrend demanded to know, seeming slightly mollified by the success of his plans.

'The Sliveen report the Dave and this other champion, a female calfling of many clans and names, feed and recover near the site where she slew Angrbult ur Threshrend.'

'Midtown, coolio.'

'You are familiar with this quarter of the human settlement, Superiorae?' asked Guyuk.

'Sure. We're golden, boss. We just keep him down there and away from us. Might even be able to lure this jackass into a trap.'

Compt'n ur Threshrend turned back to the majorae.

'That thing old Angry Bull did, messing with the Dave and his bitch. Can you do that, Mandy? Could you teach me?'

M'randm ur Threshrend's lips peeled back from the fang tracks that occupied most of his head.

'I cannot teach you, no, Superiorae. You have not yet matured enough to practise the technique. But all of the Clan Threshrendum currently in Manhatt'n sensed the contest between our fallen one and this female calfling. The knowing of it is common. Angrbult ur Threshrend engaged in a contest of *randorii* with her.'

'Dunno it,' said Compt'n ur Threshrend.

'You would not,' Lord Guyuk explained. 'M'randm ur Threshrend is correct, Superiorae. *Randorii* is an ancient combat discipline of the empath clans. It is a contest, always fatal, between the most skilled and knowledgeable Threshrendum. You are an eon from mastering it. Do not forget that only a few turnings past you were not even Threshrendum, but mere thresh.'

'Yeah, yeah, everyone's down on the new guy. So your randy-roaring technique. It'll shut down the Dave when he tries to go all Flash on a motherfucker?'

M'randm ur Threshrend appealed to Guyuk.

'I do not understand, my Lord.'

'I think the Superiorae asks whether the *randorii* is an

appropriate counter to the Dave's ability to move with great and terrible swiftness.'

'Ah,' the older empath said. 'It is. The Dave and his companion do not simply *move* with this noted swiftness, you see? It seems a matter of their thinkings rather than their exertions. Hence, the *randorii*.'

'I see,' said Compt'n ur Threshrend, turning his attention fully to Guyuk. 'Looks like some motherfuckers gonna be getting some respect for Team Threshrend then, doesn't it?' And back to the majorae. 'You done good, Mandy. Make sure all my threshies who are cool with this *randorii* kung-fu thing know about it before you go back topside, though.'

'The knowing and thinking of it already spreads fast through the clan, Superiorae. But I shall do as you insist.'

'Dude, that's all I ever ask.'

Lord Guyuk had to concede that as difficult and annoying a counsellor as the empath had become after absorbing the minds of so many different humans, his advice was sound. Guyuk was now convinced that humans were no longer the unvarying herd of cattle written of in the scrolls. To have raised themselves so far above their natural station in the absence of the Horde, it must be the case that just as a legion was composed of officers and lower ranks, so too must the clan of humanity.

Thresh-Trev'r had been useful in the way of a very crude and simple tool, but Compt'n ur Threshrend had the tactical and strategic capacity of a regimental commander; and a regiment of Grymm too, not just Hunn. His plan was indeed unaffected by the abrupt and unexpected intervention of the human champion. Or champions, Guyuk reminded himself.

'You see, we're cool,' said Compt'n ur Threshrend after Lieutenants Grymm escorted the Threshrend Majorae from Guyuk's chambers. The lord commander did not need to pause to translate the strange human vernacular. He knew the Superiorae meant the attack could proceed as planned.

'And so we return to the Above?' Guyuk said.

'Totes.'

The lord commander grunted in satisfaction. He had also learned this was a human term appropriate for signalling affirmation.

'My homeboy there,' said Compt'n ur Threshrend, indicating the door through which the Threshrend Majorae had just disappeared, 'tells me the Dave is still scratching his nuts around midtown. We're gonna keep him there, maybe even kill him, for bonus points.'

They returned to the great chamber where the Lieutenants Grymm awaited them, a cohort strong, drawn up in armour and weapons, a band of Sliveen scouts attached this time, again at the insistence of Compt'n ur Threshrend who would have them maintain a screen around the lord commander's party.

And who was Guyuk to quibble with such sound tactical advice? Sliveen would deploy with them. Not the Diwan's Finest, of course. They were still engaged in a greater mission. But the scouts waiting in the chamber with Lieutenants Grymm and a Master of the Ways were old and experienced veterans of a hundred encounters with foe like the Djinn and Morphum. They would serve well.

The chamber was a vast rock-ribbed space with vaulted ceilings, stained black by volcanic smoke, which drifted up from rents in the stony ground. Dark mouths yawned open all around the cavern walls, leading away to other chambers, to regimental barracks and training plains, down to the dungeons, up to the palace and out to the marches and salients of the other clans ur Horde. The strongholds of the Horde were vast indeed, greatest of all the contending sects in the UnderRealms. And yet . . .

The lord commander held his thoughts close, lest the heresy undo him. There was no denying the vast scale of the human settlements he had seen, both through the visions of the Diwan, and with his own eyes on the island stronghold of Manhatt'n. Where once he would have ventured forth trusting to the power and prowess of his elite guard, he could not now find that confidence which attended his ascent through the ranks of the Regiments Grymm. Lord Guyuk knew that, just as any normal human who encountered one of his warriors must surely be slain, his entire guard detail might not survive an encounter with one of the war bands of the upstart cattle.

As he donned greaves and plate and, this time, hefted his honourably scarred and battered shield, the lord commander could not help but feel some measure of anxiety. Not for himself, for he had long ago accepted his own death in battle as the inevitable consequence of walking the one true path, but for the Horde as a whole and, if he were honest, for all daemonum. Unlike most of his kind he had been afforded an opportunity to study the ways of modern man. The little unnamed thresh, now raised to the rank of Threshrend Superiorae, had provided Guyuk with ample opportunities to ponder the changed nature of these creatures. The lord commander could clearly discern in humanity not just the brute savagery of a Hunn dominant in frenzy, but more worrying, much more worrying, the reserved and guileful warcraft of the Grymm. These creatures, this livestock raised so far above its place, would not simply fight battles of resistance, or even of conquest and subjugation. They would make war of a scale and intent to annihilate everything they deemed *dar ienamic*.

Standing next to the lord commander, Compt'n ur Threshrend did not bother to armour himself.

'You carry no shield, I note, Superiorae,' said Guyuk. 'You don no mail, while warriors with honour to shame you clad themselves as though for the last great battle.'

'Meh,' the Superiorae shrugged. 'Chain mail chafes like a bitch and it won't even stop vanilla-flavoured 5.56 millimetre. And fuck armour-piercing or tracer fire or fucking HE rounds. I played a lot of fucking *COD*, man, I know this shit. Best defence is being somewhere else.'

Guyuk was sorry he'd mentioned it.

A Lieutenant Grymm stepped up, smashing a mailed fist against the iron plate and boiled grosswyrm leather protecting his upper body.

'My Lord,' he roared, as though making up for the stealth and quiet discipline they would have to practise in the Above, 'if it please you, the Master of the Ways pronounces the path clear.'

'Proceed then,' Guyuk grunted, acknowledging the officer's salute with a crashing blow of his own.

The Scolari Master was lightly armoured but even that was unusual. When they took the scrolls, the most learned of the Grymm put aside the trappings of their warrior days. And of all the disciplines, the navigators of the paths between the realms had, until recently, been amongst the least worldly and practical. After all, with the Horde sealed off beneath the capstone, there was scant call for their arcane knowledge. Only a sect with a memory measured in dark eons would have bothered to maintain the learnings of these particular masters. Guyuk knew that many of the other sects had not. This promised the Horde great advantages, tactical and strategic, against both human and daemonum enemies.

The Master of the Ways intoned his chant of guidance, reading from a long scroll, dense with runes and lines of dried ichor. Guyuk was sure he saw some of those lines shift and twist on the parchment. The Lieutenants Grymm stood motionless against a small section of chamber wall, heavy with edged metal and thick protective armouring.

The path to the human realm opened silently, a bloom of negative space, a blackness of infinite depth through which they must pass. As the Master of the Ways intoned his incantation the maw opened wider, like the mouth of *dar Drakon* as it swooped down on its prey. With the portal wide enough to take the cohort six abreast, the Captain of the Guard drew his war cleaver and lead the first rank toward the rift between the worlds.

Next to Guyuk, Compt'n ur Threshrend gave himself a shake, as if throwing off a surfeit of nervous energy. It was, Guyuk thought, a peculiarly human gesture. The empath danced from one hind-claw to the other and grinned, showing off its fang tracks as it turned to the lord commander.

'This is gonna be cool. I always wanted to be on TV.'

07

Dave wouldn't care to wager his annual bonus on it – and couldn't anyway, since he'd already blown his wad on those hookers from Reno – but he thought maybe the crowds were thinning out. Maybe people were getting smart and getting themselves off the damned streets. He couldn't be sure, but the masses around Times Square seemed thinner, and moved with more purpose. He could hear gunfire and sirens and screaming, could hear them up and down the island if he wanted to. There were still huge numbers of people bumbling around in a panic, but perhaps they were starting to get themselves inside, under cover.

A good thing, too. Sundown was well past. The full dark of night upon them.

Lieutenant Trenoweth leaned over the hood of a patrol car, marking X's onto a tourist map of Manhattan while Dave and Karen waited impatiently for him to tell them where they could best apply themselves. A chainsaw started up as city sanitation workers struggled to clear the intersection and surrounding streets of the tons of butchered meat they had made of the war band. The snarling whine of the chainsaw dropped into a deeper, meatier resonance as steel teeth bit deeply into dead flesh. Someone screamed, but it was a cry of revulsion rather than terror.

'Come on,' said Karen, jiggling impatiently in her boots and leathers. 'Clock's ticking here.'

Dave passed her a couple of energy gels one of the cops had scored for them from the Walgreens just a short distance up Broadway. Trenoweth seemed just about ready to give them something to do when his phone rang. He checked the screen and ignored it, pocketing the big-ass Android while it was still buzzing for his attention. Dave heard more of the handsets going off around them. Canaries in the coal mine of the twenty-first century. He and Karen exchanged a glance, wordless, but containing a clear desire to somehow speed everything up. Officer Delillo jogged over with another cell phone, passing it to her boss.

'You better take this, Lieutenant.'

'Trenoweth,' the cop answered the call, pissed off and short. 'What? Stop. Slow down and say again . . .'

He took in what the caller had to say, listening more attentively, and second time around the shock and dread on his face looked more deeply etched. He muttered a few words that sounded like 'thank you' and cut the connection, unseeing and oblivious. He passed the handset back to Delillo and drifted back to the tourist map weighed down on the hood of the patrol car by a couple of police radios and a riot baton.

'What?' said Dave.

'Lieutenant Trenoweth?' Karen grabbed him by the arm and turned him around with force enough to make him stumble.

'Hey!' Delillo protested, but Karen ignored her, focusing her gaze on the senior officer. Dave blinked as he thought he saw her connect to the cop, but not because she'd laid hands on him. It was in her eyes. They held Trenoweth at some level below the physical.

He came awake all at once, as though slapped, or splashed in the face with ice water.

'You gotta get over to Park Avenue,' he said, his voice insistent but strong, completely unlike the stunned abstraction with which he'd spoken only a moment earlier.

'Five hundred and thirty, Park. There's monsters over there . . .'

He stopped for a second and looked at Karen as though seeing her for the first time and not much liking what he did see. But he pressed on.

'Hunn, Sliveen, two Threshrend and leashed Fangr. A couple of war bands. Not a Talon, maybe a cohort at least.'

She nodded and started to turn away, 'We're on it,' she said.

'Wait, I need to brief you,' Trenoweth called after her, the confident timbre of his voice faltering again. She was already striding away.

'No, you don't,' she yelled back over the crowd noise. 'Come on, Hooper.'

Dave was still staring at Trenoweth. He looked like a man who'd seen something he could never understand, or knew something now that he hadn't a few seconds earlier. Something deeply wrong with the world, or within himself.

'She was in my head,' he said so quietly that nobody else could possibly hear him. Only Dave, and only because he was dialled in on the cop's channel.

'Yeah, she does that,' he said.

'No,' Trenoweth said. 'You don't understand. She was . . .'

But he trailed off, unable to explain. 'You better go,' he

said, moving onto something he could account for. 'There's monsters. Lots of them, inside a building. They're inside. Pulling people out of their homes. Pulling them apart.'

The horror was leaching back into his expression.

'She'll tell you,' said Trenoweth, his gaze troubled, following the retreating figure of Karin Varatchevsky. 'She knows about it now.'

Dave was about to say something stupid, like goodbye or good luck, but Trenoweth could not hear him. He had been stilled, caught outside whatever strange, unknowable quantum stream Dave and Karen slipped into when they warped. She'd hit the accelerator again.

Hefting Lucille, aware of her sub-aural humming again, he found Karen halfway up the block, headed west. She held a couple of mountain bikes aloft, one in each hand, as though showing off a clutch of shopping bags, triumphantly secured at a difficult sale.

'Come on,' she cried out, her voice easily pitched over the background rumble and whine of the city's soundtrack on pause. 'We trashed our last ride. Need some new wheels.'

The foot traffic was definitely lighter, and he had an easier time of it, hurrying through the living statues. He could see in their faces and the resolved aspect of their flight – suspended as it was – that these people were not blindly scattering and fleeing in terror. Most of them seemed to have destinations in mind. Specific paths to deliverance. Karen came out to meet him, stepping down from the sidewalk where she'd taken the bikes. Stolen them, to be clear about it. One looked like it belonging to a courier. It sported tote bags emblazoned with a logo he didn't recognise. The other owner was anonymous. Possibly dead. Karen had snapped the chains securing both bikes to a rack outside a 7-Eleven, pulling the steel links apart like taffy.

'Someone might need those,' said Dave, strangely troubled by the theft. Some bastard had stolen his son's bike once. It left a bad feeling.

'Someone does need them,' she said. 'Us.'

She passed him the courier bike and threw a heavy motorcycle boot over the other one, looking more than a little incongruous in her torn and gore-stiffened leathers. But then he looked kind of weird pedalling away in his black combat coveralls.

'Put your hammer in there,' she said, pointing at the heavy canvas courier bags.

He passed Lucille's long wooden shaft through a couple of loops on one of the bags. They were probably for document tubes, but worked just as well for enchanted war hammers.

'About ten minutes ago two full war bands hit an apartment building. Better part of a cohort, with two Threshrendum that we know of. Witnesses reported a couple of big toad-like daemons squatting in the foyer, eating the doorman. There are Sliveen up high somewhere, firing down on the approaches.'

Dave steadied himself on the bike as he stood on the pedal to get going. It'd been twenty years since he'd last ridden one.

After a moment or two of wobbling and almost knocking over a whole family, immobilised in their flight toward whatever safety beckoned them on the west side of the island, he settled into the once familiar rhythms of rising and falling pedals. But it wasn't just familiar; it felt natural, the bike a part of him. He was soon moving at speed, catching up to the accelerating figure of the Russian spy, trying not to focus too closely on the shape of her ass. She was psychic after all and . . .

'Eyes on the road, douche bag,' she said in a loud, hard voice.

Dave swore under his breath and concentrated on not crashing into anyone or staring at her derriere. He found he could even enjoy the ride, knowing he'd never been this fast or agile as a teenager. As the frozen city swept by in a blur he decided he could ride as well as Lance Armstrong, well enough to win the Tour de France, unless they blood tested him for magic nanobots or midi-chlorians or whatever.

They shot back up 5th Avenue, weaving a path through the stationary river of traffic, before cutting east up 46th. Karen briefed him in during moments when they didn't have to concentrate so much on avoiding the thousands of obstacles that lay between them and their goal.

'These ones employed a different attack profile,' she yelled back over her shoulder as they swept around the corner and onto Park Avenue. She reminded him of one of the SEALs, the way she talked. The double carriageway and divided traffic streams offered an easier passage here. Dave pulled level with her at the start of the 50s, where a whole block was clear. It was inexplicable, until they came upon a Fangr carcass, shot down on the median strip. Dave cast about quickly, looking for its leash holder, but found nothing.

'The Hunn and Fangr smashed their way into this place,' Karen said, keeping her eyes on the road, dodging around the tail of a yellow cab. 'All the other attacks, all of the ones I saw through that Threshrend we put down, they were out in the open, for everyone to see. Maximum horror, maximum chaos. But these ones hit the apartment block and most of what happened then happened out of sight. At first anyway.'

'Then what?' Dave asked as they slowed to negotiate the cross-town traffic at the next block.

'Then they started throwing people out of the windows. Or bits and pieces of them anyway . . . Kids,' she added, and he could hear a tightness in her voice. The first sign of weakness or at least of human frailty he'd seen from her.

She pulled up at a particularly thick traffic snarl and Dave thought she was about to dismount and push the bike through the blockage, but she didn't.

'Come here,' she said, making it an order. There was none of the softness or invitation he'd grown used to hearing in the voices of women after the Longreach.

'What?' He almost jumped back when she surprised him by reaching for his face.

Karen frowned.

'You're a tougher nut than the others but . . .' He felt her fingers on his forehead. In his freshly regrown hair. She fixed him with her eyes and . . .

Fuck.

He understood what Trenoweth had been trying to say. This woman wasn't just doing some Vulcan mind-meld party trick. She'd invaded him. Conscious and unconscious, id and ego. Memory, imagination, identity. She'd fucked them all, and not in a good way. For an excruciating instant, lasting less than a second, but feeling as though it dragged on for unbearable hours, he was all but gone. Erased from the world, at least as a wholly sentient being. It was as though she'd consumed his memories, his thoughts, his entire sense of self, leaving the merest shred behind to witness the . . . the rape of his mind.

It felt like he'd been defiled with great force and no regard for how he might feel about it. But now he knew what she knew, what she had taken from Trenoweth.

Dave felt as though he'd been gut punched. He was sick

with it. Dizzy. Too shocked to attend to the fact that for the split second she'd been inside him, negating him, the world had stuttered back into motion around them. Just for that moment. And then she was out of his head and the warp bubble expanded again and he knew, that not only was she doing it, but that she was drawing directly on him to do so.

He already knew that Karin Varatchevsky could not warp in exactly the same way he could. But she could dial into him somehow to achieve the effect. And he knew now why she called it orbing. She was more of a *Charmed* fan than a Trekkie.

'Don't do that again,' he croaked.

'If I have to, I will,' she said, without apology. 'Now you know what we're headed into. I don't have to waste time explaining.'

She took off again, pedalling away from him, accelerating at an inhuman pace, driving the bike forward with legs that could probably kick a car or a small truck out of her way. Dave followed, speeding after her just as quickly, even as he struggled to regain his balance and composure.

He knew why they had to move so fast. He knew because she knew.

Trenoweth had taken a call from the commander of the Midtown North Precinct. The man was desperate. Dave could actually hear the voice in his head, as Trenoweth had heard it over the cell phone. The commander had already wasted time and lost lives tracking them down. He needed Hooper and the woman he'd heard about. The one with the sword. He needed them a quarter hour ago at 530 Park Avenue. Everything they'd told people, to get off the streets, to stay inside and lock their doors and they'd be safe, it was wrong. These monsters – Trenoweth knew them to be Hunn, Fangr, Sliveen and Threshrendum because he'd learned that as soon as Karen had forced the entry to his mind – these fucking things had deliberately come in off the street. They'd rampaged through the building, not just killing the occupants, but displaying them as trophies. Draping them from smashed open windows. Throwing bodies and body parts into the street below. Men, women and children. They seemed to have taken particular care to ensure the children – the nestlings – could still be identified as such, and not just as smaller, random lumps of waste meat.

The imagery was stuck in Dave's head. Burned into his skull right behind the eyeballs, and there was no getting rid of it. No avoiding the connection to his own children. He almost lost control of the bike when he rode too close to a bright red hatchback that was well outside its lane. It could have been changing lanes. The driver – a young woman, his eerily improved memory recalled, unbidden, her shoulder-length black hair pulled back in a ponytail, tear tracks glistening on her cheeks, a small lap dog on the passenger seat beside her – was not watching where she was going; fixed instead on mashing her fingers against the glowing screen of a phone held in a cradle fixed to the dashboard.

Dave hit her side mirror, catching it with the edge of his knee, and immediately after by the full force of Lucille's heavy steel hammer head. It exploded in a shattering spray of plastic and glass, knocking his centre of gravity sideways. The wheel of the courier bike wobbled and caught in a rut or pothole. He was travelling at such speed that he had no time to think about what he was doing, only to sense the loss of controlled forward momentum, the sudden chaotic forces attempting to rip the handlebars from his grasp and tear him from the seat. As a teenager he'd had a similar experience; attacked by a neighbourhood dog, a thick snarling torpedo of teeth, gristle and bone which shot out of a vacant lot at him, snout down, head punching into his front wheel and tearing the bike out from underneath him. The dog would have done for him, if it weren't for his brother, riding behind him, materialising over his bleeding body, wielding a fence paling like a battle-axe. Andy took out that mongrel's eye.

But that was long ago and Andy was gone. That whole world was gone. And Dave discovered that he was a good twenty yards down Park Avenue, still pedalling furiously, his balance regained without conscious effort.

He wanted to chance a look back over his shoulder. Part of him worried what would happen if and when those sharp splinters of plastic and glass found soft targets. Had he just accelerated a hundred jagged little missiles to some lethal velocity?

He would never know, because he was already too far gone and far too late to stop and inspect any damage he'd wrought. Karen was half a block ahead of him, forging on through cross streets into the high 50s.

East 55th.

East 56th.

The wider boulevard of E57th, where she threaded the needle between two large buses. A gaudy red double-decker, some tourist thing, the upper floor open to the sky, and one of the familiar blue and white Metropolitan Transportation Authority buses. He'd already passed dozens of them, including one which had either broken down a few blocks back, or been abandoned by its driver and passengers. Dave aimed his bike at the spot where Karen had passed between them, intending to blast through and trust to providence on the other side.

But as he flashed into the gap between the grillwork at the front of the red double-decker and the exhaust puffing from the ass-end of the MTA vehicle, his vision blurred and pixelated and the world roared into motion. His shoulder caught on the grillwork of the tourist bus and he was thrown back to that day from his childhood, the bike wrenched from under him with incredible force.

08

Dave flew over the handlebars, tumbling through a swirl of colour and sound, all distorted by the same migraine kaleidoscope he recalled from the encounter with the empath daemon fifteen blocks downtown. He heard the teeth-rattling thump and crunch of steel on steel, the crash of shattered glass, honking horns, sirens, gunfire, screams. Part of him, the part of his mind sitting on its ass and chilling like Buddha, made a note to go back and fetch Lucille from wherever she ended up, because he sure as shit didn't have her anymore. He had no idea what would happen if she landed on somebody.

He was airborne, flying free, and then he was not. Another thump and crunch, this time not just heard but felt as an eruption of pain and damage through his body when he slammed into something.

A town car. One of those big-ass stretch limos. All polished black panels and tinted windows. Or they had been tinted. Now they were shattered and starred, destroyed by the impact of one uncontrolled superhero landing. He felt the big, heavy car shunt sideways under the impact, a fraction of a second before he felt bones breaking and shearing and splintering throughout his body. Ribs, shoulder, forearms, wrist, hands, hips, spinal discs. The sound of it was enormous. Buckling steel panels, exploding safety glass, his own screams, incoherent at first, but resolving in a torrent of obscenities as he crashed to the hard ground and rolled and rolled and broke a few more bones here and there. White-hot pain lanced through his stomach and up his damaged spine into his neck, his face, his skull. He felt organs tearing and knitting back up again. He screamed and swore as bones rearranged and reset themselves. He was sweating, pouring out torrents of rank-smelling moisture from every pore as his body turned up the furnace to repair itself. The migraine and pixelated aura were gone, and he rolled like a log, grunting rather than screaming now, until he fetched up against the gutter.

Not for the first time in his life.

'Fuck this for a bag of dicks,' he said, low and guttural, still short of breath and clenching his jaw against the pain and the shock.

Dave Hooper lay in the soft damp litter which had collected against the kerb, and a madly inappropriate thought occurred to him; that it was wrong for there to be any litter on Fifth Avenue. In the gutter or not.

'Hooper? You alive?'

Varatchevsky. The Russian.

No.

Karen, the all-American girl.

No.

Ur Threshrendum. She was ur Threshrendum now. As he was ur Hunn.

But it was just Warat.

Karen Warat, reaching down, hauling him up by one arm.

He cried out in surprise and real agony. That shoulder

wasn't quite finished healing. She let go of the injured limb and grabbed a handful of tattered, bloodied coverall, bunching her fist in the thick, tough fabric and using that to pull him to his feet. The material started to tear under the strain but then he was up and he felt her hands on his head again, the finger pads oddly cool and soft, but her palm ridged with rough callouses.

'No,' he said, and pulled away, instinctively. But it was too late. She'd forced her way inside him again, reduced him to a vessel. What little of him remained could feel her shaping him, working his anatomy like a meat puppet. He felt her willing his bones to mend and flesh to heal. The pain, or rather the discomfort of recovery, the prickling fever and maddening itch of it was more intense than ever before, denser and hotter, but after half a moment it was done and he was able to stand without her support.

'You'll be needing this,' she said, handing him Lucille. No problems for her hauling that heavy bitch up, then. He felt the rightness of it as the hardwood shaft smacked into his hand, felt himself drawing on some of the weapon's power, but without understanding how. The city was in motion around them again, but the crowds were not. He had fetched up against a stretch of pavement outside some antique shop. It was closed, as were most of the street-front businesses, some of them with security grilles locked in place, some with only polished glass between them and the world gone mad. They were in a very tony part of town, Dave knew, as he regained his balance. Jewellery, high-end fashion, cafes with small stupid food on big stupid plates, all the things he'd promised Annie she'd have when she married him. Just some of the many things he'd failed to deliver. Karen Warat, he was sure, knew this part of town well.

'Come on,' she said, already leaving him behind as she ran toward the apartment building at the corner of Park and 61st. She had the sword out and the long, evil-looking blade flashed and glinted under the lights of Manhattan.

The city hereabouts wasn't deserted. It wasn't possible in a city this size. But as Dave started after Karen he didn't have to fight his way through foot traffic. The closer they came to their destination, a medium high-rise condo, maybe twenty storeys tall, the fewer people they passed fleeing from it. He ran as fast as he could, and even without being able to slip the heavy chains of normal time, that was plenty fast enough to carry him toward the carnage that had cleared the streets. Ahead of him, Karen was a dark shadow blurring around and sometimes over abandoned cars and yellow cabs. Her boots landed on the hood of a taxi with a dull, hollow boom. The cab sank on its shock absorbers before rebounding enough to lift an inch or two off the asphalt. The driver had already abandoned the vehicle in front of a big-ass cathedral, right next door to the besieged apartment block. Both passenger doors stood wide open in back.

Dave ran without regard to saving energy, trusting in the vast quantities of meat he'd only just consumed, and the energy gels he'd shotgunned like understrength beers. He wasn't warping past the few frightened New Yorkers fleeing this latest horror, but to their eyes he must have moved with animal swiftness, because they pointed and gasped as he flew past. He'd seen the same reaction to Karen ahead of him.

She was already at the police cordon hastily thrown up around the scene of this latest atrocity, and Dave, dodging around another abandoned car, frowned when he saw her slide into cover. She slammed into the side of a blue and white cop car, shunting it sideways and forcing the cops who'd already taken shelter against the vehicle to crab walk after it. He could hear them cursing her, could hear her telling them to shut the fuck up.

The patrol car rocked as a giant harpoon speared into the roof, blowing out every window. Dave almost tripped over his own feet as he tried to arrest his forward momentum. Smaller bolts rained down on them from high above. He recognised them, or rather Urgon did, as the arrakh-mi fired by Sliveen crossbows. Another spear-length arrow, a shot from a great war bow, punched into the police car, detonating the flashing lights on the roof. Dave didn't need to be told twice. He dodged into a doorway across the street, getting out of the direct line of fire, just as a couple of bolts sparked off the pavement where he'd been standing, stupidly, gawping at the scene.

Five patrol cars ringed the entrance to 530 Park Avenue, and one large white truck that he took for some kind of tactical unit transport. It was riddled with war shots and darts and, before getting his ass out of the firing line, Dave had counted seven dead men, dressed identically to him in black combat coveralls. Their bodies lay sprawled around the van, which was still running, occasional puffs of exhaust coughing from its tailpipe. Other bodies, some whole, some roughly hacked and torn into parts, lay in the road, or hung from open windows of the white art deco apartment block. Still others lay atop the crushed and crumpled vehicles where they'd landed. Or perhaps where they'd been thrown, as improvised missiles. The once white facade of 530 Park Avenue was disfigured with thick runnels of blood, shockingly red in the artfully arranged spotlighting that would once have shown the building's architecture off to elegant effect.

Lucille's killing song was loud inside his mind, but soothing, especially after the violation he had so recently suffered at the hands of . . . what? His partner? His ally?

Neither felt like they caught the truth of Colonel Karin Varatchevsky. Trinder had pronounced her a very dangerous woman, and that was surely true. He'd also called her the enemy, which possibly was not true. Or not exactly. Still, right then Dave was not much concerned with working through yet more relationship issues, and listening to Lucille's hymn allowed him to shut out the violent mayhem he could clearly hear coming from within the high-end condo. Having a superhuman ability to hear conversations well beyond normal range was a mixed blessing. Not everybody loved Super Dave and it sucked ass having to hear them go on about it. But now his super-hearing was a form of torture, as he cowered, helpless to do anything about the cries for mercy, the screams of horror and of pain he alone could hear.

If Karen heard them, it didn't seem to bother her.

The police fired back at the Sliveen, who seemed to be scattered from the ground floor to the rooftop of the condo. A daemon scout had even holed up in the tower of the cathedral next door. Handguns and a couple of shotguns roared, making life hazardous for any daemonum closer to the ground. The single shot crack of what Dave guessed to be sniper fire swatted at those higher up. He saw a Sliveen topple forward, out of the church bell tower. The giant, insect-like carcass bounced and skidded down the old stone facade, catching here and there on some irregular facet of the building. Newton's Laws finished the job in spectacular fashion at street level where the Sliveen's bony carapace cracked and explosively blew apart on the steps of the cathedral.

Next door, at 530, glass shattered, masonry fell and iron-tipped arrakh-mi bolts clanged and sparked off the road in reply, or banged into the steel panels of the police cars. For one mad moment the vehicles reminded Dave of circled wagons in an old western. From his hiding place he watched Karen arguing with one of the cops. Sheathing her katana, she reached out and grabbed the guy's face.

'Whoa.'

Dave knew what was coming. He knew too that he wanted no part of it.

The cop, who had resisted fiercely whatever she'd been saying, suddenly changed. His whole demeanour, as outlined in his posture, even crouched so low in cover, switched from resistance to compliance at her touch. Or so it would seem to anyone other than Dave, or perhaps Trenoweth. He watched as the officer handed over his weapon, a submachine gun of some type and, presumably, a bunch of reloads for it. The small, dark objects looked like unusually large pistol magazines. Dave didn't think beat cops packed that kind of artillery, but maybe he'd picked it off one of the dead guys. There was plenty of dead guy stuff lying around. Another cop handed over his weapon too, a pistol, although Warat didn't appear to reach out and touch him in any way.

Dave edged out of cover and tried to warp. The way this clusterfuck was killing people, it was worth trying. 'Karen,' he yelled. 'We've got to get in there.'

A force ten hurricane blew through his head. The pain blinded him, loosened his bowels and forced him to his knees. Looking up through the blurry haze he could just make out another Sliveen on the roof of the building far above, shooting down into the street. He was sure he heard SWAT snipers in other buildings nearby start firing at the exposed creature.

A medic appeared from out of the blizzard of pain, dropped down next to Dave and tried to assess him. With great care he pushed her away. Careful not to break the black-clad, body-armoured woman.

'What the hell is wrong with him?' a voice asked. Male, gruff.

'He needs a teaspoon of harden-the-fuck-up and don't-be-so-fucking-stupid.'

Karen. She was angry enough that he fancied he could detect the merest hint of a Slavic accent underneath her carefully curated American voice.

'I told you not to do that,' she said. The faint echo of Mother Russia gone again.

As his vision cleared and the pain receded he saw she'd abandoned the cover of the patrol car and joined him in the entryway of the building across the street from the condo. He wondered how she'd made it across, if she'd been as fucked up as him.

The two cops she'd left behind sat with their backs against the side of the vehicle, watching her with moon eyes, their legs splayed out in front of them, their posture and attitude akin to public drunkenness. A condition with which Dave Hooper was not unacquainted.

The situation out on the street was chaotic. Corpses and parts of corpses everywhere. Body parts hanging from trees on the median strip: human and daemonum, but mostly human. Emergency vehicles, mostly police cars, pin-cushioned by Sliveen bolts and war shots. Ragged, uncoordinated gunfire duelled with volleys of *arrakh*.

Karen appeared to ponder their situation for a moment,

looking about her, calmly taking everything in. To Dave's eye, the Russian agent could just as easily have been contemplating a difficult seating plan at a dinner party.

She made a decision. 'Sergeant, are you in charge here?'

The cop she addressed was a squat, potato-headed character. He crouched as far back in cover as possible, while still firing his weapon at any monsters he caught sight of. The muzzle flash lit up their hiding place with flat white light every time the pistol cracked.

'Just my squad,' he said. 'You guys going in? They told me you'd be going in. Said you'd know what to do.'

'Yeah,' said Dave, eager to take charge, to start kicking this pile of shit into some sort of order. 'We'll go in.'

'In support of your men,' Karen added, qualifying his reply. She was still searching the street for something, and her expression changed when she found what she was looking for. A couple of pumper trucks surrounded by firefighters eager to do their job. They were sheltered from the worst of the Sliveen's assault by the angle of the street corner. She looked satisfied.

'Sergeant . . . Mahoney,' said Karen, checking his name tag. 'Just wait here for a moment. I have a plan if you'll bear with me.'

'Can't take any action until the incident commander gives the go ahead anyway,' Mahoney said, pointing to a tall man in a black polo and a baseball cap about fifty yards away. He was speaking into a walkie-talkie while sheltering behind the bulk of an ambulance. There was a dead body at his feet.

'We don't need a plan,' said Dave, feeling his impatience getting the better of him. 'We go in, we kick ass.' He tried to get up only to find Karen's hand on his arm. She reached inside his head and pushed his thoughts aside again. Pushed him back down.

'Hooper, your stupidity is wearing me out,' she said. 'Just sit your ass down for a second.'

Suddenly feeling numb and extra stupid from her touch, he did indeed fall back on his ass, just as she had ordered. He wanted to tell her to fuck off, to get out of his head, but he couldn't even manage that. It was like she'd stupefied him by laying one hand on his arm and *pushing* him somehow. Pushing what she wanted into his head.

He stared dumbly at the two cops she'd pushed a minute earlier. They were still gazing after her with the dopey expressions of contented milk cows – exactly how he felt now. He fought to throw it off as Varatchevsky ran to the firefighters. It was hard, like trying to wake up after a night on the tiles, but he concentrated and felt at least some of the fog clearing. She covered the distance to the fire tender as fast as a big cat chasing down its prey. The officer in charge over there, a woman Dave saw, jumped, startled by her arrival.

Dave felt a tightness in his stomach, wondering if Karen was going to push them too. But she didn't appear to. He finally forced himself all the way out of the stupor. It was not pleasant, nor easy. The fighting continued around him, the gunfire picking up as a Hunn warrior leaped from a first-floor window, nuts out, landing on the roof of an abandoned sedan, snarling and whirling a heavy mace above its head. The car crumpled under the impact and the beast, immature but still massive and dangerous, jumped toward the median strip. A heavy volley of fire caught it midair, spinning it around, punching out fist-sized lumps of hairy meat. It landed in a tangle of limbs and jangling armour amidst the shrubbery dividing Park Avenue. An automatic weapon opened up, and then another, the harsh industrial chatter of machine-gun fire throwing off showers of sparks as the bullets chewed into chain mail and armour plate. The Hunn didn't get up again.

Maybe it'll get a line in a song, Dave thought. An epic ballad of a Hunn with big balls and no brains, killed by its own dinner.

He located Karen again, surrounded by firefighters who seemed to be in furious agreement with whatever she was saying, but not because she'd pushed them to it. They didn't look like they'd taken a big hit off her wonder bong. A few nods, a fist bump and drivers mounted their trucks of their own volition. Dave heard them gun engines, and start to edge the big tenders closer to the police barricade. A few bolts pinged and thumped into the shiny red panels of the trucks, but didn't slow them. The rate of return fire from the police increased sharply in reply.

Water cannon, much like the ones Dave knew from the fire boats out at the rigs, swivelled to bear on the building. Firefighters hopped down on the lee-side of their trucks, carrying a collection of axes and other cutting tools. They looked grim but resolved. Dave was beginning to get a really bad feeling about this. It started somewhere near the base of his nut sack, and climbed up into his body.

He dialled in on their conversation with Varatchevsky. Her voice was all corn-fed Midwestern goodness, of course. Not a trace of the steppes in it.

'We are not unstoppable or invincible,' Karen told them. 'Contrary to what that dumbass might have told everyone.' She jerked a thumb in Dave's direction. 'There is something in there, some sort of creature, and it's stopping us from going in as hard as we might. But it's not stopping you. It's not even affecting you. Just us. We can't do what we have to until you take it down. You have to get in ahead of us and kill it. It's not a warrior daemon, it's not even very dangerous, not to you. Just us. Once you've killed it though,' she paused and scanned the entire group, making eye contact with all of them. 'Once *you* have killed it, we will go in and slaughter every motherfucking monster in the house.'

They cheered and roared.

'Fuck yeah!'

That came from one of the firemen, a man-mountain toting two axes like a baton twirler. Warat's speech and the big man's emphatic endorsement carried all of the others along, even the smaller, unflappable-looking woman in charge.

'Chief Gomes?' Karen said.

'Yes, ma'am?' She did not appear to be suffering from the push, or whatever it was.

'I want a steady stream of water spraying across the third floor,' Warat said. 'If anything sticks a head out, I want you to hose them down, drive them back. Is that possible?'

'It'll make a hell of a mess inside,' said Gomes. 'But I suppose that's not an issue, is it?'

'No, it's not.'

Dave was fully recovered, or at least he felt close to it. The paramedic tried to examine him again, but he gently pushed her away. Very gently. 'It's okay,' he said. 'I'm good. But if you've got anything to eat, I'll take that. It'll help. Seriously.'

He had to get over there, had to stop Warat before she sent these poor bastards in ahead of them. What the fuck was she thinking? They were going to die. All of them.

The medic shook her head. She had no food to offer, but

Sergeant Mahoney produced half a pretzel from one of his pockets. It was wrapped in greaseproof paper. He shrugged, a sort of apology. 'I was halfway done when all the shit came down.'

'Carbs and salt,' Dave said. 'Two of my favourite food groups. Thanks.' He took the loop of salty bread, still warm from the policeman's pocket, and stuffed it into his mouth, wishing for a cold beer, and feeling a little guilty for doing so. He chewed and swallowed as quickly as he could without choking, watching the tides of fire flow back and forth, the iron rain of bolts and war shots coming down, hot lead and tracer rounds going back up, raking the building facade. He watched Karen Warat whip a dozen men into a killing frenzy. Or, more likely, into a madness for their own doom.

'Stay here,' he said and took off as quickly as he could without hitting warp.

09

Dave exploded from the stone portico into the free-fire zone. The whole world seemed scoured by bullets and archaic missiles. There was none of the luxury of sweeping through in a slow-motion ballet dance. Dave moved as quickly as Karen, but crossbow shots and bullets still blurred past at supersonic velocities. He was aware of bolts and even war shots zeroing in on him. Iron barbs bit into concrete, throwing sparks. War shot punched deep into the soil of the gardens along the median strip. He had no doubt that if one of those big-ass Sliveen harpoons ran through his chest it would tear out his heart and lungs. He'd seen it happen more than once already, and he doubted a Snickers bar and a nap would do much good. Lucille keened a high, crazed hymn which helped to keep him focused on the end run.

Karen could see him coming now, they all could. The expression on the faces of the men, and those few women, huddled behind the protective bulk of the fire tender were aghast and open-mouthed, even though they had seen Warat move just as quickly a few minutes ago.

He charged in through the last of the arrows he'd called down on his head, struggling to pull up before running into anyone and knocking them clear across the street, or into the side of the fire truck. Dodging around the guy with the twin axes at the very last moment, Dave put his own shoulder into the truck with a bang that rocked it back on its axles.

His audience was stunned and mute.

'Never gets old, does it?' Dave grinned.

He expected to hear Karen, complaining about all the fire he'd drawn on them, but instead someone else, a man, shouted over the staccato uproar of gunfire.

'Who gave the order to move these trucks in?'

It was the incident commander, the guy in the black polo Sergeant Mahoney had pointed out. He'd run in at the same time as Dave. Slower of course, and from another direction, but he'd timed it well, using the distraction to lessen his chance of being targeted. He was red-faced from the sprint, but even more so from his rage. He was shouting, almost spluttering with it.

'You cannot redeploy assets without –'

Karen reached out, and tapped him on the forehead with one finger. He stopped ranting and his eyes went blank, fixed on her with vacant but profound absorption.

A few of the firemen stepped back, as if on instinct. The commander looked at Karen as if she might give up the meaning to everything that had happened here. But if she didn't, that would be cool too. As long as he could just look at her. Forever.

'What the hell did you do to him?' Dave said. 'Is this what you did to Trenoweth? To me. Fix it, now!'

'No, I will not,' said Karen in a voice free of any regret. 'I had to push him a lot harder because we don't have time for this. People, your people, are dying in that building, Hooper.'

She addressed the group which had gathered around them. 'Who's the ranking officer here?'

A cop in sergeant's stripes looked from the lobotomised incident commander to Karen and back again. 'Yeah, uh, yes, ma'am?'

'Sergeant, once the water cannon are going, you need to go in with your shooters. Support Chief Gomes and her volunteers.'

Gomes hefted her axe and nodded to a dozen men and women in helmets with their own axes. 'We're good.'

Dave said, 'No, seriously you're not.' He didn't know whether the sergeant, or even Gomes for that matter, were truly acting on their own, but they paid him no heed at all. Everyone was locked in on Varatchevsky. He was starting to understand why all of the sects kept their pet threshers on call.

The sergeant keyed his radio. 'All units, covering fire on my mark.'

'Karen, come on,' Dave pleaded, hating the weak sound of his voice. He knew what she was doing, the effect she had on them, because Urgon knew. She was ur Threshrendum, and the role of the empath daemon was to channel the warrior spirit, the *gurikh* of the Horde's fighters before battle. To amplify the fears of the enemy, and the bloodlust of its own sect.

She didn't need to touch any of them. She'd tuned them all like a fucking radio. He could even feel her will pushing at his, trying to shape it, but he threw off the effect with a grimace. It felt awkward and difficult, like heaving a weighted bar off his chest in the gym. The sergeant issued a string of orders, none of which Dave could decipher beyond guessing he was building some kind of assault formation. The firefighters hefted their axes and even a couple of chainsaws like a Hunn war band brandishing maces and swords.

'Open fire!'

The world cracked open with the full-throated roar of metal on metal hammering away against stone and marble. Water cannon opened up, forcing Sliveen archers back from the windows. Here and there Hunn and Fangr still threw bodies out the windows from further back. A grandmother here, a stockbroker bitten in two there. A baby went out, followed by a small boy, both of them alive and screaming until they hit the sidewalk. If the orcs had intended to terrorise the human cattle, it was an ill-advised tactic. It served only to enrage them. Somewhere under his skin, Dave could feel Karin Varatchevsky channelling that rage into a killing frenzy. In his fists, Lucille sang her approval.

The already monstrous roar of gunfire grew. An explosion halfway up the building face blew out windows and rained broken glass into the avenue.

Gas line, Dave thought.

Fire broke out higher up in the block, but the water cannon did not lift their aim from the lower floors where they proved useful at suppressing the Horde's archers.

Another pumper truck powered up its cannon and sprayed solid jets of water across the avenue, into the ground floor windows and doors, sweeping away a few Hunn and Fangr which had been waiting to receive the charge.

Dave shook off the last of his fugue and placed his hand firmly on Karen's shoulder. He spoke in the Olde Tongue without realising what he was doing.

'These are not warrior dominants. We dare not . . .'

Karen casually took his wrist and twisted, snapping it downward. It broke with a sound like a dry twig underfoot.

Pain flared, followed by the dizzying heatwave of accelerated healing. It distracted him long enough for her to order the attack.

'GO, GO, GO!'

Karen swung out of cover and took aim at the building, a pistol in one hand and the stubby little submachine gun in the other. It barked and strobed, but she squeezed off single shots from the pistol with such rapidity it was hard to believe she wasn't firing a second machine gun. She dropped back into cover when the SWAT teams made it across. As Dave rubbed at his wrist, something huge and heavy crashed to Park Avenue in front of the apartments. He felt the impact through the soles of his feet.

A dead Hunn, a big one, leaking thick daemon ichor from a dozen gunshot wounds, all precisely targeted at the face, throat and the thinner mantle of bone beneath its shield arm.

Dave stood, dazed and unsure of what to do. A war shot, huge and impossibly fast, slashed past his head and exploded as it struck the gutter, spraying him with splinters of Drakonglass. That focused his attention. He felt the little cuts and scratches on his face healing immediately, stinging and burning as they closed up.

He had to get in there – they both had to get in there – or every one of those men and women was going to die screaming. And for what? Why was Karen doing this? He knew Trinder would smirk and tell him, 'She is what she is, Hooper.'

Under the maelstrom of modern firepower three teams of eight men followed behind black shields. The shields looked to be bulletproof but Dave presumed the plexiglas ones probably weren't. He had no idea whether they'd provide any protection from *arrakh*. They reached the front door and pushed in behind the flash and crump of stun grenades.

Gomes and her firefighters crowded in behind them, all racing for the same double doors. Dave thought they'd be cut down in the street, but Karen had one thing right. The water from the fire cannon created an effective screen and, along with the massed firepower, shielded them until they forced their way inside.

With the monsters.

'Fuck this,' he said. She might be a stone killer from the KGB but he'd be damned if he was going to let her use these people as her personal peasant militia.

Gunshots and screams echoed back across the street, amplified by the acoustics of the marble and granite foyer.

He tested his wrist, slapping Lucille against the palm of his injured hand. Aside from a slight twinge, it was healed.

'You said we don't have time for this,' Dave shouted over the gunfire. 'So we'd better go, right? No point letting them have all the fun?'

He grabbed her upper arm again as if to drag her along should it prove necessary. He was ready to jam the hammerhead into her face if she tried anything, but this time, Warat did not stop him.

'Now we go,' she agreed, but without any sense of urgency to catch up with all the men and women she'd just sent to their deaths. Even so, she did not hesitate. When they took off, they ran across Park Avenue, leaping bodies and cars, soaked by blowback from the pumper sprays still hammering the lower floors.

He wasn't moving at warp, but he still travelled impossibly fast, sprinting, leaping, dodging one way and another, just like he had in high school football. Except for the magical sledgehammer and the crazy, hot Russian killer and all the daemons of Hell, of course. In other circumstances he might even have enjoyed the experience of his reclaimed physical prowess, had it not been for the carnage through which he had to pass.

Approaching the front of the building he could see, without having to count, all the cops from an earlier response effort, dead, splattered and gutted in the road save for one of them. The survivor was screaming, run through with the long lance from a Sliveen war bow. It had pinned him to a car, a little hatchback which had rear-ended a grocery truck. His back was to the building and Dave just knew that he'd been shot while trying to help the occupants of the car escape. They were mostly gone, except for the driver. She was hunched over the wheel, her head draped in the shroud of a deflated airbag while her would-be saviour spasmed and jigged on a skewer, screeching. The avenue was thick with the dead, mostly human, but leavened here and there with some grotesquerie from the UnderRealms. The Sliveen Karen had shot down. A couple of Fangr, chewed up by shotguns blasts. A headless Hunn, perhaps their leash holder. Human blood ran freely, pooling and drying in great lakes on the tarmac and sidewalk. Daemon ichor flowed thicker and slower, but still it flowed. Dave leaped and rolled as Karen did something to the submachine gun that ejected the empty mag with a flick of her wrists.

The volleys of the daemon archers on the upper levels of 530 had fallen away, but not completely. As though emboldened by Karen's example, the rate of fire from the cops seemed to pick up. It sounded heavier too. As though new weapons had been added to the arsenal. Dave saw more men in body armour and tactical gear pushing into the contested space with them, using fire and movement to advance. They carried long arms, assault rifles firing three round bursts that sounded like trip hammers. They ran through the rainbow spray from the fire trucks. The shouts of the police, which had earlier been ragged and confused, became gradually more orderly and directed.

Dave knew that it was not just their training and their bravery. It was the human Threshrend running at his side. He could feel it coming off her. Waves of heat that got into his own blood and drove him on with the same power as Lucille's battle hymn. He wondered if she was just as able to put the fear on the Horde.

If they had any fear, of course.

A small flurry of iron bolts fell behind them, triggering another torrent of gunshots from Karen. She ran, aimed and loosed fire all at once, a fluid blur of lethal intent. No daemon crashed to the ground this time, but she looked satisfied with her work, and Dave had reason to be glad, again, that she hadn't opened up on him with a gun back at the consulate. No more bolts or javelins hit the road near his feet. They had timed the run perfectly, unless you were some poor bastard getting torn apart inside, Dave thought. Waiting for us to drag asses to the fight.

Karen squeezed off another of those concise bullet storms as they neared the foyer, and this time he saw the result through a window: a Hunn and two Fangr, edged weapons drawn, dancing like spastic marionettes. For one mad, distracted moment Dave was seized of a memory; Annie scolding him for using the word 'spastic'. It was cruel, she said. Not as cruel as this bitch, Dave thought, when Karen cut the three daemonum down before they could carve into a group of shooters hiding behind their plexiglas shields. The orcs had probably drawn blades as soon as they caught sight of the strange, transparent shields: more of a provocation than a defence.

As Dave and Karen made the ruined entryway, the once beautiful frontage of 530 Park Avenue disintegrated under the destructive fire aimed against it. High windows shattered and spilled long fangs of glass into the street. Lumps of broken stonework rained down on him, some of them hot and smoking. Dave kept his head down and ran, his legs pumping with machined speed, his knuckles white where he gripped Lucille. He grimaced as he sidestepped a messy pile of body parts and gore. No clothing, he noted, in a flat internal voice that sounded a lot like a recording of madness. Probably somebody who'd been hauled out of their bed or the bath. The pile of meat and bone looked too big to have been a kid. But the remains of children defiled the street behind him. He shut his mind to them with an effort of will such as he'd never had to exercise before. In doing that, he also felt the amplifying effect of Karen on his *gurikh* fade away. No biggie. He didn't need her encouragement to kick these hairy fuckers to actual pieces.

The ruin he would make of the creatures which had done these things would not avenge the atrocity. Dave knew that.

But he was going to ruin them anyway. Hooper recognised the swelling chorus in his head as he charged into the building. Something Lucille had learned from him, or his memories. Something she seemed to have chosen just for this moment, to carry Dave along with her.

The 'Ride of the Valkyries'.

10

The cohort was no mere detachment of bodyguards assigned to protect Lord Guyuk ur Grymm. They would die to a daemon protecting him, of course, but they were also a fighting force in their own right – just like Lord Guyuk remained a warrior as well as the commandant of Her Majesty's most elite forces. And so they emerged upon the feeble human host and overwhelmed it in moments.

The Way Master opened his portal far enough from the target that the Lieutenants Grymm were able to deploy their war bands for an encircling manoeuvre before the humans knew what was happening. There were few if any of the calfling soldier clan here and the Grymm swarmed the field with great ferocity and speed. They flowed through the hard, strange, angular landscape as if they had trained since the nest for it. Sliveen scouts assaulted high points where they might direct fire and movement while also watching for the approach of any main-force enemy factions.

Guyuk was gratified to see that at least some of the cattle knew their place and marinated themselves in bodily pastes and juices upon comprehending the danger which had found them. They screamed and howled and tried, most ineffectually, to flee. It was an excellent palliative to the despondency which had threatened to overtake him of late. While it was hardly necessary, he drew his great war cleaver, Vier's Bane, and set about with an economy of violence dictated by the inconvenient necessity of sparing most of the wretched creatures. Compt'n ur Threshrend was adamant about that. He evinced no faith in even the Grymm to separate the useful from the useless in the heat of slaughter, so best to slaughter as few as possible.

It made for an admirable and undeniable logic. Even so, the lord commander had to revel, if only for a moment, in the meaty bite of his great blade as it cleaved asunder a dark-skinned, rotund calfling, waddling away as fast as its stumpy little legs would carry it. The screams of the cattle were pleasing, but lost for the most part beneath the battle roar of his thrall. To be fair, one of the prey did make a nuisance of himself, producing a tiny handheld weapon – one of the guns Compt'n had spent so long explaining to the lord commander – and firing it, wildly, inaccurately, but nonetheless with some effect. The noise of its discharge was outsized for such a ludicrously small contrivance, yet one of the tiny war shots hammered into Guyuk's shield and managed to stagger him. Just slightly, but there was no denying the impact. He saw another shot hit a Sergeant Grymm of Pike. Having no shield behind which to shelter, the sergeant took the blow square upon his bone cage. Bright white sparks flew from his chain mail, which disintegrated around the entry wound.

And enter it did, the tiny shot punching through good strong mail and twice boiled grosswyrm leather. It did not kill, or even drop the sergeant, but the force spun him around and arrested his charge, delaying for a second the ultimate demise of the upstart calfling. He died, screaming on the end of the warrior's pike, as was only appropriate.

There was a short interlude of violence, and all resistance collapsed.

Little pride was to be had in the victory, Guyuk told himself as he used the edge of his great round shield to carve one of the last fleeing humans in two. The shield's iron edge was chamfered to a quarter-claw thickness. Keen enough to slice through boiled wulfin-hide armour when wielded by a strong arm, well trained to the task. Used in such a fashion upon the unprotected bodies of the calflings, it was a spectacularly gruesome kill. Bloodwine and sweetmeats fairly exploded from the fragile bag of thin skin, painting the lord commander in hot gore.

Not a killing to sing about, or record in the scrolls, but it did afford an opportunity to practise one's self-denial. His head reeled with hunger, and long tendrils of acidic drool swung from his fangs. Not one morsel did he take from the quarry, though. Nor did any of his guard. They encircled their prey, as identified by the Superiorae, crushed all resistance with swift resolve, then stayed their claws and blades.

The cohort had emerged many leagues from the centre of the metropolis where the human champion and his thrall were heavily engaged by the diversionary attacks of Compt'n ur Threshrend. Still, the incredible scale of this settlement was of an order to daunt even the strongest mind. Was it so great that even a regiment might not fully invest it? Guyuk pondered this as a form of meditation to still his rumbling stomachs. He hawked a thick gob of digestive phlegm to the unnaturally level ground. From where he stood, the whole of the sky seemed filled with the towers of humanity. Projects, the Threshrend called them, and the word seemed freighted with a dark significance. These man-made ranges were indeed the project of a malign and terrible power. Even as Guyuk looked upon them he saw the small flashes of light and fire which he knew to be the tale-bearers of the human's ranged weaponry; the guns of the calflings, such as he had just encountered. There was no sense of massed and coordinated fire, but the occasional streak of magick light – of the cursed 'tracer' rounds – indicated that the attention of the armsmen was focused on the war bands which even now rampaged through these Projects a league's distance moonwise.

'Secure the prisoners,' he ordered. 'Do not damage them.'

Sergeants Grymm and their thrall hurried to his bidding. Again, Guyuk was pleased with the discipline and forbearance of his warriors. Were this a cohort of Hunn he had no doubt the ambush would have been a slaughter pit, with all of the calflings torn apart and every inferior Hunn drunk on their juices. Perhaps even the officers. His warriors Grymm, however, did not so much as raise a mailed fist to the terrified prisoners, in spite of the frustrations which attended the herding of them into some sort of order. They managed to make themselves understood with basic gestures and the occasional snarled word or two of abuse, even though none of the calflings understood the Olde Tongue. Guyuk doubted their ignorance mattered much when all he required of them was to gather in a bunch where they might be given their instructions. A cleaver banged on a shield. A pike used to create a barrier. These were enough.

'Nice work, boss.'

The Threshrend Superiorae appeared, holding a severed limb from which he stripped the meat by drawing the long bone through his blurring fang tracks. It was a disturbing thing to watch, threshrendum at their repast – all whirring fangs and flying scraps.

'It was simple work, Superiorae,' said Guyuk, plucking the flayed limb from Compt'n ur Threshrend's claws. 'And you complicate it by feeding your face while my warriors practise self-abnegation.'

'Threshy's gotta eat,' said the tiny empath, completely without remorse or shame. 'I can't think on no empty stomachs. And this next bit is where Threshy needs to be thinking like a motherfucker.'

Guyuk tossed the leg away, putting all of his many frustrations into the throw. The bone flew some distance and hit one of the larger human chariots with a bang. A prisoner screamed, the high-pitched shriek becoming a moan which fell away when the creature fainted with fright. The prisoners, a score of them on a quick headcount, huddled close together under the yellow glow illuminating the staging area in which a number of beastless chariots stood idle. Guyuk had learned not to flinch from the artificial lamplight of the human world, which, unlike sunlight, posed no dangers to his kind. He could not help his immediate inborn reaction however, and his hide crawled in revulsion under the lamplight. It did not improve his mood.

'Be about your responsibilities then, Superiorae. We are a good few leagues from the Dave here. But I'm sure you would not wish to contend with him or any main-force human military faction which might deploy.'

'I'm on it, boss,' said Compt'n ur Threshrend, his spirits obviously lifted by the fresh kill he'd just enjoyed. 'Lemme at 'em.'

'Hi. I'm Threshy, but you can call me Master.'

As great as the shock of ambush had been, the survivors of the attack were still capable of surprise. Stripping the leg meat from one of them like a southern fried drumstick had the desired effect. It freaked them the fuck out. Speaking to the captives in their own language gave them something to hold on to in their witless terror. He was to be feared, but unlike the giant, hulking beasts around him, he was different, if only in being able to communicate. In that one, special way he offered deliverance, perhaps even salvation.

The car lot on the edge of the Bronx, or what the soul once known as Compt'n thought of as the Bronx, sat next to some sort of bullshit community college. The main building was painted with rainbows, the internationally recognised symbol of being totally fucking lame. Compt'n knew it. Trev'r knew it. Even the roiling stew of minds he'd sucked out of the captured Navy SEALs back in Omaha knew it. Except for one dude, whose sister had been an artist or something. He didn't mind rainbows. The fucking sissie.

'So, who's the segment producer tonight?' Threshy asked.

He knew his fang tracks and monster chops weren't best suited for mouthing human words but he thought he did a pretty good job of it. Even if he sounded a little like a drunk doing a Sean Connery impression.

Sho, whoosh shegment prodoosher tonight?

The calfling known as Compt'n had been familiar with the jargon of media, having courted soft coverage of his academic output for many years, especially when his work with the military on the Human Terrain System burned so many bridges back to the world of academe. Unlike the dumb medieval brutes in Guyuk's cohort, unlike the lord commander for that matter, he did not find himself in an unfamiliar, alien world when they'd emerged from the UnderRealms. They came up, as planned, right on top of an outside broadcast unit covering a couple of war band attacks on the housing projects at the northern end of the city.

Compt'n knew of the WYNY broadcast truck from the Threshrend Majorae which had seen it earlier, without knowing what it had seen. The van sat in the car park of the college a safe distance across 3rd Avenue from the shit brown vertical slums. Or it had been a safe distance, when the only danger was from the war bands currently tearing through those slums. In one of the strange, recursive echoes that came from having consumed more than half a dozen human minds and all of their associated memories, the projects were oddly familiar to Compt'n ur Threshrend. Not because he had ever laid eyestalks on them before tonight, but because they'd been used as art assets in *Grand Theft Auto IV*, a video game Trevor Candly had played obsessively before thresh had sucked out his brains – and sucked in the memories of the phantom digital New York all but burned into that poor quality grey matter.

'Fuckin' awesome game,' said Threshy to himself, someone else's nostalgia getting the better of him. 'So, like I said. Who's gonna do Threshy a solid, and save their worthless fuckin' lives tonight?'

The huddled survivors of the lightning raid didn't rush to collaborate. Not because they were bravely resisting his offer to sell out, but because they were still too terrified to speak.

'Okay. I get it,' he said. 'Everyone's kinda freaked out right now. I totally understand y'all losing your shit and everything. You probably figured my homies and me, we're gonna torture you and eat you and stuff . . .'

He let that hang, watching them cower, making sure they understood. From the way they did some extra cowering he figured they got his drift.

'And we will totally do that . . .'

Zing! A few screams. Some cursing. One guy even fell to his knees and started begging which was both funny and awesome.

'Unless . . .'

And he paused again, holding up his hooked claws.

'Unless somebody mans up and tells me who is producing for WYNY tonight?'

He jerked a claw back in the direction of the news van, just in case some of the slower kiddies needed hand puppets to make it all clear to them.

Somebody, a woman Threshy thought, said something, but mixed in with all the moaning and crying and caterwauling it was hard to tell.

'Say what?'

'You ate him!' a woman said, her face an abject fright mask. She'd been crying – was still crying – and her cheeks were stained with running eyeliner.

'Oh,' said Threshy. 'That guy? Oops. My bad.'

Guyuk, who stood a short distance behind him, draped in entrails and painted with blood, glowered down on the prisoners. He stepped up beside Threshy and the terrified captives recoiled as one.

'Do they resist, Superiorae?' the lord commander growled. 'Shall we make an example of one?'

'No. No resistance here, dude. Just a lot of peeps filling their pants is all. Chill out. Let me work my monster mojo, okay?'

Guyuk skinned dark, ragged lips back from his fangs. It probably wasn't helping to calm down the cattle, but Compt'n ur Threshrend decided to go with it.

'So, who was that spoke up just then? A smart motherfucker doesn't want to get eaten by my bro here, I bet.' He indicated the horrifying figure of the lord commander looming behind him.

A skinny white woman put up a very shaky hand. She wore jeans and some sort of photographer's vest, the pockets full of batteries and cables and shit, looked like.

'Hey! Props to you, bitch. You gots more balls than all these ugly-ass monsters put together. You get to live.'

Her face contorted into a grimace some way between a nervous tic, a sick and weakly grin and a horrified wince. Some of her fellow prisoners, thinking they'd just lost their lives through timid silence, suddenly threw up their hands, raising their voices, offering to help.

'Whoa, back the fuck up,' said Threshy. 'She definitely gets to live.' He pointed at the skinny woman. 'And y'all maybe gets to live if she does good.'

Were it possible, the woman's pallid features lost even more colour as she understood the weight of responsibility that had just landed on her.

'Come on down, darlin',' said Threshy, beckoning her with one of his fore-claws. If he were a true Threshrend Superiorae he would have been able to reach out and twiddle her fucking dials like a master DJ, damping down her fear, amping up her calm. Or the other way around, if that worked for him. But the tiny thresh he had once been had never had a chance to grow into those skills, not fully, and so Compt'n ur Threshrend had to make do with cunning and another form of mind game.

'Come on,' he said, in as gentle and encouraging a fashion as a daemon hell toad with a forest of eyestalks and chainsaws for teeth could manage. 'Come on over here. I'm not going to eat you. Just your friends if you don't help me out.'

The woman faltered at that.

'Come on. What's your name, sweetheart?'

'Polly,' she answered, her voice quavering. 'P-Polly Farrell.'

Threshy was sorely tempted to mock her little stutter, the habits of Trev'r nearly outweighing the needs and judgment of Compt'n. But in the end, the will of Compt'n ur Threshrend was enough to overpower the strength of that initial Trev'r imprint.

'So, Polly. Y'all look like a photographer or some shit like that? Is that your thing?'

She shook her head, so violently it seemed in danger of coming loose.

'N-no. I'm just the intern. They got me to carry all this for them.'

Her hands fluttered over the bulging pockets of the vest.

'Okay, that sucks for you. Being an intern, I mean. Lotsa work. No pay, right?'

She nodded, a little more self-contained now and obviously taken with his knowledge of intern lore, in spite of her terror.

'Yeah. Where I come from, you know, Hell, we call that slavery. It's hell popular down there.' He grinned at his own joke. 'See what I did there?'

But if he meant to set Polly at ease with the quip, the sight of his fang tracks, encrusted with gore, did not help. She started shuddering.

'Whoa, sorry. Bad joke. Okay. So, Polly. This is like really fucking important to me, and to this ugly mountain-sized motherfucker behind me.'

Polly Farrell risked a glance up at the towering figure of Lord Guyuk ur Grymm, but shied away from the awful vision.

'Dude,' Threshy stage whispered back over his shoulder in the Olde Tongue. 'Dude, you're freaking her out with the entrails and shit. Think you could, like, clean up those bowels you got hanging off of you? That'd be golden. And maybe practise your line, for your cameo later.'

Guyuk growled, but used his cleaver to flick off the heaviest strands of intestine and viscera.

'Are we golden now, Threshrend?' he asked in a tone of voice that implied they'd better be.

'As Kanye. Thanks. So, Polly,' he said, changing back to English as he refocused on the intern. 'Here's the thing. I need to negotiate with the mucky mucks. You know, your leaders and shit. But every time we try and talk with them, they drop a fucking bomb on us. Soooo . . . I figure, since I don't have like a Twitter account or a blog or anything because, you know . . . typing . . .' He held up his bloodied claws and wiggled the hooked talons at the ends. 'I figured maybe we could just, you know, go on TV or some shit. Could you help us with that? Could be a promotion in it for you. Maybe you might even get paid or something, and I would totally not fucking eat you as well.'

Threshy leaned in as if to impart a secret and he saw her mustering every reserve of courage she possessed not to rear back. Good for you, he thought. You hardcore biatch.

'I won't even eat your friends over there,' he whispered. 'If you can help out. Do you think you can help out?'

She threw a desperate, almost despairing glance back at the small circle of captives. Some called out.

'What's going on?'

'What's it saying?'

Others had fallen into a fugue state, staring hopelessly into the distance.

'I . . . I'd need the camera guy. And the sound guy,' said Polly.

Threshy sucked air in through his fang tracks.

'Man, I hope nobody ate them.'

Immediately inside the foyer, five cops and the dual axe-wielding firefighter lay in spreading pools of blood next to a quivering Hunn and two bullet-riddled Fangr. The fireman's axes were matted with coarse hair and clotting daemon ichor. The wounds which had killed the men were grosser, uglier than the bullet holes in the monsters, but they were all just as dead. Except for the Hunn, which was twitching in the last moments of its life. Karen put a bullet into the big orc's melon without even pausing to aim as she walked past. The action had no more significance for her than picking lint off a lapel. Then she paused and backtracked. She put another round into the monster's giant flaccid dick. Shrugged. Moved on. The loose bands of cops and firemen still on this floor, mopping up, tending to the casualties, jumped at the first shot, but not the second. They settled when they saw it was her. Dave was dumbfounded to see them so obviously relax. She'd sent them in here, killed them all to be honest, and yet the observable composure that passed over at the sight of her reminded him of a Mexican wave at a sports ground.

'Are you doing that?' he asked. 'Chilling them out?'

'Yes,' she said, without even attempting to dissemble.

'Well fucking knock it off.'

'No. They need it and we need them. And you're not going to do anything about it because you'll get more civilians killed.'

She was right. He honestly didn't know which was worse. Sending these guys to their doom, or brainwashing them into liking it. He stared, whey-faced at the corpses on the floor near the concierge desk.

At least they died happy. Sort of.

'Fuck me,' Dave muttered. 'You turned them into pod people.' If Trinder found out about this, Hooper had no doubt he'd order a sniper to put a bullet into Karen's brain. Bad enough when she was Agent Romanoff. Worse now that she'd morphed into Rasputin too.

Karen stopped to scavenge weapons from the dead officers. Or ammunition, anyway. She'd discarded the submachine gun, keeping only the pistol and she moved quickly from one body to another, stripping them of ammo. 'Armour-piercing and tracers,' she said, checking the contents of one magazine. 'Not your standard load.'

Nobody objected. They just continued doing their jobs. Dave recognised Mahoney and the paramedic who'd tried to tend him earlier. They worked on a screaming fireman and they had the same dopey, satisfied 'just-fucked-by-Karen' look about them as everyone else.

He gripped Lucille a little tighter. He could hear the terrible sounds of close-quarter battle and atrocity coming from the upper floors. Most of the cohort which had initially stormed into the building had not been at the windows firing down on them, or in the reception area, waiting to receive the attack. Hunn and Fangr rampaged, unseen, slaughtering the residents on the floors above them. He could hear it. War hammers and axes smashed open heavy doors. Giant, horned feet kicked at makeshift barriers of furniture piled high in doors and hallways, shattering the feeble defences. Bone cracked open, sucked clean of marrow. Closer to them, shotguns blasted away followed by submachine-gun fusillades smothering the growling death roars of the Hunn. He had to close his mind to the garbled, babbling horror of defenceless human beings begging for mercy, pleading for their lives which were ending in blood and terror.

Instead, while Karen stripped the dead and rubfucked the feeble minds of her cult followers, he tried to work out the numbers, to get some idea of what they faced. Two Hunn war bands. That meant anywhere between four to a dozen Hunn in each band, with each of the warrior daemons controlling a leash of two or three Fangr. He had no idea how many Sliveen they had with them. There could be as many again of the giant insectile stealth daemons and from the tattoos of the ones he'd seen shot down, they weren't untested, unnamed fighters either. The first one had been inked with the stories of battle against four other sects.

There could be as few as two dozen *ienamic*, or anywhere up to a hundred of them.

'Would you stop humming that stupid song,' Karen said as she stuffed the last of the pistol mags in a pocket of her motorcycle jacket. Dave hadn't realised he'd been subvocalising his duet with Lucille.

'Fucking Wagner,' she added, muttering mostly to herself. 'Fascists and their fucking oompah music.'

Dave stopped humming. Lucille didn't.

Ugly organic splatters painted the wall behind the

reception desk and a thick smear of blood covered the black and white granite tiles in front. The polished stone desk was shattered as though by the blows of great war hammers. Filthy footprints or claw marks spoiled the once pristine public areas of the exclusive condominium. Hundreds of stray bullet holes pockmarked the walls, but older, more primitive weapons had wrought great damage too. Twilight fire flickered from the destruction, ignited by the fierce fighting. Karen took note of it.

'Armour-piercing I approve of,' she said. 'Tracers, not so much.'

Dave, the safety engineer, figured it out without being told. The tracers were a fire hazard in a building already ablaze within a dense city. With the firefighters busy playing at Conan the Barbarian there was no one on hand to quell fires great and small. He held Lucille in a firm but supple grip, ready to swing on anything that came at him. Including Karen. She held the katana in her right hand, blade pointed at the floor, angled slightly away from her, the pistol in her other hand. Nine reloads sat in the zippered pockets of her leather jacket and biker pants, clinking softly against each other when she moved. He hadn't consciously counted them as she picked them up. It was just one of those things he knew about these days.

'Why are we waiting?' Dave asked.

Warat sighed, making no move to join the fight upstairs. 'Americans. No sense of patience at all. Do you know anything of Russian history?'

'No,' he said, not hiding his impatience, which he had plenty of.

'How about your own Civil War?' she asked, kneeling down to search one of the cops again.

'Not much,' he said. 'I don't have a war boner like a lot of guys. Lots of people died. That's all. Lots of people always die. Like tonight.'

Satisfied, she stood up with a radio in her hand and unplugged the earpiece. The speaker, at low volume, began to give a running play by play from the battle upstairs. It was incomprehensible to Dave. The radio chatter reminded him of Omaha, warping through cornfields, trying to find Emmeline.

He tuned the radio out. He was getting better at that too, dialling down certain channels.

'They'll die,' Dave said. 'Your little fan club. They'll all die. That's the only fucking history lesson I got here tonight, Karen, or Karin or Ekaterina. Whatever your name is. Lots of people are gonna die because they can't deal with this shit, and for some reason you won't. They'll end up like these poor fucks.'

He waved a free hand at the desecrated corpses.

'Poor fucks, we can get more of,' Warat said. 'The world is full of them. Even this country. Especially this country,' she added wryly. 'Do you know where they can get more of us?'

'That's a bullshit argument,' he shot back, raising his voice. His anger got the better of him.

'Shush, now,' she said, as if cooing a baby. She moved quickly. Not just with the animal swiftness they both possessed, but with the surety of someone trained to move that way. She drove a fist into his solar plexus, punched all the air from his body, left him doubled over and gasping. Partly from shock, but mostly from the precisely aimed blow. She was possessed of enormous strength, like him. But unlike Dave she was familiar with honed violence. He had been punched more than once in his life. Starting with the beatings his old man liked to hand out, he'd taken more than his fair share.

Handed a couple on too. But no man had ever hit him as hard as Warat just did. Not even Marty Grbac that time he'd busted his nose and laid open his cheek for taking the name of the Lord in vain. If he had to guess, Karen Warat was throwing about eight or nine times as much power into a punch as any man who'd ever put one on him.

She hadn't hit him to shut him up or stop him from charging off and messing up whatever plan she had, however. She'd hit him to distract him long enough to put one hand on him more gently. As he collapsed to his knees and tried to find some air to breathe in, he felt her cool fingers on his head.

'Be still and be quiet,' she said.

And she pushed. Hard.

It was only a short time later that Dave regained the ability to speak and to move, but it was not quick enough. More people had died. Warat was seated in a chair by the stairs, her katana between her legs. She breathed slowly, and gazed into the middle distance, reminding Dave of his wife – no, his *ex*-wife damn it – when she was doing yoga, or meditation, or whatever the hell it was. It would have been spooky were it not for the even spookier detachment of Warat's pod people, who simply went about their duties after she'd decked him as if nothing had happened.

'What do you hear?' she asked, coming out of her semi-trance.

'What the fuck do you mean?'

Resentful Dave climbed to his feet. Cautious Dave kept his distance from her. Lucille, too, seemed to vibrate just below the level of perception, like a warning bell struck some time ago.

'I mean, what do you hear? On this floor? The next one up. Anything? Because I'm not getting anything. Threshers are somewhere nearby, but I think they're a few floors up now.'

Dave had shut himself off to what was happening inside 530 Park while he was down. It was too hard, not being able to do anything about it. He'd withdrawn into himself to wait out whatever Karen had done to him.

'The fuck should I do anything to help you, you murderous bitch?'

'If you want to help these people, Dave,' she said, her voice light and calm, where his was full of dark resentment and barely restrained fury, 'you'll do as I ask. I know your abilities. Better than you do, I suspect. Now shut the fuck up, listen hard, and tell me what you hear upstairs.'

Dave was inclined to flip her the bird and get himself upstairs and into the fight, but her eyes held him.

'I'm not going to push you into it, Dave. It gets harder every time with you. It's like you're building up a resistance. It wearies me, to be truthful, trying to push you around. If you'd just do as I ask, I promise, we'll kill everything which needs to be killed a good deal quicker.'

Rifles still cracked outside, singly and in short barking bursts of automatic fire, but the massed thunder that covered their charge into the building had abated. Dave was close to storming off and leaving her here but it was the fact that she didn't push him, that he could tell she had withdrawn whatever hold she might have had over him, that gave him pause.

'Come on,' she said. 'People dying.'

He frowned and tuned out the sporadic gunfire and concentrated on the eerie calm around them, letting his senses expand, almost as though he was detaching from himself, drifting up through the floors above them.

He listened to gunshots, war shouts and terrible screams. Edged weapons powered by honed muscle and fury snapped through bone, and sliced open flesh. He heard radios. The small unit Karen still carried. Other radios carried by her fighters. She wasn't forcing them to fight. She simply drew on the empathic power of dar Threshrendum to amplify the natural human bent toward savagery and vengeance-seeking. At the same time she dialled down the fear and uncertainty that was just as natural a reaction. Dave didn't think she was having that effect on him, but he could feel it in the ether.

Emergency Services Unit teams spoke in their own tactical language, which Dave did not understand. He could also hear the firefighters. They had their radio channels. And when they didn't, they shouted and roared at each other as men in battle always had. He heard all of that.

Karen smiled, breaking in on his thoughts.

'I didn't expect that,' she said, as though she'd heard what he'd heard.

Of course she had.

'They're actually scaring these *ublyudok*. The Hunn weren't expecting a pit fight. Just dinner and a show.'

'These what?' Dave said, thinking he'd missed the debut of some new horror.

'These bastards. Your countrymen are giving a good account of themselves, Hooper. The Horde warriors are surprised. They were ready to die at our hands. Yours and mine. But not to be killed by the entree.'

Dave ignored her and concentrated again, searching with mounting frustration for any sign of the Threshrendum which had turned off his warp engines. Kill those things and

Karen was right, they would blow through this place like a hurricane.

He could hear the dial tone of a landline phone, knocked from its cradle. White noise, probably from a television or radio, in a room somewhere to his left. He could hear water running, splashing on a hard stone floor two storeys above them. A clock, an old one, ticking. But nothing else nearby. No grunts or snarls. No bones crunching between powerful jaws. No chewing. No screaming.

'This is murder,' Dave said, reining in his need to get going, a need for kinetic violence that Lucille was only too happy to sing him toward. 'They're not dying for us, Karen. We're killing them.'

'This is war,' she said. 'You should be familiar with it by now. Your country has visited enough of it upon the world.'

Dave had no response to the taunt. He'd said much worse in the years after his brother had been lost to the war. Much worse. Instead he spoke softly, while most of his attention remained detached, elsewhere, seeking their prey.

'Karen?'

She opened her blue eyes and looked at him. 'Yes, Dave?'

'Don't ever touch me again.'

She smiled.

'Why, Dave, I'll bet that's the first time you've ever said that to a girl. But I'll bet they've said it to you more than once.'

'I'm serious.'

'I know. And these are all the fucks I do not give,' she said, holding her arms wide and letting her own irritation and impatience show through for the first time. 'Stop whining and get on with it.'

'Whatever. I'm not the killer here. You are.'

'Trinder told you that?' she asked as she rose out of her seat. Her boots crunched on shards of broken pottery. A vase which had once sat atop an antique table, now reduced to splinters.

'No, well yes, but my common fucking sense tells me that too. You're trained for this, or shit like this anyway. I'm not. I'll do whatever needs doing in here, as best I can. But I'm not your tool.'

'Well, arguably you are a bit of a tool,' Karen said, but without any obvious malice.

'On your left, on your left,' the radio squawked. A heavy axe thumped against a wall or a door. Dave heard wood cracking and screeching. Karen closed her eyes again, reciting something under her breath. He heard a sound like a chicken or a joint of beef being pulled apart. And screams. Gunfire roared. He didn't need any Spidey senses to hear that. Everyone in the foyer could hear it, and yet, they just went about their tasks. Karen continued muttering, or praying, or whatever she was doing to maintain things.

'Third floor clear,' a voice on the radio said. 'I need medics in here. Officers and firefighters down.'

A male voice, urgent, but not nearly as garbled with fear or even excitement as it should be.

'Continue with clearance,' another voice on the radio.

Karen came back to herself. 'I suppose you do not play chess, Dave, but let me explain what is happening now. You and I? We are the most valuable pieces on this board and we'll find the Threshers by using our pawns. We find them, fix them in place and we take them off the board.'

The radio squealed and squawked as two different signals competed for the same channel. Karen turned her radio down a notch.

'Panic,' she said. 'Can you feel it?'

He could. She breathed deeply, exhaled, and the feeling cleared like mist burned off by the sun.

She can wind them down. Or wind them up, he thought. Her little toy soldiers. Just like that.

The radio squawked. 'I need more men. I've lost half of . . . oh, shit.'

There was a blood-curdling scream. Inside his head.

'Our cue,' Karen said, moving fast again. Gun forward, sword ready, a weird mix of iconography. Gunslinger, samurai, biker babe from Hell. Dave's boots made small ripping sounds as he ran across the drying blood on the floor. She seemed to avoid stepping in it without apparent effort. Taking the stairwell next to the lifts, Karen climbed to the third floor in a series of leaps and turns. Dave followed.

12

'They're close,' Karen said. 'The way they reach out and touch us, it has a limited range. It manifested at less than a hundred yards before. I know them, Hooper. I was very intimate with that Thresher.'

'Jesus,' he said. 'That's nasty.'

She waved it off. 'I'm a veteran of the GRU and the New York art mafia. I've done worse.'

They broke out onto the third floor. The smoke-filled hallways looked like a hospital corridor after a mass casualty event. The wounded were propped up against walls, illuminated by the flickering firelight that trickled forth from cleared apartments. There was more shadow than light for the dead, stacked like cordwood in the corners where they wouldn't get in the way. The lights were out but enough of the first responders carried their own torches and emergency lamps that Dave didn't need his night vision. Warat advanced with the gun in her left hand and the sword in her right. A ripple of movement flowed away from them, down the hallway. Karen's surviving pod people, turning toward her, gazing as if rapt. Dave found that spookier than stalking the Horde in the dark.

She stopped and froze in place. Chief Gomes, her white shirt splattered in blood, knelt on the floor in front of an open door next to her own gore-matted fire axe. She was trying to staunch the bleeding of one of her comrades. The entryway of the suite was blocked by a quartet of dead firefighters. Dave expected her to rage at them, especially Karen, but she didn't. She smiled when she saw the Russian.

Karen mouthed a word to her. Where?

Gomes inclined with her head down the hallway and whispered back. 'To the left, ma'am. All the way down.'

'Sorry,' Dave said as he slipped past, but Gomes just pressed harder on the bloodied poultice she'd stuffed into the sucking chest wound.

'S'okay,' she said, as though he was a few minutes late for a coffee date. 'Had to be done.'

'Hooper,' Karen said. 'Down the hall, on the left. Corner apartment. It will be in there somewhere. Just like down on the street. I'll hold it. You kill it. It had guards, but they're mostly taken care of. Mostly.'

Dave nodded and moved forward. A dead Fangr, its head taken off by gunfire, had been kicked out of the way and fetched up against a door. None of the casualties paid him much attention as he slipped past. They all looked to Karen. He was certain if she suggested they throw themselves at the Thresher to distract it for him, they would.

Pain swelled in his temples with each step, like knuckles grinding in on the soft spot. He felt pressure building behind his eyeballs and a sick feeling of dread, but he recognised it as coming from somewhere outside him. He ran one hand up and down Lucille, tested his grip, and felt better for it. She was back to humming one of her own tunes and it filled him with warm content, like a long pour of good bourbon in front of a fire on a cold night.

Doors stood open here and there, some of them smashed off their hinges. One propped open by a dead cop, a Sliveen bolt in his throat. Bullet holes riddled the walls, interspersed with large gaping rents where the axes had missed. Brass casings littered the floor, sticky with the coagulating monster gruel that puddled around his boots.

The survivors of an ESU fire team gathered around the doorway at the end of the hall. They looked like hell, slumped over each other, against the walls. One of the men was sitting with his legs out in front of him, trying to reload his weapon, a submachine gun. He'd lost a hand and he used his remaining hand to seat the magazine in place. It looked like someone had fashioned a tourniquet from a tea towel and tied off his bleeding stump. He kept at the task like a small boy, the tip of his tongue just out of his mouth, fixated on the most difficult part of gluing together a model airplane.

'I'll take it from here, boys,' Dave said. His voice was thick.

To a man they all looked to Karen for confirmation.

'Okay,' one of them said, after a moment. The man with one hand persisted with trying to load his weapon. What the hell was gonna happen to that guy? He probably wouldn't be partying in LA with Jennifer Aniston or Paris Hilton, Dave thought.

He stood in front of the door now. Took a breath and tried to discern what lay behind it.

Dave listened.

The steady if laboured breathing had to be a Thresher, for sure. A pair of grunting, snorting sounds, as if someone had a sinus infection, those must be Hunn, perhaps a couple of them. And maybe their leashes. Going straight through that door was gonna get bloody. Dave knew it in his bones. Hadn't stopped any of these guys though. He glanced back toward Karen and found her a few steps away, the pistol holstered somewhere, her free hand up, palm out. He recognised the attitude from the struggle she'd had with the Thresher back at 42nd Street. There were no special effects, no streamers of colour or distortions of space and time. She stood, one hand out as if about to wave to somebody. Some of the survivors gathered a short distance behind her, watching, transfixed. Even the wounded had dragged themselves down the corridor to be closer to her. Iron filings drawn to a magnet.

Dave shook off the shudder that wanted to run down his back. They reminded him of the walking dead in Omaha. Not the Tümorum, but rather the meat puppets raised by the Revenant Master. A different kind of Muppet, he snorted nervously to himself.

If one berserk Hunn with a couple of blades got in amongst them it would slaughter them all, those that didn't go down in the crossfire.

'Okay,' he said to Karen. 'I'm going in.'

'No you're not,' she said. Her voice was strained and her eyes appeared to be sunk deep in shadow. 'You're standing around out here scratching your ass. Now get going. This one's strong. Three Hunn somewhere,' she added with a grunt. 'No leash.'

Awesome, Dave thought.

He used Lucille to open the door, pushing on it with the steel head, ready to start swinging if anything came at him. It was unlatched and swung open slowly. A couple of ESU shooters, one of them bearing a pump-action shotgun, formed up on his six and he stopped for a second, surprised that he was now thinking things like 'They formed up on my six.'

His brother used to say shit like that. Like he had faith in it, too.

Shit like that got his brother killed.

'It's okay,' Dave started to say, 'I got this . . .'

He wanted to warn them off. There was no point in getting anyone else killed for such a meagre return. They couldn't move as quickly as him, even with his warp drive crippled. They couldn't mix it up with the Hunn when they ran out of bullets. And they weren't even doing this of their own free will. Not entirely. Not with Karen pushing them around. He wasn't being noble. They'd get in his way, stop him from busting out his biggest, baddest Hulk Smash for fear of catching them by accident. And he had enough guilt to be getting on with for now. The dead were piling up around him so high you couldn't see past them.

'Karen told us,' they said in unison, like horror movie twins, and that was creepier than anything he'd seen so far.

'All righty then,' Dave said. Karen had told them. There would be no warning them off. 'Just don't shoot me in the ass.'

The apartment, a vast and airy space, was trashed. Hooper moved through upturned furniture and shattered electronics. Tall windows looking out over Park Avenue and East 61st spilled enough city light inside that neither of his wingmen needed their night vision goggles. Not in the main living area at least. Blood had pooled in the carpet and was partway gone to the consistency of molasses. A dark trail led away from the lounge and veered into a dark-panelled room.

'Let's go then,' said Dave. Bert and Ernie followed obediently.

The blood trail ended in a grotesque mound of meat and gore piled atop a billiard table.

Man, that felt is ruined, Dave thought. He couldn't help it. His mind had to go somewhere and he didn't want to contemplate the mess on the table. The billiards room, or library – bookshelves reached up to the plaster ceiling – was all but demolished. Hundreds of books lay torn and crushed as though a bomb had detonated in here. Great, obliterating axe blows and the heavy crunching impacts of maces and mauls had destroyed all the shelving. Dave had never been much of a reader after high school. Sports and reports mostly. But he keenly felt the violation of this room. The Horde had rampaged through here for the pure moronic joy of it. He knew that, because he felt in his own meat Urgon's pleasure at the thought. He thought he could make out the scraps of a uniform in amongst the butchery on the stained and ruined surface of the pool table.

'A cop, you reckon?' he said in a quiet voice. 'One of your guys? Maybe the concierge?'

He was talking to the ESU guys but was surprised by Karen's voice. Not in his head, thankfully. She'd followed him in, without her entourage.

'Just the hired help,' she said.

'Well, nobody who could afford to live in a place like this, that's for damn sure,' Dave replied. His own voice sounded sad to him. He worked for people who lived in places like this, and even if he didn't like them much he wouldn't wish such an ending on them. It seemed especially mournful to him that the hired help, as Karen called them, had died in their place.

The Russian turned a slow half-circle, sweeping the room with her katana. Clearing it.

'Little thieves are hanged,' she said. 'But great ones escape.'

'Is that Russian?' Dave asked. 'It sounds Russian.'

'Very,' was all she said. 'It's this way. Keep moving.'

French doors, reduced to splinters and crystal fragments, hung off their hinges at the entrance to a second kitchen. A space for caterers, Dave supposed. Everyone should have a space for caterers. The demolition work in there seemed perfunctory, uncaring, without the gleeful spirit animating the rampage in the library. A stone bench sundered by one or two mighty blows. But no bodies. He pushed into the kitchen. Feeling bad about it, but not enough to stop himself, he opened the fridge. Inside was a sad collection of bean sprouts, rice, tofu, and detox drinks. Not even a single imported beer.

He expected Karen to give him an earful but she pushed past his elbow and reached in for the tofu brick, never taking her gaze off the middle distance where she remained focused on the Thresher. She said nothing, but he took her snack attack as permission to fuel up too. The only thing that even halfway appealed was a block of cheese. Some sort of cheddar, wrapped in a cloth so you could tell it was worth paying extra. He grabbed it out and scarfed it down as quickly as he could, feeling better for having done so. Matter of fact, he felt so much better after eating it that it might have been a good idea to linger and take on some more fuel, even it was just hipster gruel. But Karen had already moved on.

He closed the refrigerator and followed her into a small laundry closet where she stood, staring at the wall. The muppets trailed after him, as if leashed. Dave was certain he could hear the steady, rhythmic breathing of the Threshrend on the other side of the wall.

'It's in the bath,' Karen hissed, red-faced and bug-eyed,

sounding as though she was suffering an asthma attack. Her breathing was ragged and the ESU guys seemed to come out of a trance. One of them fumbled his weapon and dropped it. The machine gun discharged and his offsider swore, confused and distressed, like a man coming awake from a night terror.

'Shit!' Dave spat, heaving Lucille up and swinging with all of his might and hers at the wall. Masonry and wood splinters exploded into the adjacent bathroom, opening up a massive breach and distracting the Thresher enough for Karen to gain the upper hand.

'NOW,' she yelled at him. 'Kill it.'

Dave didn't need telling twice.

He threw himself at the opening. Dived right through it, ignoring the scratches and abrasions he picked up. They healed as he sailed over the squat, toad-like figure of the Threshrend daemon. Warat was right. It was in the goddamn bath. Not just squatting in the big spa-style tub, but enjoying a splash. With bubbles. Or it had been until Karen had target-locked on it and commenced their duel. Dave rolled as he hit the hard granite of the bathroom floor. It was wet and he slipped trying to get to his feet, but he still moved a lot quicker and with more freedom and agility than the Thresher with its ass jammed into the hot tub. He could not see the Hunn who were supposed to be guarding it. Lucille keened a high, sweet killing note as he swung for the bleachers. He meant to split the thing in two, but his range wasn't good. Nonetheless the glancing blow with the cutting edge of the steel head sliced the creature open from crotch to neck. It squealed like a stuck daemon pig as a steaming tide of Threshrend guts and tubing spilled into the tub. A reverse swing punched the steel fist into its ugly skull, which burst apart with a loud, wet pop.

Dave felt the creature's death as a great mass lifted, not from his chest or shoulders, but from deep inside his head.

A roar behind him. He turned on the three Hunn which had lain in ambush for him in the walk-through closet between the bathroom and the master bedroom. They struggled now to get inside.

They were also blood drunk. Shit-faced and reeling with it. Their gross free-swinging genitalia flapped and slapped in Dave's face as they struggled to have at him.

He charged them, his face distorted by disgust and something more. By contempt and a strain of shameful remorse. He hadn't loosed these things on the world. He knew that. He'd been sleeping off an epic debauch with a couple of five-star hookers when the Longreach had broken the barrier between the realms and let monsters back into the world.

But still . . . the dead were piling up, weren't they?

Before he could finish the Hunn and wash away just a little of his guilt – guilt he totally should not have been feeling – a storm of automatic gunfire ripped into the orcs. It was Karen, freed from her duel with the empath daemon, firing both machine guns she'd taken from the ESU muppets. Tracer rounds and armour-piercing. A lashing torrent of white fire that she directed at the Hunn nearest her. The armour-piercing slugs blew through rudimentary chain mail and leather breast plating. The tracers set the daemon on fire, incendiary rounds hitting home with dozens of tiny, flaring explosions which quickly merged into a flaming pyre. A smoke alarm shrieked and sprinklers opened up in the bathroom and the walk-through, but they did nothing to douse the small inferno. The two surviving warriors flinched away, forgetting Dave altogether.

He had seen plenty of fires in his line of work, but nothing like this. The flames did not spread. The small, intense blue-green inferno was strangely contained, never making the leap from the burning remains of the Hunn to the lacquered joinery or the carpets of the closet or the clothes hanging in there. He saw the plastic wrapping shrink on some freshly dry-cleaned suits nearest to the pyre, but that was all.

'Huh,' he said. 'That's weird.'

And then he and Lucille set to laying some righteous payback on the two remaining Hunn.

13

'Now we kill as champions,' Karen said. 'Until the second Thresher finds us.'

'You mean until we find it? Right?'

Her expression told him otherwise.

'The only certain way to find an ambush is to spring it,' she explained. 'And so . . .'

They warped.

The noise of the dying city fell away, replaced by the sibilant hiss and droning hum of a world held in suspension. The bizarre, self-contained flames that licked at the corpses of the slain Hunn danced no more. Dave could still feel the heat coming off them, and he sensed that he could pass his hand as easily through frozen flames as living ones. But he wasn't that dumb.

'Wait,' he said. 'So, this thing . . .' He twirled his finger around, indicating the warp field. 'You really can't do this on your own, can you?'

'No,' she confirmed. 'But I can borrow the ability from you. As long as we're within range of each other.'

'And that range is?'

'Unknown.'

'Okay. Just thought it might be useful to know.'

'It would be.' She sighed. 'But later. For now, we should put down as many daemonum as we can before we move into the range of the other Threshrend.'

'It'll be upstairs, right?' Dave said, looking at the ceiling. 'At least, what, a hundred yards or so up?'

'A few floors, yes.'

'All righty then. Let's get to work.'

They took their time. Leaving Karen's followers behind, stopping back in the kitchen to fill themselves with more fuel. Dave couldn't come at the tofu, but he found tins of tuna and sardines in the cupboard.

'Your breath will be enough to wither the enemy,' Karen said as she finished off the last of the tasteless white goop.

'Whatever it takes,' Dave grinned, wiping olive oil from his chin. 'Except tofu.'

He licked the oil from the back of his hand, dug the last sardine out of the final tin with one dirty finger, and then drank the remaining oil in that tin for good measure. He had reason to ponder Zach's good sense while he ate. Again. The Navy SEAL had been right more often than not. They weren't in a video game. There was no power bar telling him he was running at fifty or sixty percent. Both he and Karen had eaten massively before, mostly fat and protein too. But how much energy had he burned since? How much was left and what reserves had they just consumed? His metabolism seemed to be settling down fast after New Orleans. It'd burned like a runaway nuclear reaction when he first woke up after the Longreach. It wasn't doing that now, but he was still having to consume four or five times as many calories as he'd once eaten. When he was a fat bastard.

Zach had told him he would need to know all this one day. All this and more. And here Dave was with no fucking idea. He'd been hungry after the fight with the unnamed Hunn at Broadway – and after healing himself, a process over which he had no control. He did not feel as hungry now, after scarfing down the tinned fish and cheese, a combination which once would have made him gag. But he did not feel sated either. Not even close. He knew he should keep eating, but they had to be about their work.

Naively, Dave had expected to enjoy it, if only in the grim way that finishing a hard, unpleasant job was enjoyable. Warping through the condo, revenge-killing orcs who couldn't fight back? What's not to love? But he was forgetting why it was necessary. On the next floor he had a reminder, as they chanced upon the remains of what looked, from the decorations, like a kid's party – before three Hunn and their leashed Fangr had turned the apartment into a charnel house. They were caught now, in the warp field, eating the last of the scraps.

Even Karen, who seemed unaffected by the most hideous of scenes, blanched at this and went about the business with a cold efficiency. She drove the tempered steel chisel point of her sword into the nasal cavity of one beast after another, with enough force to punch it out through the back of their skulls. Dave had room enough in the high-ceilinged apartment to work up a good swing with Lucille, who was singing a fine sweet song of vengeance, keen to get in amongst the foe. But, like his companion, he gave in to no flourishes or extravagant gestures, simply crushing the skulls of the Hunn and their slaved *daemonum inferiorae* like a worker on a production line. Whenever his eyes strayed to a corner of the room where the children or their carers had died, he quickly averted them again.

They left the apartment in less than a minute.

Karen could tell him when a group of monsters or an individual daemon was nearby. She could sense them. Dave found he could too, if he concentrated fiercely, but he had nothing like her radar for picking them out and he deferred to her amplified senses. In this way they passed by those apartments where the doors remained locked and the inhabitants unmolested, or where entry had been forced and the occupants slain, but where no members of the Horde remained.

Lucille seemed to understand his dark mood, and her battle hymn quieted into a lament after a while, a soothing tune that settled his frayed and raw emotions. In this way they moved from floor to floor, dispatching the beasts without passion or relent, until, eight floors later, they found their second Thresher in a large apartment with an open floor plan.

Dave had just half a moment's notice when Lucille came fully alive in his grip again, her murder song suddenly roaring up out of the funeral lamentation he'd been humming along with. He heard Karen call out her warning.

'Hooper! It's here . . .'

And then his vision fell apart and they dropped out of warp and into a wild storm of pain and disorientation. It passed, quickly, but not before their exit from the suite was blocked by a wedge of snarling Hunn, while other daemonum poured out of the rooms where they'd been hiding. Dave heard the crack of Karen's pistol, firing rapidly, muzzle flash stabbing out into the dark. Her aim was good and she dropped the better part of a whole war band which had come screaming through the double doors of a room to her left. Headshots, all of them. Sparks flew when one round struck a helmet, but the extravagant fireworks he'd come to expect when hot lead hit chain mail and armour plate were missing. Monsters roared in fury, screeched in shock and pain, and fell to the hard wooden floor with great muffled thuds and thumps. But more of them came on.

Dave was briefly aware of city lights flashing on a 400-year-old katana blade and then he was swinging his own weapon with barely directed savagery. Unlike Karen he had no combat training. But he did have Lucille and he could still move with terrible speed. He fell back on his football training, the only real training he'd had in the art and science of physical confrontation – a couple of weeks judo classes as a small boy notwithstanding. Dave ran straight at the nearest war band, the closely packed threshing machine of yellow teeth and bared talons that Karen hadn't targeted.

'HUNN UR . . .'

He hit them before they could get their war chant rolling, scything into the group with Lucille, who seemed to glow in the pale electric light pouring through shattered windows and billowing silk curtains. Lucille's cutting wedge swept aside the initial thrust of half a dozen blades and axeheads, splintering an ironwood shaft, and smashing aside the sharp and hungry steel with a discordant clanging. And then he was in among them, swinging wildly, jabbing, lashing out, feeling the blunt fist of Lucille's hammerhead crushing armour, the thick axehead crunching and tearing through boiled leather and chain mail. Claws raked at him, a blade ran through his shoulder and he screamed, but he fought on, a mad turning gyre of violence. He pistoned out a kick and connected with the unprotected balls of some unnamed Hunn. They popped like rotten melons. The Hunn roared in pain and outrage as it doubled over, unable to control itself. Before Dave knew what he was doing, Lucille described a tight, blurring arc, impacting the back of the Hunn's skull, blowing it apart in a hot burst of gore. He swung again, and again, the magical weapon beginning to describe fast, whirring loops that broke legs, severed arms and cleared a fighting space around him.

Lucille's battle song swelled inside his head. An aria of killing. Dave burned with healing heat and with the energy of his counter-attack. He was dimly aware of crashing glass and breaking wood, of indiscriminate destruction, but none of it mattered. He gave himself over to Lucille's hungers. As she had when he'd fought and defended desperately against Karen at the Russian consulate, the enchanted weapon seemed to need only his touch to unleash bloody mayhem. Dave felt himself less the perpetrator of this terrible violence than its channel. He did not use the weapon. She used him.

And then it was done.

'Through here, Hooper.'

He fell back to earth, found himself on his knees, bloodied and corporeal, surrounded by piles of dead monster meat.

'Whu . . .'

He croaked, desert-mouthed and gagging on it.

'Where? What?'

The words were barely audible, but Warat seemed to hear and understand.

'Through here,' she said.

He found her in a bedroom, extracting her magical sushi sword from the ass of a mid-sized Thresher which had tried, in the final moments of its cursed existence, to climb out through a window that was way too small to afford it an escape route.

'Damn,' he grimaced as the sword came free and she

flicked off the intestinal gore. 'That's nasty.'

'We need to fall back,' she said. 'Gather reinforcements. Send them ahead . . .'

In spite of the toll taken by the combat and the damage done, Dave arced up.

'No way,' he said. 'We're not doing that again. You're not sending a bunch of your little meat puppets into the next ambush just to give us a heads up.'

The Threshrend let go with a gurgling moan as it died. A gush of foul-smelling bodily fluids poured out of the gaping wound Karen had made of its ass. She ignored the mess as she advanced on Dave, but not menacingly. She looked a picture of reason and poise.

'Hooper, be real, we need to –'

Lucille came up between them, the oversized steel head dripping gore and blocking Karen's path, preventing her from laying hands on him.

'We need to get on and finish these bastards,' said Dave. 'Without getting anyone else killed. Is there another Thresher in the house?'

He could try to fire up the warp drive, but he was starting to dread the pain and madness that came with it when a Threshrend empath got inside his head.

Karen returned her katana to its scabbard and reloaded the pistol she'd used to cut through the first wave of attacking Hunn.

'You're not thinking straight, Hooper.'

'Maybe not, but I'll do my own thinking from now on. You just keep your distance and tell me, is there another Thresher? Because if not, I say we hit pause and grab a snack.'

Karen raised her eyes to the ceiling, and frowned as

though displeased by a crack in the plaster she found there.

'That was a helluva fight we just won,' Dave explained. 'But they weren't even Hunn dominants. They didn't have names. And we handled them without getting all Speedy Gonzales about it. We can take these things, Karen. We can.'

She jacked the slide on the handgun. Still frowning.

'And if the next ones are dominants. Or Grymm?'

The window behind her crashed in before he could answer.

Two Sliveen scouts swung in, one firing a crossbow from its free hand, the other flicking a brace of throwing stars directly at Dave's face. It was only the fact he already had Lucille up to ward off Karen that saved him. The enchanted maul twitched and bunted away two of the dark, spikey missiles, but missed the third, which sliced open his ear before embedding itself in the wall behind him. He tried to warp, instinctively, but the world broke up in shattered mirror shards and bright silver spikes of pain to go with the scorching sensation that burned half of his head.

He heard the handgun bark twice before the sound of gunfire was lost inside a louder maelstrom, an eruption that blew him forward off his feet. The ruined apartment whipped around him in a dizzying blur and he landed on something soft and hard and moving.

Karen.

'Get off me,' she grunted, and Dave felt himself thrown into the air again, with such strength that for a moment he worried he might fly out of a window and drop all the way to the sidewalk.

Trinder had wondered in LA whether he might survive such a fall.

Dave remembered that, as he also remembered partying with Paris Hilton and lunching with Brad Pitt and having drinks with Pitt's ex-wife.

And Dave's ex-wife, where was Annie? How was –

He crashed into something again, and this time the impact was nothing but hard angles and machined surfaces. He'd landed in the kitchen. His vision was clear again but what he saw made no sense. The apartment was bigger. Much bigger, as though the owners had knocked down a wall, and extended their living room into the neighbour's place next door. That was understandable, he thought groggily. This place was a mess. They needed to renovate.

His head swam and the floor seemed to shift underneath his butt. He was sitting down? Why was he sitting down on the job?

Work to be done, Dave. They'd roared at him in their big dumb booming voices. *What the fuck, Dave? Are you on board for the big win or what? There's six billion fucking barrels down there. Let's just go git 'em!*

But he wasn't sitting down on the job in Houston or out on the Longreach. He was in New York. With a Russian lady. And there weren't six billion barrels of oil here. There were Grymm. Six billion Grymm.

No. Scratch that, he thought as his wits returned to him.

There were a dozen of them. No. Thirteen Warriors Grymm. They muscled into the apartment through a breach in the wall. Flames licked at the ragged edges of the hole, which had not been there a moment or two before. Plaster dust choked the air and Warriors Grymm scrambled through, climbing over shattered masonry and around the twisted, buckled licorice whips of steel I-beams warped out of shape by . . .

An explosion.

There had been an explosion.

Dave shook his head and jumped back to his feet, throwing off the last of his disorientation. The Grymm had lured them here. Another Guyuk trap most likely. And he'd stepped into it again. Only the flames, which even the Grymm cringed away from, and the twisted steel beams prevented the elite daemonum warriors from swarming the apartment. The Sliveen were down, one shot and the other opened up like a piñata by Karen's sword work, but she was out of ammunition and fighting two of the Grymm on her own. The daemons held cleavers and wielded them with greater speed and skill than any ham-fisted Hunn, dominant or otherwise. Karen was moving so quickly to block and deflect and parry that she was just an impression of movement rather than something you could perceive and analyse. Dave had a flash of insight, understanding that she was using and being used by her weapon, just as he had been by Lucille. The bright blur of razor sharp steel rang like bells and neither of the Grymm were able to close with her for a killing stroke of their own. But nor could she break through their defences.

Another Grymm emerged from the breach and joined the assault on Karen. She started to give ground against them. Dave took a step in their direction, meaning to charge into the fray with Lucille, but he realised with a start that he no longer held her. He could hear her, muted and far away, but the mad beauty of her song was not in his head. It was nearby but distant. Another Grymm, this one armed with a war hammer of its own, made it through the tangle of steel and fire and ran straight at Karen, horned feet pounding on the hardwood floor.

For the briefest instant they were all silhouetted against

the backdrop of the burning city and then Dave was charging into the fray too. He was exhausted, all but drained, and he wasn't sure how he'd moved so quickly. He was dizzy and confused and not completely certain what he was doing, just that he'd picked up the nearest heavy object he could find and set his course for the daemonic threshing machine bearing down on Karin Varatchevsky. The words of his old football coach came back to him. *Leave nothing in the tank Dave. Nothing in the tank.* Well, he was running on fumes when he slammed into them with an enormous crash, like a truck running a stop light, and then three of the Grymm and one large, brushed steel refrigerator were flying through space, out of the window and tumbling down, end over end to the street far below. Dave almost followed them out into the void, but felt himself jerked back at the last second. Karen's fist was bunched up in the collar of his coveralls, which ripped under the strain. He choked as she drove a kick into the remaining warrior, not targeting its well-protected centre mass, but the knee joint of its leading leg, which was planted firmly to provide a solid base for the mighty swing of its war hammer. Dave heard the joint come apart with a wet, crunching explosion of shattered gristle and bone. The Grymm's shout of pain and surprise died to a gurgle on the point of her sword.

It was too late though. There were too many of them. Lucille was nowhere Dave could see and only a faint mournful sigh reached him from where she lay. He had nothing more to spend in this fight. Karen was hunched over, trying to draw in a ragged breath, her eyes dark hollows as more Grymm poured into the room. Her gun was gone. She had trouble holding her sword. They were done. Nothing left. No reserves to draw on.

It was time to die, the hero's journey over.

14

Nobody ate the camera guy, but he did have a Sliveen bolt through his thigh, an injury he'd picked up attempting to flee. Threshy was torn between relief that the asshole hadn't escaped, and irritation that he couldn't do his job properly. The Grymm were not equipped to tend the wounds of human captives, or even remotely disposed toward the idea. In the end, they were all going into the blood pot, so why bother? If one died and spoiled there was always another tasty, slow-moving snack to replace them.

Polly, the helpful intern, put another down-payment on her deliverance by suggesting they patch the cameraman up with the first-aid kit in the news van, and another woman, a midwife who'd been making her way home to the towers when she was caught up in the ambush, helped with cleaning and binding the wound. The camera guy wouldn't be running any marathons, or even putting any weight on the injured limb for a long time, but they found a couple of plastic milk crates for him to sit on and that was enough. His sound man was missing, most likely fled, but the ever-obliging Polly proved more than equal to the task of holding a boom mike.

Compt'n ur Threshrend had his press conference.

A pre-record.

He wasn't dumb enough to go live and call down an air strike on their asses. And, as a bonus, if he fluffed a line he could go back and do it again. The Grymm led their prisoners through the grounds of the college, away from the car park which Threshy judged to be way too exposed. Thousands of residents in the project towers had a direct line of sight down on them, even if their attention was wholly taken by the war bands running amok inside the housing development.

A playground area behind the main campus building, with good overhead cover from a stand of elm trees, promised enough space to corral the prisoners off camera, deploy the guard and record the presser. Guyuk was so much taller than Threshy that framing the shot was not a simple exercise. Camera guy, who was more than willing to cooperate for a chance at not being chewed to pieces, eventually declared himself satisfied with Threshy in the foreground, Guyuk looming over him a few metres behind, silently mouthing the line of script he'd been given. A shield wall of Lieutenants, Sergeants and warriors Grymm blocked most of the rainbow motif that would otherwise have rendered the shot even more strikingly perverse.

'People of Earth,' roared Threshy, before collapsing into fits of giggles. Threshrendum physiology had not evolved to express delight in humour of any sort, and it was a toss-up who was more unsettled by the empath daemon's lulz: the Grymm or their terrified captives.

'Threshrend!' barked Guyuk when his patience ran out, which was pretty quickly. 'Compose yourself.'

'Sorry, boss,' wheezed Threshy, still attempting to get some control over his laughing fit. 'Sort of ass-planted into the ironic butt crack between reality and perception there.'

The calflings exchanged confused and worried glances.

The lord commander flexed his fore-claws, giant muscles bunching up and down his arms, causing the elaborate artwork tattooed into his hide to move and twist with sinuous grace. He gathered his temper with an obvious effort of will and growled, 'Get on with it. Or do you forget the Dave is about in this settlement?'

Threshy bounced up and down, eager to please and only a little sobered by the mention of Hooper.

'Okay. Okay. I'm on it. And don't worry about the Dave. We got his number. So, Polly? We good, here?'

She nodded nervously.

'Still recording.'

'Okay.' Threshy banged his fore-claws together, and took a deep breath. 'Okay. Just edit this bit out. Take it from "People of Earth". Okay?'

The light on the news camera glowed green. Polly dipped her head to him. The prisoners watched on anxiously.

'People of Earth,' said Threshy, managing to control his mirth. 'I am Compt'n ur Threshrend, dar Superiorae dar Threshrendum ur Grymm. I speak for Lord Commander Guyuk ur Grymm, and through him for our Dread Majesty, She of the Horde.'

He let go a nervous breath and it came out like a serpent's hiss, which was totally in character, so he went with it. As far as possible, he knew he had to be more Compt'n than Trev'r, but it was not easy. The imprint of the first mind absorbed had shaped all that came after.

'Your greatest city lies prone before us. Like a bitch . . . Gah!'

He threw up his claws and stomped a few feet away. His

video crew stood easy, or as easy as they could on the lip of the blood pot.

'Come on, Threshy,' he muttered to himself. 'Get into fucking character. You can totes do this.'

He heard Guyuk's low animal growl and spun quickly on the lord commander, whose patience he was sorely testing.

'My bad! It's just the, er, the rituals of the calfling speaking ceremonies, they are not simple, my Lord. No, some crazy-ass complicated rituals we're into here. But, just gimme some space. I don't want to fuck this up. It'll bring the Hammer of fucking Dawn down on us.'

A lie, but one he could sell. Guyuk had never played *Gears of War* and any mention of mysterious human dawn hammers was more than enough to quiet an uppity daemon with a sunburn phobia. The lord commander said nothing, but relaxed out of his formal stance. Behind him, armour plate clattered softly and chain mail clinked as the solid shield wall of warriors Grymm relaxed slightly out of their own rigid postures.

'Sir? Maybe if you forget about the audience and just tell me?'

It was Polly again. Sweet, helpful Polly.

'Yeah,' said Threshy. 'Awesome. Thanks Polly.'

Man, it'd be a real shame to have to eat her brains later.

'Okay. Can you cut from my intro? Pick it up from "She of the Horde"?'

The two humans exchanged a wordless look which spoke loudly to the weirdness of whatever they'd got themselves into.

'Sure,' said Polly. 'We'll pick it up from the Horde. Mike? You good to roll?'

The cameraman adjusted himself on the makeshift seating

of the milk crates and agreed that he was. He shouldered the camera, and Polly moved the boom mic back in, just out of shot. Threshy moved back to his mark, took a moment, and continued on as though he'd never interrupted himself. He heard the Grymm Guard snap to attention again.

'Okay. So . . . *Your great city lies prone before us.* The least of our Horde makes play within its walls. We are not the dumbasses . . . Fuck! Can we do that again?'

Polly signalled for him to just go on.

'We are not the idiot foe you met in Omaha and New Orleans. We are the Grymm ur Horde and we could end you this night. The war bands my master Guyuk ur Grymm has unleashed on this city, they are nothing. The least of our untried, untested ranks. Know this, just one of the warriors you see behind me . . .'

He turned aside to give the camera a better shot of the Grymm shield wall.

'. . . just one of them could kick the ass . . . D'oh! . . . Fuck. Okay. All right. Let me go again . . . Just one of them is . . . would . . . Damn. Polly,' he said, dropping out of character. 'I'm trying to say my guys back there are like these awesome fucking death ninjas compared to these losers we got running around town tonight chewing on people and shit . . . but I'm like . . . what's a good way of saying that, you think?'

Polly Farrell seemed to take a few seconds to process the question, or maybe just the fact of being asked it.

'Well,' she said, 'I guess you could say something like "Just one of my Lord's Grim soldiers is the equal of", what, a score of those other ones?'

'Coolio,' said Threshy. 'That works. You could do this for a living. Ha! See what I did there? Again? Okay. Here we go.

From the top . . . Just one Warrior Grymm is the equal of an entire, untrained war band. And the Grymm are legion.'

He really liked that bit. It reminded him of his cunning plan to totally fuck up the Dave.

'You cannot hold out against them. There is nowhere safe. My lord commander . . .' he indicated Guyuk who knew enough to play along by growling at the camera, 'can place his forces wherever he chooses, whenever he wants. You are not safe in your strongholds, your homes, anywhere. You know . . .'

He almost said 'You know I'm not bullshitting you', but stilled Thresh-Trev'r's tongue at the last moment.

'You know this to be true. And we will prove it to you, night after night until you submit to the will and the protection of Her Majesty.'

He paused for a moment to let that sink in.

'There is only one path . . . Let me do that again, Polly . . . There is but one path to redemption. Submit to She of the Horde. Pay Her the tribute She is due, and She will deliver you from evil.'

Threshy had to concentrate fiercely now as he channelled Compt'n over all the roiling minds he had consumed. His vision greyed out at the edges with the effort.

'The Horde is not the worst of what is yet come upon you. The UnderRealms are limitless. The dangers infinite. You cannot stand alone. Submit to Her will and find deliverance. Resistance is futile.'

He almost lost it again at that, but managed to hold in the wild braying laughter that wanted to burst out between his fang tracks.

'She will lay waste to another two of your cities. Then you will come to terms with Her.'

Threshy swivelled his eyestalks toward the Master of the Ways who opened a new portal at the signal. The camera swung in that direction at the gasps of astonishment coming from the prisoners. A protean cell of negative space hovered over the painted asphalt of the playground.

'GRYMM UR HORDE!'

The roar of the lord commander's guard sounded as loud as cannon shot. The shield wall turned as one and marched into the portal, disappearing through the rift between worlds, one by one.

Lord Commander Guyuk ur Grymm leaned forward as the camera swung back on to Threshy. This was his cameo.

'I'll be back,' he snarled in heavily accented English.

'And . . . we're out!'

The small green light on the strange device blinked out. The wounded calfling, the 'camera-human' lowered his equipage, and the warriors Grymm came stomping back through the portal into the Above. It all struck Lord Guyuk as a bizarre contrivance. To give the Threshrend his due, however, he seemed entirely comfortable orchestrating the foolishness.

'It is done then, Superiorae?'

'Done and dusted, my Lordiness.'

'Excellent.' Guyuk barked an order at his senior Lieutenant. 'Gather the cattle. We shall withdraw to await the –'

'Whoa . . . Back that up,' said Threshy. 'Ain't no cattle being gathered up here tonight.'

Guyuk's expression was cold.

'Say you what, Superiorae?'

'They gotta go, boss. We promised them freedom if they

cooperated and shit, and they cooperated. And shit.'

Guyuk, who alone amongst the highest councils of the Horde had forced himself to think of the cattle as more than just livestock, still had trouble comprehending the Threshrend's intent. These captives, after all, did not hail from one of the human war clans. They were no armed faction. With no power to demand honourable consideration, they were not entitled to such. Lord Guyuk needed no empathic link to a Threshrend daemon to know that human war clans fought fiercely across the metropolis this night. He could hear the crash and thunder of their weaponry within bolt shot. The night sky, normally a dark cover under which daemonum might pass unharmed by the foul heat and light of the sun, was no cover at all. The iron Drakon of humanity roared across the stars and spat terrible fire down on any war band foolish enough to be caught in the open.

As his thrall was right now.

Compt'n ur Threshrend had assured him the men would not fire on them whilst they were protected by proximity to so many calflings. But that was surely even more reason to hurry them through the portal back to the UnderRealms? A lesser commander would have damned the eyestalks of his impudent consul and backhanded the underling through the rift himself. But Guyuk knew they were engaged in the first moments of a long war, not merely a hard battle, and Compt'n knew more of this enemy than any of Her Majesty's most venerated officers.

'Why must we release these captives then, Superiorae?' he asked, his voice tired but patient. 'And be sharp with your answer. I would have us quit this field with all dispatch now that our mission be done.'

'Well, you see, it's not all done, boss. My intern still has to cut the package together, and then we gots to be sure it drops into the channel and . . .'

'Threshrend,' growled Guyuk.

'I know, I know. Two things. The ritual of communication is only half done. I need to be sure it's like, nailed, right. And . . . this is important . . . we didn't come here to just frighten peeps, as much fucking fun as that always is. We came to confuse them. To, you know, sow confusion in their ranks and shit. And I promise you, dude, we let these guys go' – Compt'n ur Threshrend gestured toward the captured cattle – 'and they'll go bleating and mooing and shit about how the Horde can't be all bad and we can be trusted. And because we *are* bad and we totally *cannot* be trusted, we can totes use that against them later. You see? I'm not being merciful. I'm being a sneaky motherfucker.'

'Sneaky is acceptable,' Guyuk conceded. 'But what now of these rituals? This package that must be cut?'

He raised his war cleaver.

'Whoa. No. Different kind of cutting. Just lemme check.'

The Threshrend scuttled over to the pair of human adepts who had assisted with the ritual. They conferred in the wet, garbled tongue of the cattle while the other calflings watched on in fear, aware somehow that their fate was being determined. The warriors Grymm encircled their lord commander, looking to the skies for iron Drakon, watching the ground approaches for any sign of human soldiers. Above them, Sliveen scouts flitted across the uppermost battlements of the large stone keep painted in the noxious colours of the sky ribbons one heard of in the Above. Guyuk wondered how the campaign progressed elsewhere in the vast city. It vexed him that he could not follow the small and relatively simple incursion on a sand table or even the Diwan's altar, as he might a much greater battle. It was not a care for his own safety that pulled him back toward the portal; rather the promise of attending to the reports of his scouts. Unlike Compt'n ur Threshrend, he was no empath.

At that moment, the Superiorae turned away from the calfling adepts and fairly skipped back into the lord commander's presence.

'Oh man,' he said. 'This is gonna be awesome.'

'I await the awe, Threshrend.'

'Oh, I'm bringin' it. Be cool on that, Super G. Threshy is bringin' the awesome. And the intern. Here's how it's going down. My lady friend there, Polly . . .'

'The female calfling?'

'Yep. She don't look like much. She's no Kardashian. But man, she's Lara fucking Croft when it counts. She's willing to come back down with us, do the edit on her lappy, and come back in return for us letting the others go.'

'She makes this demand of us? Of me?' growled Guyuk.

'Dude, no way. Not a demand. An offer. A trade. It's like I said, *mein Führer*. We gots to put some money in the favour bank, build up our trust deposits, right? So we can take it out and spend the motherfucker when we need it. You follow?'

'No.'

No, Lord Guyuk ur Grymm did not follow. Who was this unarmed calfling breeder to be making demands of him?

The Threshrend actually raked its claws down its face in frustration.

'Look! We were always going to let the cattle go. It's part of the plan. The sneaky fucking plan. And having this Polly chick pimp out my bit? Also part of the plan. And if we take her back down, give her a peek at just how much fucking pain we gots to lay on these motherfuckers, then that can totes be part of the plan too.'

The Threshrend crouched as he drew closer to Lord Guyuk, although he seemed less worried about being decapitated by the supreme commander of the Grymm – a genuine possibility – than he was by the prospect of being spotted by the human's iron Drakon.

'Just work with me here, *jefe*. Can we, like, put on a parade or something? Throw a couple of Hunn legions onto a training field, even though they don't, you know, train or anything? But we kit them up, balls out, and my intern here – that's like a slave, if it helps you come at the idea – my slave relays visions of the awesome fucking power of a fully operational Death Star back to the meat sacks.'

'This Death Star . . .?'

'Sorry, poetic license. What I'm asking, big guy, is for a simple May Day parade. Couple of Hunn regiments maybe. We can loop the footage if you want. Scare the shit out of the cows. We tell 'em that's what coming next time. Into their fucking cities. Right inside their bedrooms. Whole legions, whole fucking regiments of the Grande Horde. Not just a couple of pissant war bands of unnamed pussy Hunn. They will lose their fucking shit. Not all of them. But enough. Enough to start begging for mercy, suing for terms and shit. It will fuck them up. Right now they're united. You gimme this, and I'll crack them like a rotten egg. Come on, do it for Threshy. Do it for the Horde. Get on board for the big win. You know Her Majestic Awesomeness likes results.'

There was no denying that, of course. She of the Horde did

indeed preference victorious results. Guyuk considered the plan. As he understood it, through Compt'n ur Threshrend's impenetrable babbling, the Superiorae intended to further his exploitation of this calfling breeder to undermine the cattle's solidarity. It was not far removed from the traditional role of Threshrendum, he supposed. Unable to serve in honourable combat, they schemed and connived at disrupting the foe, thieving their resolve, diminishing their warrior spirit through empathic subversion. He could not claim to fully understand what Compt'n ur Threshrend was about, not in the minutiae of tactical details. But he did understand the strategic importance of sowing discord and spreading an exemplary terror amongst the cattle.

'I concur,' he said at last, turning to the senior Lieutenant Grymm. 'Release the captives. Send them on their way with ransom for safe passage from all of our host who would assail them.'

'Except for the intern,' said Compt'n ur Threshrend. 'She comes with us.'

15

It was almost like a date, except he was a razor-toothed Hell daemon intent on enslaving all mankind, and she was his captive. Actually, that wasn't so far removed from some of the memories Compt'n ur Threshrend had consumed when he sucked Professor Raymond Compton's brains right out of his melon. That had to be why he found himself . . . well . . . nervous as he escorted Polly Farrell to the reviewing platform which afforded such sweeping views across the training plains of the Regiments Select of Her Majesty's Grymm.

The area was smaller than the training ranges used by the mainline formations of legions and Regiments Grymm, and indeed the forces wheeling and manoeuvring below them were not the three Select, but merely standard units of Grymm. Still, they looked hella impressive stomping about down there under a lowering sky the colour of bad blood and old bruises.

And they were a hell of a lot more impressive than any rabble of Hunn old Guyuk could have dialled up at short notice. Even base legions of Grymm practised and drilled manoeuvre warfare to a much higher standard than their more numerous Hunn allies. A Hunn's idea of manoeuvre was a bellowing charge with jaws agape on the off chance something might fall into their cakehole and make a convenient meal of itself.

'So these bad motherfuckers you see down here, that's the Grymm,' said Threshy, trying not to sound as though he was striving hard to impress her, even though that's totally what he was doing.

Even though that's totally what he was *supposed* to do, what he'd promised Guyuk he'd do, because that was part of the plan.

It wasn't like he was trying to impress her because he had a little monster boner for this tweedy chick who put him in mind of Fred from *Angel*.

Professor Compton had had a thing for Fred from *Angel*. And when she'd turned into Illyria? Oh man . . .

Threshy could not help but wonder what Polly Farrell would look like in skin-tight blue leathers and big hair.

Gah! Focus, Threshy, focus!

What she looked like right now was a slightly nervous nerd, but Threshy was certain her nerves, such as they were, could be put down to being exiled, even if temporarily, to the UnderRealms, where everything wanted to eat her. He was pretty certain she didn't have first-date nerves.

'Where did you learn to speak English?' she asked, her voice quavering just a little in spite of her best efforts to keep it steady.

'Off TV. Comcast runs cable to Hell. I mean, you have to deal with Comcast, which is its own kind of Hell. But, anyway, those regiments down there, that's like better than 30,000 daemon warriors, all of them trained like super samurai but with the strength of King Kong. Or maybe, I dunno, the Hulk. And that's just a sneak peek at some of the Regiments Grymm.

Man, the Hunn are bigger and meaner . . .'

And all of them as dumb as a sack of fucking war hammers.

'And then you got your Gnarrl, who are like army engineers, and your Sliveen, your Threshrend of course, and your Fangr. You got 100,000 Hunn coming at you, it means you really got all of them *and* about 300,000 or 400,000 leashed Fangr too. Can you see why you guys are like doomed, if you don't make friends with the Horde?'

'But you want to eat us!' she protested.

'No way,' Threshy said. 'Not even.'

'But I saw you. I saw *you*, Threshrend. You ate that poor man before. Back in the city.'

'Oh, let's not bicker and argue about who ate who,' Threshy said, trying to sketch a boyish grin. Trevor Candly had been convinced his boyish grin could get him out of any trouble.

Polly shrank back and Threshy remembered that his fang tracks might make Trevor Candly's boyish grin look a little grotesque. She didn't run screaming, but that was because he had a Threshrend Majorae nearby, suppressing her fear reflex, amplifying the unusual reserves of courage he had first detected in her back in Manhattan. That was why she was only a little anxious, instead of batshit cray-cray with fear. He could have done all that himself, of course. He wasn't a complete noob at the empath game. But Compt'n ur Threshrend wanted to stay focused, and he didn't need to be distracted by a lot of psychic busywork like keeping Polly Farrell from falling to pieces.

He was already distracted enough by imagining Polly Farrell wrapped in a tight, electric-blue leather jumpsuit.

Fuck. What was wrong with him? He shouldn't be having these feelings.

'So, have you, er, you know, got enough recorded?'

Polly seemed to remember the smart phone she was holding.

'Oh. Yes. I have. Thank you. I should probably just do my editing now though.'

'You sure you wouldn't like to see the palace or anything? Or the Engineering Works? The Gnarrl got some kick-ass stuff over there, you know.'

He cursed himself inwardly as the words left him. He'd insisted the Gnarrl be kept well out of sight. A simple thresh, even a Hunn dominant, might be impressed by ironwood siege towers, or fleets of ballista, by the rolling fortresses armoured in Drakon-scale or the covered siege engines of the Horde's engineering specialists. Polly would only see a lot of out-dated medieval bullshit; the sort of toys that boy scouts might lash together as a team-building exercise. None of it would put her in mind of the awesome power of a fully mobilised Grande Horde.

'No, that's okay, Threshrend,' she said. 'Really, I should be getting back to your library. You said all I had to do was cut together my report and I could go.'

Compt'n ur Threshrend's forest of eyestalks all drooped at once, but he pulled himself together. This was crazy. She was his captive, possibly his dinner. Not some fucking Tinder date.

She was part of the plan. And she was sticking to her part of that plan, even as he tried to distract her with offers of a trip to the Drakon rendering pits, or a promise to get her a ringside seat at a Shurakh contest in the Hunn barracks.

Might as well just throw her into the blood pots, you idiot.

'The library, yeah, okay, I suppose we should get back to the library.'

'People will be getting worried,' Polly said.

Threshy had to stifle a snort of nervous laughter, even as part of him couldn't help but admire this chick's fucking moxie. It wasn't all down to the Threshrend Majorae topping up her natural reserves of courage. Threshy's own radar told him Fred had a cast-iron pair of Hunn nuts on her.

Polly! Her name is Polly and she is not wearing a spanky blue leather catsuit that I want to peel off her delicious little bod with my fang tracks.

Peeps had a lot more to worry about than Polly running a little late. The Horde was going to eat their world, and Threshy had the carving knife.

'Okay. You're right. We'll book it back to the library. Ha. See what I did there?'

She sketched a perfunctory smile, more of a facial twitch, really. And he died a thousand little deaths inside.

You fucking idiot, Compt'n, just shut the fuck up!

'I just wanted to make sure you got all the vision you needed,' he said weakly.

'Thanks.' She gave him a measured look. 'You seem to know a lot. About TV production. For a monster, I mean.'

Threshy turned his back on the Regiments of Grymm which swarmed like black geometric storms over the vast bloodstone plains of the training grounds.

'I understood TV production actually was full of monsters,' he said and both his hearts soared as she let him have a genuine smile.

'That's funny,' she said, without laughing.

She didn't laugh, but she said I was funny. Fred said I was funny.

No, Illyria.

No!

Polly.

He let go of a ragged breath he hadn't known he'd been holding.

'Okay. Let's go, Polly.'

He took a furtive pleasure in saying her name, but lost it as the pair of Lieutenants Grymm detailed to escort them and vouchsafe the calfling prisoner crashed their horned feet on the Drakon-glass flagstones of the reviewing platform. The Threshrend Majorae assigned to maintain Polly's Zen cool was doing a hell of a job, because she didn't flinch.

'This way?' she asked, indicating the nearest archway leading back into the main tower of the Grymm Lord's Keep, from where Guyuk ur Grymm commanded Her Majesty's most elite forces.

'Yeah. Don't get too far ahead of us.'

Threshy trailed after the young woman in a complete funk. He was starting to regret having the Threshrend – he couldn't even remember the fucking thing's name – chill her shit out. He was starting to think he might have preferred it if Polly Farrell was appropriately terrified and extravagantly grateful to old Threshy for keeping her safe from all the big bad monsters.

An image bubbled up out of all the human thoughts and memories he had consumed, gurgling to consciousness and breaking the surface like a fart in a poison mud bath.

Princess Leia chained to Jabba the Hutt in her space bikini.

When he imagined himself as Jabba – not that fucking hard, really, – and Polly as Leia, Threshy felt a stirring in his loins. This was a new thing. He hadn't even realised he had loins before. Physically, he was still very young, not long out of the nest. Normally, if he had survived into adulthood it would have been many years before he could even think about breeding. But now, apparently, he had loins. And the motherfuckers were stirring inside him.

What fresh Hell was this? Those Scolari douche bags who'd made him eat that fucking moron Trevor and set him on this path hadn't said anything about this shit.

'Wait up, Polly,' he called after her.

It had been an age since the lord commander had called upon the Archivum Scolari. It was not far removed from his quarters, being directly accessible from the Lord's Keep by any one of five bridges which reached between the two towers. And it was not as though Guyuk shared the prejudice of the last lord commander against knowledge preserved upon stone tablets and within the bound volumes and bundled scrolls of grosswyrm vellum. Lord Traabal ur Grymm was famous for taking the heads of Scolari whose advice displeased him, roaring, 'I think with my meat!'

And he did not lie. If he'd actually done a little less thinking with his meat he might have seen his loyal deputy Guyuk coming for him with a blade. Guyuk had struck at the lord commander, as was his right and duty, because the old fool was weakening, if not destroying, the Grymm with every Scolari master whose head he took. Furthermore, upon taking the commander's chain for himself, the newly ennobled Lord Guyuk had it proclaimed amongst his thrall that he afforded the greatest urgency to binding up the wounds and filling out the ranks of the Scolari Grymm.

As the oldest of scrolls cautioned, in the knowing of things lies the mastery of them all. Or as Guyuk had ordered inscribed upon the redesigned livery of the Consilium, commissioned to mark the nightfall of a new era, *Knowing Things Is Useful*.

So it could not be said of his era that he turned away from knowledge. Only that he had not the time to pursue it as he might, given the burdensome duties of Her Majesty's Lord Commander of Grymm. Those duties, onerous in the rare interregnums between wars against the lesser sects, were crushing indeed now he had the human Horde with which to contend as well. The latest from dar Diwan ur Sliveen both thrilled and appalled him as he stalked past long ranks of Praetorian Grymm guarding the passages of the keep. Each guard would crash out a salute as the lord commander drew level, smashing mailed fist into iron breastplate, creating the effect of a slow war drum. Spent seer-stone chips glowed malefic red to light his way as he brooded on the Diwan's latest revelations; vast panoplies of battle had she laid out for him while Compt'n ur Threshrend tended to his schemes; slaughter on a scale to unsettle the scribes of even the most ancient war scrolls.

The Superiorae had sown an exemplary terror amongst the peoples of the American sect, and done so without spilling oceans of daemonum ichor across the Above. Or not the Horde's ichor, to be more accurate. Many legions of the lesser sects had been lured into battle with the Americans, and in every instance they had been utterly destroyed.

Ay, but there was the rub of it.

For all of the success of Guyuk's lures and entrapments of the Morphum and Djinn and the other bastard sects, for all the success of the Horde's strange new stratagem Compt'n ur Threshrend called 'insurgency', the lord commander's gall simmered at the inability of any daemonum force to engage the calflings in open battle.

We are the calflings, herded toward slaughter, he grunted to himself as he crossed the lower viaduct to the Archivum and twinned ranks of Praetorian Grymm on either side of the bridge crashed out salutes, so many of them now that they sounded like some diabolical war engine of the Gnarrl. One of the war hammer ploughs, or the great rolling fortresses bristling with rock throwers. Guyuk did not put these troubling thoughts to one side as he acknowledged the salute of the Captain Grymm and strode through the portcullis of the Archivum. Leaders did not flinch from sharp truths. They allowed themselves to be cut by contemplation of the realities, to bleed a little in worrying about all that might go wrong. Better to do so before battle than after, when it was always too late and the bleeding too great to staunch with mere thoughts.

He found the Superiorae and the human female in the great domed library of the Masters Scolari. The atmosphere was hushed, the silence broken only by the rustle of scrolls, the scrape of bone quills on wyrm-hide parchment and the occasional bizarre exclamation of the Superiorae dar Threshrendum ur Grymm in the strange wet tongue of the calflings.

'Fuckin' awesome. This is made of win. Yeah, fucking win, baby!'
What was the Superiorae saying?

The human, Polly ur Farr'l, did not so much as flinch at Guyuk's approach. That was explicable, he supposed, because the Threshrend Majorae was enhancing her natural *gurikh*, which she apparently had in abundance, but surely not such abundance that being cast into the dark heart of the UnderRealms would not undo her fragile mind.

She said something in her own language.

'I really don't think we need the star wipe.'

Did she speak to Compt'n ur Threshrend of magicks, or dread technology? They both seemed intent on the small iron box with human magicks contained within.

'But I love the star wipe,' Compt'n said, seemingly in protest, leaning so closely over the creature's shoulder that the lord commander wondered how he contained the urge to bite off her head and have at the sweetmeats inside. Indeed, the Threshrend's tiny half-formed loins were engorged and trembling with the very prospect.

'Attend me, Superiorae,' Guyuk growled, slowly.

Polly ur Farr'l looked away from her magick box, her comput'r, and regarded the lord commander with equanimity.

'I think your boss wants you,' she said.

'He's not the boss of me,' Compt'n ur Threshrend declared.

'Threshrend!'

'Coming, boss!'

The female returned to her labours, some arcane series of devotions made to the magick box, which reminded Guyuk of the ritual gestures the Diwan had performed over her seer stones earlier. The Farr'l was not in the leastways intimidated. Guyuk glowered at the Threshrend Majorae, squatting quietly, concentrating its thoughts on her. Was it necessary to imbue her with such confidence that she had not even the slightest terror of his presence?

The Threshrend inclined its eyestalks in the direction of the Superiorae, as though that explained everything.

'Is she nearly done?' Guyuk asked. 'I am wont to press on.'

The Threshrend seemed distracted, his attention divided between his lord commander and his prisoner.

'Do you hunger for her, Superiorae?' Guyuk asked.

It was as though he had caught the empath in some illicit observation of Her Majesty's own thoughts. His eyestalks went rigid with surprise, possibly even fright, and he appeared to become aware of his loins for the first time.

'No!' he said, not at all convincingly.

'We have plenty of prisoners in the dungeons. Get yourself something to eat down there if your appetite distracts you.'

'Appetite?' the tiny Threshrend said, as though Guyuk had spoken in some foreign tongue and the translation had been especially difficult. 'Oh, right. Yeah. She totally embiggens old Threshy's appetite, boss. For, like, eating her and stuff. Yeah . . .' his thoughts seemed to wander off again as he contemplated their captive. 'Yeah, old Threshy would love a piece of that. I would just . . . eat . . . her . . . up.'

'Your treachery is admirable,' Guyuk rumbled quietly, 'but ill timed. You yourself have explained we need this female to deliver our message and vouchsafe our honour and trustworthiness until such a time as we might be positioned to strike at the unwary calflings. Her path does not lead to the blood pot, not yet.'

That caught his attention at last. Lord Guyuk even imagined that the Superiorae was alarmed by the idea of his prisoner going into a regimental stew. Good. It was his idea, after all, to spare her for other uses.

'You're right! You're like totally right, G-Man. No blood pot for Fred . . . I mean, Farr'l. My bad. My mistake. If I confused you when I said Fred. Because I meant Farr'l. The wretched calfling Farr'l. Yeah. Fuck her.'

Guyuk had little to no sense of what his pro-consul meant, but that was not unusual. Not for the first time did Guyuk have cause to regret the choice of the first human soul the Scolari had given his Threshrend advisor to consume.

'I wish to return to the Above as soon as you are finished stitching together this cloak of lies,' Guyuk said, inclining his furrowed brow toward the calfling woman. She busied herself at the thin iron box of magicks. Really, it was more akin to two lids hinged together than a box with a lid.

'Sure,' Compt'n ur Threshrend said. 'She's just wrapping now. We can make it back to the Big App with her in five, I reckon.'

'We shall not return to . . . Manhatt'n,' Guyuk advised him. 'Not with the captive woman. If she is the adept you think her, she will have no need of a sizeable thrall to escort her to the Above. The two lieutenants currently assigned her watch will suffice.'

The Threshrend's eyestalks actually drooped in reply.

'Oh, okay then, but they're not gonna eat her when she's done are they? Because that's not part of the plan and –'

Guyuk struck him with the back of his fist. A light flick, but quick enough to snap the creature's head to one side and induce a whip-crack motion in all of its eyestalks.

'Gather your wits about you, Threshrend. It was you who determined that this female should go under our protection. My lieutenants are tasked to ensure nothing eats her. Or has your hunger robbed you of memory along with your wits?'

The empath was staring at him as though he had never been struck by a higher daemon. Lord Guyuk admonished himself, not for the loss of control, but for not having thought to strike the creature earlier. Superiorae and Pro-Consul adeptus he might be, but Compt'n ur Threshrend still answered to his lord commander.

'I would have thought you had gorged yourself to point of utter satiation in the Above, Superiorae,' he said, applying the balm of his proper title. 'But it seems you are possessed of a hunger every bit as demanding as your . . . *personality*.' He made the effort to draw out the human term Compt'n had taught him. 'Order sustenance from the regimental kitchens before we take leave. I would not have you distracted during our audience with Her Majesty.'

If Guyuk expected the empath to be surprised or even perturbed by the news of their summons to the palace, it was not to be. Still rubbing his skull where the lord commander had cuffed him but lightly, the Superiorae did not even react to the summons. Instead he asked, 'So, the lieutenants, they'll get her safe home? Polly, I mean.'

Guyuk frowned at the unusual phrasing, but put it down to all the personalities at war within the Threshrend's thinkings.

'They are tasked to deliver her wherever she demands or desires. They will die in her thrall, if needs be.'

'Okay,' said Compt'n ur Threshrend. 'I can live with that.'

'Oh, Threshrend,' Guyuk rumbled, 'You cannot imagine how my hearts flutter with relief to hear that.'

Compt'n ur Threshrend regarded his lord commander with cautious reserve.

'Your sarcasm's coming along real nice, boss. A little more work and it'll sting nearly as much as your bitchslap.'

16

Another explosion, a series of them, like a string of lethal Chinese firecrackers, burst over the Grymm struggling through the breach in the apartment wall. Gunfire ripped into those warriors who had cleared the opening and closed most of the distance to Dave and Karen. Armour-piercing and tracer rounds.

For illuminating targets and destroying personnel, Dave recalled from another reality. The SEALs had chanted that, like a children's poem.

When?

Once upon a time, he thought.

Some of the Grymm caught fire at the touch of the incendiary rounds, consumed by the same strange blue-green flame that had torched the bodies of the unnamed Hunn below.

'The fuck?' Dave muttered as more dark figures poured into the room. They wore body armour, helmets and night vision goggles and it might once have given them an intimidating, otherworldly aspect, but now it marked them as members of his tribe. His Clan.

They were men.

And, you know, maybe a hot monster-killing babe or

two. He wasn't sure whether equal opportunity laws covered special operations teams.

Dave wondered if Karen was okay, but he was too far gone to check. He closed his eyes and drifted off to the sweet, sweet sound of human gunfire.

Guns, he'd decided, weren't so bad after all.

The penthouse didn't look like a normal apartment. It looked like the big white box an apartment came in. A big white box with a white leather couch. These guys obviously didn't have kids. For a long time after he woke up, Dave just lay there, looking at the drip someone had hooked up for him.

He felt as if he was bleeding out, but of course that wasn't possible. The fluid was going in. All of his wounds were either healed, or healing in fresh pink swatches and ridges of scar tissue which would fade away over the next hour.

He found a few energy gels in pockets he didn't even know he had. He could feel his body burning the calories as soon as he sucked down the warm, sweet-tasting jelly. Like throwing drops of gas onto a roaring bonfire.

The power was back, the penthouse clean and brightly lit. No sign of the SWAT team or ESU or whoever had saved their asses. No sign of the medics who'd plugged this drip into him.

'Eat this,' Karen said, and he jumped a little as she emerged from the kitchen.

'What is it?' he asked, as his head fell back on the padded arm of the white leather couch. He'd painted this fine piece of furniture with so much of his own blood and sour sweat it seemed a shame not to finish the job. Warat, or Varatchevsky, was carrying something which looked heavy, although the weight did not bother her. She looked as though she'd been awake for a while longer than him. Her leathers were filthy and torn here and there, but her face and her hands were clean, freshly scrubbed. He could smell the soap.

'It's a ham,' she said. 'I would have made eggs for the protein, but there was no power until two minutes ago.'

Dave waved a hand around in the warm glow of electric light.

'Well, power's back now. So where's my eggs, woman?'

It was a tired shot at lifting the mood. She took neither offence nor amusement from it. Instead, she used her katana to carve a massive hunk of cold meat sheathed in fat from the leg of ham, a whole leg including the hoof too, with only a few slices missing.

'Jesus Christ, Karen. I just watched you stick that all the way into a monster's ass.'

'I cleaned it off,' she said. 'No cooties. See?'

She sliced off a huge chunk of pink meat and took a fist-sized bite of it.

The streets far below throbbed with the red and blue lights of the emergency services. Sirens rose and fell, but there were so many sirens all over the city it was impossible to say which were headed toward them. A lot, Dave guessed. A lot of ambulances anyway. Did they put dead people in ambulances? Would they bother, when the dead were piling up all over the city?

The penthouse afforded views far to the north and west and it seemed as though hundreds of fires burned out of control. He twice saw military aircraft swoop down from the night sky, unloading high explosive weaponry, rockets and bombs, on less built-up areas. It looked like a news report out of Gaza or Syria. Except that those rockets were falling on an American city. On *the* American city. Hours ago he would have run to the windows, gaped in horror. But he'd had his fill of more intimate horrors. Instead he collapsed on the white leather couch and fed on little tubes of energy gel until he no longer felt like he might fade out of existence.

'How long . . . ?' He trailed off, not even sure where to begin.

'Not long,' she said. 'You've been out of it less than half an hour. ESU took down the last Thresher at the same time they rescued us.'

He stared at her like she was a puzzle he couldn't quite figure out.

'But we killed that one. You stuck it in the ass.'

She shook her head.

'There was a third. On the floor above. Remember? You were just asking me about it when the Grymm set off that satchel charge.'

'They what?'

He felt even dumber than he just had, as though he'd woken from a nightmare, but was unsure whether he was actually awake, or still dreaming.

'The Grymm set off a charge, blew a hole through the wall,' she explained as she carved off more ham. 'It's a proven technique in house to house fighting. Your forces used it a lot in Iraq and Afghanistan.'

'Where'd they get a bomb?' he asked, and then waved his own question away. 'Forget it. It wouldn't be that hard, would it?'

'No, it wouldn't, if you knew what to look for, and they did. They're learning. The ambush was simple, an old tactic. They let us spring the first stage and when we survived they launched the second attack. The real one.'

'Jesus, that first one felt pretty fucking real to me.'

Karen gave him the ham bone, keeping the heavy flank of pink meat she'd cut off for herself. He took the offering with a hand that was scabbed and scarred and held together with fresh pink skin that itched ferociously as it healed.

'The last Thresher was old,' she said. 'Cunning. He did something. Shielded his mind, but also mine. That's why I couldn't feel him or the Grymm.'

'Or the Sliveen,' Dave added.

'No, nor them,' she conceded.

'So, Karen,' Dave said, resolved to press on. 'Do you see you were wrong?'

She looked at him, her head tilted just a little to the side.

'I was not wrong,' she said, without bothering to ask what he meant. 'The tactic worked.'

'But you didn't need to push those guys into beating the bushes for us. We could have found those Threshers without sacrificing so many people. And if we'd lost more of them, we'd have been fucked, wouldn't we? There'd have been nobody to help us when the Grymm ambushed us. You should think on that next time.'

She stared at him, not offended. She appeared to be giving the question her honest consideration.

'No, you are wrong, Hooper,' she said at last. 'If we had done it my way, we would not have needed our asses pulled out of the fire. We would have probed for the Threshers, located them, and killed them. Your squeamishness nearly got us killed. But you are not a soldier, are you?'

'No,' he said. 'I'm not. But even soldiers are people, Karen. Their lives aren't forfeit just because they signed up.'

'Their lives are forfeit the minute they sign up.'

'How very Russian,' he said sarcastically. He wanted to eat. Needed to. Saliva was shooting into his mouth, but he swallowed it and pressed on. He needed to say this. 'Nobody signed up for your militia tonight. You pushed them. Don't do that again. Not here. What you do when you go home, that's your business. But if you want Americans to die for you, at least have the decency to ask them. They might surprise you.'

There was no heat to the exchange. He was exhausted and all he wanted was for her to understand. She did not push back.

The ham joint was still cold from the refrigerator, in spite of the power failure. More saliva shot into his mouth as he bit into it, disgusting him a little bit and undercutting all his noble feelings about putting Varatchevsky in her place. He couldn't separate the memory of so much torn human flesh from the clean, smoked meat between his teeth. His empty stomach cramped, but he kept chewing and swallowing and trying not to remember. There was no joy in the mere consumption of fat and protein, but it was necessary. With each mouthful he could feel himself healing. His strength was not yet returning. It wouldn't until he was at least halfway recovered from the damage of combat.

They spoke while they rested up, but their conversation was flat. An exchange of information. Nothing more. Tallies of the dead, casualty counts on both sides.

Thirty-seven cops.

Nineteen firefighters.

The civilian death toll, still unknown, but high. Very high.

Dave ate and recovered his strength. Karen too. There was no alternative. They were spent.

They discussed fighting styles. A leashed Fangr was, in many ways, easier to deal with than one unleashed by the death of its master. They tended to run berserk when freed. Unnamed Hunn were invariably savage, but stupid. Sliveen were vicious and cunning. The Grymm, when faced outside warp, were horrifying. Dave had no doubt that were it not for Karen, they'd have killed him; and Karen for her part conceded she could not have survived the encounter without him throwing a fridge at them.

'I didn't really throw it,' he shrugged. 'Used it more like a battering ram.'

They swapped details of the effects of different types of human weaponry. They ate. Dave eventually got up and found beer in the fridge, but Karen made him drink water.

'To hydrate.'

She led him through a tactical discussion of how best to deal with empath daemons in future.

'If you are unwilling to risk a few pawns, we will need a ranged option,' she said. 'Snipers, air support or even artillery in the open. Infantry or *spetsnaz* or *Zaslon* operators, to clear urban environments like this.'

Dave had no idea what a *Zaslon* operator was. He could hear again the ghost of a Russian accent in her voice when she used those Russian words.

He was too exhausted to say what he really thought, that she was worse than anything Trinder had said of her. But he didn't have to. She would already know. With Karin Varatchevsky, just thinking something was enough. She would know. She'd also know he thought Trinder was full of shit.

Dave didn't even bother cataloguing his injuries. He just ate his ham, and finally found himself enjoying the calorie-dense fat with a particular relish. He waited for the furnace inside him to burn the fat away. The windows of the penthouse rattled with the force of an explosion going off within a mile or so. They ignored it. When he'd finished a gallon of tap water, Karen let him have that beer. She drank from a large porcelain jug while reclining in the single-seater across from him, her boots up on the coffee table. Or what he assumed to be a coffee table. It was a machined block of stainless steel weighing a ton and had probably cost its own weight in gold.

Lucille lay on top it. Karen had fetched the maul up from the site of their death struggle with the Grymm and laid it out next to a bowl of nuts.

'What are you drinking?' Dave asked, mildly interested. 'A milkshake?'

He wouldn't mind a milkshake. There was only the one beer.

'Raw eggs, protein powder, creatine and cocoa.'

'Okay then. Enjoy that.'

He ingested mouthfuls of pink pig meat, wondered at the lives of the people who'd lived in this penthouse and what the hell was happening across the city beyond it.

A phone rang. Not the apartment landline, as he first thought. A cell. Karen frowned, her eyebrows knitting to form a single furrow between them. If she'd done Botox, Dave thought numbly, she couldn't do that frowny thing. So she hadn't done any Botox. Good for her. He ate some more ham, tearing the meat from the bone with his teeth as though ripping into a giant drumstick. Karen put the revolting protein shake down on the stainless steel slab, leaving a ring. A phone in a ruggedised case appeared from deep inside her gore-stiffened biker jacket.

'Wow. Is that a BlackBerry?' Dave said. 'Did the KGB pick 'em up cheap on eBay or some –'

'Shut up . . . Yes?'

The first comment she directed at him, the second at whoever had called her. Dave had half-expected her to say hello in Russian. *Dasvidaniya Tovaritsch*, or *Stolichnaya Ivan* or something like that. But he supposed it could just as easily have been a call from her made-up life. Her cover. Except she probably wouldn't bother answering that anymore, would she?

The crease between her eyebrows grew deeper, and the line of her mouth thin and tightly pressed.

'Sure,' she said, almost spitting the word out. She passed the handset across the stainless steel table. For a second he didn't know what she meant him to do.

'It's for you.'

From her expression, she was as surprised as he, and pissed off with it. Although Dave was pretty pissed off that he had to lever himself up from where he'd been lying, exhausted, stretched out on the couch eating his ham and drinking his beer. Fuelling up. Totally fuelling up, not being a lazy, irresponsible slug while the city died around him.

'Super Dave,' he said when he had the phone – yep, a BlackBerry – up to his ear.

'Hello, Dave. It's Emmeline.'

. . .

What the fuck?

'Uh. Hi . . . Doc,' he said. Each word more uncertain than the one before it. 'How are you? Besides, you know, alive,' he said, recovering a little. 'After I rescued you and stuff.'

His confusion was as deeply felt as his astonishment. They had not parted on the best of terms. The only thing that could have surprised him more was big gay Igor commando-roping in to give him a kiss.

'Yes. I'm alive, thank you,' said Ashbury.

Dave's bewilderment was mirrored in Karen's face. Or rather, Karin. He assumed from her furious expression that this cell phone really was a Russian government unit. Probably specced out the wazoo with all sorts of security that Ashbury had just poked through to say hello.

'I suppose I should say I'm sorry for my performance in Omaha,' said Emmeline, sounding anything but repentant. 'You did save my life and I rather prefer being alive. So thank you.'

'Jeez, don't choke on your *joie de* fucking *vivre*, Doc.'

He put his thumb over the mic, or what he thought was the mic and mouthed at Warat.

Is this your phone? Like, your spy phone?

Uploading an empath daemon to your cortex made for easy lip reading. She rolled her eyes, but nodded. Yes, it was her spy phone. *Cool*, Dave thought as he sat up a little straighter and poured the last of the beer down his throat. He was reviving. His whole body still burned with a low-grade fever as it repaired itself, but he didn't feel as though he was in the last stages of viral pneumonia anymore.

'Fucking NSA,' said Varatchevsky, under her breath, but loud enough that Dave didn't need his Spidey senses to hear.

'We need to meet,' said Ashbury.

Dave turned all of his attention back to the woman on the phone.

'Can't get enough of Dave's special sauce, eh, Doc?'

Emmeline's grinding teeth were probably audible to Karen across the table. He heard elevator doors open outside the penthouse. A low burble of voices. Medics or cops, he supposed.

'For fuck's sake, Hooper,' Ashbury said. Her voice sounded much sharper and familiar for it. 'Listen to me, you witless man-child, I am sorry for being such a petty bitch in Omaha. It was wrong of me and unworthy. But you have been a complete dick and people are dying for it.'

He felt as though she was about to say *'Again'*. His face flushed, more with irritation than shame or guilt. Guilty Dave was on a break. But he saw the smirk sketched on Karen Warat's features and it punctured his usual defensive reaction to being made to feel at fault.

'So what is it you want, Doc? Oh, and my friend Karen isn't very happy about you calling me on her phone.'

'Your friend is the agent of a hostile power.'

'Well she's hostile to monsters and that asshole Trinder but that don't make her unique in this conversation, does it?'

'Oh God, look, Hooper, just shut up, and . . .'

He heard the phone being taken from her and a new voice came on. Deep and richly toned, but constrained, as though the man talking could not allow himself to truly speak his mind or let his feelings get away from him. Certainly not after Ashbury had let hers run free.

'Dave, it's Captain Heath.'

Warat was up from her seat, but not headed toward the kitchen. She'd picked up her sword and the pistol she'd taken earlier from the cop. He was probably going to get into a heap of trouble for that. If he was alive. She seemed to want to check on whoever had arrived, and Dave left her to it.

'Hey, Cap'n,' he said, feeling a little dumb. 'How's things?' Even dumber.

'Things are not well, Dave. But you know that. We're inbound for New York. We'll be there in less than an hour and we need you to meet up with us.'

Dave found his heart was beating faster than it had all night. He had just fought monsters for three hours, and had come closer to being killed – like really killed, game over, no credits – than at any time since he'd fronted Urgon. But now his head was a helium balloon that might possibly lift off his shoulders and float out the window, drifting away across the burning city.

'I'm sorry,' he said. 'Did I miss the bit where we're best friends again? If we hugged it out over a couple beers it must have been a shitload of beer because I don't recall that at all.'

His heart started to slow, but his words flew out faster and louder.

'What I recall is you chewing my ass ragged and turning me out on fucking cable TV as the dipshit who got all your guys killed back in Nebraska. What I recall is Big Gay Igor trying to punch out my fucking lights, which is okay because he punches like a girl and you can totally fucking tell him I said that and . . .'

He stopped.

Everything had stopped.

'Karen! Fuck! Did you just warp me out of my call?'

She appeared back at the door of the penthouse.

'Oh excuse me. Did I interrupt your tantrum? You might not have noticed but one of Trinder's little friends was just outside. The half-breed they put into my gallery when they tried to grab me.'

'Wow,' said Dave. 'Seriously? Half-breed? I'm appalled. You're quite the bigot aren't you. Is that like a Russian thing too?'

'Asking me if being a Russian makes me a bigot rather makes you an even bigger one. Now let's get out of here before she comes back with the rest of the men in black. By now Trinder's probably turned a Thresher into a double agent just to put a leash on us.'

He pointed at the phone.

'Hey. On a call here? Or I was until you hit pause.'

She clicked her fingers in an unnecessary theatrical gesture and they dropped out of warp.

'Your apology is accepted, Dave,' Heath said.

Hooper stamped on the brakes again, throwing them straight back into super slo-mo.

'Fuck's sake, Karen! He didn't hear a thing I said. Just, "I'm sorry".' He shook his head at the unfairness of it all. 'It was a sarcastic sorry. *Sarcastic*. Not a real sorry. I didn't apologise and now Heath thinks I did.'

'God. The snippy old British bitch is right. You really are a man-child.'

'She's not old. And she's not snippy. She's got autism.'

Karen dropped into a pantomime East London accent. 'Ooh, fancy a bit of hot English crumpet do we?'

'What are you, my wife now? . . . Ex-wife . . . Soon enough.'

Karen dismissed him with a flick of her sword.

'Your thoughts, not mine. Just find out what they want, Hooper. They're obviously playing way up the food chain if they can break into my phone. They might be able to deal with Trinder. And if they don't, I will. Understand? Because we don't have time for his shit anymore. So talk to your one-legged friend. Get whatever information you can and then we're gone. There's still plenty of monsters out there. If we don't put them down hard, they'll be all over us, everywhere. Fast.'

She clicked her fingers again and they dropped out of warp. He wondered how she was doing that, riding on his ability. He couldn't even feel her do it, which was how he'd lost track of his rant at Heath.

'We were all under a lot of pressure in Omaha,' Heath continued, as if he hadn't been interrupted. And as far as the navy officer knew, he had not been. 'I'm sorry too, Dave. I didn't handle it well. Nor did you. But no messing around now, we are in trouble, Dave.'

He could hear the difficulty Heath had getting those words out, and it spiked his own need to take back the apology he hadn't actually offered. His jaw was still clenched with an almost biological need to spit a lot of angry words back down the phone. But as long as Rational Dave knew he hadn't apologised, he supposed he could put up with other people believing Contrite Dave had, especially if it cleared the air. That's what being a grown-up was all about, as he'd explained to his boys more than once, 'Sometimes your mom is just plain wrong, but it's easier to say sorry and pretend she's right.'

And easier still not to say sorry and pretend that you had.

'So,' he said, exhaling a stale, beery breath. 'What's up? You know, besides orcs eating New York, and zombies in LA?'

'Just that,' said Heath. 'Everything that's happening. It's following a playbook. A playbook written by Compton about how to collapse a whole society. Or a civilisation.'

'Oh, right,' Dave said. 'Well that sucks.'

Shit, he thought. Were they gonna blame him for this too?

17

'No, we're not blaming you, Dave.'

Heath's voice was level, but Hooper had come to recognise that precisely measured delivery as a sure sign that Captain Michael Heath was not being pathologically honest anymore.

As a jet roared low overhead, Karen returned from another hurried trip to the kitchen with two blocks of cling-wrapped food. Cheese and something that wasn't cheese.

'Pâté,' she said. Her lips moved, but he heard the word inside his head.

He grimaced and indicated he'd prefer the cheese. It wasn't American cheese. It didn't glow in the dark. But it looked less likely to make him gag than the small brick of creamed liver she quickly inhaled. Dave put the block of cheese in a pocket, trusting the cling wrap to keep it clean. He would eat it as soon as he could, but he couldn't talk to Heath with a mouthful of cheddar. At least he hoped it was cheddar and not some bullshit imported hippo cheese or something. The sort of people who lived in big white boxes like this, they'd eat artisanal hippo cheese for sure.

'We don't know how they got the information from Compton,' said Heath. 'We don't think he's collaborating with them. We think he's dead, Dave. But they probably tortured him first.'

'Well that's all right then,' Dave said. 'Wait. That didn't come out right.'

'I know what they're doing,' said Karen, loud enough for Heath to hear. 'Or what they did.' She'd downed that disgusting shit brick of raw offal as fast as Dave would neck a beer after a day's work.

'Is that Varatchevsky?' Heath asked. 'The Russian?' he added.

'Yeah, it's her,' said Dave. 'And, yes, she's a bitch. But she's a useful bitch. You'd like her Heath. She's all about sacrifice.'

Especially other people's.

'We can discuss her later,' Heath said, but Karen took the phone from Dave, who was happy enough to give it up. He didn't want to get caught in this crossfire.

'No, we can discuss it now, Captain,' said Karen, leaving Dave to wonder if she'd heard what Heath said on the phone, or in his head. 'You know where we are, what's been happening. If you broke in on this phone, you can track it. You're also capable of turning on a cable news channel. So do not dissemble, Captain. You are aware of our situation. Hooper and I just put down a large cohort and survived a reasonably sophisticated two-stage ambush that resembled nothing so much as one of your vertical envelopment exercises.'

She thumbed on the BlackBerry's speaker and Dave heard Heath reply.

'Colonel Varatchevsky, I have no interest in you or –'

'Well I have an interest in you, my Captain,' she shot back, cutting him off. 'Agent Trinder is coming for me, and he will come heavy. That's not an insurmountable problem, but it is a problem, or rather a distraction I don't need. Hooper is with me by his own choice, and in Trinder's view that makes him compromised. So unless you want to lose your asset I suggest you race Trinder up the chain of command until you find someone who can shut him down. Go all the way if you have to. We're leaving now. We have monsters to kill and this apartment will soon be full of Clearance agents or, more likely, Hellfire missiles. Call us back when you have something.'

She cut the connection and hit warp.

'We have to get out. Now,' she said.

Dave picked up Lucille and juggled the cheese block while he peeled off the cling wrap.

'Seriously? Missiles?' he said. 'Trinder'll be pissed at me, sure. And he'll always be pissed at you, but . . .'

Karen pointed out the tall windows at the tracer fire ribboning up into a sky painted with flashes of bomb bursts and explosions. Infernos great and small engulfed skyscrapers and neighbourhoods alike. The violence seemed not just sweeping, but universal, as though it was eating the city whole.

'You think anybody is going to notice one more explosion?' Karen said. 'Come on. Move.'

Dave didn't think Trinder would blow him up just to get to Varatchevsky, but the cheese was really hitting the spot, so he had no excuse for sitting around anymore. Besides, she was right about one thing. If Trinder couldn't get over his hard-on for Karen he was going to be a distraction at the very moment they couldn't afford it. Heath might be able to help with that.

Then again, Dave had signed that consultancy contract back in LA. Trinder might not fire a rocket up his ass, but he might narc him out to the IRS. Not a first-order issue right now, granted. But those guys were as bad as daemonic carnivores and he really didn't want to give them any more reasons to get on his case.

Would Karen object to him giving his lawyer a quick call? If Boylan hadn't been eaten by Tümorum zombies or some stray Fangr he'd know what to do.

'Hey, can I use your phone again?' he asked.

'We will call Heath when we're clear of the building,' she said, heading out the front door.

'No, I want to call my lawyer. Or agent really. He's more of an agent . . .'

Dave trailed off at the glare she shot him.

'Maybe later,' he said.

Damn. It was like he didn't even have these superpowers, the number of people telling him what he *couldn't* do. He had really thought that getting free of his wife meant getting free. Not so much, it turned out.

Bloody footprints marred the carpeted hallway outside the penthouse, but it was otherwise unmarked and undamaged. The battle hadn't reached this floor. The elevator doors were closed, and wouldn't open again until they dropped back into normal time, but that didn't matter. Taking the elevator would be a dumb-ass move.

'Stairs,' she said.

Trinder's Clearance agents were four flights down and seemed to be withdrawing.

'They're covering a tactical retreat,' Karen said as they carefully threaded their way through the living mannequins. They were dressed for the office. Dark suits and ties instead of combat coveralls. They didn't even wear body armour. Dave recognised the little Asian chick. Agent Nguyen.

'There'll be another team in the stairwell on the far side

of the building,' Karen said. 'And more covering the elevators and any external fire escapes. They want us in that apartment, Hooper. A fixed target.'

'Bullshit,' he said, but without conviction.

'They're going down, not up. This one made us, while you were yapping on the phone.'

She had stopped in front of Agent Nguyen and, before Dave could stop her, reached out, placed a finger on her tattooed forehead and closed her eyes, murmuring something.

Hooper slapped her hand away.

'Whatever you're doing, don't. I thought we discussed this. It's really uncool.'

'It's insurance,' Karen replied, as uncaring as ever about his opinion. 'She'll be fine.'

Dave frowned and switched Lucille from one shoulder to the other.

'You make it very hard to like you, *Karin*.'

'As hard as this will be for you to hear, *Super Dave*, getting you to like me has never been a life goal. But getting out of this building is. And the cheese. I'll take some of that too.'

He broke the remaining block in half and tried to give her the smaller piece as they threaded carefully down through the knot of agents. She took the larger portion. If this was a date, it would be their only one.

Dave expected to see the other agents he knew by name, Comeau and the Madigan woman, but, apart from Nguyen, the agents here were just anonymous off-the-rack suits.

Three flights down, Karen announced she was going to drop out of warp.

'But I need you to pick it up, straight away.'

'Why?' Dave asked. 'I mean, why don't you just do

whatever you're doing, daisy-chaining it off me or whatever. I can't stop you. I don't even know how you're doing it. Fuck, I don't even know how I do it.'

'I need you to take over because it burns energy too fast when I drive. It's inefficient. So I'm going to hand off to you. Pick it up quick. We want them to think we're still upstairs.'

Dave didn't object, but he did shake his head.

'I can see why Trinder wanted to take you out,' he said. 'He just couldn't have you in the game, his game and yours, could he?'

She stopped at the turn between the seventh and eighth floors. The stairwell was pocked by bullet marks and a few splatters of daemon ichor. The fluorescent light was harsh, making the lines of her face seem longer and harder, her cheeks hollow and her eyes sunk deeply into her skull.

'But we're not in that game anymore, are we, Dave? We have our own game now, right?'

Karen's voice seemed empty of all human feeling. Dave was sure that if she didn't get the answer she wanted, one of them would not be leaving this stairwell. He was also sure there could be no lying to her. He could feel her, inside his head.

'Right,' he said. 'I was just saying, is all. But yeah, that's his game, not ours.'

Her eyes searched his face, and deeper than that.

'Okay,' she said, satisfied at last. The moment passed.

He held up Lucille and Karen tapped the blade of her katana against the steel head of the splitting maul. It rang like a chime and he felt a shiver run up his arms.

'You feel that?'

'Yes,' she said. 'But I don't know what it means. Do you?'

'No.'

They swapped responsibility for maintaining the warp field and hurried down the remaining floors, stopping briefly to check on survivors. Chief Gomes was still there, supervising the care of her men and women. Dave was pleased to see Sergeant Mahoney had made it through as well. The cop was on the fourth floor with that paramedic who'd tried to treat Dave earlier. They were suspended in time over the body of a civilian, a middle-aged man. Mahoney looked on as the woman applied CPR.

'That thing you did to me, earlier,' he said to Karen. 'You know, speeding up the healing process . . .'

'No,' she replied. 'I can't. Not for them. They're not like us.' She almost sounded sad.

The penthouse exploded as they stepped out onto the street.

Dave had dropped out of warp just before they re-entered the foyer. The bodies there had all been removed, although he had no idea where. Hysterical women and children, and a few hysterical men, huddled together out of the way of the emergency services. Paramedics had the floor now. Everyone deferred to their orders and requirements. An intact ESU SWAT team stood watch over the triage process. Their commander nodded to Dave and Karen when they emerged from the stairwell, but otherwise made no move toward them. The last of the fighting at 530 Park Avenue had concluded half an hour earlier. This was mopping up.

Dave saw the rockets. He'd looked up as soon as they walked out onto the street. A reflex action, which allowed him to spot the hot, bright smoking trail of two missiles as they streaked into their target.

The roar of detonation was shockingly loud and uncomfortably close. It lit up the streets around the condo for three blocks. Karen's instincts, or training, served her better than Dave's unthinking reaction, which was simply to flinch and watch the enormous bloom of orange and yellow fire that erupted from the top floors. She dived back under cover in the foyer, yelling at him to move his ass. He could see debris spiralling down through the concrete canyons, the first shards of glass arriving before he'd even thought to step on the accelerator again.

The world stopped.

'Don't waste your energy,' Warat yelled out. 'You'll need it.'

But he needed it now. He could see a young boy in a Teenage Mutant Ninja Turtle shirt and tighty-whities caught out in the open, staring up, paralysed by the spectacle. Hooper ran out, remembered to bring himself to a full stop before gently picking up the boy, who looked to be about Toby's age. He checked the descending debris field and the other potential victims caught under it. They were all moving to safety. They'd be fine. He decided he had time to walk the kid back inside the foyer, where he stood him in front of the ruined concierge station, like a small statue.

'Did it occur to you that you could have killed the kid, accelerating him like that?' Karen said, unimpressed with his public service.

'Nah,' Dave shrugged. 'It doesn't work like that. I'm pretty sure, anyway I piggy-backed Heath before and he didn't die.'

The boy gasped and nearly fainted away as Dave let the warp bubble collapse and the flaming debris rained down outside. Dave held the child up as other people came running in to find shelter.

'Be cool, kid. You can tell all your friends Super Dave saved you.'

Something landed with a massive boom nearby and, although he hadn't seen it, Hooper was certain that stupid coffee table had just touched down. His reassuring grin faltered and died as he saw the kid's face fall.

'My friends are . . . They were upstairs. They're all gone.'

'Nice work, Super Dave,' Karen said into his ear. 'Let's roll.'

'Sorry,' he said to the boy, but it came out so small and quiet that the child didn't hear. He simply stood, his eyes awash with tears, his whole body shaking. A few moments ago he'd reminded Dave Hooper of his son, and now he did so again. Little Tobes, six years old, shaking and crying because Dave hadn't turned up after school the way he'd promised. Toby bullied again, as he had been every day for a month before Annie got the truth of it from him and Dave promised to do something the very next day. Promised to take names and kick ass. Failed to take names and kick ass. Failed to even show up before the little rat bastards had got to his kid again.

Failed to rein in his anger. With those little cunts. With himself.

Failed.

He slammed the memory back down deep where it had lain, unexamined for years. But not before he had to contemplate the shame of what had come next. He had been angry, mostly with himself for letting the boy down again, but of course Bad Dave was having none of that and Bad Dave had roared at his own son about little Tobes bringing this on himself because he hadn't just hauled off and hit the bully the way his old man had taught him to.

Karen's voice cut through his fugue.

'Yeah, you've got a lot of atoning to do, shithead. But you can't do it one little urchin at a time –'

Had she been reading his mind?

'– there's a whole world to save first. Starting with this city.'

Of course she had. He walked away from the kid, muttering an apology. Karen marched over to the SWAT team, which was crouched at a row of broken windows, taking cover while watching the chaos in the street.

'Do you have a cell phone I can borrow, Officer . . . Pombier?'

She read off the squad leader's name tag.

'The hell was that?' Pombier asked, looking up as though he might see through the ceiling. 'They told me you guys took care of everything.'

'That was something else,' Karen said. 'Can I borrow your phone? It's important. See if I can stop that from happening again.'

More flaming wreckage crashed down in the street. Pombier was a heavily built, slab-shouldered man. He wore a black baseball cap instead of the bucket helmets of his comrades. Dave thought the big cat on the logo might have been some sort of unit badge, until he realised the cat was chewing a baseball bat. Pombier was a fan of the Detroit Tigers.

'Damn. Okay.'

He keyed a pin into an older-looking phone in a hardened case before handing it over.

'Get under cover!' one of his men yelled into the street.

'Thank you,' Karen said, ignoring the mayhem outside.

As best Dave could tell, she hadn't pushed Pombier. She hit a few buttons on her phone, brought up a number, smiled, and keyed it into the sergeant's cell.

'NSA doesn't have all the cool tricks,' she said, as they waited.

'What do you mean?' Dave asked, still recovering from his encounter with the boy.

Karen spoke to whoever picked up at the other end of the call.

'Captain Heath. Yes. It's Colonel Varatchevsky. We need a time and a place to rendez-vous. And you need to get Trinder off our asses. I mean it. He just blew up some very expensive real estate because we were standing in it.'

Dave couldn't hear what Heath said in reply, but Karen didn't take the news well. She didn't speak for nearly a minute, instead listening and occasionally saying 'yes' or simply nodding her head.

'Fine,' she said at last. 'Twenty-three hundred hours. The Armoury on Lexington. I can explain then.'

She handed the phone back to Pombier.

'Thank you, Sergeant.'

'He didn't want to speak to me?' Dave asked.

'He didn't need to speak to you. He's going to unplug Trinder, or try anyway. And we're going to meet up at the National Guard Armoury on Lexington Avenue. Until then we have work to do. Your friend Compt'n just released a sex tape.'

'What?'

'Yes. He's fucking with everyone.'

18

As was so often the case, Lord Guyuk ur Grymm was not entirely sure of what the Threshrend spoke. From the tenor of his delivery he thought the empath was speaking purely to fill up the silence in his head, lest the voices of those souls he had consumed echo too loudly inside his skull. The lord commander was learning to indulge his pro-consul in such moments, grunting occasionally as though he attended more closely to the Threshrend's endless prattle than was actually the case.

'I mean, if we had some fucking YouTube down here we could like have our own channel and shit. We could be fucking coining it, man . . .'

The stomping of hardened feet and the scraping of claws on the stone tiles of the palace forecourt made it easier to ignore Compt'n ur Threshrend's babbling. Should he return to discussing the stratagems and tactics of the war in some useful manner, Guyuk would return to paying him heed. For the age they spent traversing the long march to the palace, the Superiorae babbled incessantly about the calfling Farr'l, and her role in his plan, and how important that role was, and how he simply couldn't have her eaten by any old daemon, and how he hoped everyone understood that, especially the two Lieutenants Grymm assigned to escort her Above. Lord Guyuk had thought him addled with hunger, but now simply thought him addled. Naturally, he had not told the Superiorae of the experiments now underway in the Consilium, where other Threshrend, veteran empaths, consumed the thinkings of scores of captives, but Guyuk had reason to hope the masters' investigations might prove fruitful. He was not entirely sure Compt'n ur Threshrend was not losing his minds.

For the moment, however, Guyuk was content to march at the head of the lieutenants' detail, the Threshrend scurrying along beside him, hurrying to keep up. The dark red skies of the Demesne ur Horde were streaked with far-off Drakon smoke and low drifts of volcanic plume. The dense, black tendrils obscured the uppermost towers of the palace. The great court was largely empty, save for a few war bands of Grymm who drilled at close quarters, and a Dread Company of Gnarrl constructing scaffolds for the ritual abasement of *dar ienamic* captured in the Above. Not Men, of course. Such human prisoners as the Grymm had taken in Manhatt'n and Om'haa were in the pits awaiting interrogation.

The great iron racks and triangles where Gnarrl hammered and strained to fashion the traditional installations of torture would soon host captives from the Sectum Gargui and Qwm, taken for trophies at the chaotic edge of battle.

Once, Lord Guyuk would have fumed at the impudence of the rival sects, daring to tread upon ground the Horde had claimed, even if by right of traditional fief. The human cities of Manhatt'n and Om'haa might well lie within lands claimed by other sects once upon an eon, but those lands now belonged to She of the Horde by right of occupation. No Djinn or Kravakh or Qwm immediately stood forward to defend them when the Horde first entered. Hence they were now the property of the Horde, no matter how furiously the other sects and clans might contest the claim.

As the outer wall of the palace loomed over them, Guyuk wondered whether it was judicious to have the Threshrend along for this audience. She of the Horde had already encountered him, of course, but in a lesser form, when She questioned the mere thresh after it first returned from the Above. But so much had changed since then, most particularly to the little daemon. Simple thresh had matured, and been elevated not just into Threshrend, but into Daemonum Superiorae. That would not normally be of concern. Quite the opposite. But as the lord commander knew well, the course of Compt'n ur Threshrend's maturation had not run true. There could be no doubting the intelligence and utility of the souls it had taken up, or most of them anyway, even if they were mere cattle. Guyuk had come to understand the foolishness and hazard of that particular form of bigoted blindness.

No. As he crossed the bridge over the burning moat, and took the salute of the Praetorian Grymm at the palace gates, Lord Guyuk ur Grymm worried not that the empath would have nothing to contribute to this meeting, but that he might have altogether too much.

Threshy wasn't a fucking idiot. Those assholes G had running his regiments might have thought so, but they were dancing to Threshy's funky disco tunes now, weren't they? Nine Talon of Grymm were already in New York, hitting points of critical failure while the city fell apart around them. Hundreds of cohorts, and even augmented Talon, from all three Regiments

Select stood ready to jump into another forty-three cities around the world, fourteen of them in North America. The Diwan dar Sliveen had her bad-ass ninjas in place too. They were all just waiting for the word. His word. And he was just waiting on word of Polly. Pretty Polly.

He hoped those Grymm assholes hadn't got hungry and decided to take a bite out of her. He knew, in his head, they wouldn't dare. It probably wouldn't even occur to the unimaginative pricks. They had their orders and to a Grymm, orders were better than a barrel of fried chicken.

But still. Threshy couldn't stop thinking about her and how she was getting on. Her story would be on the air by now. It'd be on the net. It'd be viral. Like the fucking super flu. Polly would be Captain fucking Trips.

When would he get to see her again? He really needed to see her again. Even though he knew it was wrong. He was a monster. And she was just monster food.

He tried to put it out of his minds as they passed under the enormous portcullis. It helped that he almost shat himself as ranks of Praetorian Grymm saluted with a crash of iron-shod spears on cobble stones, and mailed fists into breastplates. Sparks flew from the ground contact, creating a small storm of thunder and lightning which lit up the long and gloomy tunnel. Perhaps Guyuk was right. Might have been better to chill back at the cave while *el jefe* handled this one. Threshy knew he was the motherfucking King Kong of Nobel Laureates among these intellectual pygmies. He'd eaten the finest brains to prove it. But because of that he also knew he'd been cursed by the very act of raising himself from dumbass thresh to ass-kicking Threshrendum.

Fuck that doughnut-eating moron. Why'd he have to eat

Trevor Candly's brains first?

Ha, because the Scolari ass-fucked you.

'You said something of the Scolari, Superiorae?' Guyuk rumbled a few steps ahead of him.

Had he?

Fuck, sometimes he didn't know when he was thinking aloud. And that was the problem.

'Nope. Not me, boss.'

What was going to happen when the Low Queen cracked open Threshy's little ol' egghead and drank up all the noggy goodness? She did that. He remembered it from his last encounter as mere thresh. And that hadn't even been a pop-in to the palace. He'd only been admitted to an audience chamber and She of the Horde hadn't even revealed Herself in Her full Majesty.

Well, it was hard to say, really.

Like, for reals. His head hurt bad when he tried to think about it.

The queen wasn't like some super bug in the old Alien movies or nothing. She was more like . . .

Pain flared inside his skull as he tried to recall the details of their last meeting.

Nope, won't be doing that again.

'G-Man. Is this trip really necessary? You don't think we could've Skyped in or something? You know? While we were totally kickin' up on the frontline for the glory of the Horde and shit?'

'She of the Horde has summoned us to audience, Superiorae.'

What? And that's it?

They passed out of the tunnel and into the first of the inner courts. Polished Drakon-stone, the colour of heart's blood, stretched away into the distance, at least double bowshot length. Another wall rose up ahead of them, topped with crenellated battlements and towers spaced at regular intervals to command the approach across the inner court. The gulf between the outer defences and the palace proper was not entirely devoid of features. Here and there Threshy saw that the plain of Drakon-stone was interrupted by jagged eruptions of rock, as though broken fangs had bitten through the surface of the world. The inky black, razor-edged rock formations were festooned with debris of some sort, rags and . . .

Bones, he realised. The bones of *dar ienamic*. Staked out under the sky where they might be picked clean by winged carrion eaters.

He couldn't help it. He imagined himself on those rocks.

'G-Man, I think you should do the talking.'

'An excellent suggestion, Superiorae,' the lord commander grunted. 'Abase your thoughts before the Low Queen. She will take from you what she will, and ask of me what she must.'

'Awesome,' said Compt'n ur Threshrend. 'Engaging total abasement mode now.'

For once, the empath daemon was as good as his word. He did not speak again as they crossed the Nemesis Plain. The stomping cadence of the Lieutenants Grymm seemed even louder as it rolled away from them across the Drakon-stone. The bones on the *càrn dar ienamicum* were nearly white, Guyuk saw. It had been some time since the hungry stones had been fed, but they would have their fill soon enough. He would see to it, and Her Majesty would be pleased.

The entrance to the second curtain wall was not as grand a portal as the first. The tunnel was narrower and ran a crooked course through the heavy fortifications, switching back on itself a number of times, narrowing to vicious choke points at random intervals, opening up into unexpected killing pens at others. No Praetorian Grymm lined the walls in this passage, but they were present, watching the procession from above where they might rain fire and death upon any who attempted ingress without permission. Even Guyuk himself would die in here if She ordered it, or if he was simply foolish and forgetful enough to seek admission without first being summoned to audience.

Emerging into the second court, the lieutenants took a minute to rearrange themselves in good order before resuming their escort. The architecture of grand statements gave way to the practical and unspectacular, at least in this part of the palace. Carved Drakon-stone yielded to simple cobbles and pavers. The eye swept not over great vistas, but was hemmed in on all sides by barracks, armouries, stables, pot houses, training squares, blacksmiths, foundries, forges and cell blocks. Praetorian Grymm hacked at each other with heavy ironwood training swords, not even coming to attention as the lord commander of their Clan strode past. They were the Palace Praetorian, sworn only to She. Hammers rang on hot metal in the smith shops, the heat of the dangerous furnaces leaking out of the wide doors and windows. A wagon rolled past, piled high with meat for the kitchens. Human cuts, Guyuk saw, but already slaughtered and so marked for the barracks, not the tables of the court. Her Majesty and the Royal House would dine only on the finest and freshest of produce.

Guyuk and Compt'n ur Threshrend wound through the maze of the second court, the empath daemon almost running alongside the lord commander to stay in touch. The Threshrend lived under Guyuk's protection in regimental quarters, but here, were he to be separated from the escort, he could find himself cut down. There was no call for Threshrendum to be about the inner courts.

The small procession drew up in front of another gate, the lieutenants crashing to attention when challenged by the Praetorian Watch Captain. Mailed fists pounded at armoured chests, raising an uproar that reminded Guyuk of the guns used by men to such ill effect.

'Who seeks admittance?' roared the captain, flanked on either side by two Praetorian Sergeants, their blades already drawn.

The senior Lieutenant Grymm stood forward.

'The lord commander seeks admittance to audience. He comes in company with his Pro-Consul adeptus, Compt'n ur Threshrend, Superiorae dar Threshrendum ur Grymm.'

The Captain of the Guard glowered at the empath daemon as though offended by the very idea such a creature might seek admittance. His nostril slits flared and a low growl rumbled from his throat, but there was no question of denying their admission.

'You vouch for this unworthy creature, my Lord?' the captain snarled.

'Of course,' Guyuk said. Form was so tiresome, and yet it was everywhere. It was everything to the warrior clans.

'You are relieved,' the captain told Guyuk's senior lieutenant. The officer did not demur in any way, saluting again, and standing down. The entire detachment stood down with a rattle of armour and weaponry.

'Come,' the captain ordered. Two sergeants banged spear shafts together, then drew them apart, and pushed open the heavy iron doors leading to the Sanctum Royal.

19

Dave had thought, as they'd raced toward 530 Park Avenue, that the city had taken the first hits from the Horde and walked through the blows. Absorbed them. He'd thought New York was counter-punching, getting its people off the streets and its fighters on to them. He realised now that he had been wrong. Or something had changed.

'Fucking Compton,' he said.

Karen didn't bother asking what he meant.

They simply ran. They didn't warp because using the weird temporal distortion was draining and Dave was going to have to learn to call on it sparingly.

They still ran faster than any human being had ever run, or ever would. Any normal human being, at least. No stitch built up in Dave's chest as he sucked down air for the furnace inside. No pain shot up through the soles of his feet to his ankles and shins. A light sheen broke out on his forehead but otherwise they may well have been going for a slow walk to a favourite bar. Five blocks down Park, heading toward the meet-up with Heath, he was surprised to find his idle speculation on their speed resolving into a series of simple equations that hung, suspended in his conscious memory of high school and college math classes. It was the same effect he'd experienced in New Orleans, when calculating the speed and trajectory of his attack on the Sliveen atop the church steeple. He didn't even ask the question, not really, but the answer presented itself. They were moving at seventy-six miles per hour, he discovered. As fast as cheetahs.

He wished he'd taken Zach's advice and found the time to measure exactly what he was capable of doing. His abilities seemed to be changing, evolving, but from what and into what remained a mystery.

They sprinted downtown, mostly sticking to the raised garden beds that divided Park Avenue. These formed a natural conduit through the dense, tangled traffic that jammed up the streets and the crowds thronging the sidewalks and spilling out onto the road, making the traffic snarl even more chaotic.

'This is worse than before,' he shouted at Karen.

'It's Compt'n,' she said with the pronounced inflection on the name, biting down on the second syllable, holding it deep in her throat and squeezing the 'n' sound out through her nose. A characteristic of the Olde Tongue as it was spoken in the demesne of the Horde.

Whatever that asshole had done, it had turned millions of people out of their homes and into the streets. This was not the frightened but relatively organised rush to safety of the hour after sunset, when the first attacks had begun. This was anarchy, an unholy free-for-all akin to NOLA after Katrina.

The MetLife building loomed ahead of them, ten blocks downtown, squatting across the avenue. Fires throughout Manhattan filled the streets with a thin screen of smoke, fuelled by a dozen larger columns in the distance, each spawning a separate re-enactment of 9/11. Under happier circumstances the crowds might have put him in mind of New Year's Eve, or a giant street party, but the heaving masses had no unity or even basic coherence. Wide-eyed, flushed with panic, they surged and boiled and seethed. Businessmen argued with cab drivers who consulted their smart phones and radios. Mothers battered their way through with strollers laden with supplies, beneath which you might see the head of a screaming child. Towed along in their wake, sometimes dragged by the arm, were the boys and girls too old to ride. Through it all, the entrepreneurial spirit of the Big Apple burned, with vendors selling food, water, weapons and offers of transport to safety. One guy even had T-shirts and hoodies emblazoned with the 'Battle of the Apple'. Most featured an anime-style Hunn holding an apple, taking a bite and spurting bloody spray across the white fabric. Dave wondered how he'd had them made up so fast, and what sort of idiot would spend time doing that when he should be running for his fucking life.

Someone who needed the money, part of him thought. Or someone who thought ahead.

The lights of a dozen police and fire vehicles strobed, their sirens screaming, amplified authoritarian voices ordering people to clear the way.

It was all for naught.

The roar was so painfully loud to Dave's augmented sense of hearing that it made his head swim and he almost tripped and fell.

Ahead of him, Karen sprinted like a parkour adept, occasionally leaping from the raised garden beds to land on the roof of a car or a cab when her immediate passage was blocked by knots of people clambering over the median strip. Dave followed her lead, launching himself onto the roof of a bus at one point, landing with enough force to dent the panelling with a dull boom and rock the heavy vehicle on its tyres. He was dimly aware of muted screams and cries of terror coming from within. Probably passengers terrified a monster of some sort had just landed on the roof and was about to peel it open and start scooping them out like fat sardines. He ran along the roof and leaped over a chasm the length of two town cars to crash down on the ass-end of another MTA bus. He landed hard and blew out the rear window with a loud bang. The physics of this was all wrong, he thought. Speed, mass, acceleration, deceleration, all wrong – and then he barked a single sharp laugh. Of course it was all wrong.

Where the fuck you been, Super Dave? What part of this is right?

He jumped from only halfway along the top of this platform to avoid ploughing into a tree when he landed.

He'd made up some ground on Karen. She was finding forward momentum hard to maintain through the increasingly impenetrable densities of the crowd.

Dave heard his own name called out many times, sometimes by folks holding cell phones up to catch a picture of him.

'We might have to get off Park,' he shouted as they pounded up a relatively clear length of the median strip. The monster corpse he'd seen hours ago, while racing in the other direction, was still acting as a potent talisman, clearing a space around it.

'Won't need to,' Karen shouted back.

He followed her gaze forward and almost stumbled again. Something was happening ahead. Something awful and vast. He could not say what, but he could see the pressure wave that travelled through the tightly packed masses. They convulsed with it, visibly flowing away from the older building in front of the MetLife, although Dave was certain that 'flowing' was too gentle a word for whatever was happening five or six blocks ahead of them. He knew that hundreds of people would be dying up there, crushed and trampled underfoot. The howling uproar reached them half a second later, a wall of sound, as tens of thousands of voices cried out in shock and fear. Dave almost groaned at the sudden pain of it, as though someone had jammed chopsticks in his ears.

Then it was gone, muted as though he'd turned on a pair of noise-cancelling headphones. Good ones, like he used to wear to watch the game when his boys were noisy toddlers. Karen said nothing. She didn't have to. She was in his head again. Doing something to shield him from the noise. She didn't look back, didn't ask permission or forgiveness. She hurtled onwards, less sure of her course through the bedlam, occasionally using her speed and strength to shoulder aside anyone who got in her way.

'Try to orb,' she called back over her shoulder without turning around. 'We have to get up there. Something big is happening.' A man in a suit with one arm torn at the shoulder flew bodily through the air as she elbowed him out of her way.

Dave braced himself for the trauma of failure and pain if there should be a Threshrend nearby, but there was none, and instantly they passed from the insensate madness of the riot and into near perfect stillness. The man Karen had sent flying was arrested in midair, his face an absurd caricature of surprise. Whatever Karen had been doing to protect Hooper from the ear-shredding volume, she stopped, and Dave immediately noted that the mysterious dreamland of warp was not as quiet as usual. The low background rumble was louder.

They stopped sprinting. Whatever the Horde was up to, it would not be able to advance its cause as long as Dave maintained the warp field. He unwrapped the last of the cheese from the penthouse and broke off a hunk for Karen.

'Thanks,' he said. 'The noise was putting the zap on my head.'

'I know.' She took the offered food. 'You're going to have to learn to control that.'

'Yeah. Sure. I'll get to that in my downtime. So what the fuck's happening up there?'

Karen turned back toward the two buildings that sat across Park Avenue, the ugly modernist tower of the MetLife dwarfing the old world charm of the Helmsley Building in front of it. Karen angled her head a little to the side as though she might be able to see around it.

'I'm not sure, but I think the problem might be in Grand Central.'

They started to move again, and Dave was struck by the unpleasant image of forcing a path through a human jungle. The heat was ferocious, coming off so many bodies, so closely pressed in on each other, running wild on what was already a warm evening. The stench was worse, bad enough to make eating the last of the cheese difficult. Dave forced it down anyway. They would need all of their reserves of energy.

'Why Grand Central?' he asked.

'Tactics,' she said. 'I think having delivered the shock and awe, they'll target transport and communications nodes now. I think this Compt'n thing means to collapse the city, Hooper. And if it works here he'll do the same everywhere. If it works here it'll be *easier* everywhere else.'

They were forced to thread their way through the traffic

for half a block. The leading edge of the human pressure wave had reached this far up and further compacted the crowds. After finding their path blocked, Karen climbed on to the bonnet of a taxi and from there they made better progress, only returning to the median strip or the avenue proper when it proved impossible to jump from one platform to another. Sometimes the crowds had flowed right over the top of the traffic. Sometimes the energy of so many people all moving in one direction had served to tip over a vehicle. Dave couldn't look at their faces. They seemed more animal than human. He did marvel at the spectacle of a minibus wreathed in unmoving flames when he first saw it. The fire looked like an especially brilliant hologram, but the heat coming off the flames was real, as was the horror of the people trapped inside.

'We have to save them,' he said, more as a reflex.

Karen didn't even bother with a second glance.

'We can't. The fire will burn us just as surely as them. Maybe we'd live. But we'd be hours recovering, and a lot more people would die. It's a war, Hooper. Get used to it.'

He might have argued with her, even as recently as a few hours earlier. Now he turned away and tried not to think about it. When he popped the bubble those people would die screaming and there was no way to save them without losing many more.

A Threshrend reached out and touched them in front of the Helmsley Building, throwing them back out of warp. The stampede had mostly cleared the ground at the intersection of Park and E46th Street. Mostly. The steady, straight line progress of Park Avenue disappeared into a viaduct in the base of the Helmsley and hundreds of bodies lay scattered there. Many still moved and twitched in their death throes. Many more were completely still. Some had been trampled to a bloody gruel. A child tottered about, screaming for her parents. An old man hugged himself and rocked back and forth over the body of somebody who hadn't survived the terrified rout.

Karen dived to the left as soon as they fell out of warp. Dave dodged in the other direction, half blinded for a few seconds by the pixelated smear of his migraine aura. He swore as he tripped and rolled. The headache was already huge and pressing against his skull. It took a few seconds to clear after he popped the warp bubble. He cringed and made himself as small as possible against the side of a delivery van, waiting for the rain of Drakon-stone-tipped war shots and iron bolts.

None came.

'We're clear,' Karen yelled from her cover, crouched down low beneath the chassis of a garbage truck.

Dave looked back up the avenue. The wide, double carriageway was still packed with crowds of terrified, fleeing New Yorkers. Road and foot traffic had merged entirely, creating a perfectly solid gridlock of stationary metal and heaving humanity. The crowd roar was still enormous, but this far removed from the worst of it he was not pained by the volume. Paradoxically, things looked much worse here, where he could see individual bodies and the ruins of burning vehicles.

He pushed himself up and followed Karin Varatchevsky into the dark stone maw of the twin tunnels running under the Helmsley Building. She had drawn her katana and pistol and advanced cautiously into the pooling shadows, no more handicapped by the dark than he was.

'Is this a good idea?' Dave asked. 'I'm no expert, but isn't this a great place for an ambush? Cut us off in here? Without warp?'

'It's an excellent spot for an ambush, Hooper. I commend your steep learning curve. But there are no *monstrs* here. I would sense them.'

'Like you did with that last Thresher you totally didn't sense back at the apartment?'

She ignored him.

The way she said 'monstrs', he definitely heard the original Russian in her voice. Hundreds of corpses lay in a thick carpet on the roadway that ran under the Helmsley, all of them trampled.

No.

Not all of them.

A few he saw had been cut down by edged weapons. Some were feathered with arrakh-mi bolts. The ground around those bodies was clear.

'The Horde was here,' Karen said. 'Not long ago either. The Threshrend is somewhere close, however . . .'

She trailed off as if feeling for something more.

Dave stopped and knelt by one of the victims of the daemonum warriors. A man in casual office clothes, now soaked in blood and gore from the slash that had opened up his torso. A single dart protruded from one of his shoulders and Dave figured he'd been hit a short distance away and had then run until he was caught and cut down. Or rather, Urgon Htoth ur Hunn surmised as much, for he was the more knowledgeable in such matters. It was likewise Urgon who recognised the dart as not being of Sliveen origin. He wasn't even a voice in Dave's head. Not like Lucille. But he was there. Always.

'Karen,' Dave said. 'Come here.'

She reversed a few yards, watching for the appearance of the ambush she'd just assured him they hadn't walked into. Dave wasn't sure whether she was being careful or reckless.

'What is it?' she asked.

'This bolt,' said Dave. 'It's not from a Horde crossbow. Not Sliveen or Grymm.' He placed a boot on the man's chest and grimaced as he pulled the bolt free of the body with a wet, tearing sound.

'My Thresher wouldn't know one *arrakh* from another,' she said. 'So, the little monster voice inside your head is telling you we've got new friends to play with?'

He frowned as he examined the bloody shaft and the design of the arrowhead.

'Maybe,' he said. 'This looks like it's come out of the Savat *arrakh*-works. See, it's longer than a Sliveen bolt, and the arrowhead is wulfin bone, not iron-tipped or Drakon-glass.' It was a relief of sorts not to have to translate everything he'd just said.

'Qwm Sect,' Karen said. 'Well that's just super.'

'Yeah.'

Dave tossed the shaft aside.

'Urgon didn't think much of the Qwm,' he said.

'Neither do I,' Karen said, and started back toward the far end of the tunnel, moving through the field of the dead as quickly as she could. Lucille hummed in Dave's hands, but she was no more or less roused to her usual blood madness by the find. The Threshrend was still near, he thought. He was pretty sure he could sense the eagerness of his girl to be cracking that particular head open. But she gave no sense of being aroused by the promise of imminent slaughter on a much grander scale, as she normally did when they drew close to *dar ienamic*. As they passed out of the tunnel on the other side of the Helmsley, even that died away.

'I think we could warp again,' Dave said.

'I think so, too,' Karen agreed. 'That Thresher's out of range. I can feel it.'

20

A Talon of Hunn had infested the Grand Central Station. Four cohorts, more than a hundred of the big-ass dominants, led by a BattleMaster ur Hunn. They had no Threshrend in support, however, and so Dave and Karen came upon them as a divine wind, a wave of mutilation, or some other metaphor Dave couldn't quite put his finger on. He'd dozed through high school English, and barely passed Writing for Engineers at college. He had a T-shirt once upon a time that he loved dearly.

Once I couldn't spell engineer, it said. *Now I are one.*

Annie made him stop wearing that, of course. 'It makes you look like a moron, Dave,' she said, before adding that he didn't need any assistance on that front.

'Hey, Super Dave . . . a little help?'

Karen's voice broke into his reverie. He'd recalled Annie teasing him – and that's all it was back then, just teasing – with surprising fondness.

'Sorry,' he said. 'Off with the pixies.'

'Well how about giving me some help here with the man-eating daemons.'

'On it,' he said, and swung Lucille's splitting wedge at the skull of the nearest Hunn warrior. It came apart with a satisfying detonation of bone and flesh. Destroying the Talon was not much of a challenge, not like clearing the apartment tower and fighting through the ambush had been, even though these Hunn were full dominants, named and scarred, inked with the legends of all the battles they had fought. There were Grymm and Sliveen here as well. They first put down the Sliveen ranged around the upper concourse, before killing the four lieutenants, one for each cohort, Dave presumed.

The rest of it was what his old man would have called a job of work. Not that his old man had much experience with actual jobs or work of any sort. Each cohort had dispersed to a different quarter of the station where they were about the business of murder and destruction when Dave and Karen came calling. His control of the warp field was such now that the encounter was less a fight than an execution. They went from one daemon to the next, Dave smashing heads with Lucille, who was singing a giddy, trilling song of delight he'd never heard before, while Karen lopped off heads with *Ushi*, or drove the chisel point of the magic sword up into the nasal cavities of those she could more easily reach.

'I'm getting bored of jumping up and down,' she said at one point, leaving Dave for a few minutes before returning with two pistols and reloads she'd taken from the bodies of some transit cops. For the next five minutes, Grand Central rang with the metronomic reports of Karin Varatchevsky double-tapping a couple of dozen Hunn dominants.

'Damn, it's like grubbing out my backyard,' Dave grumbled, as he methodically cracked skulls, although he hadn't owned a back yard since Annie had split, and he hadn't been all that diligent about keeping it tidy anyway.

The reduction of the Talon took up the better part of a

quarter of an hour, at least as experienced by Dave and Karen. To the surviving witnesses, to the handful of cops and a small squad of soldiers still holding out against the attack from behind the ticket windows, it would appear as though that wave of mutilation, invisible but unsparing, swept over the monsters while they drew half a ragged breath.

'Hey,' said Dave, as a thought occurred to him. 'Gimme a second, would you?'

Karen nodded and went on with her last few executions. She wasn't tiring, but she did look like she was glad to be nearly done with it. Dave checked around for any stragglers he might have missed, found none, and ran upstairs to the Apple Store. A couple of genius types in blue T-shirts crouched behind their genius bar, giving rise to the valid question of just how smart they were if they hadn't bugged out yet. He was curious to see the effect of the warp field on the screens of the laptops and iMacs which were still powered on. They all looked as though they'd frozen in the middle of a screen refresh which, he supposed, they had. Leaning his magical sledgehammer against one of the blonde wood display tables, he laid his hands on the keyboard of one of the larger Macbooks. It came to life.

'Oh, fucking sweet.'

But his simple joy at the discovery soured when he found he couldn't access anything online. All the files and apps on the computer's drive were available. The internet was not.

'What the fuck, Hooper? Are you that much of a fan boy?'

Karen had followed him upstairs after finishing off the last of her cohort. Her katana blade was dark with daemon fluids. She was frowning at him, but he could see she'd figured out what he was trying to do. Or she'd just read his mind again.

'I thought I'd see if we could get net access inside the

bubble. I wanted to watch that Compton video you told me about. Dumb idea, I suppose.'

She shrugged, conceding his point.

'No. It was worth a look. So the laptop worked when you tried to use it, but only the laptop?'

'Yeah. I can't get anything external.'

He shut the lid, frowned, and opened it up again. Angling the screen just so it lined up with the other two on the bench. He was hoping to find an iPhone at the set-up table, but there was only an iPad in its box. Still wrapped.

'I want to get a phone,' he said, almost apologising.

Karen surprised him.

'Good idea. You can get me one too. Mine's compromised.'

She took out her BlackBerry, removed it from the thick protective case and used the butt of her sword hilt to smash it to pieces on the nearest bench.

'I should have done that earlier,' she said.

'I think they keep all their stock out the back,' mused Dave, irrationally pleased to be getting a new phone. His old one, which he'd lost back on the Longreach, was only halfway through contract. 'Might take a while to find. And set up. I think we should ask the geniuses.'

'Fine,' said Karen. 'But make it quick. And don't get the ones that bend.'

Dougie, the senior genius, was at first shocked to find Super Dave had popped into existence, right in front of him. Shock became relief upon finding out he probably wasn't going to get eaten tonight. Relief morphed into concern that he might get in trouble if he just gave away a couple of brand-new phones without taking a credit card number or even a driver's license.

'Jesus Christ, Dougie,' said the junior genius, Carlos, 'just give them the fucking phones, man, and let's get out of here.'

'We need them set up,' said Karen.

'Who's this?' asked Dougie.

'Agent Romanoff,' said Dave. 'And she needs a phone too. Hers got hacked by Hydra.'

The set-up was faster than Dave expected. A few minutes compared to the usual half hour. While he waited for Dougie and Carlos to work their particular brand of magic, Karen ran back down to the concourse to talk with the soldiers and cops they'd seen holed up in the ticket booths.

'There you go,' said Dougie, handing a couple of the latest iPhones to Dave. Carlos threw in a pair of Lifeproof cases.

'Thanks fellas,' said Dave. 'Stay frosty, okay? And I wouldn't be headed uptown if I was you. It's a fucking mess.'

'But where can we go?' Dougie asked. All the competence and calm he'd displayed while rushing the phone activation was gone.

'Seriously? If they have gun stores in Manhattan, I'd make my way there tonight. Or if you have a secure space out back, just lock yourselves in until dawn. Things'll get better when the sun comes up.'

They were thanking him when he winked out of existence in front of them.

They made better time on the southern side of Grand Central. The crowds were still ferocious, but they weren't massing as badly as they had been uptown. At least not on Park Avenue. They were turning on each other though. Fighting for the buses still running. Looting food stores and diners and even high-end restaurants.

Dave and Karen were free running again, saving energy. Dave could tell he'd drained himself maintaining that warp field. He was comfortable at the pace they were running – felt like he could keep it up for hours – but he worried that if they ran into real trouble he didn't have enough gas left in the tank or dilithium crystals or whatever he needed for the warp core. Not for taking on a hundred-plus Hunn at once.

He wanted to stop and eat, but he was starting to wonder where he could do so. Every second food outlet they passed seemed to be under siege or had already been cleared out. For the first time it occurred to him that hunger could be as much of a threat to him as the blade of a BattleMaster.

'Cops confirmed the Horde are hitting transport and communication,' Karen shouted over the noise of the mob. 'Emergency services infrastructure. Hospitals. Fire stations. But not cop stations. They sound like Hunn and Grymm too. Main-force infantry deploying in Talon order. And they're avoiding counter-force operations.'

'And in English that would mean?'

'They're refusing battle with cops and military units in the city. They're even withdrawing in the face of half-organised civilian resistance. Gun clubs, gang bangers, anyone with enough firepower, they just won't engage. The city's big enough that there's plenty of other targets.'

'There were cops and soldiers back at Grand Central,' Dave shouted.

'Not many and not well organised yet. They would have been chopped to pieces if we hadn't turned up.'

They were moving quickly, but not as fast as they had

earlier. The median strip which had provided a highway through the middle of the crush was now as crowded as the pavement and roadway. Car horns blared and sirens howled. Dave heard gunshots and occasionally automatic weapons fire, but it sounded distant. They veered left at E37th, a cross street with slightly less congestion, and Karen led them over to Lexington. The going here was easier and they made good time until the mobs thickened up again near their destination.

The crowd here moved with a sense of purpose tinged with fear, responding to police guidance to stay off the streets and proceed to the armoury. Casualty checkpoints protected by street cops, detectives and ESU officers triaged people in a methodical manner. Street vendors sold their wares while food carts fed people under the watch of heavily armed police officers.

Dave stopped for souvlaki, and Karen did not object. She was also becoming worried about how much energy they had burned through. A uniformed cop with an assault rifle made sure they were fed when he recognised Dave. Getting away, they still had to warp momentarily when the crowd surged around them.

On E31st Street they found a quartet of Hummers with a motley collection of bikers on Harleys, all armed, moving down the street toward the river.

Karen nodded her approval. 'Someone made a good call, arming them.'

'This is America, nobody had to arm them,' Dave said. God knows his brother alone could have armed a whole chapter of the Hells Angels.

Overhead they could hear the hammering blades of helicopters and other aircraft mixed in with the sound of jets roaring over the city. He tracked a steady stream of helicopters a few blocks off to his left.

More troops, he hoped, or an effort to get people out.

They covered the last five blocks in a flash.

'Whoa,' said Dave, pulling up a few hundred yards short of 25th Street. 'Might be time to hit pause.'

The hulking Armoury of the 69th Regiment was besieged, but not by the Horde. Thousands of civilians crowded the streets around the dark stone flanks of the massive fortress.

The crowds were so dense there was no easy avenue of approach to the main entrance. A platoon of infantrymen, with rifles unslung and bayonets fixed, held the gaps between half a dozen Humvees parked in a loose half-circle to secure the entryway, a double-height stone arch deep enough that it formed a tunnel of sorts into the stronghold. Occasionally the soldiers would part just far enough to allow a few civilians through. The press of the crowd was so great those lucky enough to be permitted entry had to be dragged from the crush by squads of troopers while other soldiers and some cops reinforced the blockade. Whenever this happened the screeching, caterwauling protests of the mob were amplified into a white squall. The noise sounded less like human cries than a force of nature. Dave put an end to it, imposing stillness on the world.

'Jesus, what a mess.'

'It'll be happening all over,' Karen said. 'People are trying to go anywhere they might feel safe.'

'How we gonna get through that mob?' Dave asked, not at all certain that she wouldn't do something very Russian like cutting a path through with Sushi the magical sword.

'I don't know,' Karen said. 'But let's find out.'

They were able to get within two hundred yards of the barricade before further movement became impossible. There were no vehicles to use as stepping stones and they were too far from the clear area behind the semicircle of Humvees to make it in one prodigious leap. Not without taking the chance of landing on someone and probably killing them. The exploding rear window of the bus he'd jumped on to was a recent memory.

'You ever crowd surf?' Karen asked.

'Er, maybe. When I was drunk but . . .'

That was all she needed. The one-time gymnast backed up a few yards, measured her run and before Dave could protest she'd launched herself at the crowd, reminding him in her last three strides of an Olympic athlete attacking a raised balance beam. He half expected her to perform some double reverse overhead twist, but she merely bounded into the air, landing on the shoulders of a big, thick-necked man, with an agility that should not have surprised him. What did surprise him was the way the man didn't flinch or buckle, but then why would he? He was only experiencing the transfer of energy for a fraction of a second.

Karen did not pause or look back. Like a fire walker moving across a glowing coal bed, she hurried over the crowd. Dave had done something similar, he supposed, back in New Orleans, when he was only just unwrapping his brand-new gifts for the first time. He'd leaped and climbed onto the high, steeply pitched roof of a church to go after a Sliveen archer which had been using the steeple as a sniper's nest. In that first rush of wonder at the changes which had so transformed him, he hadn't doubted for a second that he could do such a thing. He'd seen it was possible and he'd gone for it. Watching

Karen disappear across the heads of the crowd he could see this was possible too.

If the laws of classical physics hadn't changed – okay, yes, objectively they had – and the kinetic energy of a non-rotating object of mass, 'm', travelling at a speed, 'v', was still . . .

'Oh fuck it.'

He followed her across the top of the crowd. It was surprisingly easy and the chances of anyone exploding when he hit play again were probably very small.

The 69th Infantry, New York's own 'Fighting Irish', was a regiment of such storied renown that the staffs bearing its colours were one foot longer than the standard length authorised for normal and much less vaunted units. From Bull Run to Baghdad, the 69th had fought. On this dark night of September, they fought in the concrete canyons of their home town; one understrength light infantry battalion supported by two superheroes, elements of the Emergency Services Unit of the NYPD, a fifty-strong detachment of the Patriot Guard on Harley Davidsons and an FBI SWAT team which, coincidentally, had just a few days earlier been tasked with arresting one of those superheroes.

But that was before she was special.

Dave landed in the area kept clear by the platoon and their improvised stockade. The bikers of the Patriot Guard had been present for his brother's funeral, which was more than Dave had managed. They mingled with steel workers, gang bangers and a trio of heavily armed drag queens. Dave hurried up the steps, eager to put the desperate scenes behind him. He caught up with Karen in a vast auditorium space, filled with cots and blankets and hundreds of refugees. They were all caught outside the warp bubble, and he could see the fear and exhaustion on their faces as though each had been photographed especially to haunt him. But he could also see that the animal terror which animated the mob outside was not present in here. For the moment, these people felt safe, or at least a little safer than they had a short while ago. Such a profound difference, he thought. A few steps and they were delivered from evil.

Maybe.

'We should probably find Heath and the others, or at least whoever's in charge, before I flip the switch again,' Dave said. 'We can get some food here, fuel up.'

'This way,' Karen said, heading off at a fast walk that was closer to a jog. He followed her through the crowds of displaced New Yorkers. Most were women and children, but a surprising number of them were grown men too. Single guys, like him.

'Who are these guys?' he called after Karen.

'Family, I'd say,' she called over her shoulder, not slowing or looking back at him.

'Lot of guys,' he said, swerving around a cot on which a man in an expensive suit sat with his head in his hands.

This time she did stop and turn around.

'You really are a dinosaur, aren't you? A quarter of the complement of this regiment is probably female. Could be more. They'll have brought their partners in too.' She shook her head, as if amazed at his ignorance. 'Just keep up, would you?'

'You seem to know this place well,' Dave said as they left the auditorium and plunged into a long stone corridor with rough-hewn walls. 'Did you, like, spy on it or something? I mean, no biggie if you did. We all got our jobs and stuff, but . . .'

She laughed at him.

'No. I didn't spy on them, Hooper. The army rents out these spaces all the time. Deb balls, fashion parades, gallery shows. I've been here before. As a curator, not a spy.'

The corridors were poorly lit and over crowded, but nowhere near as catastrophically as the streets outside. The military personnel they passed wore battle dress uniform. Dave could recognise that sort of thing now. His brother would be amused. The soldiers all wore sidearms and many of them carried assault rifles. He saw magazines and hand grenades clipped to webbing and many of the troops wore helmets with night vision rigs. For every soldier he saw, there were another two or three civilian-looking types carrying a motley assortment of weapons and gear. They turned off the main hall floor and proceeded down a crowded corridor. Those not in gear were in the process of shuffling past with tablets, files and maps. At one door a line of men and women in civilian gear stood waiting to talk to a soldier inside.

'They're arming anyone who can be halfway trusted with a weapon,' Karen said. 'I approve. This, at last, is very Russian.'

She turned down another corner, past a drinking fountain, through a hallway covered on both sides by pictures and paintings which depicted the unit's long history.

'Not Russian. Just practical,' Dave said.

'Okay,' Karen said as she put her head around a door to peer into an office. 'We found them.'

21

The small band of gallant heroes, of scientists and soldiers tasked with saving the world, was watching TV in a tight conference room. Dave and Karen wouldn't have to crawl over a table to find a seat but it was close-quarters filled with bad coffee, stale sweat, and leftover pizza. Dave kept them in suspense, literally, for a few moments longer while he scoffed down some pizza and checked out the scene in the cramped briefing area. Heath was there, looking even more severe and judgmental than usual, and Emmeline, bruised and scraped and bandaged back together after Omaha. She looked like she'd dropped a few pounds. She looked kind of hot, actually, a little sleeker and all roughed up like that. It took the polish off her very English . . .

'Hooper,' Karen snapped. 'I'm right here.'

He threw up his hands.

'I'm just getting ready is all. I didn't do so well last time I spoke to these guys.'

Zach Allen and Igor, big gay Igor, had crammed in as well. They were outfitted in full combat harness, and both men packed serious-looking weapons, assault rifles with underslung grenade launchers. Pouches for the bomb throwers were heavy with fat, bullet-shaped rounds. Igor also carried over his shoulder the long brutal-looking sniper rifle he'd used to put down the Tümorum. Compton was missing, of course. Another man in the same grey digital camouflage as the soldiers sat at the head of a dark wood conference table which dominated the cramped confines of the room. From his age and the fact that he was the only one sitting down, besides Emmeline with her injuries, Dave supposed him to be some sort of higher-up.

'You know him?' he asked Karen.

'Yeah, sure,' she snarked. 'He's the guy in the army uniform. Moscow totally told me to keep a close eye on him. Are we done?'

No, he wasn't. Now that the moment had arrived, Dave knew he really wasn't ready for it. Annie would laugh, harshly, but he'd never been one for conflict. Dave was happiest when he was . . . happy. As dumbass simple as that sounded. And falling out with people, feuding with them, carrying grudges and measuring slights, all that shit, that wasn't the path to happiness. He hated it. In his heart, he just wanted to get along. But others weren't like that. Not his wife, and not the crazy KGB *monstr huntr* he seemed to have fallen in with, that was for damn sure. And none of these guys, either. Not Heath with his Old Testament severity, nor Emmeline with her uppity fucking Asperger's, and certainly not Igor. Not with everything he loaded into that swing he took at Dave back in Nebraska.

Maybe Zach, though.

Zach was one of those rare Christians who seemed to practise all the preaching. He didn't look it, encased in body armour and weaponry, but he was the forgiving type. His brand of faith left him no option.

Dave dropped out of warp, causing the map of Lower Manhattan which covered the table to flutter slightly in the breeze of displaced air.

'Hi. Thought we'd pop in.'

The older guy seated at the desk jumped in surprise. He was unused to having people materialise in front of him with no warning.

'The fuck?' he gasped, before seeming to realise what had happened. 'It's him, right?'

'Yes,' said Emmeline. 'It's Super Dave.'

'And Aeon Flux,' said Igor, studiously avoiding eye contact with Dave by way of staring at Karen. She was worth staring at, Dave thought, but not if your tastes ran to Töm of Sweden. Maybe Igor was diggin' on all the leather she wore.

'Dave, thank you for getting here,' Heath said. 'I'll assume it was a hell of a commute.'

He used a remote to pause whatever they'd been watching on the television, some video of a juvenile Thresher by the look of it. 'This is Shane Gries, Colonel, US Army. He is the acting commander of all forces south of 42nd Street.'

'Mr Hooper,' said the colonel, but like Igor his eye was drawn to the striking figure of the woman with Dave. Torn and bloodied leathers, filthy blonde hair tied back in a rough ponytail, a vicious-looking antique samurai sword angled across her back.

'Where is Colonel Rowe?' Karen asked.

Gries sighed. 'I'm afraid he is dead, decapitated by one of those things wielding a machete the size of a light pole.'

'This is my, er, friend . . . Karen,' Dave said. 'She kills monsters too.'

'We know who she is, Dave,' Heath said, and turning to

Karen, Dave thought Heath might salute her. The moment had that sort of feeling about it. Instead, he offered his hand in an unusually casual manner. 'Colonel Varatchevsky, I'm Captain Michael Heath, US Navy.'

She hesitated for a brief moment before taking his hand in hers. 'Gentlemen, I'm sure I'm delighted to meet you.'

Dave had half expected her to let the cover fall away. But she didn't start speaking in some thick Slavic accent. If anything her waspy, New England manner was preppier than ever.

'This armoury has always been a special place for me. I was MC here for the Michael Kors show during Fashion Week.'

'And how are you, Doc?' Dave asked Emmeline, aware of how difficult she'd be finding her proximity to him. 'You doing okay? With all your scrapes and bruises and . . . you know crushing on me and stuff.'

The high colour of her cheeks turned a deeper shade of red, the colour spreading down her neck. He heard Karen snort in amusement.

'Hooper,' she said slowly. 'I'm fine. Just leave me be. Let me do my job.'

'Zach,' Dave said, taking Em at her word. He couldn't bring himself to say Igor's name, simply nodding in the big man's direction. The giant commando, for his part, seemed content to play his role by staring into the middle distance like some anonymous spear carrier.

Karen clapped her hands, startling everyone.

'So. This isn't awkward at all. Colonel Gries, you've got an angry, terrified mob at the door, which I can guarantee you will act as a giant honey pot at some point in the next few hours, drawing the ravenous Horde down on you. And Captain Heath, you've no doubt had all sorts of adventures since you lost Captain Duhmerica here to the blandishments of the charming Agent Trinder. So perhaps you'd care to bring us up to speed while Colonel Gries figures out how to avert the horrifying massacre that's shortly to unfold on his doorstep.'

Dave broke the uncomfortable silence which followed by saying, 'She's not really with me.'

'She has a point about the crowd,' Gries said to Heath. 'I've armed anyone I think can be trusted and pushed a roving perimeter out five blocks up to 31st Street, extending out to the East River and into Manhattan as far as Madison Square Garden. That is the closest thing I have to an LZ and the pilots tell me it is hairy enough getting in and out of there.'

'It was pretty sporty coming in,' Zach offered, not looking at Dave. 'A lot of people tried to get out on the bird we flew in on. That sucked.'

Colonel Gries continued, 'Is there anything your people can do to help with that? I only have the one battalion here, and a quarter of them are still outside the gates, trying to get through with their families.'

'All those guys in the auditorium?' Dave asked.

'My acting command is a collection of National Guard soldiers who are part-time by nature, plus whatever other units from the other services I am in contact with. I told my guard counterparts they could bring their families in here when we mobilised. It meant three-quarters of them turned up on time, rather than half, and more than a few of the dependants are veterans who were willing to help. Who was I to turn them back? I need every trigger puller I can find.'

'Just asking, not judging,' said Dave.

'Michael, we'd better fill him in on Compton,' Emmeline said. Like Igor, she wasn't looking at Dave either.

Heath nodded agreement and Emmeline picked up the remote and pointed it at the flat-screen TV on the wall. But she didn't restart the recording.

'What do you know, Dave? About Compton?'

He exchanged a glance with Karen.

'I haven't had time to catch up on my TiVo.'

'All right,' said Emmeline. 'You've been busy. Just watch this.'

She hit play and the video rolled. Something that looked like Monty Python's giant hell toad with a buzz saw in its mouth and maybe two dozen eyestalks swaying above it started to talk.

'People of Earth!' it barked. 'I am Compt'n ur Threshrend, dar Superiorae dar Threshrendum ur Grymm. I speak for Lord Commander Guyuk ur Grymm, and through him for our Dread Majesty, She of the Horde.'

'Damn. It didn't sound much like Compton. Did it?'

'We haven't had time to run linguistic software over it,' Emmeline said. 'But no, apart from the little bugger calling itself Compton, er. . .'

'Compt'n,' Dave and Karen both said at once, correcting her pronunciation.

'Okay,' she said. 'Apart from that, this is the Compton playbook.'

Emmeline pointed at the screen. 'Everything that's happened in the last six hours, the massively distributed attacks on soft targets by militia-style irregulars, the initial *non*-targeting of comm networks to allow them to spread confusion and terror, the avoidance of contact with counter-force units . . .'

Dave looked quickly over to Karen. She'd used just that phrase. She was concentrating on Ashbury, however.

'Compton war-gamed all of these tactics years ago,' the exobiologist explained. 'Before he'd even done the Human Terrain studies. It was what brought him to DoD's attention.'

'I don't get it,' Dave said.

Karen answered before Heath or Emmeline could.

'Professor Compton built scenarios,' she said, her impatience with having to explain it to him clear in her voice. 'Worst case scenarios. For instance, if bin Laden wasn't a dumbshit goat fucker who fell ass backwards into a puddle of oil money, if he got smart and really zeroed in on all the points of critical failure in a modern post-industrial society, what would he hit? He wasn't even partway there on 9/11. Your friend Compt'n worked out the blueprint for going all the way.'

Dave saw from Heath's nod that she was right.

'But how would you know . . .'

She brushed off the question.

'Everyone tries to get inside the heads of their enemies. For you it's Islamists. For us, too. But also Chechens, Georgians, Ukrainians and whoever stands in the way of the born-again Russian Empire.'

Everyone was staring at her now. Coming from Karen in that cultured north-eastern accent, which sounded as though it should be doing radio spots for organic yoghurt, it was just one hit too many from the crazy bong.

'Okay. So, say it's Compton,' he conceded. He didn't want to, because that path led back to Omaha and his decision to rescue Emmeline instead of going after the neckbeard from Hell like he'd been told. 'You must have, like, counter plans or something?'

'There's always plans, Mr Hooper,' said Colonel Gries. 'But they rarely survive contact with the enemy. If you look out a window you'll see why.'

'There's more,' Heath said. 'You're missing a fairly obvious point.'

'I am?'

'Of course, you are,' Emmeline put in. 'The video. Who shot it? Cut it together. Released it? The Horde haven't got around to hiring a PR company yet.'

'Oh,' said Dave. 'Right.'

She restarted the playback again, fast-forwarding a minute or so until it came to vision of a young woman. Emmeline paused the image.

'This is Polly Farrell. A post grad media and communications student interning at WYNY. She says she was part of a group ambushed and captured by the Grymm. She interviewed a demon that spoke English in an uneducated American dialect. She described the creature as sounding like a "mall rat".'

'Like the one I spoke to on the plane?' Dave said.

'Yes. It was strangely well versed in media management, however,' Emmeline went on. 'It demanded the news people shoot a press statement for it, and promised to release all the captives if its demands were met.'

'And did it? Release everyone?' Dave asked, assuming the answer was no; it ate everybody.

'Yes,' Emmeline said. 'It did. And now the survivors are all doing their own interviews, supporting this . . .' she struggled to find the right words, '. . . this Compt'n creature's claims to only want to negotiate a ceasefire in good faith. If we don't negotiate, the attacks will escalate, and not just from the Horde.'

'But it can't talk for the sects,' Dave said.

'No. It's talking about them,' Emmeline replied.

'It's a class-A clusterfuck for sure,' said Colonel Gries. 'The president is en route to a secure location. The vice-president is already buttoned up somewhere. Congress is supposed to be debating a declaration of war against the Horde. The debate is more than a little demented, and is being held up by a move to impeach the president for letting these things loose in the world. President Obama's recalled all US forces from overseas. All of them. The world is losing its shit because of course these damned things are coming up all over. And now, just as they're hitting us in the nuts, the usual idiots and peacemongers are bleating about the need to negotiate and compromise with an enemy that is literally eating us alive.'

'Here in the city,' Heath said, 'the terror has worked. We're gridlocked. The attack on that apartment you suppressed? It was being live tweeted and Facebooked as it happened.'

'Who the fuck bothers tweeting when there's a monster at the door?' Emmeline said. 'Honestly. There's natural selection at work, right there.'

'And now they're hitting the value targets,' Heath said. 'Collapsing the infrastructure. It's following Compton's blueprint almost point by point. In his original war game he didn't have infantry formations or heavy lift assets to play with . . . Big planes to move people around,' Heath explained when he saw Dave's confused expression. 'If this really is his plan in operation, he has those assets now. Or something just as good. As everything has fallen apart, making it difficult to deploy our own forces in any sort of order, the Horde have been putting company-sized formations directly into critical nodes.'

'We saw that at Grand Central,' Dave said. 'We stomped them pretty hard.'

'Yes,' Karen added. 'That attack vector has been closed down.'

She seemed more at home with all this than Dave, and for their part Heath and his guys seemed cool with that. Had everyone forgotten she was a Russian spy?

'I had a squad down there,' Colonel Gries said. 'They reported that back to me. Said it was like the entire enemy force blew apart like magic.'

'Only the magic of American steel,' Dave said, holding up Lucille, but getting no booyahs in return.

'The squad leader was very grateful,' the colonel went on. 'Asked me to pass on his thanks. He said he didn't get a chance to say thank you properly before you left.'

'Tell him *dasvidaniya*,' Karen said.

'So what are we gonna do?' Dave asked. 'There's hours until dawn. And the Horde aren't the only sect here. We found some Savat arrows on the way over.'

Heath closed his eyes.

'Savat? You've never told us about them.'

Dave's patience threatened to fail him.

'You know how that works, Heath. Until I saw them, I didn't know. Now I do and so do you. Savat are like Sliveen. They're just part of a different sect. The Qwm.'

Igor snorted.

'The Qwm Sect,' Dave rounded on him. 'Not the Cum Sect.'

Igor came off the wall where he'd been leaning, bringing his sniper rifle up like a crude club.

'The fuck you . . .'

'Chief!' barked Heath. 'Outside if you can't keep it together.'

'Sorry,' Dave said. Holding his hands up. 'Let's just get to the fucking bit where Dave's sorry and we all agree he's an asshole and then we move on.'

Karen's smile curled up one corner of her mouth 'I don't think we need to *get* there, Hooper. You,' she said to Igor. 'You're the *pedik* he's been obsessing about, right?'

'What the hell do you mean obsessing?' Dave snapped.

Igor moved toward Karen and Hooper with deadly intent. 'The fuck you just call me?'

'Stand down,' Heath barked. But it was too late, the anarchy they'd fought through to get here was loosed upon the room, with angry voices climbing on top of each other. Zach tried to hold Igor back. Emmeline buried her head in shaking hands, and actually seemed more scared than despairing, which only served to fan the heat of Dave's shame spiral.

'Shut up. All of you,' shouted Karen and she *pushed*. Hard. Everyone gasped, even Dave. It was as though she'd slapped them all into silence.

'Because of his brother, this one,' she said pointing at Dave when she finally had the floor, 'is a festering mess of guilt and remorse. He could make a Dostoyevsky character seem like the world's happiest Lululemon shop girl.'

'No, Karen,' Dave said, his heart seeming to lurch to a halt, but he could no more stop her speaking than he could quell the nausea which suddenly roiled in his lower gut. It left him feeling hot and cold all at once, his skin tingling with a low-grade electric shock, and dizziness threatening to tip him off his feet. She'd been inside his head. She knew what he was thinking, even when he tried to hide it from himself. He dropped Lucille, the steel head hitting the floor with a bang.

Igor had fallen back to the wall, the sniper rifle scraping

against the hard stone surface. Zach looked shocked, as though Karen had reached inside him and squeezed, which she had. Even Heath, who'd appeared sanguine about her presence and her true status, was staring at the Russian woman like she was a land mine he'd just stepped on.

'You haven't told them, Hooper, because you're ashamed. You think you're ashamed of your brother, but you're ashamed of yourself.'

She didn't lash him with the words. She sounded almost as though she felt his pain and gave something approaching a fuck. It eased the pain not at all.

Dave said 'No,' again, but it was only a small sound, lost under the background buzz of a thousand voices and the thudding of a helicopter hovering nearby.

'Sit down,' she said, putting a hand on his shoulder. The will to stand up to her, to stand up at all, left him in a rush and his butt crashed down onto the table. The room swirled around him, lost all cohesion and he blinked away the first tears as they came. It was as though she had stripped him of a lifetime's emotional armour, exposing the raw and seeping wounds beneath.

'Don't . . .' he said. The dull thud of the chopper blades faded away, but if she heard him, it meant nothing to her.

'No,' Karen said in a quiet voice. 'I've been putting up with this since we met. You've been putting up with it most of your life. It's time we both unburdened ourselves of it.'

Everybody was watching him. Emmeline through her fingers, her hands still shaking. Colonel Gries, with one raised eyebrow at the insult done to his antique desk. Heath was Sphinx-like, measuring and almost certainly judging, but giving none of it away. Zach, true to his nature, looked almost as though he felt sorry for Dave. Igor did not, but he was no longer restraining his need to let fly. Hooper wiped the tears from his eyes with the back of one hand. It was crusty with blood and served only to smear the mess over his face.

'Dave hasn't told you about his brother,' said Karen, 'or not the whole story anyway.'

'Don't. Please.'

'He's even used him as an excuse for why he has such an aversion to all things military. Did you ever wonder about that, Captain?' she asked Heath. 'Why someone like Hooper seemed to regard the glorious armed forces of your proud republic as little better than a war machine devoted to enriching the board of Halliburton and, say, the petrol company which pays his rent? It seems a little out of character, don't you think? For such a good old boy?'

'His brother gave up his life,' Heath started to say, his voice leaden with disapproval.

'Yes, his brother. The fallen hero.'

'*Colonel Varatchevsky*,' Heath said, and there was no missing the warning tone in his voice. 'If you're going somewhere, best get there now.'

She laid a hand on Dave's shoulder again and he flinched away.

'It's better this way, Dave,' she said. 'Trust me. *Vot gde sobáka zarýta*. This is where the dog is buried.'

She addressed everyone then, but concentrated on Igor.

'Corporal Andrew Galloway, nee Hooper, was gay. Just like you, sweetheart,' she smiled at the SEAL. 'Super Dave here, when he was just plain Dave, couldn't handle that. It's not all his fault. If you'd ever met his father, there was a bigot for the ages. So unmanned by his son the cocksucker that he walks out. Dave, now the man of the house, blamed Andy for breaking up the family. Ma, bless her apple pie, loves both her boys and just wants everyone to get along. She was a saint, that woman. But Dave here gives his gay brother hell. "You'll never be a real man, why can't you just man the fuck up, bro." That sort of thing. Andy, who loved his brother, proves him wrong by signing up for the most manly job there is. Pulling a trigger. Four years later this family tragedy reaches its dramatic high point when Corporal Andrew Galloway, nee Hooper, is shot to pieces and blown to Hell by Sunni insurgents in beautiful downtown Baghdad.'

She playfully ruffled Dave's hair while he wept silently into his hands.

'So, Igor, don't be hating on your redneck friend here. He doesn't hate you because you are *petookh opooscheny*. He hates that he found out you're gay before he could pack up all of his nasty feelings and jam them away in the corner of his tiny tortured mind where he keeps his dead brother.'

22

Dave didn't know he had retreated into numb stillness until Karen spoke up and he realised her voice, her breathing, was all he could hear. That and the background rumble of a world caught on the cusp of some inexplicable quantum shift between what was and what might be.

He'd warped.

'What?' she said. 'Too harsh?'

Dave let his hands fall and blinked away the blurriness that cut him off from the world. A world he had stilled without even noticing. He sat on the conference table in the cramped briefing room, deep inside the armoury. Karin stood over him, her arms crossed, head tilted a little to one side, considering him. The others were all looking at him, frozen, their expressions a mix of concern and even sympathy. Igor's face was unreadable.

Dave sniffed and wiped at his nose. He coughed, not trusting himself to speak yet.

A deep, shuddering breath leaked out slowly.

'You're a bitch,' he said, without feeling. He was all out of feelings. Like he'd just made a bonfire of them all and the only thing he felt now was burned.

'Yeah, but I'm the bitch who'll get you through this. And you're the bitch who will help all of these good people through, and as many as we can save outside the walls of this place.'

'All of the things you just said. They were all . . .'

'They were all true, Hooper. You can't hide that from me. I wish you could. You're a lousy date.'

He stared at her, too wrung out to be appalled. One of the things he always detested about Annie was her ability to see through his bullshit. She didn't need to be a mind-reader, all she had to do was spend enough time around him to read his patterns and that had been bad enough. Karen did it in a second.

'You know it all? Everything?'

'I'm afraid I do, and I wish I didn't. Being inside of your head? It's like getting jammed into a bag full of unwashed shorts. With great power comes skidmarks. If it makes you feel any better about the mind fucking, I was trained to read people on first contact long before I unlocked my new achievements. I'm just quicker at it now, and a little more accurate.'

He snorted the briefest of laughs at that, the sad little chuckle sounding wet and throaty. Another shuddering breath; slowly sucked in, this time.

'Shit,' he said. 'He followed me around, like all little brothers do. I drove him off because . . . well . . . I was an asshole. I couldn't help it.'

He had to shut up, before he fell apart again.

'Yes, you were,' Karen said, not letting him escape responsibility. 'And you've been an asshole ever since. You've forced a lot of people to pay for your mistakes, Hooper. It has to stop.'

'I'm sorry,' he said, and for one of the few times in his life he managed to say it without sounding resentful or sullen. She wasn't nearly as impressed with that as she should have been.

'Make your apologies, but make them count. You want to be forgiven, you have to earn it, starting now. We can't stay in here.' A sweeping hand gesture encompassed the infinite scope of the warp bubble. Or the orb, as she called it.

Karen picked up on his thought without him having to express it.

'I don't understand it any more than you do, Hooper. But we both know it drains you. It drains us both. And the more you rely on it, the worse it gets.'

'But I feel like I'm finally getting some real control over it,' he said, frowning. 'And I don't know that I want to go up against the orcs without it.'

'Neither of us graduated Dux of Hogwarts. But the same way I know all about you and your brother, and all your other skanky little secrets by the way, I know that whatever power or energy leakage you suffer when you orb is growing. Something is changing. Don't argue with me about it, don't even ask me about it. Just trust me.'

'The rest of them,' he waved a hand at the others, caught in stasis around them. 'Can you read them, like me?'

She smiled. A genuine smile.

'Not as easily. You're more of an open book to me. A comic book.'

'But you can read them?'

'Within limits, yes. I don't get a transcript of their thoughts, like I do with you.' She looked around the crowded office. 'Your crippled captain there is worried everything is coming apart. He's even more worried, terrified actually, that we might be the only ones who can stop that from happening. He has doubts about you, Hooper. Less about me. I'm a known unknown, as we say in my business. But you? You're the key, but you're a key he doesn't know how to turn. He blames himself for Omaha, and worries that Trinder will either waste your abilities, or . . .' she smiled again, a wintry stony-hearted expression, 'or he'll waste you.'

She made a trigger-pulling gesture, just in case he didn't get it.

'Your boyfriend over there . . .' she nodded at Igor, 'is feeling gravely disappointed in you because you are, let's face it, a bigoted asshole.'

'But I'm not really! I'm not even very conservative.'

'Hooper? Please. Psychic powers here? Anyway, a sincere apology would patch it up with him. Fess up that you didn't handle your brother at all well. Blame your old man if you want. He'll totally relate to that and it's not untrue. As for this poor bitch . . .'

Karen's smile turned unpleasantly feral as she considered Emmeline.

'She's almost passing out trying not to fellate you. It's another thing you're going to have to learn to control. She deserves better. We all do.'

'But I can't control it,' he protested. 'They all want to suck my dick . . .'

He hesitated.

'That fellate word you used means dick sucking, right?'

She laughed at him.

'Do us all a favour, Hooper, and turn off the porno show in your head. God knows you'd be helping me out.'

Dave shifted uncomfortably on the edge of the desk. 'But you said it doesn't affect you.'

'I said you have no effect on me. It doesn't mean you don't disgust me. You just don't cause my ovaries to explode like you do with her and all the other woman you meet.'

She paused, considering something.

'Except for those who are pregnant, have been through menopause, or are menstruating.'

'Gross!'

'Oh grow up.'

Karen frowned but not just at him.

'Let's think this through. Apart from lucky old me, you present as an overpowering sexual totem any for woman who can bear you children. But this is a tenth order issue,' Karen said, coming out of her reverie. 'One you can deal with later. Right now we're going back to the real world, where you are going to make your apologies and we will figure out how to pull this back from the edge.'

'Okay,' he agreed with some reluctance. She was right. He needed to get back on side with these guys. In large part he'd signed up with Trinder to spite them, not just because of the sweet deal Boylan had cut.

He worried about Boylan too, with things not looking so great on the west coast.

'Before we go back,' he said. 'Where were we? I lost my place.'

'You were about to apologise to the world's most dangerous gay man.'

'Look, I'm sorry,' said Dave, wishing that he'd had the ability to stop time, or to step outside of it or whatever, when he'd been married. A lot of his fights with Annie had spiralled out of control because he didn't have time to stop and think before he let his mouth run off. If he could have hit pause and figured out exactly the right thing to say to defuse the ticking time bomb, maybe they'd still be married. Then again, if they were still married, there was no way Jennifer Aniston or Paris Hilton would be looking to throw a leg over him.

– *Dave!*

He jumped a little. That was Karen's voice. Inside his head. And Karen's heavy motorcycle boot grinding down on his toes.

'Excuse me,' muttered Emmeline, pushing herself up out of her chair and hurrying from the room.

Heath sent Zach after her with a flick of his eyes.

'Igor,' Dave said. 'I'm sorry about Omaha. I'm sorry I was such a jerk about you being a . . . gay guy. I learned my . . .'

He stopped and paused. Initially for effect. It seemed like something a good actor would do. But thinking about what he had to say next actually made him think about what he had to say next.

Dave sighed. Igor's stony face did not move.

'Look. My ma was a good lady. She raised me and my brother right. Or tried to. She did fine with Andy. He turned out good. But me, I was always my old man's son, and my old man was an asshole. Not that there's anything wrong with assholes, I don't mean to be, you know, homophobic about them. But my dad, he was a cunt . . . Sorry, Karen.'

Karen was too busy face-palming to reply.

'Anyway, all I wanted to do was say sorry, Igor. I know I'm not a good man, but I'd . . . I want to be. I was a shit husband, a terrible fucking father, every bit as bad as my own. I was a bad son and the sort of brother my brother did not deserve. The hell of it is, I can't do anything about what's done. All those people who meant something to me, I've lost them all. But if you let me, and I know you got zero reason to, but if you let me, I'd at least like to try make things right with you . . .'

He almost added '. . . *and your people*,' but thought better of it at the last moment. Instead, he said, 'Andy, my brother, he woulda liked that. He'd think better of me for it . . . And he'd probably think you were hot.'

Igor snorted a laugh. Not much of a laugh, but it was better than a punch in the face.

'I'll tell you what,' the big SEAL said. 'I won't shoot you in the head first chance I get. We'll see how that works out. Take it from there.'

'Sounds fair enough.'

Colonel Gries spoke up over the top of them.

'This is very touching I'm sure, gentlemen. My congratulations on your betrothal, but we still have the issue at hand. The fucking end of civilisation as we know it.'

Heath was also impatient to move on.

'The video,' he said. 'The creature calling itself Compton.'

'It's a Threshrend,' Karen said. 'Although it's small to have matured into the adult state.'

'You killed one, did you not? When Trinder came for you?'

She shrugged off the suggestion.

'I finished it. Trinder's people shot the hell out of it first. I grabbed a sword, this sword, and took the top of its head off because it was blocking my exit. That's when I joined the Justice League.'

'You didn't pass out or anything?' Dave asked.

'Nope. I felt something happen, as soon as I killed it. I felt myself . . . powering up I suppose. And I used that to get the hell out.'

Heath gnawed at his lip as he thought it through.

'Dave seems to have inherited the memories or knowledge

of the Hunn he killed. What about you, Colonel?' Heath addressed Karen. 'Any idea what's happening here?'

He pointed the remote at the TV screen.

'Simple explanation? They took your guy to the dungeons and tortured everything they needed out of him. But because it's a Thresher calling itself Compt'n, it's more likely they used an empath daemon to extract what they needed.'

'It still sounds like torture,' said Colonel Gries.

'Yeah,' Karen said. 'I think they ate his brains.'

There was a slight pause before Heath reacted.

'They what?'

Igor grimaced, Gries swore and even Dave made a face as he tried but failed not to think about the bit with the chilled monkey brains in one of the Indiana Jones movies. He hadn't liked Compton much, but that didn't mean the guy deserved to die as an hors d'oeuvre.

Karen leaned back against the wall, her chin on her chest and her brow furrowed as she thought it through.

'Yeah, sorry,' she said. 'I'm pretty sure they did. Or rather that Thresher calling itself Compt'n did. Both of the Threshers I fought with had been in empathic connection with Compt'n. I suspect all of the Horde Threshrendum in the city have. He's using them as a surveillance net and a rough command and control channel. I couldn't tell for sure until I got some face-time with . . . Threshy,' she grinned. 'It calls itself Threshy. That's cute. But yeah, the ones I put down, the others I sensed through them, as far as they're concerned, Lord Guyuk ur Grymm raised Threshy on high after it . . . "took up" the soul of a calfling called Compton. And some others too, it seems. Some random guys they captured . . . probably in New Orleans, and some . . . calfling dominants, warriors, I'm afraid.'

'Damn,' said Heath.

Igor cursed silently.

'That would be the SEALs they took prisoner in Nebraska,' Dave said. 'The ones I got captured.'

'Stop playing martyr to your conscience, Hooper.'

It was Emmeline, returned with Zach Allen, who looked flushed and uncomfortable.

'You don't have a conscience and you're not very good at pretending,' Emmeline said.

'Are you okay?' Heath asked.

'I took care of it,' she said, without elaborating. 'And while pondering the origin of this Compt'n creature is fascinating, it's not advancing our cause. It might be important, but it's not urgent.'

'I agree,' said Heath. 'We've confirmed our suspicions are well based. That's enough for now. We need to move on.'

'National Security Council is in emergency session right now,' Heath said. 'We're scheduled to brief them in about forty-five minutes. Assuming we still have the link.'

He threw an inquiry at Gries with a glance. The army commander nodded.

'Our comms are good. We can head over there now, if you want. Get you set up.' Gries pushed his chair away from the desk and climbed to his feet, patting the sidearm on his hip the way Dave sometimes patted the wallet in his back pocket, just to check it was there.

'Good idea,' Heath said. 'I expect civilian comms to be aggressively degraded soon enough, if the Horde stick to the scenarios Compton originally war-gamed. He's leaving the communications grid intact for now, to spread the virus.'

'The what?' Dave asked as they all moved toward the door.

'Fear,' Karen said. 'Fear and uncertainty, escalating with every tweet and Tumblr and Facebook post. Mass media will Astroturf the horror to lock in their audience. The audience will amplify the effect across all the social media channels.'

She let everyone pass her as they filed out into the hallway, taking care not to let Sushi the magical sword brush up against them. Maybe it wouldn't chop off an arm or a leg on general principles, but Dave noted the effort she made, even as she continued to answer his question.

'The Thresher's video adds to the effect by introducing elements of doubt. Are the Horde the true enemy? Can we negotiate with them? What might be worse? Is that what you're thinking, Heath? Professor Ashbury?'

Emmeline nodded and Heath grunted in the affirmative. Dave nearly smiled, because he knew that Karen didn't really need to ask.

'Something like that, yes,' Emmeline said. 'When he judges the moment to be right, he'll try to collapse the same communications networks to impede our attempts to use them to re-establish control and order.'

Hooper frowned as he followed Em and the others back toward the main area of the armoury. Green cots were laid out, row upon row stretching from the guarded front entrance, under the massive ceiling, to the midway section of the drill floor. Beyond them Dave could see a series of tables at which clerks processed the endless flow of paperwork. To the left of that line half a dozen bicycle couriers stood waiting with their bikes. Colonel Gries, tall and limber, strode over to them, shook their hands and spoke to them for a few moments.

'You said civilian comms like phone lines,' Dave said. 'Your military communications are separate from that, aren't they?'

He sidestepped a quartet of pre-schoolers who had just made friends, playing hide and go seek under the cots. An older girl, maybe eleven or twelve, chased after them. He popped around her as well, tuning out her orders for her sister to behave herself.

Zach shook his head, sidestepping a mother using her stroller as a bulldozer. 'We have separate systems but a lot of it is networked into the civilian communications grid. The enemy doesn't have to touch our systems if they go after the civilian network. It'll degrade our capability enough, reduce our ability to coordinate.'

'Without that coordination they can achieve local superiority over any force they target for destruction,' Igor added.

'Below that,' Karen nodded to the couriers speeding out into Manhattan. 'They have the empaths to provide a command and control net. So far as we know, I am the only the empath you have.'

Emmeline made a face somewhere between a frown and contemplative musing.

'We're working on that,' she said. Dave thought she seemed much less uptight than she had been back in the office. Maybe the cramped confines . . .

'True enough,' Zach said, interrupting his train of thought as he grabbed two nearby army guys. 'What are you? Specialists? Do you have tasking?'

'Negative,' they said in unison, a bit put off by the navy chief's garb.

'You do now,' Zach said. 'Sir, rations?'

Heath nodded. 'Definitely. Rope in anyone else you need.'

'Follow me, boys, you've just volunteered for chow detail,'

Zach said, taking them in tow before they could argue.

'Meet us in comms,' Heath said.

Zach nodded and disappeared with the two soldiers, weaving through the crowd.

Dave had trouble buying it. Communications was not his thing but he had to factor it into everything he did for the oil company. Most of the civilian gear he had used proved to be tough enough. He said as much.

'This isn't bullshit,' Emmeline said. 'It's the asymmetric principle, turning your enemy's strengths against them.'

The professor, still bandaged and bruised from Omaha, looked like someone driving through heavy rain late at night. She was concentrating fiercely, but the awkward, self-conscious heat which he'd felt coming off her earlier had definitely dissipated. She was able to look him right in the eye. She hadn't done that very often since she'd fessed up to having a powerful hunger for Dave's all-meat buffet.

'Every time the Horde or one of the other Clans has faced a prepared modern military –'

'They're sects,' Karen said, correcting her before Dave could. 'Clans are the subgroups.'

'Excuse me, but didn't the Djinn call themselves the Djinn Sect? Not clan?' Emmeline said. Dave and Karen shared an eye roll.

'Yeah, but they're jerks,' Dave said.

Karen nodded.

'Everyone says so.'

Emmeline waved her hand at the Russian, 'Fine. Every time *the orcs* have deployed in traditional battle order they've been destroyed. As you'd expect when medieval infantry take on modern, networked forces. It's the same problem every insurgency has faced since 1945. Compton war-gamed scenarios to bring the tactics and strategies of the most successful insurgents to the continental US. Just in case.'

'What? Just in case the Taliban got a foothold in Denver?' Dave asked, detouring around a family who'd made a little fort of their cots. A brigade of infants howled and whined. Colonel Gries, still at the long line of paperwork tables, pointed to a quartet of soldiers who crossed the drill floor in order to sort out one argument on the verge of descending into fists. He had to raise his voice to be heard over the noise of so many people crammed in together. 'Do you know how crazy that sounds?'

'No crazier than what's going on out in the streets right now,' Igor said. 'Or in here.' He shook his head at the scene.

'Okay, so just bottom line it for me,' Dave said.

'Bottom line,' Heath said, letting Dave catch up with him so he didn't have to shout over the crowd. 'There is a very good chance this Compt'n creature and the other one, Guyuk or whatever it calls itself, there's a very good chance they could do quite terrible damage before we put them down.'

'I don't see it,' Dave protested. 'I mean, yeah, shit's real bad outside right now. And in LA too, right?'

Heath nodded. Dave heard his name spoken again and again as they crossed the large, open area. Sometimes people pointed. Sometimes they stared. He saw one or two move toward him, but they fell back as Karen glared at them. He wondered if that was all she did.

'But the sun will come up in a few hours,' he said. 'The Horde and the other sects will retreat underground, or across the universe or wherever the hell they go, and we'll have a whole day to prepare for them. They're not invincible. A shotgun will take the head off a Hunn a lot easier than a battle-axe. Hell, even a decent pistol will put them down if you hold your nerve and your aim. I know the army can't be everywhere. But let's remember where we are, the country with more gun owners than licensed drivers.'

'Is that right?' Ashbury said, looking sceptical.

'I dunno,' Dave admitted. 'But it sounds right. These things aren't immune to bullets, and they're totally not immune to missiles and tanks and bombs and shit. Hell, if you don't own a gun you could rig up a flamethrower with an aerosol can and a Bic lighter. That won't just scare off a monster, it'll torch them, right?'

He looked to Karen for confirmation and she nodded, slowly.

'Yes, but I wouldn't recommend it.'

'You're missing the point, as always,' Ashbury said. 'Hooper, I doubt I need to explain this to Colonel Varatchevsky, but you seem determined to be obtuse. Yes, one helicopter gunship can make a dreadful mess of a tightly packed company or regiment of monsters. Assuming they don't shoot it down with harpoon-sized arrows, or some bloody dragon doesn't barbecue the pilot. But helicopter gunships, unlike bows and arrows, don't grow on trees. They are complicated technologies, needing skilled operators and vast support systems just to get off the ground. So too with every weapon we might pick up to fight them, right down to the simplest handgun. They are the weapons of an advanced civilisation, Dave, and advanced civilisations are hyper-complex, interdependent and riddled with points of critical failure.'

'Okay,' said Dave. 'Point taken. I'm not being obtuse. But I think you're underestimating people's resilience. You in particular, Heath. Weren't you paying attention in Absurdistan?

We bombed and shot the shit out of the beards for ten years. It might have fucked them up, but it didn't destroy them.'

Igor chipped in.

'The reason places like Fallujah didn't disintegrate when we kicked in the door and tore everything up was they were pretty much fucked up before we got there. The Triangle, Syria, Afghanistan, we just brought a different kind of Hell.'

Igor lifted his stubbled chin in a gesture toward the city outside the solid stone walls of the armoury. 'That's not Fallujah out there. Or at least it wasn't when the sun set. Tomorrow? You're gonna see just how fragile civilisation really is.'

They arrived at a cordoned-off space and were met by Colonel Gries, emerging into another space filled with computers, maps, and heavy green phones. Along the far wall, flat-screen televisions projected a series of newsfeeds. One of the screens, with a camera above it, ran a test pattern. Inside, the noise abated a notch while the heat climbed from the concentration of electronic equipment.

'Make a hole!' someone shouted outside. A moment later Chief Allen stepped inside and in less than a minute the table was set up and two extra chairs produced. Lunch trays just like the ones Dave's sons used in school appeared, loaded with food.

'B Rats,' Allen said. 'Ration packs. Not heated, just slopped on there. Sorry. They've got a truck stacked with them.'

'It will do,' Karen said. 'And we thank you for it.'

She took a large spoon and pitched in, swallowing without chewing. Dave had to put Lucille down before he could eat. He was feeling hungry, but not as though he might die from it, as he had felt in New Orleans on that first day or so. Again he wished he'd taken the time to do all those tests Zach had suggested. He knew his metabolism was adjusting to his changed circumstances, but he had no idea, really, of how much he had to eat and when. He would talk to Karen about it, when they had time. She seemed to have a much better understanding of this stuff.

Once seated, he stared at chicken breasts coated in cold, gelatinous, yellow gravy. He shrugged and sucked them down like he would an oyster, clearing the tray within a minute. No sooner was it cleared than another one appeared, placed in front of him by a soldier who stood in awe of Super Dave. There was nothing really enjoyable about the meal. Steel pitchers of water were set in front of them followed by a heavier sergeant, clasping his hands together.

'We've got orange juice concentrate,' he said. 'If you have time I can make some.'

Dave spied a pot of coffee brewing across the room.

'Coffee would be better,' Karen said, reading his mind.

The heavy-set sergeant nodded. 'On it.' Zach shook the man's hand on the way out and thanked him, before unfolding another camp chair across from Dave and Karen. Igor joined them, laying his massive sniper rifle across from Lucille.

Dave thought he could hear Lucille cooing at the rifle, flirting with it. He gave the enchanted splitting maul a sideways look of disapproval.

She continued to court the uncharmed sniper rifle.

The smirk Karen gave Dave let him know she was still reading him like a comic book. He took a moment to vividly imagine giving her the finger and her smirk grew into a smile. Emmeline observed the exchange with mortified fascination.

'It's considered rude to converse in psychic whispers at the dinner table, you know.'

'Sorry,' said Dave, chastened.

Colonel Gries turned to Captain Heath. 'The comms guys here tell me we're five by five.'

Heath nodded. 'Are they sure?'

'They set this up in less than two hours,' Gries said, gesturing at the contained communications cell. 'National Command Authority should be able to get through to us.'

'So long as the phone lines hold up,' Zach said, sipping coffee from a green paper cup.

'Shouldn't they have hardened satellite comms here?' Emmeline asked, checking over her iPad.

'This is a guard unit, ma'am,' Colonel Gries said. 'Not SOCOM or a signal battalion.'

Zach and Igor both pulled black objects from their gear.

'Iridium provides,' said Igor.

Dave recognised the bulky satellite cell phone that the oil company sometimes used on the rigs.

'Marvellous,' Emmeline said. 'How did you get hold of them?'

'We're SEALs,' Igor answered. 'If we need it, we get it. Kinda like Captain Gravy Train over there.'

'Nothing but love for you, Iggy,' Dave said.

'I doubt that,' Igor poker-faced him back.

Another pair of loaded trays arrived.

'The empty trays,' Dave said to the soldier bringing the food. 'Still have them?'

'Yes, sir.'

'Get some bread and throw it on top to sop up the gravy. In fact, if you have any more gravy, throw that on there as well.'

'Oh-kay,' the soldier said. 'Got it.'

Emmeline gave Heath an iPad and a stack of papers.

'This hard copy, it's the same data as the pad?' Heath said.

'Yeah. Just in case,' she said. 'I've also put an executive summary up there on our screen. They will be able to see this in Washington, do a screen-cap to supplement the download.' She pointed to a flat-screen closest to them which displayed the same data as her iPad. Most of it made little sense to Dave. He was starting to recognise the shorthand used by the military to designate various units and bases, without yet understanding which units and bases the writing referred to.

Karen interpreted for him.

'Not far out in the Atlantic is an Amphibious Ready Group,' she said. 'I suspect they are trying to decide whether to reinforce Colonel Gries or attempt to evacuate him. That red line over the map on the far screen that looks like a crumpled condom is his collapsing perimeter. The red boxes with an X in them represent the known location of an enemy unit. Some of the data is minutes old. Some of it, hours.'

'Hold on, sorry,' Dave held up his hand. 'A collapsing perimeter? That's bad, right?'

Zach shrugged. 'There are some benefits to being on defence.'

'Yeah,' Igor said, contradicting him. 'It's bad. We don't want to be here when it collapses completely.'

They fell silent, leaving Dave to ponder the list again.

The military jargon was opaque but the names of the cities meant something to him. New York, New Orleans and LA in red. Des Moines, Houston and Chicago in black. A bunch of foreign cities in red too. Some he recognised: Jakarta, Melbourne, Lyon, Kiev. Some he didn't. They sounded Arabic, or maybe Russian.

As he scanned the red list of cities under attack, or which had been attacked, his heart suddenly slowed. Everything slowed. And stopped.

'Hooper?'

It was Karen. The only person who could talk to him now. They were inside the bubble again.

'Hooper? What's up?'

He stared at the screen, unable to swallow the mouthful of cold barbecue beef he'd scooped from the latest lime green lunch tray. Dave chewed the food mindlessly. Took a sip of water. Forced it down his throat, never taking his eyes off the board. He checked the colour code again. Emmeline had provided little squares with a legend to describe their meaning.

Red meant a location currently under attack. So the Horde or one of the other sects was back in New Orleans.

Black meant unconfirmed reports of attacks within the last two hours.

Blue meant an attack which had been beaten off. There were names from all over the world in blue. Omaha headed the list. Some had an asterisk next to them but he didn't know what that meant. His eyes kept returning to the red list. It was long; much longer than he'd expected. Not because of all the foreign place names. There were only nine of them that he could see on the big screen. All major cities, although he guessed there'd be plenty of minor attacks overseas that weren't catalogued for US commanders or headlining on Emmeline's home page.

No, most of the red list appeared to be made up of American place names. Emmeline, or whoever she'd detailed to do the job, had added the state in brackets after each.

Sacramento, Portland and Seattle on the west coast were joined by Little Rock, Memphis and Jefferson City in flyover country. Down in Texas the Dallas–Fort Worth metroplex struggled while San Antonio had a reminder to remember the Alamo. From Detroit to Muncy, and back to Tuscon in Arizona, up to Colorado Springs where weed prices were skyrocketing, and eastward to Kansas City, Missouri, all under attack.

There wasn't enough space on the screen to include every location under attack, confirmed or not. A line at the bottom of the red and black lists instructed him to 'See Annexe 3. More follows'.

Next to the screen, a pair of soldiers had been busying themselves with butcher paper, copying the information in neat black text.

'Hooper? What is it?'

'It's my kids,' he said, before adding, 'and Annie,' as an afterthought. He pointed at the last name on the red list before the instruction in block capitals to go check out annexe 3.

Camden Harbor. ME.

His finger had a blob of congealed gravy on it. He wiped it off on his filthy coveralls.

'That's where they are. At her dad's place.'

His voice sounded flat in his own ears.

'Her father,' Karen said. 'Does he hunt? Will he have weapons and ammunition? Does he have any military service?'

Dave shook his head. He wanted to vomit up the pre-packaged ration meat he'd just scoffed down. He'd known the orcs were crawling up out of the ground all over. He'd known Annie and the boys were as vulnerable as anyone. Why was it he had to see the name of their town on this whiteboard before he'd finally accepted what that meant.

'Old Pat's a fisherman,' he said. His voice caught and rasped in his throat. 'Retired. He might have his duck hunting shotgun, but he wasn't a mad shooter, and Annie didn't like having the boys anywhere near guns. One of the few things we all agreed on.'

Karen spoke between mouthfuls of beef and noodles.

'It's a confirmed attack. Ashbury or Heath will have details.'

Heat flickered at his temples, the first sparks of anger.

'They didn't tell me.'

'They probably didn't know.'

'Bullshit.'

'If they wanted to hide it from you, they wouldn't have left it on the board,' she said, the voice of reason. 'It's just too much information, Hooper. Ashbury is trying to do her job and Compton's now, as well as not jumping you. It's a . . .'

She trailed off, seeming to lose her thoughts as she took in all of the information on the whiteboard.

'What?' Dave asked, his anxiety and guilt starting to mount toward a point where it would tip him into action.

Karen held up a hand, focusing on a couple of place names that had to be Russian.

'But,' she said, when she was ready, 'the way she's formatted this, the fact that Camden Harbor made it on to the board probably means the attack was reported and confirmed recently. Earlier confirmed attacks are in the annexed material.' She turned around, looking for something; finding it in Emmeline's hand. The sheaf of briefing papers.

Three long strides carried her across the room. She carefully removed the documents.

'I'll bet paper cuts at light speed would sting,' she said.

She took only a moment to scan the index, quickly finding what she wanted.

'Here. A confirmed report of a platoon-sized force besieging the town centre. No contact since confirmation. Where are your kids?'

'A mile or two out of town,' Dave said, very close to

warping out of the room, the armoury and New York.

Karen appeared to think it over, but not for long.

'It could be a random attack. We don't know if this is the Horde or some other sect. This report doesn't even give us the clan. But it could be a trap too,' she said, still sounding as though she was weighing up options for an evening out. Dinner, or a movie, or an ambush.

'Why a trap?' Dave asked.

'Because of the Threshrend. Compt'n. Did he know where your family was?'

'No idea,' Dave admitted.

'Well if he did, the Horde do. And these guys aren't tactically illiterate. Or at least, this particular Thresher isn't. They know you're not going to get much support, if any, should you decide to strike out on your own for this place.'

She held up Emmeline's briefing paper.

'US military and emergency services are going to be focused on New York and LA. And anywhere else our little friends pop up in force. Those Qwm we might have come across earlier? They could well lay claim to this territory in the Above. If I was Compt'n or Guyuk, I'd let them have it, for a little while. The Qwm pour in forces, and get chewed up in the meat grinder over the next few days. It's a win-win for Threshy and Guyuk. They could even convince a few idiots to submit to them if they swept in and helped clear out the other sects. Anyway, bottom line, you're on your own if you go off the reservation.'

'You wouldn't come with me?' he asked.

She didn't answer immediately. He knew that when she did she would answer as either Karen Warat, or Colonel Karin Varatchevsky.

23

The crushing weight of the queen's presence, which Compt'n ur Threshrend recalled from his last audience with her, his only audience, was infinitely worse here in the Sanctum Royal. As superior as his intellect might be now, he had no idea how a being so boundless, so powerful, had crammed Herself into the tiny chamber where she had received him in his former guise as a simple empath nestling. At that time, he had been hardly mature enough to string two coherent thinkings together.

Thoughts, Threshy, they're called thoughts. Only podunk daemonum fools call them thinkings.

He struggled to get his own thinkings under control lest they betray him and he find himself half gutted and tossed onto the fangs of the sacrifice stones they'd passed walking across the first inner court.

For once, Thresh-Trev'r, that half-forgotten and long-ignored soul who had led him out of the wastelands of ignorance and unknowing, came through.

Eat the pudding eat the pudding eat the pudding eat the pudding, burbled Thresh-Trev'r. A line from the calfling Trevor's favourite TV show, and now a Zen koan to refocus the mind of Compt'n ur Threshrend away from distraction and disaster.

Eat the motherfucking pudding, Threshy told himself. And nothing else. He tried to keep his mind otherwise blank. A tabula fucking rasa. Because this bitch was going to . . .

'Superiorae?'

Her voice was as a quiet as a blade tip slipping into a vein, but the thunder of it filled all existence. Guyuk kneeled beside him, his neck ritually exposed for the killing stroke. Threshy had gone for the full abasement package, snout in the dirt, ass up high, ready for a kicking by the Captain Grymm.

'Y-yes, Majesty.'

He could feel nothing of Guyuk's thoughts or feelings, nothing of the captain's. In all the worlds there was only She of the Horde and He of Threshy.

'Be at ease, little one,' She soothed. 'You have served us well.'

'Oh sweet fuck!' he gasped. 'Thank you thank you thank you.'

'You may rise. You may both rise.'

Guyuk rose smoothly to his feet without a sideways glance, the great muscles of his elephantine thighs bunching as they pushed him up. Threshy was a little more ungainly as he struggled to his hind-claws, grunting with the effort. He was really gonna have to stop eating fat people. Panting with a little exertion and a lot of latent panic, he risked a glance in the direction of the throne.

The audience chamber was vast, receding into echoes and darkness. Here and there, individual paving flags of Drakonstone gave off an eldritch glow to help navigate through the enormous hall. But otherwise all was darkness. The throne glimmered, barely perceptible in the dim, red light. The faint glow caught on jewels and polished bones, on edged metal and fang-toothed spearhead, and it seemed as immeasurably large as the room itself. It was less a seat than a platform upon which the grotesque –

No! Not the grotesque! The really, really pretty, and, er, smoking hot, yeah, that's right the smokin' hot . . .

– form of the Low Queen rested. And moved.

Eat the pudding eat the pudding eat the pudding.

Threshy dropped his eyes as soon as they beheld a hint of her true appearance. Part of him, the part which saw these things through human eyes, had expected an enormous Hunn with boobs. Or the bitch from the boss battle in *Aliens*.

Instead, he now understood that he had not met the queen in the receiving chamber of some minor palace or royal residence that first time. He'd only met part of her.

The queen was a huge, seething blob of evil protoplasm, a mound of hell jelly writhing with tentacles and mouths, shot through with veins of daemon ichor as wide as streams in flood. As horrific as was her corporeal form, her psychic presence was worse. She annihilated sentience. If she chose to she could take him up into herself without even bothering to extend a single, snaking tentacle to pull him into her maw. Or one of the many, fang-rimmed maws which drooled and chewed across the seething expanse of that giant blob monster.

So, thank fuck, she didn't do that.

Nor did she repeat her trick of playing with him like a glove puppet. Instead She of the Horde merely asked Lord Guyuk to report.

The lord commander was grateful to be allowed the privilege of standing in Her Majesty's presence. Long eons had he risen through the ranks of her loyal Grymm and long eons were bad for the knees. He carefully hid any discomfort, of course, along with any relief.

Relief he felt in great measure though, thanks to Compt'n ur Threshrend, who seemed to have curbed his natural rambunctiousness at exactly the right moment. Or perhaps She of the Horde had curbed it for him. Guyuk was no more immune to the majesty of the Low Queen than anyone. Just being in her presence was an overpowering experience. How much more crippling would it be for an empath like Compt'n?

'I would hear tell of this human city we have lately invested, Lord Guyuk.'

She did not refer to them as calflings, or cattle, the lord commander noted.

'I understand that having taken it, we are now to withdraw?'

'Yes, your Majesty.' Guyuk bowed deeply. 'The other sects have attempted to bring battle to the human host and to invest their cities as demanded by the dictate of the war scrolls. They have been, each and every one of them, destroyed in the attempt.'

'This pleases me, of course, my lord commander. I am always gladdened to see the lesser sects reduced. And yet, we have bested them and bested the human foe they proved themselves unworthy of, and still we withdraw? Do you shy from the human champion. Or his apprentice – this female with the long blade?'

'The champion is not at issue, my liege. Not the Dave nor his acolyte. We are confident we have found a way to contain any threat posed by them. And we have a scheme in claw which may yet bring him here, before you, in chains. But the pro-consul advises your Majesty that when the sun rises the human forces will almost certainly attack the city with all of the destructive magick and ferocity we saw them lay upon the Djinn, and which we know they have also levied upon the other sects throughout the lands Above.'

The queen was silent for a moment, and Guyuk was aware of Compt'n ur Threshrend suddenly shivering beside him. Or at least shivering and moaning with more violence than he had been a few moments earlier.

'So I see. Your pro-consul does indeed believe so. And knowing his soul as my own I commend your plan. We shall endure the mockery of the lesser sects while they impale themselves upon the human defences. But attend to me, Lord Commander,' the queen said, her voice now sounding as though it emanated from somewhere much deeper inside his head. 'I would not want to be embarrassed in this. The mocking taunts of the usurper queens I suffer for as long I understand there to be some prospect of deliverance. But that prospect should not be long in coming.'

'Of course not, your Majesty,' Guyuk hurried to reply. 'The Superiorae is of the opinion that all serious human resistance can be negated within a turning of the moon.'

'Really? Despite their champions and their mastery of profane magicks?'

She fell quiet again, and again Guyuk was aware of the Threshrend shuddering and even spasming beside him. He sounded as though he were choking, or about to vomit up some undigested meal. The uncomfortable interlude went on much longer this time, and when it was done, the empath collapsed.

'I understand, Lord Guyuk,' the Low Queen said at last. 'You have obtained for the Horde a most remarkable advantage in your little adept. Keep him close. The souls he has taken up are weapons of a keener edge than any blade in our royal armoury. It would behove a prudent lord commander to secure even more such advantages.'

'Plans are in train, your Majesty,' Guyuk assured her.

'The Dave and his court?' she said. 'Compt'n ur Threshrend does not think so highly of them as one would imagine, given the travails they caused us.'

'Indeed, your Majesty. But on this matter, one of the souls lately taken up by my pro-consul counted himself a fierce rival of the Dave. I feel that enmity has survived to colour the judgment of Compt'n ur Threshrend.'

The pro-consul in question seemed to have passed out in a puddle of his own pastes and waste waters. Guyuk wondered at the trial he had endured under the all-seeing gaze of Her Majesty. It was known that She could look so deeply into you, taking everything she found, that when She was done you were left as an empty gourd. He hoped that was not true of the Threshrend. He had use of him yet.

'I understand that, Lord Commander Guyuk. I have spoken with the Superiorae of this. I know him better than he knows himself, and while I am possessed of confidence in the schemes you have plotted with his connivance, I counsel wariness. This champion, and his new acolyte: my Scolari are disturbed by them. The scrolls offer no guidance, and little commentary. They gave no warning that we might encounter more than one nemesis of the Dave's ilk. Now, on closer reading, the Consilium fear more human champions are yet to reveal themselves. The Superiorae will not knowingly mislead you in this matter, but that is not to say he knows enough to mislead you. Trust his word, Lord Commander, but trust your judgment. I do, for now.'

Guyuk shifted uncomfortably from one foot to the other. An audience in Her actual presence was not unlike bearing up under the heaviest Drakon-scale armour. It sapped the strength and eventually the will.

'Of course, your Majesty,' he said. 'Have you any reason to doubt the Superiorae's schemes?'

He was aware of a shift in the giant, translucent mass of the Low Queen. When she moved it occasioned a great slithering and sucking, and even a few instances of grinding, cracking noises as rocks shifted under her bulk.

'It is a bold scheme, and I approve of it. As fearsome as these technological magicks of the humans undoubtedly are, Compt'n ur Threshrend believes the . . .'

She paused.

'. . . the civilisation, the great collection of all human sects which gives rise to them, lacks resilience. Unlike the Sectum Inferiorae we do not fight their weapons and armour, my Lord. We assail their civilisation.'

She fell into quiet, as though contemplating what she had just said.

'The pro-consul is wise to advise this, I feel. It is a truth he holds close.'

'The pro-consul has thought much on this, your Majesty. I have detailed plans if you would have them of me.'

'No,' She said. 'That will not be necessary. I have already had them of young Threshy.'

For a terrifying second he was adrift and alone in the endless void. For an even more terrifying second he was not one soul in the dark, but many, all of them screaming and raking at each other. Then Threshy fully woke up on a thick, soft wulfin-hide rug and found Guyuk looking down on him. Looking almost concerned.

'Are you recovered, Superiorae?'

Threshy groaned weakly.

'Oh, man, I'm about a thousand fucking miles from recovered. We got anyone to eat? Or drink.'

To his surprise Guyuk passed him a tankard of bloodwine. Not hot and freshly decanted, but warm enough to be pleasant. His head swam as he necked it down, and he burped when he was done.

'Thanks, G. At the palace . . . did I . . .?'

He honestly had no memory of the visit. In previous lives he'd known a few nights like that. Not as a mere nestling thresh, naturally. But Trevor Candly and one of the SEALs had known of partying to the point of obliterating blankness. Not that he'd done much partying at the palace.

'You did not disgrace yourself, or me, Superiorae.'

'Phew,' said Threshy, exaggeratedly wiping non-existent sweat from his brow.

'So, Her Maj? We cool?'

'We are indeed,' said Guyuk. 'You do not recall the audience?'

Threshy pushed himself up off the rug, already feeling about a thousand percent better, and wondering if the G-Man might have a little more of that bloodwine lying around.

'Oh I remember the walk over there,' he said. 'And the tour of Castle Wolfenstein. Everything gets hazy after that. But those Praetorian cocksuckers didn't throw us on the rocks. So we must have done good, eh?'

Guyuk bristled but made an obvious effort to chill himself out.

'The Praetorian Grymm are the finest warriors the Clan –'

'Yeah yeah, the finest, the most badass, the least likely to suck a dick. I got it. But they freak me out, man.'

As he came fully to his senses he realised they were not in Guyuk's private chambers, but in some other bitchin' crib.

'Whoa, G-Man. Who pimped out this contemporary domicile? It's fucking phat, dude.'

The cavern roof soared to a height at least three times his own, which was why old Guyuk was able to perch on a comfy sitting rock without having to bend his head. But the sitting rock, the wulfin-hide rug, and a long stone feasting bench with a single cold meat platter were just a few of the touches. Threshy scrunched up his suppurating, wart-filled face in something approximating a human frown.

'Is that . . . Oh my fucking god. It is! You got me an Xbox! And a TV!'

His excitement peaked and dipped very quickly when he realised there was nowhere to plug them in. And no electricity down here, even if some well-meaning Sliveen scout had ripped a socket out of somebody's lounge-room wall on the orders of the lord commander to procure the magick artifacts for his favourite pro-consul.

'Well it's the thought I guess,' Threshy said, his disappointment getting the better of him until he saw the pile of tablets and phones on a plinth in the corner.

'Whoa! These won't need power. Just yet.'

He hurried over and plucked a big-ass Samsung from the pile. His fore-claws were not well suited to using the device. Not at all, in fact. But it gave him an idea.

'It was an oversight,' Guyuk said, 'not preparing quarters for you, Superiorae. You should have had your own when you were raised above the common Horde. The Master Scolari further suggested we provide you with this plunder. You have spoken frequently of this Box of X and the Scolari are most interested in the amulets of power all of the humans, high and low, seem to wield.'

'So these are all mine now? That's cool. Uh, we'll need to wash the blood off the screens. And maybe we could get a generator or something, to hook up the Box of X?'

He smirked.

Guyuk meant well.

'But you know what I could really use, G-Man? If I'm gonna actually use these things.'

'Broadband?'

'Well, yeah. Totes. But I could really use an intern. You know. A slave or two.'

He clacked his talons together, showing how poorly fashioned they were for controlling human artifacts.

'Interns will be captured,' Guyuk promised. 'But now we must discuss the greater plan. Our advance forces invest the village of the champion and we must deploy in good order to engage him should he step into the lure.'

'Yeah, yeah, the greater plan. I'm all over that like a cheap Chinese suit. But remember how we were talking about interns. You know who's a really cool intern. Polly ur Farr'l.'

24

'Hey!'

Emmeline jumped as the papers she had been about to hand to Heath disappeared.

'What the hell?' the navy captain exclaimed.

'Sorry,' Dave said. 'But I gotta go.'

'At ease,' barked Colonel Gries over the small uproar which followed, with everyone talking over and across each other.

'What the hell is going on, Dave?' Emmeline asked. 'Did you just magic away my file?'

'No,' Dave answered. 'Karen's got it.'

The Russian spy showed no shame as she held the papers aloft for Heath and Ashbury. Igor eased one hand toward his sidearm but remained seated at the table. Chief Allen looked like a spectator at a tennis match, his head snapping back and forth as he followed the ball between the players.

'This is unacceptable,' Heath said darkly. 'Return the classified documents, Colonel Varatchevsky. And don't do that again. Not unless you'd prefer to deal with Agent Trinder.'

She smiled.

'I apologise, Captain Heath. No harm meant.'

Emmeline looked ready to start listing all the ways Karen

had put herself in harm's way, but Dave jumped in.

'Look, we don't have time for this.' He pointed at the red list on the whiteboard. 'Camden Harbor, Maine. Mean anything to you?'

Both the SEAL and the scientist frowned at the board.

'It's a small coastal village,' said Emmeline. 'A tourist town in New England, I think. Maybe some fishing too. Why?'

'My family,' Dave said. 'My boys,' he clarified. He was forever clarifying Annie out of what he considered to be his family. 'They're up there. So, what? You didn't know that?'

The scepticism leaching out of his voice could have burned a hole in the hardwood floor.

'No,' said Emmeline.

'No,' Heath added. 'That was . . .' He paused. 'That was Compton's responsibility.'

'Fuck,' Dave spat. 'Why? Aren't you doing his job now?'

He was glaring at Emmeline.

'Are you fucking kidding me?' She laughed. Not a real laugh. Just a short, sharp bark. 'Have you been paying attention? We've been a little busy, Hooper. The background check on you was an administrative detail. And Compton, God rest his nit-picking soul, was all about the administrivia. Not Michael or me. Compton. The location of the post office box you neglect to mail your alimony to every month really wasn't our concern.'

'Maybe it should have been,' Dave suggested acerbically.

'And maybe you should have paid your fucking alimony,' said Emmeline, the colour in her cheeks rising fiercely.

Fuck that. Dave's stomach turned over and burned with the bitter acid of resentment. He paid most of his alimony. When he could afford to. He threw a despairing glance at Karen. She seemed to be the only person in the room who'd clued into how serious this was. Gries's men and women were obviously aware of the confrontation, but doing their best to ignore it and get on with their work.

'Okay. So Compton ran a standard background check on Hooper,' Karen said, throwing her hands up like a cop walking into a fight over a parking spot. 'Trinder probably ran a deeper one. And your lawyer, the hobbit . . .'

'Boylan,' Dave said.

'Yes, he would have too. Millions of people will have been running checks on you, Hooper. There's no reason for you to presume malign intent because it was Compton. Or because Heath and Ashbury left that to him. It was his job.'

Dave felt his head beginning to swell like a hot air balloon. He'd been looking to Karen to support him, but this was a piss-poor excuse for support.

'But it's Compton,' he protested. 'He hated me before he turned into a fucking daemon, and now he knows where my kids are. That's why Camden's on that list, Karen. He knows where they live.'

'Maybe,' she conceded, then seemed to consider it. 'Probably.'

'Dave,' said Emmeline, her voice changed, dragging his attention back onto her. 'I'm sorry. You're right. We should have known. I should have known and . . .'

She was blushing now, but not with anger. Dave waved away her self-reproach, a triumph for Grown-up Dave over Asshole Dave.

'I'm sorry, Em,' he said. 'I shouldn't have snapped at you. Wasn't your fault. Let's blame Compton. I'm good with that.'

The military personnel were grim-faced: Heath

thin-lipped, Zach looking a little ill. Even Igor appeared concerned at some level. He wasn't braced, ready to drop into a shooter's stance anymore, but he was frowning mightily.

'Still, I gotta go,' Dave said again. 'I gotta get up there. You know that, right?'

He was talking to Heath and Emmeline, not certain which of them was the boss now. Karen watched the SEAL, looking into the man's eyes, her own mind unreadable. But she was reading him, for sure.

Dave wished he could borrow that ability from her, the way she seemed able to steal his warp facility from him. But that was a one-way street. He could only guess at what Heath and Emmeline were thinking. He couldn't know, unlike her.

'I don't need you here for this,' Heath said at last, twirling a hand to take in the Armoury.

'But we'll need to know where you are and what you're doing,' Emmeline added. 'We need to know we can call on you if we have to.'

Dave almost said, 'You sound like my wife', but wisely kept that thought to himself.

'I got a phone,' he offered instead, remembering the new iPhones he and Karen had secured from the store at Central. He fumbled it out of a pocket, almost dropping it. 'It's not bent,' he said to Karen.

Heath shook his head.

'You can't rely on the cell networks. Chief Gaddis?'

Igor pulled the Iridium phone out and tossed it to Dave who caught it with ease. 'Know how to work that?'

'Used them in my job from time to time,' Dave said.

'We have a batch of pre-set numbers in there – one of them will be my phone,' Zach said.

'How are you going to get up there?' Emmeline asked.

Before he could answer, Karen had spoken over him.

'You can't warp. Not that far, not for that long. If you made it at all, and I doubt you would, you'd be drained when you got there. We both would be.'

'So you're coming with me?'

'Sure,' said Karen Warat. That was all she said, but there was a whole world of meaning behind that one word. He knew to be wary of Varatchevsky. He knew Trinder was probably right about her. But Warat? Dave thought he could trust that woman. She seemed to have an understanding of things that wasn't necessarily prescribed for her by some controller in Moscow or the GRU or whatever.

He tried to not think on it. It was an uncomfortable experience knowing that she knew his mind as he did, possibly even better. She wouldn't be subject to the lies and evasions with which Dave habitually faced the world. He flicked a glance at her, guiltily, as though he'd been caught imagining her undressed.

And then, of course, he did do just that, and he blushed.

She rolled her eyes. 'Oh for fuck's sake.'

'You won't even get out of the city,' Zach warned, unaware of the unspoken exchange between them. 'Bridges and tunnels are jammed solid. Some of them are free-fire zones.'

'How did you get here, Captain Heath?' Karen asked, choosing to ignore Dave for the moment.

'By Osprey, landing on the deck of the USS *Intrepid* about four hours ago, Colonel,' Heath said. He pointed at the collapsing perimeter screen. 'I'm afraid we no longer hold that LZ and I'm not sure I want to chance Madison Square Garden.'

'It's the only aircraft with the range,' she said.

'You presume a great deal.'

'Well, you could find us an aircraft, or Hooper could call up a news station. Network or affiliate. It wouldn't matter. You know they'd all send a chopper. For him.'

'Oh, checkmate,' said Dave. 'You're even better than Boylan.'

'No,' Karen said. 'From what I know of Boylan he would have got the chopper and a development deal with all the merchandising rights.'

Heath rubbed both hands on his face. Dave distinctly heard the rasping sound of a five o'clock shadow.

'Michael, you have to let them go,' Emmeline said. 'It's his children. He's going to go anyway. You know that. Send Igor and Zach with him. Two more guns won't make a difference here, but they might up there.'

Heath checked his watch. Half an hour until he had to brief the NSC. His face was sombre and his voice flat when he spoke to Dave.

'Do you know they're alive? I have to ask.'

A hot wind blew through Dave. The muscles in his jaw bunched as he ground his teeth together. What the fuck was Heath . . .

He felt a cool hand on the back of his neck.

'Chill out,' said Karen and all of the heat and pressure seemed to drain from his head as though she'd pulled a plug. He shrugged off her soothing touch.

'I said don't do that to me, Karen.'

'You say a lot of stupid things, Hooper. This situation isn't helped by you letting the little cartoon angry man inside your brain run around Hulk-smashing everything. The captain is offering to help. Take his offer. It's the best you'll get tonight.'

'Thank you, Colonel,' Heath said, looking a little puzzled by her. He'd obviously seen the effect she'd had on Dave, deflating the worst of his temper with a simple word and a light touch. Perhaps he'd also been briefed about the effect she'd had on those cops and firefighters she'd pushed at 530 Park Avenue.

Pushed them all the way into their fucking graves, thought Dave, not caring if she could read that too. The head of steam he'd been building up had dissipated as soon as Karen had laid those cool fingers on him, but he was not about to just chill the fuck out and let things be.

Merely irritated now, rather than dangerously enraged, he set the satellite phone down on the table, unlocked the iPhone and entered the number for Pat O'Halloran's house, surprising himself by recalling it with ease. But of course he could recall almost anything with ease these days. Even things he'd never known.

Nobody spoke. He had two bars of reception. It should have been enough, but after half a minute or so the attempt to connect dropped out. Dave frowned, trying again.

'The civilian cell phone net is not reliable,' Emmeline said gently. 'It's not even the Horde taking down towers and relays. It's just 300 million people trying to call at once.'

'I'll keep trying,' Dave said, putting the phone away for now. 'I still have to go.'

'I know,' Heath conceded. 'I would ask that you take Zach and Igor, as Emmeline suggested. They'll liaise with any military assets we need to call on.'

'And keep an eye on me.'

'In your dreams,' Igor muttered.

'You cool with this?' Dave asked him.

'Ours is but to do and die,' the big SEAL answered in a slightly louder voice.

'Zach?'

'Somebody's got to carry your chocolate bars, man.'

'I'll try to get you some usable intelligence on the situation in Camden,' said Emmeline. 'I'll need those new phone numbers of yours.'

Karen grinned. A sardonic expression at best.

'You'll need Dave's number. Not mine.'

'Oh whatever,' said Emmeline, rolling her eyes toward Heath. 'Remind me to ask the NSA for her cell number, bra size and credit card details later.'

'Ladies,' Heath sighed. 'Please. Colonel Gries, are you in contact with the *Iwo Jima*?'

'Yes,' he said. 'It is spotty but I am in contact with them.'

'Ask them to task an MV-22 Osprey urgent to . . .' Heath looked at the map. 'The roof of this armoury?'

'Very bad idea,' Gries said. 'Worse than Madison. Your best bet would be the cleared area by the United Nations Building. Large enough to handle the Osprey plus they have a perimeter that is, for the moment, holding.'

Dave and Karen looked at each other, then at Zach and Igor.

'Piggyback,' she said. 'Just like you did with Captain Heath.'

'What?' Dave said, a little stupidly.

'You do that a lot,' Karen said. 'Contrary to what you think it is not very cute or charming.'

'I suppose I get to carry Igor then,' Dave said.

Igor broke into a huge smile. 'I am always on top.'

'Dude,' Zach said. 'I am really cool with not knowing.'

'And you get to ride the sexy Russian colonel,' Igor said.

'Gentlemen, how about just a little fucking decorum here,' Heath said, his own well of patience upon the edge of depletion.

'Yes, sir,' Igor said. 'Of course, sir.'

'Okay,' said Heath. 'Chiefs, the Osprey will have food, ammo and a Growler onboard if you need it. Make sure these two keep fuelling up until you get there. As for you, Colonel,' he said, addressing Karen directly, 'I'm putting a good deal of faith in you. Ordinarily I'd use whatever force necessary to detain you for the federal authorities. There is still a warrant out for your arrest, you understand.'

Dave scoffed at the suggestion of detaining her.

Karen might have shrugged, or she might merely have been rolling her shoulder to settle her katana into its scabbard.

'And ordinarily I'd use whatever force necessary to evade your authorities, Captain. But we passed through the looking glass a while ago, I think. Nothing is ordinary anymore, is it?'

Emmeline interposed herself into the exchange.

'No, Colonel,' she said. 'But be aware that our priorities are not universally shared. Agent Trinder and the Office of Special Clearances are not much interested in having you running loose. Nor the FBI. Pretty much any local law enforcement you encounter will try to detain you if they realise who you are. We would prefer you let our men handle any such difficulty.'

Zach gave Karen his stone face, Igor smiled.

'We're well-known charmers,' said the bigger man.

'I promise,' Karen sighed theatrically. 'No killing the anonymous extras. Anything else?'

'Yes,' said Emmeline. 'It would assist us greatly in not being arrested and eventually jailed for aiding and abetting the escape of a foreign intelligence agent, if you didn't use this opportunity to escape.'

Heath threw his hands up to forestall the point Karen was about to make.

'We know,' Heath said. 'The only one who can stop you doing anything is Dave, and he doesn't seem inclined to. Nor are we, Colonel. We all know that we're well beyond that. But do us a favour, if you're still drawing breath tomorrow, don't just disappear. All right? If you're going to embarrass anyone, please let it be Trinder. Not the Professor or me.'

Her smile, which Karen so often used as a cover to conceal something, like an old-fashioned lady's fan, suddenly lit up, as though Heath had flicked on a switch.

'Oh Captain, rest assured, a choice between inconveniencing you and humiliating Agent Trinder is no choice at all. I will, as one of your most celebrated fascist warmongers promised, return.'

'And you, Dave,' Emmeline said, seemingly satisfied with the word of a spy. 'Be careful and good luck.'

Heath stood forward and put out his hand. Dave took it carefully and shook.

'I can't make any promises,' Heath said, 'but I will try to get you what support I can. We have . . . other assets in play.'

'Thanks, man,' Dave said, taking care not to crush his hand. 'But Emmeline's right, a couple of extra guns might make all the difference, and I got those already.' He nodded at Igor and Zach. Turning to Emmeline, he leaned in without thinking to give her a kiss on the cheek.

'No,' she said, throwing a hand up in alarm. 'Don't. Just be careful, like Michael said. And get your boys. Your wife too.'

'Ex-wife.'

'It hardly matters,' she said. 'Go on.'

25

It was always weird hearing a recording of your own voice,
and Threshy was in the unusual position of having more than
one internal voice now, none of which sounded like Daffy
Duck with a mouthful of chainsaws. That's what he sounded
like on-screen, however. No denying it.

'Dude, change the channel,' he told the terrified calfling
behind the bar. The man, who wasn't the barkeep, struggled
to use the remote with shaking hands and numb fingers.
Compt'n ur Threshrend could feel the guy's panic wanting to
slip the leash. His fear was a barely caged animal, wild and
ready to bolt. Still, he was better able to work the tech than
Threshy or any of the sabre-clawed daemonum in the bar.
And so he lived. And changed channels.

By way of contrast, the barkeep, who had not done as
he was asked and had made a nuisance of himself with a
sawn-off shotgun, was dead, an arrakh-mi bolt through one
eye. The other patrons of Fightin' Phil Luton's Sports Bar,
on an isolated stretch of highway well north of New York,
were gone, taken under to the blood pots. Even so, the bar
was crowded with the cohort of Warriors Grymm assigned to
escort and protect the lord commander. The ceiling was low,

forcing Lord Guyuk to perch on one knee as he watched the giant flat-screen behind the bar.

There were at least another two dozen televisions they could have been monitoring, watching multiple news feeds from all over the world, but Guyuk confessed himself vexed by the human magick which was not magick.

'Conjure me but one vision at a time, Superiorae,' he growled after a frustrating few minutes of trying to follow Compt'n as he summarised the various news feeds he'd had the surviving human set up for him.

'Not a multi-tasker, eh, chief?' Threshy said. His mood had vastly improved since he'd learned Polly Farrell was drawing breath. 'Fair enough. All the research says it's bullshit anyway. Let's just grab us a seat at the bar and watch the big screen. Our man Chumley here can fetch us some more pork rinds.'

The man's name wasn't Chumley, but he looked like a banker to Threshy, and Chumley seemed a good name for a banker, even a comparatively young one like this. Guys like Chumley had owned the world before the Horde returned. Threshy knew that. None of the other cattle whose thoughts and memories the empath daemon had sucked down, along with the warm, sweet pudding of their delicious brains, had much liked guys like Chumley. One of the SEALs blamed the Chumleys of this realm for his old man 'losing the farm' and dying drunk and poor. The Scolari Compton had resented them for gathering the rewards which should have been due to him. It was interesting to ask all the voices which spoke to Threshy what they made of poor Chumley's fate – trapped in an isolated drinking hole off US Route 1 playing step and fetch it for a cohort of Grymm.

For most of them, it seemed payback was a welcome bitch.

'Yo! That one, go back. We want to watch that one,' said Threshy.

'Yes, s-sir,' Chumley stammered and waved the stick at the screen, mashing buttons.

He lost reception altogether for a second, and moaned a pitiable apology.

'I'm sorry, sir, so sorry . . .'

'Just fucking fix it,' said Threshy. 'And hurry up with those pork rinds.'

Pork rinds, it turned out, were even more delicious to the daemon palate than to human taste buds. Chumley found the right channel and opened another packet of salty treats for his captors.

'B-beer?' Chumley asked.

'W-what?' Threshy asking, mocking his stutter.

Chumley took a deep breath and visibly steadied himself. 'Beer,' he said. 'I could get you and your friends some beer. To go with the p-pork rinds.'

'Sure,' Threshy said. 'Why not. Pause that.' He pointed one fore-claw at the screen and Chumley did as he was told.

'What transpires, Superiorae?' Guyuk asked. 'Is there a problem? The magick lantern no longer dances with light.'

'Just getting some beer,' Threshy said. 'To go with the pork rinds.' As much as a Threshrend daemon could shrug, without shoulders, he did. 'It's a special libation, boss. To go with this delicacy.'

He scooped up a few of the scratchings and threw them into his gullet.

'Oh,' Guyuk said, 'I see. Excellent,' and he reached forward with one massive arm, draped in chain mail and armoured with vambrace, to scoop the rest of the deep-fried snacks toward himself. The lord commander had a powerful taste for pork rinds and insisted they locate a supply to present to Her Majesty.

'Would a b-bucket be okay for the beer?' Chumley asked, holding up a plastic pail. 'It's just, your . . . claws . . .'

'Yeah, got it. We're disabled,' Threshy said. 'You don't have to rub it in, Richie Rich. Just fill the bucket. And find us some more pork rinds.'

Chumley hopped to his orders and within a minute they were able to enjoy their show with beer and snacks. The plain and earnest face of Polly Farrell, lately returned from the demesne of the Horde, the only human being to make a round trip to the UnderRealms as far as anyone knew, filled the giant screen. She was talking to somebody from WYNY, a sure sign she'd recorded the interview shortly after making it back, escorted by the Grymm. No way this lucky bitch was going to be playing in the minors from now on. She'd be talking to Larry King or Oprah or someone like that next. Not bad for an intern.

And some time soon, thought Threshy, *she's gonna be interning for one horny little empath daemon.*

Guyuk had picked up a few words of English here and there. Mostly military terms. And now 'beer' and 'pork', which he mispronounced as 'prork'. But he was no more able to follow the twitterings of the released intern than she could have understood him. Being the only daemon able to translate the Olde Tongue to English gave Threshy an advantage he was keen to use while he alone still possessed it. He had no doubt Guyuk would have other Threshrendum follow his example and directly ingest the thoughts and memories of select human captives. The old devil hadn't said anything like that, but Threshy could sense the deceit and potential betrayal coming off him. Tough shit. Let 'em try.

None of those other softcock mind-readers were likely to snack down on the premium grey matter he'd managed to score, were they? Not top-shelf mad scientist and Navy SEAL brains. Fuck, he could bullshit people in German and Chinese and half a dozen languages now. He knew how to make doughnuts, do a PowerPoint for a grant application and clear a room full of armed men. Or at least, he could do those things if he had an opposable thumb instead of these stupid talons.

Chumley delivered the bucket of beer as Polly said, up on the enormous screen,

'. . . they took me down to their world . . . They call it the UnderRealms and they talk about it as if it's right underneath us. But I don't think it is.'

'Smart bitch,' Threshy said, as he translated for Guyuk. 'And hot, really hot,' he added in English, just for himself.

He picked up the beer bucket and tipped it messily into his maw. It did go well with those pork rinds.

'More beer,' he roared at Chumley, who hurried to comply.

'S'good,' Threshy told Guyuk. 'You should have some. It's no bloodwine, but trust me on this. Beer and pork. It's a good reason to not kill every last motherfucker up here.'

'I don't think their world is even physically part of our reality,' Polly continued. 'I'm not a science major, but I think there's some sort of dimension thing happening and these portals or wormholes, or whatever they use to travel back and forth, are a bit like the points at which different universes touch each other. But, like I said, I don't know.'

'Ha, you knows plenty, pretty Polly,' Compt'n ur

Threshrend said, or tried to. The beer went to his head quicker than bloodwine hot from the jugular, causing him to slur his words, but not so badly that he could not translate for Guyuk.

'This is disturbing, Superiorae,' the lord commander said around another mouthful of pork fat. 'This creature, a mere slave, not even one of their most learned Scolari, has intuited this from her short time in our realm? Perhaps we were wrong to let her go. What more might she tell the human warrior caste? They will surely interrogate her.'

'Oh for sure. But that's cool. She'll tell them what we want her to. Watch.'

The camera cut away to the interviewer, some anonymous haircut trying to look as though he wasn't freaked the hell out by asking this girl about her trip to monster land.

'And they just let you go?'

'Yes,' said Polly, then, 'No. They didn't just let me go. I had to promise the smaller one, the Threshrend, to make his video. In return they let us go.'

'And let's have a look again at some of that remarkable statement from the . . . er . . . spokesmonster for the Horde . . .'

The screen filled with vision of Threshy and Guyuk standing in front of a line of Grymm. Threshy was telling the world there were worse things than the Grymm in the underworld and promising to protect any who submitted to She of the Horde. Guyuk shifted his massive bulk next to him with a clanking of armour and the rattle and clink of mail.

'Yadda yadda yadda,' Threshy said. 'We've seen this bit already.'

But Guyuk was entranced by his own appearance on the big screen.

Ego-fucking-maniac, thought Compt'n ur Threshrend.

'How would we secure this magick for the Horde?' Guyuk asked, not really listening to the answer. He seemed hypnotised by himself up there behind the bar.

'Oh, a couple of thousand years of intellectual evolution,' Threshy muttered to himself in English. 'A Reformation, an Enlightenment, some materials science, some physics, maybe a little less bathing in bloodwine, a little more respect for Threshy . . .'

'What's that you say, Superiorae?'

'Oh we could catch some guys and totally eat their brains for sure, boss.'

Polly was back explaining that she didn't really expect the Horde to honour their word. She'd agreed to help them because she thought that at least she might be able to help a few of the other prisoners.

'But they let them all go. And me,' she said, shaking her head, obviously having trouble believing her luck.

'So he can be trusted, this Lord Guyuk?' the male voice asked off screen. 'After the terrible things he's done? The things he's still doing.'

'I don't know,' she said. 'But he kept his promise to me. Maybe he can be trusted but others can't. The monsters have been fighting each other forever. Maybe he wants an alliance or something. I don't know.'

'Booyah!' roared Threshy, punching the air and nearly jostling Guyuk's drinking arm as he did so. Luckily the Grymm Lord's drinking arm was as thick as a tree trunk and not easily jostled. None of the beer spilled over him.

'It's working,' Threshy said. 'They won't believe this shit coming from you or me. But from pretty little Polly, who's been all the way to Hell and back. Dude, the surrender monkeys will eat this shit with chocolate topping for breakfast.'

Guyuk belched and wiped his lipless mouth. Chumley startled at the thunderous sound and nearly fainted away.

'More beer, sir?'

'Beer! Prork!' the lord commander barked. The television was filled with images of Grymm Legions manoeuvring on the Clan's training grounds; all shot on Polly Farrell's phone cam.

'I guarantee you, G-Man,' Threshy said. 'This won't stop the cattle shooting back at us, but by the time the breakfast cable news shows are on, half of them will be crying like bitches, blaming themselves for everything and demanding their warlords stop fighting and sue for peace.'

'If this comes to pass,' said Guyuk, 'you will have done well, Superiorae. It is the role of the Threshrendum to confuse and dispirit *dar ienamic*, but the scrolls have always deemed it to be a duty of little import and no honour. Perhaps that will change if Her Majesty be well pleased.'

'Oh she'll be pleased, *jefe*. You can bet your leathery ass on that. Especially with all the losers in the other sects still rolling up to get their asses kicked wholesale by the cows.'

Guyuk came out of his reverie, almost as if he noticed where he was for the first time. The low roof, scarred by blade and bludgeon work. The pools of blood and random scatterings of body parts. The destroyed furnishing and the stone-still figures of the Sergeants and Lieutenants Grymm arranged about the wayside inn.

'We must away soon, Superiorae. The Masters of the Ways will have prepared our transit by now.'

'So we're done with this guy?' Threshy asked, jerking a claw over the bar at Chumley. As soon as Guyuk nodded, the Threshrend daemon launched himself across the pork scraps and the empty beer bucket. His roaring fang tracks closed around the human's head and sheared off the upper third, allowing him to suck out the hot, quivering grey matter. Chumley didn't even have time to scream.

'Huh,' said Threshy as he licked bloodwine and bone flecks from his slowing fang track. 'I understand the derivatives market now.'

Guyuk's eyes slitted as he watched video of the Djinn being slaughtered by human forces in the demesne known as Nebr'skaa. Guyuk did not take his eyes from the screen. He could not know what the voiceover was saying, but he could read a battle clearly.

'It is not necessary that you refer to them as cattle, Superiorae,' the lord commander said in a low voice. 'Your allegiance is not in doubt, and we defeat ourselves if we treat this foe as being unworthy of respect. They will teach us otherwise, as they have taught the Djinn, the Morphum and the other sects who sought them in the open field. We must know them as they know themselves, and so we call them as they are, Superiorae. Call them Men.'

26

It was only when the twin-bladed hybrid cleared the rooftop of the buildings surrounding the armoury that Dave could truly appreciate the extent of the disaster. The Chrysler Building, that art deco icon, was awash in flames, spilling a column of black smoke into the air. Muzzle flashes chased shadows in the alleys, barricaded by burning tyres and trash dumpsters. Tracers whipped down avenues, bouncing off the streets, adding more fuel to the burning inferno. Fires fanned out from the central focal point that was Times Square in a massive X pattern. Sown, according to the loadmaster who helped to seat them, by small teams of Sliveen leaping from rooftop to rooftop carrying fuel and fire. Sirens screamed out against the mayhem, trying to clear the streets in order to get to a place where they could do some good.

Manhattan was disintegrating in fire and chaos. Across the water, on the mainland, he could make out individual eruptions of violence. The concussive thump of explosions. Bright, almost playful coloured lines of tracer reaching out across the night, and once, as they lifted clear of the skyline and banked around the northeast, a jet of some sort sweeping in low and dropping a load of bombs which detonated like a string of giant firecrackers. But this was a muted echo of the savagery unleashed on the island.

Full dark lay over half of Manhattan where the power grid had failed, but it was a darkness shot through with fire and lightning. Dave thought he could hear a dull roar down there, not just the noise of the crowds, like the heaving moat of asylum seekers which surrounded the armoury but a much greater, deeper roar; the thunder of millions, all crying out in terror.

'Shit,' Zach breathed next to him, shaking Dave out of his gloomy reveries. It struck him that he had only heard the man curse once before. For a sailor, Zach Allen was careful with his cussing.

They stood by the Osprey's troop ramp, which was lowered enough for a crewman to man a large, old machine gun. A loadmaster stood near them, imploring them to step back a bit further from the edge. Dave figured he could probably survive the fall but that would not do his kids any good.

Igor stood stony-faced beside his comrade, staring at the dark skies riven with a blood orange light. Dave had another moment of insight. Two right after each other. He was gonna have to buy a lotto ticket.

'Igor,' he spoke into the headsets each of them had been given.

The commando didn't seem to notice. Dave tapped his toe against Igor's boot.

'Hey. Igor.'

The SEAL came back from wherever he'd been.

'What?'

'Your, ah . . . your partner. Sammy? He's nowhere nearby is he?'

Igor levelled a stare on Dave that could have crushed coal

into diamonds. There wasn't much light in the cabin, and what there was came from small red globes, casting an eerie glow over the hard lines and deep shadows of Igor's already intimidating face.

'No,' he answered at last. 'West coast. San Diego.'

'Oh, right,' Dave said, searching for something to add. 'Well, I'm sorry you're here.' That hardly seemed enough. 'I'm sorry about everything,' he added.

Igor's expression didn't soften in any appreciable way, but he did sketch a brief shrug as he said, 'If I wasn't here I'd be somewhere else. Not at home.'

Zach returned from talking with the loadmaster and sat down. Turbulence shook the plane, forcing him to hold onto the webbing that lined the inside of the fuselage. Igor and Dave took the seats across from him and Karen. The aircraft dipped one wing and the engine noise increased. Dave tried to catch a look out of the windows but the angles were all wrong and he found himself looking up at the sky. He couldn't even see stars out there.

'Sammy will be fine, buddy,' Zach said into his own headset. 'He can look after himself. And he'll go to the base, first sign of trouble. He'll be there already if anything is wrong.'

'I know,' Igor said, before clamming up and returning to the far away place from where Dave had fetched him back.

Dave wondered then about Heath. He'd mentioned a few days ago that he had a daughter, but he hadn't mentioned her again. Where was she? Where was her mother? Were there any other kids? And what price was Heath paying for not being with them, while Dave got to fuck off and chase after his family because . . . well, because he was Dave, and that was what he did. He fucked off and chased after his own interests.

All the time. It was like his philosophy or something.

They gained altitude quickly on the new heading, seemingly unencumbered by the weight of a vehicle strapped down in the middle of the hold. Olive green in colour and festooned with equipment, it looked like a jeep from an old war movie and sported two machine guns: one large, one small. Igor, a man prone to excitement at the presence of such things, had walked past it without a single glance. His work car, Dave supposed.

The seating wasn't comfortable; he could feel the vibration of the engines and the oversized propellers boring into his spine as his ears got ready to pop. This was nothing like the luxury jet they'd chartered out of Vegas. Man, he was missing that jet like he missed the '90s. Chances of scoring a boutique beer and a nice steak on this flight? Less than zero. The aircrew and loadmaster busied themselves with their duties, not Dave's comfort. Across the aisle, Karen was consuming energy bars one after another and stuffing loaded mags into an army tactical vest. She'd secured the katana in the fuselage webbing and busied herself with the more conventional weapons Colonel Gries had provided for her. A short, stubby assault rifle and a pistol. Hand grenades dangled from clips on her armoured vest and a thick black canvas belt. She also wore a fighting knife like the one Zach had offered Dave down in New Orleans, although if it ever came down to her needing that they were probably fucked, he thought.

Dave carried no weapons besides Lucille, who seemed to be asleep next to him. She'd been singing her mad woman's opera in New York, but it seemed she'd fallen quiet when she knew he was resolved to leave the city. Gries had offered him a pistol and some quick and dirty training, but Dave had declined, just as he had when Trinder had wanted him to carry a handgun into the Russian consulate.

'You need to eat, Hooper,' Karen reminded him, without looking up.

She was right, even though he didn't have much of an appetite. Rooting around in the small backpack full of high protein snacks Zach had rustled up for him, Dave figured he could at least start with something that didn't taste like tree bark and dead monkey ass. He fetched out a couple of Atkins chocolate-orange bars, which he normally didn't mind, but he soon found himself eating purely for the fuel, ignoring the nausea and acid reflux that made him want to gag as he occasionally took in the cataclysm below.

It was worse flying over those parts of the island which still had power. He could see more. The worst of it were the vast swarms of humanity surging through the canyons of the city, reminding him of Brad Pitt's zombie movie, which reminded him of how much fun he'd had in LA with Pitt and Boylan, and just how far he was from that one, bright shining moment in the madness of the last week. Looking down on the death of the greatest city in the human world, he didn't think he'd be getting back to Brad or Jennifer or LA or any of that good shit any time soon. Looking down on the fall of New York his stomach clenched and twisted into knots which made it difficult to force down any sort of food.

But still he ate. After finishing the Atkins bars he chewed on some other tasteless protein slab while below him the high towers burned and fell and rivers of bloodwine ran hot and free in the streets. What the hell was he doing? Wasn't he needed down there?

Compt'n had somehow turned New York into a gigantic

blood pot in the space of a few hours. And Dave had made no fucking difference at all. The city was a roiling cauldron in which monsters ran free and hunted as they wished, but worse than that was the way people had turned on each other so quickly. Dave stared out of one of the small armour-glass windows, wincing against the painful flare of a massive explosion which atomised the top floors of a high-rise at the northern end of the city.

'There is nothing to be seen out there,' Karen said, not looking up from her weapon check. 'We did what we could. Now you should eat and rest. Don't torture yourself with what-ifs and what-might-have-beens. Prepare for the next battle.'

Igor flicked a weary, almost contemptuous look across the cabin at her, but said nothing and did even less, withdrawing to that far away place of his. San Diego perhaps?

Dave hadn't seen mention of it on the board back at the armoury, but then there were plenty of places in annexe 3 which didn't make the board. He unscrewed the cap from a bottle of water and washed down the mouthful of protein bar he'd been chewing. The engine noise had levelled off and they seemed to be set on a flight path now. He assumed the pilots would take them directly to Camden Harbor. It wasn't like they needed an airfield to land. This thing could set down in any sort of open field, or even on a roadway.

'How long 'til we get there?' he asked nobody in particular.

Zach answered.

'They're pushing it hard, and we won't be slowing down to refuel. Won't be much more than vapour in the tank when we get there. Call it an hour, depending on the prevailing winds. Or, you know, dragon attacks.'

'Yeah, okay, I hadn't thought of that.'

'I did,' Karen said, apparently finished with her equipment check. Like Dave, she was hydrating and protein-loading. She tapped the side of her head. '*Monstr* radar,' she said. 'I'll know if one's around. Drakon are such smug, superior bitches.'

'So you'll recognise one of your own?' said Igor, not bothering to open his eyes.

Karen gave him the finger, but casually. There was nothing behind it.

'A dragon wouldn't be able to help it,' she said, as though delivering a little TED Talk. 'She'd be pissing her britches she was so pleased with herself. So I'll know. Don't sweat it.'

'I'm not sweating it,' Zach said. 'We've got AWACS cover all the way.'

Dave dipped into the backpack for a Hooah Bar.

Karen leaned back as best she could in the uncomfortable seating, closed her eyes, and commenced eating again.

Nobody spoke for about fifteen minutes. Zach stared out into the dark. Dave forced himself to ingest as much protein as he could stomach, and then some. He didn't need to shovel fuel into the furnace the way he had when his Marvel menopause came on, his superhero Change. Back in those first hours he'd been something akin to a nuclear-powered garbage disposal. Now? He wasn't sure, but he'd heard about athletes who'd eat 15,000 to 20,000 calories a day during their most intense training periods. What was that? Ten big steaks with all the fixings? That sounded like something he could do.

Karen finished the last of her protein bars and he thought she might sleep. She still had her eyes closed, as though meditating on each bite. Instead, she sipped at her water bottle, opened her eyes and spoke to him again, ignoring the SEALs.

'The asterisks on the white board. Did you notice them?'

Igor's eyes were open now. He didn't say anything, but Dave could see him concentrating to hear them over the engine noise.

'I didn't pay them much heed. You know I don't understand most of the shit that goes on with these guys. The military. Ashbury's outfit.'

He assumed Emmeline was the boss of OSTP now Compt'n had been, well, eaten. She'd said as much, hadn't she?

'Yeah-yeah-yeah,' Karen taunted him. 'My name's Dave and I'm just here to chew gum and kick ass.' She dropped out of the cruel imitation. 'You need to step it up, Hooper. Start paying attention and controlling what goes on around you instead of being controlled by these people. The asterisks on the board and in Ashbury's printed reports marked locations where individuals, almost all of them civilians, are reported to have defeated incursions by UnderRealm hostiles.'

'So what? People been fighting these things since they showed up. Beating them too. Sometimes.'

'Yeah, with automatic weapons and high explosives,' Karen said. 'But if you'd taken the time to read the report, or even just asked Ashbury, you'd know there are five confirmed cases of what the military is calling individuals with "enhanced capabilities". Five, including us. You were number one. I'm two. There's some woman in Georgia, a sheriff in some delightfully bucolic shithole called Fester. Another guy in LA, a gang banger of some sort. Be cool to put them together and see what happens, wouldn't it?'

'Champions?' Dave ventured, feeling silly as soon he said the word. But it wasn't his choice of word, was it? That's what Scaroth had called him. It's what the scrolls thought him to be.

And that little Threshrend ass-wipe, of course. Compt'n. To Compt'n he wasn't just a champion, he was the ur-Champion. The Dave.

He remembered Karen had mentioned there might be others when they first met at the consulate. He turned to Zach. 'Do you know about this?'

'He doesn't,' Karen answered before Zach could reply. 'They haven't briefed him yet. They're still sorting out the reports they're getting in from all over the country. The whole world.'

'You said there were five,' Dave said, his mind starting to run ahead of him. He had no idea where this was going.

'And "almost all of them" were civilians,' Zach cut in.

'Gold star for paying attention, Zachy! Yes, the last confirmed "enhancement" – their term, not mine – is military. But not how you'd think.'

'How then?' said Igor. His voice had a threatening note to it that Dave had no trouble making out in the loud, uncomfortable chamber of the Osprey's cabin.

Karen smiled.

'An army chaplain. Another woman. The After Action Report was kind of sketchy. Identified her kill as a Sliveen. But I'm willing to bet it wasn't.'

'Because?' Dave was intrigued now. The idea that he wasn't alone, or at least alone in the world apart from Karen, was a lot more appealing than he would have imagined a few days ago, when being Super Dave mostly seemed to promise lots of premium pussy and free money.

'Because of you, Hooper. You put down a Hunn, right? A blood-drunk BattleMaster? And Sliveen are sect allies of the Hunn. They're all Horde nestlings in the end. I put down a

Thresher, but mine was from the Qwm Sect. The other Threshers I killed, they'd been thinking deeply on the matter. Or rather Guyuk's Scolari had. As far as the scrolls say anything, and they don't say much, it seems the first calfling with the *gurikh*, the warrior spirit, to take down a sect warrior is chosen to lead the champions. Twelve sects. Twelve champions.'

She smiled at Hooper.

'That's what Heath was talking about when he said he had other assets in play. He has other champions, like us. And one Dave to rule them all.'

The Osprey droned on for a few moments, bucking in slight turbulence. They had left the New York area behind and seemed to be flying over water. Dave had done enough of that to recognise the signs, even at night. He could see the lights of individual ships and boats, small jewels on the endless black sea.

'Damn,' he said, when nobody else seemed to have anything left to add.

'Oh there's more,' said Karen. 'Your enchanted hammer? My katana? They're not unique either. Sheriff Sheila May Robertson blew the head off of what sounds like a Hunn dominant, but almost certainly wasn't, down by . . . Buttecracke County.'

She smirked at the name.

'It's Beau-cray,' Dave and Zach both said at once.

'Whatever. The good lady sheriff is helping your authorities with their inquiries, and one of the things they're inquiring into is why her Remington now blows giant holes in anyone who tries to pick it up. Anyone but her.'

Zach looked down at his own weapon, a compact submachine gun with a long banana-shaped clip.

'So, you're saying . . .' Igor ventured, 'If I can tag me a brand-new kind of orc, I get an upgrade? My rifle too?'

The long-barrelled, big bore sniper rifle he'd used back in Nebraska was secured with the rest of his kit a little ways up the cabin. 'Because those zombies I took down, I don't recall anybody bagging one of them before. So where's my awesome zombie powers?'

Zach snorted at him.

'Tümorum aren't pure sect,' Dave said, earning a nod, possibly even some cred from Karen. 'To the Horde they're just a disease. Like foot and mouth running wild through cattle herds. Djinn use them as a weapon. But they're not part of their sect either. The Djinn are both the sect and a clan in their . . . demesne?'

He looked to Karen for confirmation of the term and she nodded.

'Their allied clans are more like, I dunno, what's the word?'

'Vassals,' Karen supplied. 'If you'd nailed a Djinn warrior, or a Sumateem scout a little earlier, I think you'd have secured your upgrade, Chief. But you were too late. That army chaplain, she took the head off a Sumateem which stuck its nose in where it wasn't wanted.'

'Jesus, a chaplain?' said Igor.

'Igor,' Karen beamed. 'How very PC of you not to say "a woman" like it was totally unbelievable. But yes, a chaplain.'

'How?' Zach asked.

'With a chainsaw.'

She let that fall at their feet like a hand grenade, before jumping on it.

'She wasn't even part of the deployment on the river. She was in town for some interfaith talking shop. Like I said, the report's pretty thin, but it seems she was at a childcare centre when the panic hit Omaha. They went into lockdown. An inquisitive orc stuck its head in and she cut it off.'

'So this preacher woman's rockin' a magic chainsaw now?' Dave said.

'Yes. Ashbury's report didn't say so, but I'll bet things got messy before they figured out not to touch it. And I'll bet she hasn't figured out to name it yet, either. Unless it's just going by Husqvarna or Stihl or something.'

'Sweet Jesus,' Zach breathed. 'The kids? In childcare?'

Karen turned her palms upward, showing him she had no information about them.

'I'd suggest the two of you start paying attention as well,' she said, addressing the SEALs directly. 'Ask questions. Don't just take everything on faith because your one-legged sugar daddy says so.'

Igor finally bristled at the provocation.

'And we should take orders from you? Just because you're like him?' He threw a scathing glance at Dave. 'You're better than us? Last time I checked you were a spy, lady. You're a liar. A killer. At least Hooper's just a fucking moron.'

'Hey! I have an engineering degree you know.'

'Oh it's true, Dave,' Karen teased. 'You know you're a moron.' She grew serious though when she turned back to Igor.

'Heath doesn't tell you everything. He didn't tell you about the other assets. The champions.'

'He's my commanding officer,' Igor said. 'He doesn't have to. Does Putin call you for a catch-up every time he decides to shoot down an airplane or invade Ukraine?'

'No,' she said, not raising to the bait. 'But there are things you're better off knowing.'

'Such as?' Dave asked. Unlike Zach and Igor he wasn't part of any chain of command. And he was all too used to being bullshitted.

'Heath thinks you've lost already,' Karen said.

The SEALs reacted, each in his own way; Igor cursing, and Zach folding his arms, as if to shield himself. 'No way. I've never known the captain to give up,' he said.

Dave said nothing. He watched the Russian closely.

'Oh he's not giving up,' she said. 'He's getting ready for the next stage.'

'Which is what?' Zach asked, sounding entirely unconvinced.

'Collapse,' Dave said, surprising them. 'Retreat. Consolidation. Counter-attack. That's why you're flying out of the fighting right now. We're not going north to rescue my kids,' he added sombrely as the realisation came to him. 'Heath's pretty sure they're dead already.'

Dave felt as though a couple of quarts of blood had just rushed away from his skin, but Karen was smiling at him, giving him a slow clap.

'And so you finally begin to wake up.'

'But my kids . . .'

'Oh he's probably wrong, Dave. I'm sure we'll get there just in time. But it doesn't change his thinking. And, you're right. He thinks we can't possibly hold everything. He thinks that Compt'n is smart enough to do real damage. Not just to stage a few mass casualty attacks, or even to defeat a modern military force. Your army, mine, even the Chinese who are throwing nukes around like firecrackers. But he's not going to do that.'

'No,' Dave said, not so much seeing it now as admitting

what he had been able to see for a while.

'Compt'n's going to collapse the support system for that military. The civilisation which created it. That's what Heath thinks. That's why he sent us up here. To preserve his assets.'

'Bullshit,' said Igor.

'Really?' Dave asked. 'You know where the rest of your teams are, Chief? I doubt they're back in Omaha, mopping up. National Guard units could do that.'

Igor shifted uncomfortably in his seat, looking to Zach for help, but he had nothing.

'Your other teams are out looking for the rest of the Super Friends,' said Karen, tag-teaming with Dave. 'Trying to put them in the bag before it's too late. Before everything falls apart. Or before Trinder gets them.'

'That asshole?' said Dave. 'What's he got to do with this?'

'He tried to kill us because he judged he couldn't control you anymore, Hooper. Trinder and Heath are of one mind, I suspect. I'll admit I'm guessing at Trinder because I haven't had a chance to read him since everything went south. But I know what Heath thinks of him. Or at least what Heath feels about him. There is a difference, I'll concede.'

She took a sip from her water bottle, giving the others a chance to speak up. Instead, all three men just waited on her as the plane bounced around in another patch of bad air.

'Go on, Dave. Think it through. Dazzle me,' she said.

'We're not just fighting the Horde,' he said, slowly. 'We're fighting all twelve sects. But the Horde are the key, because they've got Compt'n. And this Grymm Lord too. He's been smart enough to know he can't win a battle he doesn't even begin to understand. The other sects will take some time to come to that. Some of them may never do so.'

'That's right,' Karen confirmed. 'They're still rolling up in the same old way, deploying in squares on the open field. We nuked one outside of Kiev a few hours ago.'

Dave frowned. 'How do you know that?'

'It was in Ashbury's report. That you did not bother to read.'

Dave nodded, slowly. 'Okay. So the Qwm arrowhead we found in New York? How's that fit in? They weren't sitting in a field somewhere.'

'They could have a couple of regiments drawn up in some cow paddock in New Jersey somewhere. But, even if they don't, Compt'n will let them take the brunt of the fighting in the cities. Urban warfare is a meat grinder. And you are the little sausage if all you bring to the fight is a bad attitude and a spiked club.'

'Still not really getting it,' Dave said. He understood the argument she was making. A dragon was dead meat on the barbecue when it met a heat-seeking missile. A Hunn dominant could rage and roar like a grizzly bear with a scorching case of cock rot, but one bullet placed carefully was putting him down. A Regiment Select of Grymm drawn up in formal battle order outside the gates of your city was a Regiment Select of Grymm sitting in the kill box of a B-52 or a cruise missile swarm.

But all of those things – heat-seeking missiles, jet fighters and bombers, firearms – were the products of super-evolved, highly complex human societies. Collapse the society, and the magicks went away.

But that wasn't exactly what Karen meant. She was talking about purely military tactics and strategy.

Zach answered for him, sounding tired.

'I think she's saying that Compton will use the other

hordes as cannon fodder,' he explained. 'Weakening them and weakening us.'

Neither Dave nor Karen corrected his use of the term 'Hordes'.

'He might even do what we cattle do,' Karen went on. 'Seek allies and mercenaries among the natives. Aligning, at least initially, with any human forces he can convince to support him against the threat of the other sects. Or the rest of the UnderRealms.'

'The rest?' Zach frowned.

'Sure,' said Dave, getting scared, but getting angry with it. 'The orcs aren't the only things down there. You've already seen dragons and zombies and necromancers. Compt'n is right in a way. At least the sects are organised evil. They keep the rest of the daemon realm in check.'

'Oh fuck this. I call bullshit,' said Igor, sounding thoroughly pissed off.

'Whatever,' Karen replied, without rancour. 'Believe what you will. But just remember we had this conversation. And as for you, Super Dave . . .'

'Yeah?'

'We go get your kids. Your ex-wife if you really want.'

'Yeah, my boys. Toby and Jack. Does Heath really think . . . you know . . .'

'Heath is a realist,' Karen replied. 'If he's right, and it's too late for your kids, I'm sorry. If he's not and we get them, you have to decide what you're doing next. The party's over.'

27

'It's gonna be close, people. Finish your drinks, put your tray tables up. Some prayers might help too.'

The pilot's voice crackled off the intercom and they were left in the dim, red-lit cabin, dropping down through rough air. Dave clenched his teeth and his butt cheeks, wondering if they'd have enough fuel to land safely. Wondering if he'd miraculously heal after being torn apart and burned to cinder in a chopper crash. Probably not, he thought. Zach hadn't been exaggerating about the fuel. The Osprey wasn't going anywhere once it was down. Not until the crew found some more avgas, or Heath organised a supply drop.

Would Heath be able to do that? He was probably being swarmed right now. And in spite of Karen's confidence that Dave's superhero club had really taken off, he hadn't seen any evidence that the Chainsaw Chaplain or Sheriff Shotgun would be helping out.

And if Heath didn't get them a refuel, would it lend credence to Karen's theory that he'd sent them up here to preserve his assets?

He tried to breathe slowly, wrapping his hands around Lucille's smooth hardwood handle, hoping she might calm his nerves some. Karen and the SEALs had tooled up in their own way, ready for a hot landing. She wore Sushi the magical samurai sword on a strap across her back again, but like Zach and Igor, Karen cradled a machine gun in her lap. Her tactical vest carried spare magazines and dangled hand grenades like dark Christmas ornaments. A protein bar poked out of one pocket, but she mostly seemed to be carrying weapons and ammo. They'd eaten plenty.

The intercom hissed and popped and the pilot's voice returned.

'Be aware we have flames near the LZ. Looks like three separate spot fires in the town centre. Muzzle flashes evident. No comm links to the local authorities. One minute to set down.'

Zach did something to his weapon, taking the safety off Dave assumed, and a second later Igor followed. Even craning around in his seat, it was impossible to get a clear view of the town ahead of them. Impossible and frustrating. He could just make out a few lights but they appeared to be scattered in the darkness on the edge of town. Their approach vector put Camden Harbor directly ahead of them. There was little to be seen out of the cabin windows. Dave's imagination filled in the blanks. Terrible images of his boys arose, unbidden. Toby and Jack screaming, torn apart like Dave's workmates on the Longreach. Annie cursing his name as she went down trying to protect them. He tried to blink away the visions but they persisted.

'Chill,' said Karen, her hand suddenly on the side of his face. The fingers cool. Her voice in his head. Deep inside. This time he didn't flinch, letting the balm of her will wash away his fears. Calming him down. Chilling him out.

'You've done this before,' she said. 'You're just bringing it home now.'

'Hooper.'

It was Igor, still grim-faced and fearsome, but no longer directing that animus toward Dave. 'Your boys will be fine,' he said. 'We'll get them, and we'll put down anything tries to stop us.'

'Yeah. There are no rules of engagement tonight, Dave,' said Zach, patting his assault rifle. 'We just kill 'em all.'

The anxiety Dave had been feeling, a restless fear that had threatened to turn into panic, ebbed away. It would have been nice to think it was the support of these men he wanted to call friends, even if the course of his friendship with Igor had not run exactly true, but he knew it was more than that. Karen removed her hand from his face, leaving behind little more than a tingling sensation on his skin and a mild tension in his gut. She had reached right inside him again and changed something. For once, he was glad of it.

Everyone braced as the Osprey flared and decelerated. Dropping toward the landing zone, Dave's stomach tried to climb up out of his mouth, but he was used to that. He'd done a lot of time in choppers over the years, flown into some pretty hairy situations. The Osprey was larger, louder, unimaginably more powerful than a civilian helicopter, but the sensation wasn't all that different from the descent onto the deck of the Longreach when all of this started. Dave closed his eyes and tried to relax, waiting for the touchdown. When it came, it was a much harder jolt than he'd expected. The pilot cut power to the engines. The uproar died away and the blades slowed.

'Okay. I'm cool,' he said to himself. 'I'm good. Let's roll.'

The loadmaster signalled them to stand as he dropped the

big-ass hatch at the rear of the aircraft. Aircrew manned the heavy, mounted machine gun. Once the hatch thumped down on the ground, the SEALs stepped out into the night.

'Dave,' Karen said beside him. 'This is the bit where you stay calm.'

Drawing in a deep breath, he took his bearings. He could smell the smoke. Not clean wood smoke, but the chemical reek of burning plastics, cars, houses. He put it aside with a mental shove. This was Annie's home town, not his, but he had a working map of the place in his memory thanks to a couple of access visits with the boys. He knew, as soon as he'd exited the back of the hybrid aircraft, that the pilot had put down on the baseball diamond in back of the local school. He'd brought Toby and Jack here to throw them a few pitches the last time he'd visited. He knew the Public Safety Building was only a couple of blocks from here. Roads radiated out of the town centre down on the waterfront like broken spokes from a bicycle wheel.

He heard gunshots, a crackling volley, but not the automatic fire he was getting used to whenever the military opened up. Dave started to run toward the sound of battle, toward his boys, but Igor ran in front of him, a lot faster than Dave thought possible. 'Hey! We do this together.'

'Fine,' Dave said. 'Then keep up. I'm going to get my kids.'

Karen caught up with him. Clinking and jangling with all of the heavy metal she was hauling. 'Hooper, you can't charge off on your own.'

'Yeah, just chill the fuck out while we scope this,' Igor said, scanning the roofline of the school for Sliveen. Zach swept the high ground, too, even as the sound of more gunfire reached them. Was Dave the only one paying attention? Even the aircrew back on the Osprey ignored the reports of battle, busying themselves unloading the Growler.

'Sorry, but I don't have time to play soldiers.'

Dave stepped around Igor, who dropped the muzzle of his weapon.

'Hooper,' he said, 'I will put a slug right through your fucking femur if I have to. We know you'll get better. So don't tempt me. This is our job. Let us do it.'

Dave took a deep breath and forced himself to stop moving away from the chopper.

'My boys are close, and keeping them safe is my job,' he said, maintaining a tight rein on his desire to get the fuck gone, right now. 'Karen and I can warp there in a fraction of a second. Annie's old man lived on the far side of the village. It's a five-minute drive – in the direction of all that gunfire.'

He jerked a thumb over his shoulder, toward the flickering dome of light which hung over the treeline. Camden was a small village, but heavily wooded and they couldn't see much beyond the small forests which marked the boundaries of the school grounds.

'I don't have time for you and Zach to work through the SEAL Handbook,' Dave said.

Karen stepped up to him, grenades swinging from her tactical vest, but she made no move to lay hands on him or push him in any way. Gunfire and the sound of crashing glass reminded him of the apartment fight back in New York, but when he dialled in on the audio he didn't hear as much helpless screaming here. A lot of shouting, mainly men and women yelling at each other to concentrate fire. But not as much screaming.

'Hooper,' said Karen. 'Don't be an ass.'

'No,' he said firmly, ignoring the sounds of the struggle. 'I am going to get my boys, the quickest way I know how. Follow or not, fuck off or not. It's all the same to me. There are monsters here,' he said, fixing his eyes on each of them in turn. 'Remember them? Fucking monsters. In the town where my boys live? Where Compt'n *knows* they live.'

'Yeah,' said Igor. 'So what does that tell you is probably waiting for you?'

'My boys,' Dave said again. 'They're waiting for me.'

He was about to hit the accelerator when Zach spoke up.

'Dave's right,' he said. 'He should go, we'll only be a few minutes behind in the Growler, and we'll come heavy.'

A leaden ball that had been sitting in his gut lifted and floated away like a child's balloon.

'Thank you, Zach,' he said. 'I appreciate it.'

'Not a –' Zach started, but Dave had already warped.

First thing he noticed was that he could warp. There were no Threshers around to stop him. The air was warm and still perfumed with a hint of night jasmine under the burning chemical reek of smoke and fire. The stars, so infinitely far away, seemed cold in the sky. They would stare down impassively on whatever happened here.

Dave stepped around Igor and took off, not really caring if Karen followed him. He had to get to his kids. It was a physical need. He accelerated from a run to a flat out sprint, blowing through the school's parking lot, past empty bicycle racks and a couple of haphazardly parked cars, one with the driver's door left wide open, but no sign of the occupant. To his right the town's school bus was a yellow blur. He was stunned. He had never moved this quickly before. He could feel himself pressing against an envelope of sorts, some invisible membrane that lay just below the surface of reality. He could feel it threatening to give way, to tear under the stress of his impossible velocity. But he pressed on anyway.

Around him the architecture of Camden Harbor, a quaint diorama of steep-roofed New England cottages, new-built clapboard shops and converted harbourfront warehouses stretched and twisted. Dave flew over a small stone bridge and banked around the tree-lined corner of Knowlton and into Mechanic Street. The road was wider there, dropping down slightly toward the centre of town.

He slowed, dialling back the warp drive, killing the eerie, disturbing effect of moving at what seemed to be near super-liminal speed. He had no idea where that had come from, but guessed it was probably something like a normal person finding the strength to flip a car off their kid.

The town remained trapped in stasis. Fall's shimmering coat of oranges, browns and yellows had not touched the green trees, but that day was coming. In any other year, summer folks would soon switch out for those who wanted to sail the bay aboard one of the windjammers to view the Fall foliage. Dave had tried once, early in his marriage, to talk Annie into taking the boys out on one. Her father's life had been the sea, but it had also swallowed one of her cousins, leaving her with a lifelong trepidation of the water. As far as he knew, the boys had never been out on the harbour, let alone the sea.

Warping down Mechanic Street, into the heart of the little tourist village, Dave leaped over a seven-car pile-up, jumping high into the air to survey the town centre. It was as he remembered it, and yet utterly transformed. There was the familiar patchwork of streets with little cottages and grander New England homes, some of them burning, some of them dark. The shops and bars were all closed. Fire, frozen into eerie ghost forms by the magical physics of warp, poured in torrents from the upper floor of a two-storey house at the intersection of Mechanic and Free Street. A jaunty red fire hydrant seemed to glow an even brighter red in the flames, but no hoses ran from it, no tenders rushed to the blaze.

While he was airborne and without being aware he was doing so, Dave counted the seven cars, six of them pick-ups and SUVs, parked neatly in the slots on either side of Mechanic. And he counted, without realising, the thirteen vehicles abandoned or crashed, higgledy-piggledy up and down the main route into town. A little hatchback had smashed into a power pole outside the tall, barn-like edifice of the Smokestack Grill, gift-wrapping the pole with its engine block. The windscreen was shattered and a thick blood trail led away into the dark. Downed power lines fizzed and snapped, shooting sparks. Or they would have, in real time. Here, where nothing moved, bright white fountains of electrical sparks hung frozen in space.

Still in midair, Dave quickly scanned the high ground, as Zach and Igor had back at the school.

No Sliveen waited on steeply pitched rooftops, no Threshers tried to knock him out of warp.

Shit! he thought. What would happen if they did when he was a hundred feet in the air?

Looking down the gentle slope of Mechanic Street, he saw a cohort of Hunn concentrated outside the single-storey brick bunker that was the Camden Public Safety Building. Burning police cars and an ambulance cast their long frozen shadows down the street, all the way back to the corner of Mechanic and Washington, where a handful of blood-drunk Hunn ran amok in The Owl and Turtle Bookshop. Annie liked to go to readings there. Dozens of books hung over Mechanic Street in arrested trajectories, flapping toward a growing pile, already ablaze. The orcs must have had a real Eve-Of-Destruction hard-on to have set a fire like that. They didn't normally dig on naked flames. Too much chance of setting themselves alight.

Dave reached the zenith of his leap and started to drop down. He bounced once on the far side of the pile-up, vaulting into a second jump, but not as high as the first. As he rose past the first floor of The Owl and Turtle he saw, suspended amongst the dozens of titles that floated before him, a copy of *Green Eggs and Ham* by Dr Seuss. Dave plucked it from the air and turned the pages, both curious and full of dread. Jack had once borrowed this book from the library and smeared peanut butter handprints onto a torn page.

Annie had given Dave the money to pay for the damage and sent him off to make things right. Instead, he'd made the repairs himself before sneaking the book back on the shelf and spending the cash on a sixer. Of course, this copy of *Green Eggs and Ham* from the bookstore was unmarked by peanut butter or Dave Hooper's running repairs. It was new. He wondered if, like him, the library's old and battered one had been replaced.

Dave dropped the book to the ground as he landed in the middle of the Hunn laying siege to the police station. Lucille positively trilled with anticipation. They were surrounded by nineteen dominants wielding cleavers, clubs, mauls and blades, all of them matted with blood and gore. They wore full armour, too, no longer fighting in the old style, junk flapping around in the breeze. The windows of the Public Safety Building flared with muzzle flashes, and he had to take care to

avoid the lines of tracer, which even now zipped toward him
with the speed of an Aroldis Chapman fastball. The Hunn had
used the cover of crashed and burning vehicles as protection
from the gunfire, but not as much as any human with half
a brain would. Five dead monsters, all of them riddled with
bullets, one missing half its head, already lay on the ground.
He got to work, cracking skulls, bloodying up his enchanted
lady friend. Lucille seemed to shriek with pleasure every time
her blunt steel head smashed open another monster melon.
Hot brains splashed his face and daemon ichor exploded from
the shattered skulls.

The background rumble he'd grown used to in the warp
bubble seemed louder, then he realised it was more than that.

A large vehicle skidded out onto Washington Street, the
whine of a diesel motor winding up to full throttle, stopping
him in his tracks.

'Get out of the road, you dumb *zhopa*!'

He leaped again, with less control and grace than before,
diving this time to preserve his skin as a yellow school
bus roared toward him. He had time enough to recognise
Varatchevsky behind the wheel of the GMC Short Bus. She
leaned out of the window, firing into the pack of dominants
frozen out the front of the police station. Armour-piercing
and tracer rounds, unaffected by the warp, probably hyper-
accelerated by it, punched through steel plate and chain
mail with murderous effect. As Dave rolled on the asphalt,
she ploughed the short bus into the remaining Hunn like a
bulldozer. Bodies burst apart, still locked in warp, the orcs
unaware they were dying.

Speed and mass, thought Dave. Speed and motherfucking
mass.

Squealing brakes locked the tyres, mashing daemon body parts into the road surface.

The bright yellow bus, extravagantly painted in offal and blood, finally lurched to a stop. Karen opened the side door and stepped out, katana in hand.

'Okay,' she said, stabbing three-quarters of the blade's length through a Hunn's skull. '*U tebya s zhopu techka*,' she sneered at the dominant before turning back to Hooper. 'I don't know what the hell you just did, Hooper. But could you at least help me finish these last few off? *Then* we go back and get the others. And *then* we go get your boys. All right?'

'Okay,' Dave said, still a little stunned by the mess she'd made of the cohort.

28

He collapsed the imperceptibly thin membrane separating them from the world in which bullets and men, monsters and books, and buses and thought itself all moved in real time. Gunfire tore through the air around Dave's head, hammering at the flanks of the bright yellow, blood-spattered school bus. Windows shattered and men cried out somewhere nearby in shock and confusion.

He heard someone order a ceasefire, and somebody else ignore the order and unleash half a clip of automatic rifle fire into the street.

'I said stop shooting, damn it!'

Dave crouched, keeping himself out of the line of fire, or hoping to at least. Karen was already moving, a shadow flitting around the bus with feral speed. Her gun fired once, twice, sending short bursts back up the gentle slope of the hill into the remains of the small Hunn war band outside the bookstore. So intent had Dave been on blowing through the greater number of Hunn outside the Public Safety Building, he hadn't heard or noticed she'd cut down the smaller breakaway group. He felt guilty heat flush his cheeks. He didn't bother with the war band because they weren't relevant. They were nowhere near his boys, and they weren't in the way.

They were someone else's problem.

A few more rounds of gunfire, a single booming blast of a shotgun and the same voice he had heard before yelled again.

'I said ceasefire, goddamn it. We don't have enough ammo.'

The timbre or the tone of the voices changed as the man turned from whoever he had been yelling at to yell into the street instead.

'Who the hell is out there? What just happened?'

Dave shouted back, from behind the shelter of the bus. He could hear sirens now, and the crackle of runaway fires. But no more gunshots.

'It's Hooper. Dave Hooper. Annie O'Halloran's husband. Or, you know, ex-husband,' he added, feeling foolish. 'The Hunn are all dead out here. I'm coming out. Don't shoot, okay?'

He held his hands up, gripping Lucille in one fist. She had gone quiet again. Not silent, but compared to the killing joy which had suffused her only a moment ago, she seemed almost tranquil. Like she'd just enjoyed multiple murdergasms. He heard Karen swapping out a magazine on her weapon.

She didn't put her hands up, but she wisely didn't point the gun anywhere near the cops either. They picked their way through the remains of the cohort. The impact of the bus travelling at God-only-knew what relative speed had caused most of the creatures it struck to explode into large chunks of hairy meat. One of the Hunn dominants had only taken a glancing blow, however, and Dave put a kick into the side of its head as it tried to crawl away, its progress slowed by a shattered hip and severed arm.

His heavy boot smashed into its dented helmet with a tinny crunch.

The helmet collapsed and yellow-green monster brains burst out in a wet spray.

A door cracked open in the front of the PSB, spilling a shaft of electric light out into the fire-lit night. A gun barrel poked through, then a black helmet.

'Hooper? The Dave Hooper?'

'The Dave, that's right,' he answered, causing Karen to roll her eyes. 'You can come on out. It's clear. That right, Karen?' he said, quickly checking with her. 'Your radar's all clear?'

'Yeah. Sort of,' she said, not exactly sniffing the air, but obviously testing the airwaves for something. 'I'm not getting anything nearby, and my range is pretty good. I think we got them all.'

'Like we got that extra Thresher back in New York?'

'Picky, picky. I got nothing on the radar, Hooper. What about Lucy the magical hammer? She singing any murder songs for you?'

'No,' he admitted. 'You can hear that?'

'No. But you can, and that's how I know.'

He was almost relieved to hear that, but there was no time to ponder it as more men and a couple of women appeared from within the sturdy brick building where they'd made their stand. Some were cops, obviously, even though they were dressed in military camouflage and body armour. Others might have been civilians who simply took shelter in the bunker-like public safety offices. They were dressed in an assortment of odds and ends. Some of them in hunting gear. One man, toting a ridiculously long, double-barrelled shotgun, wore pyjamas.

Nobody was pointing any weapons at Dave or Karen, but nor were they rolling out with smiles, baked goods and blowjobs to say howdy. Most seemed to be staring at the bus, which was only to be expected. The engine block was crumpled in as though from a serious collision with another large vehicle, or a number of them, and the bright yellow panels along the side were painted with grotesque smears and splashes of gore. Dave realised that to them the bus must have simply appeared to materialise in the midst of the cohort, sending the monsters flying apart, quite literally.

A tall ginger-bearded man in blue jeans, a checked shirt and tactical vest flicked the safety on his assault rifle – Dave assumed it was the safety – and nodded to the two surprise arrivals.

'Well, we much appreciate your intervention, Mr Hooper and . . .'

'Karen.'

Her smile was hugely inappropriate, given the circumstances, but well-practised and utterly disarming.

'Dan Bourke,' the man in charge said, uncertainly. 'Pleased . . . I'm sure . . . Karen.'

'You the sheriff?' Dave asked.

Bourke winced.

'Head of IT. Sheriff's dead. Deputy Paulson is missing.'

'So, how come you're running this?' Karen asked, looking at the uniformed cops picking through the detritus of battle.

Bourke shrugged.

'Ex-Ranger. I was in signals, but I was a captain.'

Bourke's posse, such as they were, fanned out among the bodies and body parts, covering them with their weapons. The streetlights had failed, probably when that little Nissan had taken out the power pole, but there was more than enough light from burning cars and buildings.

'They're all dead,' Dave said.

'Best to be sure,' Bourke replied, still looking as though he wasn't quite sure everything had turned out for the best.

'Fair enough, but we gotta be going if you don't mind.'

'Whoa. Not so fast there, Mr Hooper. You seem to know who's who in the goddamned zoo and I wouldn't mind a little filling in.'

Dave felt his impatience building up another head of steam. He'd done his bit, or, to be honest, Karen had when she ran the bus over the Hunn. The town was safe, and now he had to be getting on to his family. Karen's hand closed around his elbow, and her mind seemed to flow around his frustration, restraining him physically and emotionally.

'Dan,' she said, digging her fingers into Dave's arm like clamps. 'Are these the only creatures you know about within the town? Because if there's more we do need to put them down as quickly as possible. And we're the best suited to that job. No offence.'

'None taken,' Bourke said in a tone that gave them to understand she'd been as insulting as possible. 'We weren't having much luck with them,' he conceded then. 'It was a good thing they showed up so late. Most of the town was already home and abed.'

'Bourke,' said Dave. 'Do you know of any more Hunn or any other kind of monster in town? Anybody called anything in? Especially from out Shermans Point way. That's where I'm headed.'

Bourke and Dave both started at the sound of a gun blast. Karen did not.

'Had a live one, boss,' somebody called out from up the street a ways. 'Just put him down.'

'Well be careful,' Bourke shouted back. 'All of you. No sense anyone getting killed now.' He returned his attention to Dave, who was nearly bouncing on the balls of his feet with the need to be gone. Only Karen was stopping him from warping right out of there.

'Sorry,' said Bourke. 'It's been Hell.' He sighed, and it sounded as though he was letting go of a stale breath he'd been holding for hours. 'There's no more that I know of. But the phone lines are patchy, and not everyone has cell coverage.'

'That's okay,' Dave said. He knew there was a cell tower out on the point where Karen's old man lived. He was starting to calm down a little, but not so much that he wanted to delay any further. 'You want to wait here?' he asked Karen. 'Help these guys out?'

'No,' she answered quickly, taking both of the men a little by surprise. 'Sorry, Dan. But Hooper and I will need to scout the town and you'll be wanting to deal with your casualties.'

'Ayuh,' the IT guy conceded. 'Got plenty of them, I'm afraid. Including my chief.'

He shook his head and his lips began to tremble. Dave thought Bourke might even cry, but he got it under control as another vehicle came flying around the intersection of Mechanic and Washington. It was Igor and Zach in the Growler. Bourke shook his head at the sight of them, a series of short, rapid side-to-side jerks, as though he might shake some meaning into the sight. Perhaps he expected a whole convoy to roll in behind the jeep, which bristled with mounted machine guns, but there were only the two SEALs.

As Zach stomped on the brakes, the wheels sliding a few feet over the gore-slickened tarmac, Igor leaped from the passenger seat.

'Nasty,' he said, taking in the ambience of slaughterhouse floor.

'Igor, Zach, this is Dan Bourke,' said Dave, as the SEALs stomped through the gore. 'He looks after computers and he kills monsters.'

'Is the military here, now?' Bourke asked. 'Are you the relief?'

He looked hopefully up the road, but the only sounds were the flames of burning cars and buildings, and the voices of the other townspeople as they inspected the bodies of the Hunn. The flames and horror cast a dark Lovecraftian pall over the normally picturesque downtown area of Camden. It seemed to Dave as if he'd stepped sideways into an older, bloodier New England, perhaps from the era of witch burnings.

'I'm afraid we're not really the cavalry, sir,' Zach said.

'No, we're with these assholes,' Igor added helpfully. 'I'd say we're their cab drivers, but even that'd be pushing it.'

'Chill out,' Zach said, his voice growing mellow, the drawl becoming less Midwest and more Californian surf bum. 'Mr Bourke, can you give us a quick and dirty sit-rep. What you got here? Is this it?'

Bourke appeared to really take in the scene for the first time. Like everyone else in the country he'd undoubtedly seen the news reports out of New Orleans, cheered on the army in the Battle of Omaha, and watched with creeping horror as everything fell apart after victory had been declared. The downtown area of Camden Harbor, such as it was, had been trashed. Shops burned and bodies, both human and otherwise, lay everywhere. To Dave, after New Orleans, it didn't seem all that bad. But he wasn't a local, even though he was a sometime visitor. The horror in Bourke's expression was less about the amount of damage than it was about the sense of violation and loss of confidence. The Hunn hadn't come in large numbers. Just a cohort. But they had come and they could return at any time. Like a biker gang from the lower levels of Hell.

Good reason for Dave to be on his way again, but he probably needed to hear this. And while Karen couldn't be certain of her radar, not after that Thresher in New York had punk'd her so badly, he took solace from Lucille, who'd gone back to sleep. She, at least, didn't seem to feel like there were any more daemons to kill.

'First reports came in just before midnight,' Bourke said. He sounded as though he was talking to himself, rather than Zach. 'Lucky thing that. Couple of hours earlier, it would have been a bloodbath. I was in the office. We've had server problems and because of, you know, the troubles, the chief wanted all of our communications links working. He was at home but he . . . he came in. Or tried to.'

Bourke eyes flitted up the street Zach had just driven down.

'He's up there. In that wreck outside the bookshop.'

'Do you know where they first appeared?' Dave asked. He wanted to hear they were nowhere near Annie's old man's place.

'Maybe up by the creek runs near the school,' Bourke said. 'That's where the first reports came in.'

Dave relaxed a little. That was in exactly the opposite direction to Shermans Point and Pat O'Halloran's place. He tried not to let his relief show, and nobody seemed to notice it. Up and down the street, townsfolk were emerging from their shuttered homes, many of them carrying firearms.

'The Bigfoots came in from that direction,' Bourke said.

'Bigfoots?' Zach said.

Bourke seemed to come to himself again.

'Yeah, that's what the *Pilot* called them at first, after the Longreach attack. I guess it stuck.'

'Local paper, not an actual pilot,' Dave explained, at Karen's inquiring look.

'So the Bigfoots just marched in, tearing stuff up and burning shit down?' Igor asked.

'Pretty much,' Bourke said. 'By the time they got here,' he indicated the Public Safety Building, 'I had enough guns to hold them off. Not that they seemed intent on pressing the case. I suppose they're learning to be wary of guns and such like.'

'Yeah, I suppose so,' Karen said, not sounding at all like she did.

'Mr Bourke, we have personnel we need to secure out on Shermans Point Road,' Zach said. 'It seems to me like you have everything in hand here, and you'll want to be tending to your casualties.'

'Yes, sir, I will,' Bourke agreed. 'Will you be coming back here? Will the army be coming in?'

'We're Navy,' Igor told him. 'SEALs.'

Bourke seemed to consider that, rubbing at his orange beard.

'Really? Well that's good, I guess. This being a maritime town. So the navy's coming?'

'Don't count on it,' Karen told him, deflating his sudden optimism. 'If I were you, Dan, I'd keep a good watch out, and half your guns standing to in your headquarters there.' She pointed her gun at the PSB.

'You think there'll be more? That they'll come back?' he asked. The prospect did not sit well with him.

'Just be ready,' Karen said. 'You only have to make it to dawn and that's not far off now.'

Dave realised with a start that she was right.

'I gotta get going,' he said.

Igor's hand shot out and grabbed his arm, exactly where Karen had been holding it earlier.

'This time we all go together.'

'We'll take the Growler,' Zach said, as Dave let himself be led back toward the vehicle.

Igor climbed into the rear, manning the machine gun. Dave saw now that there were two different mounts, one of them a grenade thrower. He hopped into the back of the little jeep, finding a place to sit on an ammo box. Zach and Karen took the front seats.

'Try to call your wife,' she said. 'Do it now.'

The composure Dave had felt frayed a little, just a stitch or two.

'Why? What's up?'

29

The iPhone was useless. Not even a bar of coverage and no time to go looking for WiFi as they drove away from the town centre. The Iridium unit picked up a clear signal without a problem, but when he tried to connect to old Pat's landline, and then Annie's cell phone, he hit the wall. No service on either. He felt dread like cold, black water in the pit of his stomach as Zack steered left, taking them around the headwaters of the harbour.

'No,' said Karen as he tried to warp away. He could feel her shutting him down without even laying hands on him this time.

'I don't know what you did before, Hooper,' she said, 'but it wasn't normal. You drained yourself, and me, worse than a couple of minutes warping should have.'

They passed the small park sloping down to the bay where dozens of yachts and billionaire boats were tied up. Dave had no doubt that if the owners of those vessels had been in town, most of them would have put to sea to escape the Horde.

He wondered if there were sea monsters out there, and asking the question, answered it. Yes. Yes there were. His mind, not wanting to contemplate what might be wrong at the O'Halloran place, was sliding around on its ass like a fat kid on a skating rink. 'Stop acting like a redneck *ebanashka*.

Whatever you did before. Don't.'

Dave didn't know what she meant by *ebanashka* – it wasn't Olde Tongue, so it was probably some Russian insult – and he didn't know what she meant by 'before'. Or rather, he half did. She meant when he'd pushed his warp drive to its limits and felt himself pressing up hard against something mysterious and immaterial. Or immaterial in this reality at least. But he didn't know how he'd done that or what it meant. He no more understood what had happened than Karen did.

Zach stomped on the gas as they swung on to High Street, which doubled as Route 1 heading northeast out of town. It would follow the coast for miles, through heavily wooded New England forests, but they were only travelling for a few minutes, looking for Shermans Point Road. Dave calmed down somewhat as it became obvious that there was no damage on this side of town. The power was out but more than a few places ran generators, a must-have item in the winter months when blizzards could take down the grid for days at a time. He saw lights on in lounge rooms, and even the flicker of TV sets through windows in every second or third house. Some people stood out on their front porches, all of them seeming to be armed with hunting rifles of one type or another. Igor waved to them as they roared past.

'Colonel Varatchevsky?' Zach said as he overtook a northbound Volvo loaded high with camping gear and suitcases. He had to speak loudly over the rush of the wind and the noise of the Growler's engine.

Karen's voice betrayed a hint of wariness. The SEALs had been studiously ignoring her actual status since they'd met. 'Yes, Chief?'

'You mind if I ask you something?'

'As long as you don't mind if I tell you to fuck off should I not feel like answering.'

'Fair enough. Can I ask why you're doing this, helping us, when you could have just disappeared? Gone home even. The Horde and the other monster clans, they're in Russia too, right?'

'They are,' she said, not bothering to correct his use of the term 'clans'. 'Not as many as there seem to be here, but it is early days.'

'So why are you here? Seriously. That Trinder guy has a hard-on for you and, to be fair, you are a spy. From a really hostile foreign power.'

'I hope you don't think less of me for that?'

Her tone was teasing, amused.

'A little,' Zach admitted. 'Although I guess I'd be more pissed at you if I'd known you before. You know, when you were undercover.'

They swept past a side street that Dave recognised as home to Jack and Toby's best friends, a couple of boys from their school, and another street just one block from Shermans Point Road. There were fewer houses out here and they were set further back into the trees. The night grew closer. Karen seemed to consider Zach's question, but Dave could tell she was also scanning for monster signals.

'I'm here because I'm here,' she said. 'This is where the threat is. So this is where my mission is.'

'You operating under orders right now?' Igor asked from the back, shouting over the wind that tried to whip his words away.

'Yes,' she said. 'I am to assess the threat and advise my superiors on tactics and strategy.'

'So when you're done with that, you're done with us?' Dave asked. He was surprised at how put out he sounded.

'We are all doing what we have to, Hooper,' she said, turning around to face him. The wind of their passage whipped at her hair, lashing her face with the long, filthy blonde strands. Zach slowed as they reach the turn-off.

'But you told me you thought we were past all of that shit,' Dave protested. 'Trinder and Heath and people fighting each other instead of the Horde.'

'We are, for now,' she said, breaking off for a moment to scan whatever frequencies she found the Threshers and orcs on. 'But I don't see you volunteering to defend my family or my country. For now, I serve them here, Hooper. But only for now.'

There were a couple of properties at the intersection of Route 1 and Shermans Point Road, but they were dark. Dave recalled them as being summer rentals, empty for most of the year. There was no reason why they should be occupied now. Away from the highway, full darkness fell upon them again, pierced only by the headlights of the little jeep. Igor charged the machine gun with a metallic ratcheting sound.

'Let her be, Hooper,' he said. 'She's a soldier. Like us. She doesn't get choices. She gets orders.'

Chastened by the rebuke, Dave let it go. He'd been diverted anyway by Karen's mention of family. She'd never said anything about them before, and as far as he knew from the briefing by Trinder she had none in America. In fact she'd been here so long as a deep cover agent that she probably had nobody other than older relatives back in Russia. Did they even know where she was, what she was doing? Karen had turned back to the front, probably scanning the airwaves again. They roared down a long straight stretch of road and Dave was tempted to warp just for a second, to see if he could. He didn't think Karen was blocking him anymore, trusting that he would do as he'd promised. It would be a quick and dirty way to check for Threshers, but he caught himself before the thought could go further. Zach was driving. They were all in the jeep. It would probably keep going at this speed and fly off the road.

Karen turned around again and gave him a firm shake of the head.

She knew what he'd been thinking.

That was a hell of a thing, having anyone inside his head like that. But someone like her, a spy and . . .

She interrupted his train of thought.

'I'm right here you know, *zasranec*.'

'Sorry.'

She returned to scanning ahead.

'At least you're not staring at my ass anymore.'

Further chastened, Dave tried to keep his mind from wandering again. They were getting close.

Igor grinned at him.

'Busted.'

Pat O'Halloran had done well from the fishing trade. He still owned a share of the small fleet of trawlers he'd built up, although it had been ten years since he'd been out on the water for a living. He was probably the richest man Dave had known before moving down to Texas to work in the oil industry, and he had reason to resent him for that. As careful as the old trawler man had been to raise his daughter right, Annie was still his only daughter, and he'd spoiled her rotten, at least as far as her ex-husband was concerned. To Dave's way of thinking, a good deal of the trouble in their marriage had been less about realities than expectations, primarily the expectation of one Annie O'Halloran that her husband would be able to keep her in the style to which her old man had accustomed her.

The Growler swept around the long looping curve that would deliver them to Pat's place and Dave found himself wondering less about monster infestations – it did seem pretty quiet this far from town – and more about how Annie was coping shut away up here. It made sense she'd moved in with her dad. They hadn't owned the townhouse they'd lived in in Houston. That was a company condo, so she hadn't been able to shake him down for it. Alimony took a big bite out of Dave's ass, of course, but Annie had always been one of those women for whom equality meant busting his balls to work two jobs. One on the rigs or at the office, and a second when he was at home with the boys. He almost grinned at the idea of her brow beating old Cap'n Pat into school runs and homework supervision, but the grin faded. O'Halloran had probably done it willingly, and of course there was Vietch to call on as well. Her lawyer and boyfriend.

Dave hoped Boylan had made a mess of Vietch like he'd promised.

Pat's house was comfortable, but no mansion. A solid red brick cottage in the Colonial Revival style, notable mostly for its easy access to the outer beaches of the point. It was a long way from the big city restaurants and galleries that Annie had a taste for. Hell, it was a long way from downtown Camden if you weren't driving. The walk up to Route 1 alone was a good quarter hour.

Still, he had to admit, it had one abiding advantage, didn't it?

As remote as it was from New York, where Annie would

have loved to live, it was even further from the Gulf and the Texas oil towns where Dave had dragged her and the boys, and where he still lived.

Or where he had lived, until last week.

'Anything?' he asked Karen.

'No. I think we're clear,' she said. 'How's Lucy?'

'She's cool.'

'Up ahead, right?' Zach asked as he slowed the Growler to about twenty-five miles per hour.

'Yeah. There's a track off the end of the surfaced road, leads down to the water. You can follow it all the way. There's a house with a good turning circle for the driveway. That's them. They're the only one this far down on the outer point.'

Igor swept the forest with the muzzle of the machine gun.

'Residences off to the right, on the inner harbour?' he said.

'Yep,' Dave confirmed. 'Five of them, as I recall.'

No lights flickered through the trees from that direction. No sound drifted up. Some of the houses were occupied year round, but Dave did not know which ones. He'd never really fitted in here, even when he'd visited in the years before the separation. He twirled Lucille in his hands, trying to feel if she could sense anything.

She hummed in his hands, but that was all. And she'd been doing that for days.

Zach found the track that ran through the scrub down to Pat O'Halloran's cottage. As always it was meticulously well maintained, the branches and undergrowth cut way back, the hard scrabble surface clear, if a little wet from an earlier shower.

'Still good,' Karen informed them as the twin cones of the headlights illuminated the private road.

'Yeah, think so,' Dave confirmed. Lucille was quiet.

He was beginning to worry that everything was maybe too quiet, but he had no idea how the orcs would lay an ambush somewhere like this without Lucille being able to sense them. For that matter, Zach and Igor presumably knew all about not driving into ambushes and, as watchful as they were, they didn't seem to think one was coming. The headland was surrounded on three sides by water. A couple of tiny islets lay just offshore due south, reachable by a hazardous walk across mostly submerged rocks. Nothing would be storming them from there.

It was so quiet Dave was more worried by the lack of any signs of life. The headlamps picked out the cottage at the end of the gravel road. He recognised the large front door, white-panelled and framed by the slender columns of the entry porch. Palladian windows – that's what Annie always called them when she was pestering him to replace their aluminium frames in Houston. He knew she'd also insisted on the ones at the cottage being 'authentic', which to Dave was another way of saying inexpertly made by poorly trained craftsmen. They threw back wavering reflections of the jeep's headlamps. He saw Pat's old truck parked by the side of the house, and a couple of bikes chained to the rails of the front porch. He didn't recognise them but assumed they belonged to the boys.

'Cutting the lights,' Zach said as he pulled up.

'I'm good,' Igor told him, pulling down night vision goggles.

'What about you two?' the younger SEAL asked. 'How fast does your night vision adjust?'

'It won't be a problem,' Karen said. 'Just do it. I'll cover you.'

Another thing Dave hadn't bothered to find out. How quickly did his night vision kick in?

Instantly, as it turned out. Zach cut the lights and the

world resolved itself into crystal clear blues and greys. Karen had known that because she had obviously taken the time to find out at some point. He hadn't. That was gonna change, first chance he got. First thing tomorrow, in fact, when he had the boys safely away.

Zach fitted his own NVGs and they dismounted, Igor last of all, covering them with the mounted machine gun. Dave carried Lucille in an easy, two-handed grip, ready to start swinging, but she didn't seem to think it would be necessary. He could hear small waves lapping at the shore, but nothing like the rustle and clink of leather and chain mail, or that rattle of armour plate and edged weapons. But nor could he hear any TV or radio, or see any lights on. He knew Pat kept a generator and a supply of diesel to run it.

'Think the power's out?' he asked nobody in particular. The other three crept forward, sweeping the approach with their weapons.

'And the phone lines,' Karen said.

Igor stopped, dropped and covered the way they'd come in with his more compact weapon. The barrel of his sniper rifle poked out a foot over his shoulder.

'Well,' said Dave, struggling with his impatience, 'the orcs aren't likely to be waiting in the house, are they?'

He strode between the carefully advancing special operators, stomping up the front steps, ready to hammer on the knocker.

The shotgun blast blew a hole in the door directly in front of his face.

30

Lucille saved him. She didn't start singing as much as shrieking when Dave stepped onto the porch. He was already raising his hand, reaching for the brass knocker, when the magical war hammer filled his head with the buzz of angry wasps and screaming eagles. He warped by instinct, without thought, simply to escape the horrible din which seemed to fill the whole world. He didn't transition to the weird edge-state he'd found himself in earlier, where it seemed as though the fabric of reality itself might tear under the strain. He simply slowed everything right the fuck down as the door in front of him seemed to bulge and glow. Paint blistered, cracked and dissolved. For an uncomfortably long, suspended second the hardwood distended like the surface of a balloon. Then rents appeared, forced open by glowing fireflies.

No, they were wasps.

No, they were shotgun pellets.

And Dave was diving, rolling, twisting away, feeling muscles tear and repair themselves. Losing sight of everything when he flinched and squeezed his eyes shut, as though that might protect him from the shotgun blast that was tearing through altered space toward him. The world turned and spun and fire raked at his flesh. Long splinters of pain speared through him as white-hot lead shot tore through his body.

The world sped up again and he heard screaming, not just his own. And shouting, a woman's voice. Two of them, both known to him. Karen, yelling at everyone and no one to chill the fuck out, calm the fuck down, and stop shooting.

And Annie.

Annie O'Halloran. Love of his younger life, bane of his later existence.

Annie screaming and screaming and screaming as Dave fell into darkness, pushed under by the tsunami of pain he'd just absorbed.

He came to in pain, but not the twisted agony of burning and ripping he'd felt when Pat O'Halloran had unloaded both barrels of his old Ruger 20 gauge on his one-time son-in-law. Or at the door he was standing in front of, anyway.

'I knew you never liked me,' Dave croaked, not really joking, as he cracked open his eyes. He expected to be blind. Dead.

Instead he was stretched on a couch in the lounge room of his former father-in-law. An old tarp, stiff with age and dried paint, lay under him and he suspected that Annie would have made either Zach or Igor go out to the garage to fetch it before she'd allow them to lay him on her father's good lounge.

He blinked and his eyes felt dry and scratchy, but hell, at least he could blink and he could see. He winced at the memory of the blast which had nearly taken off his head.

'He's awake,' somebody said, as Dave struggled to sit up. He felt at his cheeks, gently, gingerly with fingertips only, not sure what he'd find. A whole new face? Grotesque and misshapen, grown back over shattered bones and cartilage?

No scars. No wounds. A three-day growth.

'Dad! Dad's awake!'

It was Jack. Or Toby.

For a second he wasn't sure which. It had been a while since he'd spoken to the boys face-to-face.

'Dad, are you okay?'

That voice, higher, a little more lilting, was Toby's. He was eighteen months younger than his brother and unexpectedly musical. Annie had insisted he have singing lessons and Dave thought he could hear it in his voice now, a measured timbre that his brother lacked.

'Dad?'

And that was Jack. His voice was cracking. Dave blinked again and rubbed at his eyes. He expected to find them crusted with dried blood but somebody had cleaned him up.

After Annie made sure the couch was safe.

'Hey,' Dave said, looking for his sons in the gloom, unable and unwilling to keep the grin out of his voice. 'Hey boys. Did you see your old man on the TV?'

'Did we!' shouted Toby.

'You were on everywhere, Dad,' said Jack. Dave's vision cleared at last and he found them easily in the dark. His boys.

'Come here,' he said, or tried to around the lump in his throat.

'Boys, you mind your father, he's hurt.'

The speaker brought them up short and swift.

Patrick James O'Halloran. Boston Irish master mariner. A hard man and an even harder father-in-law.

Ex father-in-law, thank Christ.

Dave spied him standing by the cold hearth, cradling

the gun with which he'd nearly blown Dave's head off. He looked older, even harder if that were possible, and utterly unrepentant. The rest of the room came into focus. Zach and Igor standing by the windows – the *Palladian* windows – both of them peering out into the night, keeping watch. Karen stationed by the window at the far end of the room, which looked out toward the tip of Shermans Point. She was watching Dave, her machine gun held with casual ease, the handle of her katana protruding well above her shoulder.

'How long?' Dave asked.

'Half an hour,' she said. 'We were waiting for you to recover. Or die.'

He looked for Annie but couldn't see her before the boys slammed into him. Their small arms around his neck, their warm faces pressed against his cheeks.

'We saw you on YouTube,' said Toby.

'Yes, and they saw you on TMZ and Perez Hilton . . . with Paris Hilton.'

Annie.

That flat nasal voice which could pack so much more hurt into a few words than Dave could ever load up into a fist. Not that he had with her. Not once, not ever, no matter how sorely she had tempted and baited him to do it. He felt his youngest son stiffen against him.

'So where have you been, Dave?' said Annie, her voice sounding tired rather than angry. 'Besides partying with your new friends in Hollywood?'

'Well, mostly here on the couch I guess, after Pat shot me in the face.'

He tried to ease the boys away from him, but they held on tighter.

'Granddad didn't mean to,' Jack said. 'We thought you were a Bigfoot.'

'Can't blame a man,' Pat O'Halloran said, again without a trace of apology.

'I could but I won't,' Dave said. 'Am I still pretty?'

Toby loosened his grip and sat up.

'We saw you! You were like . . .' He made a sucking-snorkelling sound and danced his fingers around his face, which scrunched into a fright mask, and then returned to its normal, unblemished form.

'It was like they said on TV,' Jack said in something approaching a stage whisper. 'You're indestructible now.'

'No, he's not,' said Karen.

'That's enough.' Annie sighed. 'You boys let your father be. He's had a nasty accident. You've said hello. Now go get yourselves off to bed. You've hardly slept and he'll still be here in the morning. You will be here, won't you, Dave?'

'Hey. It was you who took the boys and fucked off . . .'

'Language,' growled Pat. 'Keep it civil, Hooper.'

Karen spoke over the top of them.

'You can have your episode of *Divorce Court* when we're out of here. You boys, go get dressed. Camping clothes. Good boots. Go now. You, Ms O'Halloran . . .'

'I'm sorry, but who are you anyway?' Annie asked. 'These two I know now,' she said, indicating Igor and Zach who remained studiously fascinated by the approaches to the cottage. 'They had the good manners to introduce themselves properly. But you haven't told us anything. Did you bring your girlfriend, Dave? Is that who this is?'

Karen snorted.

'He wishes.'

'No I don't.'

'Hey? Super Dave. Pretty sure I mentioned the psychic powers.'

'You have psychic powers?' Jack gasped, staring at Karen with awe.

'And a magic ninja sword,' Toby said. 'Holy crap. You're even better than Black Widow.'

'Language, boys,' Pat growled again. 'Keep it clean on my deck or you'll be swabbing the deck.'

Dave cringed. It had been a while since he'd been directly exposed to Cap'n O'Halloran's patented nautical sayings.

Zach decided he had to say something.

'Ms Warat is correct,' he said. 'We need to exfil. Our pilot confirms he's been refuelled. And this location is not secure. I don't want to remain here any longer than we have to. Dave, are you good to go? How are you feeling?'

Dave thought about it.

'Really hungry.'

'Of course,' muttered Karen. *'Fsyoe zaeebahnuh.'*

'Language!' growled Pat.

'Your kids speak Russian, Dave?'

'They will if you keep up the cussing like that, *pizda staraya*,' O'Halloran said. 'I've had your sort on my boats before. So I'd thank you to watch your mouth around my boys.'

'They're my boys,' Dave said.

'Could have fooled me,' said Annie.

'Why? You weren't banging Vietch back then, were you?'

Dave heard Zach say, 'God help us,' under his breath, but the white squall that blew up between the clans O'Halloran and Hooper buried it. Nobody was arguing with each other. It was more a matter of throwing words *at* each other. Pat avowing that he should never have let his daughter fall in with such a low life. Annie yelling at Dave about some Hollywood lawyer who'd been ringing at all hours of day and night, *all hours*, harassing both her and poor Pearson, making all manner of threats. Annie demanding to know where her share of his last bonus went. Annie lashing him about all the bills she could not pay, the responsibilities he would not meet. And Dave, forgetting about the boys who were still clinging to him, jumping to his feet with such speed that Toby actually flew a short distance through the air and over the back of the lounge chair with a comical cry of 'Whoa,' while Dave shouted, 'Perhaps your old man could reach into his pocket for something other than fucking shotgun shells.'

It only ended when Karen stormed across the room, spitting out the words 'Shut up shut up shut up,' as she smacked her palms on Pat and Annie's foreheads, and then gave Dave a cracking backfist. The old man's eyes narrowed at her touch, Hooper's ex-wife's bulged in shock. Her mouth flew open in a wide, soundless 'O'. Pat's lips pressed together in a thin, bitter line. Dave knew why. He was familiar with the deeply unpleasant feeling of Karin Varatchevsky reaching into his skull and squeezing hard.

'You two!' she barked at the boys. 'Go do as I said. Now!'

The boys both scuttled away. Toby seemed no worse for his maiden flight across the lounge room.

'As for you,' she rounded on Dave and jabbed a stiffened finger into his chest. It hurt, and he could imagine her driving it right through his ribs. 'Wake up and smell the hell stew, Hooper. I've put up with you bitching and moaning about this poor woman from the moment I met you.'

Annie did an actual cartoon double-take and shook her head vigorously. Dave opened his mouth to speak but Karen jabbed him again, *pushing* a little this time.

'You're a terrible father, every bit as bad as your own. But you were a much worse husband.'

She threw up a hand like a traffic cop, to forestall his inevitable protest.

'You have no secrets from me, remember. I came up here with my head full of your whining about this woman.' She pointed at Annie. 'I was expecting to find a castrating succubus because that's what you'd convinced yourself you'd married. But I've had half an hour with Annie while you've been having your power nap, and what I actually found is just another woman who married poorly. She's been terrified these last days, like everyone in the whole world, except you. You were partying, and she was here wondering when the orcs would turn up.'

The force of her censure was a physical weight that Dave could feel pressing down on his shoulders, immobilising him. It got worse.

'That drop cloth you've been lying on. She didn't put it there to protect the couch. We used it to haul your carcass in off the porch. But you just had to make it her fault didn't you? Like everything was always her fault and never yours. You're a selfish bastard, Dave. You're smart enough to know that, but you're selfish, so you won't do anything about it. You never have. In some ways, killing Urgon was the worst thing that could ever have happened to you.'

She pushed him again, hard. Forcing him to see himself as others did. Not as Super Dave. More like Super Douche.

The psychic blow was heavy enough to cause Pat O'Halloran to stagger against a wall and his daughter gasped, collapsing to the floor.

It saved her life.

31

'The attack on the village has gone as planned, your Lordship. And all the cattle have been cleared from these fields.'

'Very good,' said Guyuk, not bothering to correct the Sliveen MasterScout. Although the lord commander had vowed to give up thinking of the human foe as nothing more than a food source, he had learned that others of the Horde found it nearly impossible to do so. For now, he would have to content himself with the knowledge that he was better than them. He understood *dar ienamic*. Or he was beginning to, at least.

'They're going back to the blood pots right?' Compt'n ur Threshrend said. 'The cattle, I mean. Because I got me some powerful munchies and I plan to see to them when we're done here.'

'Yes,' Guyuk grunted, 'the blood pots. But first we must be done here, Superiorae.'

'Pfft.'

Guyuk recognised the odd noise the Threshrend made as being a remnant human gesture indicating scepticism. Compt'n ur Threshrend seemed especially fond of it.

'You can stick a big fucking fork in us, *jefe*, we are done,' he said. 'All except for the screaming and the shouting and the tasty, tasty feasting back at the ol' blood pot. And beer. I think we should totally take some beer when we go back down.'

Lord Guyuk ur Grymm marched into the Above, away from the dark portal to the UnderRealms, maintained here by not one, but three Masters of the Ways, two of them at the far end of the connection, as suggested by Compt'n ur Threshrend. Motherfucking redundancy, he called it and Guyuk recognised the sense of the practice. It would not be wise to assume that because they had the Dave isolated and at some supposed disadvantage, the damnable human champion could not yet do them great harm. To lose a Way Master, for instance, and find themselves trapped on this small peninsula in the hours before dawn would not do. If the accursed sun did not burn them from the earth, some equally accursed human magicks almost certainly would.

A Dread Company of Grymm fanned out through the forests ahead of them. Two more Talon of Hunn stood ready in the staging area at the other end of the Way, waiting their turn to pass through and join them. They would fight without leashed Fangr, lest a single dominant losing control for just a moment give them all away. It should not matter. Every moment brought more forces of the Horde onto this headland. Every moment, Guyuk hoped, brought the Dave closer to his ending.

As they stole through the night, the lord commander tried to take a measure of confidence from the success of the diversionary attack on the nearby hamlet. The Hunn there had died of course, but they had died well and their names would be added to the scrolls no matter what came of this next chapter. Their mission was done. The Dave had been drawn here, away from the main human armies, and having so easily accounted for the threat he could see, Sliveen confirmed the champion had repaired to his nest, unaware of the much greater threat he could not yet discern.

'My psychic Super Friends are ready to rock, boss, just in case you were wondering.'

'I was not wondering, no, Superiorae. But thank you for informing me anyway. The finest warriors of the Regiments Select of Grymm are of course well known for their incompetence and without your constant blathering I am sure I would faint away with worry that they would fail to escort the Threshrendum to their required station as ordered.'

'Wow,' Compt'n replied. 'That was like, wow. You laid down some choice snark there, boss. Good for you! You'll be, like, doing irony and shit soon.'

'Yes. Yes my . . . snark is coming along. Thank you for noticing.'

Compt'n ur Threshrend did indeed appear to be quite genuine in his appreciation for Guyuk's use of the strange human form of communication known as sarcasm. It was, he had learned, a particular favourite of the Dave. He seemed to speak in high snark and nought else whenever he challenged a member of the Horde. Guyuk did not intend to look foolish should he ever have to cross wits with the man.

'But be quiet now, Superiorae,' Guyuk cautioned. 'We draw closer to the quarry and this, after all, is your plan. Best that we afford it the highest chance of success.'

They advanced through the forest, the smell of salt and seawater strong in his nasal slits as he listened to the crashing boom of surf on rocks. The rumble rolled in from the darkness dagger-wise, the direction from which the sun would rise soon enough. Too soon indeed for his peace of mind. Beside Guyuk, shield-wise and a few steps behind him, Compt'n ur Threshrend hurried to keep up. Although he was the smallest of the daemonum investing the headland he was by far the loudest. Even the Hunn were able to advance on their prey with greater stealth.

'If you stomped a little harder through the dead fall of this forest I'm sure the Dave might actually hear you coming,' said Guyuk.

'Pfft. The Dave has probably fallen into a barrel of rum by now,' the Superiorae replied. Guyuk was not sure what he meant, but the empath did appear to take a little more care to soften the fall of his hind-claws.

The small hovel where Compt'n ur Threshrend had promised they would find the Dave's nestlings slowly appeared through the trees. It was an unimpressive structure compared to the great towers Guyuk had seen in Manhatt'n, but far sturdier than anything recalled in the annals of the war scrolls. One of the human chariots waited in the clearing in front. The Superiorae surprised him by leaping into the lower branches of a tree, and scaling quite nimbly into the upper canopy. The lord commander suppressed the urge to scold him or even to ask what he was doing. He had to remember that, as perverse as the Superiorae could appear at times, he was their only expert in the ways of *dar ienamic*.

We must hasten to acquire more experts, Guyuk thought, as the Threshrend scuttled down again.

'Lookin' good, boss,' Compt'n said in a low voice. 'You want I should tell my peeps to start blocking his WiFi?'

'If you mean, should the Threshrendum begin their attack? No. The last of the Hunn are still to move into position.

I fear that fate shall gift us no more than one lunge at this foe. I would not wish to strike before we are set.'

'Okay, okay, not judging. Just saying,' the tiny empath daemon said hurriedly, throwing up its fore-claws. 'It's just, you know, sunrise and everything. And I don't really tan. I burn. We all burn. Like, you know, horribly. So . . .'

'I am aware of the danger, Superiorae. But war is risk. And this is a risk which might win us not just the human realm but the greater struggle against the other sects. It is a risk worth taking.'

It was totally fucking not worth taking. Or at least, not in person. Or not in monster.

Threshy stopped and frowned, an even uglier expression on this face, riven with scars and suppurating boils, than it had been on all his previous human faces. Or the faces he'd eaten. He snarled and shook off the thought. Sometimes the persistence of his old ways of thinking fucked him up.

Like when he thought of Polly Farrell. And all the things he'd like to do to Polly Farrell with his monster loins.

He quickly pushed those thoughts aside.

He was here, and not rotting in some Grymm dungeon, because he *could* think in those 'old' ways, the human ways of those whose brains he'd sucked up like an offal slushy. There was no pay-off in worrying about what might have happened if he hadn't been spared by Guyuk.

It was enough to unsettle a motherfucker. Even a motherfucker who'd eaten the brains of a genius like Compton. Hell, even those SEALs he'd chomped had been a lot smarter than most people you'd eat. But not as smart as Compton, and that was why they were here. Because Compton had known Hooper would eventually make his way to his family.

Didn't mean Threshy needed to be here though. Or even Guyuk. They could have sent the Dread Company without adult supervision. They'd have killed every motherfucker who needed killing. And then everyone else. No need for Threshy to bother with anything but the celebratory kegger back at the palace. He didn't even need to be here to control the Threshrendum. They were all battle-worn badasses and they knew now how to stop Hooper and his little dominatrix friend from speed-whoopin' their asses like the Flash.

He sniffed at that, as the last cohort of Hunn moved quietly into position around them, the dominants slipping through the darkened forest with a stealthy silence that belied their size and the great weight of armour they all now wore. These were not mere warrior Hunn. They were dominants-exceptional. The finest of their clan. Nobody was going into this cage match with their dumb nuts hanging out.

It bugged the hell out of Threshy that he couldn't figure out how Hooper and the Russian bitch were orbing around. Or warping, to use Hooper's term. It also bugged him that he tended to think of the mysterious power as orbing, because that's how the woman thought of it, and his empathic link was to her, not the so-called fucking Dave.

Warping was much cooler.

But the fucking Consilium Scolari took their lead from the Threshrendum in the field, not Threshy, and like him, the Threshrendum were linked with Varatchevsky, not Hooper. So orbing it had to be.

Even though nobody knew what the fuck it even was. There were no such things as orb daemons or warp monsters.

The power seemed indigenous to Hooper, which was fucking bullshit.

Threshy sniffed as his nostrils caught the scent of something in the breeze. Gun smoke. Faint and almost faded. It gave him a start for a moment and he saw, and felt, that Guyuk caught it too. He could not see the bulk of the Dread Company, but he felt them suddenly freeze.

'Human weaponry.'

The Sliveen MasterScout surprised Threshy. He had not sensed him there in the shadows. Sneaky fucker.

'Explain yourself, MasterScout,' Guyuk growled quietly. 'You reported the Dave and his thrall were unaware of our approach.'

The Sliveen warrior sniffed at the night air again.

'It has been some time since the calfling weapons were used, my Lord. And then not more than once or twice. None of my scouts reported being taken under fire by their magicks. It must have happened before we arrived.'

'Ha!' Threshy snorted, remembering at the last moment to keep his voice down. 'Maybe his ex-wife shot the asshole. That'd be like her from what Hooper said. Or the Russian? Man, we shoulda just cut a deal with the bitch. Made her Queen of the Above for whacking him. She'd have done it for fucking free.'

He understood from the expressions on the faces of Guyuk and the MasterScout that they had little or no idea what he was talking about.

'Meh. Too late now. Let's just go kill 'em all.'

'You are convinced this is not some trap, Superiorae?' Guyuk asked.

'Not convinced, no,' said Threshy. 'But it's probably not.

I reckon we should fire up the Threshrend and see what happens.'

'Are the Hunn in place?' Guyuk asked the MasterScout. The Sliveen bowed.

'Yes, my Lord.'

'In that case, Superiorae have your Threshrendum engage *dar ienamic*.'

'You don't have to tell me twice, *Jefe*.'

32

Two Sliveen *arrakh* punched through the window where Igor stood watch. He was safely hidden behind the window frame, but the daemon scouts had a clear shot at Annie. Or they should have. They did not anticipate her collapsing under the cudgel of Karen's psychic hammer blows, and they were unfamiliar with the flaws of handmade imitation colonial glass of the type Annie O'Halloran had pestered her formidable father into installing. For the sake of authenticity.

Annie's ethically wavy window panes, and her unexpected collapse, meant that the pair of harpoon-sized war shots that came crashing through the glass passed harmlessly through the lounge room to embed themselves deep in the plaster wall, rather than deep inside Dave's ex-wife.

He warped and . . .

. . . cried out in pain as his vision broke up into shattered slivers of mirror glass and pixel chaff.

'Threshers!' Karen shouted as the SEALs opened fire, adding the strobing white light of muzzle flashes to the schizoidal effect which seemed to shatter the world into a thousand jagged pieces until Dave stopped trying to warp. The thundering report of a shotgun added its deep bass notes to the industrial hammering rattle of machine-gun fire. Dave heard a male voice, Igor's perhaps, shout 'Cover me,' as Hooper rolled around on the hard floor, having forgotten how he got there.

Lucille wailed and keened for his touch, but he had no idea where she was. He was vaguely aware of screams. Small, terrified screams somewhere nearby but too far away and then he remembered.

Toby and Jack.

His boys.

They were upstairs, dispatched by Karen to change into travel clothes. The realisation struck him at the very moment he heard the crunching, crashing explosion of Palladian window frames on the upper floor, and remembered where he might find his weapon. Probably lying on the front porch where he'd dropped it when O'Halloran had tried to shoot him through the door. Already moving, sick and disoriented by the Threshers' brain-spasm, he stumble-tripped across the room, yelling at Annie to stay the fuck down and banging his shoulder so hard into an internal door frame that it splintered under the impact.

He heard bones crack – his bones – and his head swam as he burned up more energy knitting them back into place. The gunfire behind him was a constant, coughing roar, almost loud enough to drown out the roars of the attackers outside. Almost, but not quite.

'Hunn. Hunn. Hunn ur HORDE.'

Arrakh missiles thudded into the brick work, their Drakon-stone arrowheads exploding in bursts of orange-red fire. Windows shattered under storms of iron bolts. The boys' screaming redoubled and Dave, whose hunger pangs had become sharp and constant, accelerated up the narrow staircase to the second floor. The board cracked under the force of his boots and he realised that if he was running toward a fight with an armoured Hunn or Grymm, or even a Sliveen, he was probably running to his death, and the death of his children. He had barely recovered from his injuries. His metabolism was burning at white heat on an empty tank. He had no armour, no weapons. Not even a knife.

He kept going.

The upper floor was dark but not to him. His night vision rendered everything into a bright clear palette of cool blues and greys. He could not see his boys, but he could hear them, sense them in their room. Something was in there with them. Dave Hooper sprinted down the narrow hallway, his boots hammering on the uneven hardwood board like a hundred horse hooves in stampede. The thing in the bedroom was stooped under the low ceiling. Too thin, too angular and insectile to be a hulking dominant or squat, brutish Grymm.

Sliveen, he thought as it bent to up-end the bed under which Toby and Jack were cowering. Dave caught a glint of moonlight on a curved and wicked blade. Half scythe, half peeling knife, it was designed to skin the hide from small prey like urmin and wulfin cubs. The boys' screams were hysterical, louder and more imperative than any of the guns firing downstairs. The rangy daemon stopped and turned, aware of the threat at its rear. Dave was afforded the merest glimpse of Toby's little face, tear-streaked and hollow-eyed, before the Sliveen scout turned fully toward him and blocked the view. The daemon whipped out a second blade, longer and straighter than the first, but nothing like the claymores or cleavers favoured by the other Clans. The Sliveen hissed and flew at Dave, blurring the air in front of it with a complicated pattern of slashes and feints and looping bladework. Had he been able to, Dave would have simply warped safely around the creature and taken it from behind, driving his fist into the base of its neck. But he could not warp, and he could not even get around the thing that had charged out of the bedroom and into the confined space of the hallway. They flew toward each other like speeding cars. In a fraction of a second they would collide and Dave would be cut into chuck steak.

He leaped.

Not at the beast, or the whirring steel, but at the floor, balling himself up, tucking in his head, passing under the threshing machine it had made, and crashing into the shins and knees of the Sliveen scout. They hit each other with a combined speed of well over a hundred miles per hour and Dave felt the bones and knee joints of the monster give under the impact.

Mass and speed, he thought. Bones splintered and cracked. Complex arrangements of cartilage, gristle, muscle fibre and meat separated at high speed with a loud popping sound. Dave did not escape entirely. A fierce, burning spike of pain raked his back, as one of the blades cut through the filthy, stiffened fabric of his coveralls and, beneath them, his flesh. But as the creature shrieked and fell backward, Dave used his body weight to trap its flailing arms and claws, and the blades beneath. He felt steel puncture his skin again, but ignored it as the tingling heat of healing sewed his flesh back together.

Then he was astride the Sliveen, face to face with its snarling features. Mouth full of broken fangs, nasal slits flaring and snorting acidic mucus at him, huge shark-like eyes black with the killing fury. Before it could roll out from underneath him, or just use its massive animal power to throw him off, Dave drove his thumbs into those eyes. The daemon shrieked, a horrible, gruesome sound as the human champion gouged deeper and deeper, feeling the membrane of the eyeballs rip under his thumbnails, and the hot vitreous fluid come spurting out. Dave roared his own animalistic *shkriia*, gripped the head of the Sliveen like a watermelon and smashed it into the hard oaken board until the skull gave way and the brains came pouring out. The creature shuddered underneath him and went limp.

He slumped to one side, and fumbled in his pockets for an energy gel, a protein bar, anything. His hunger was a fire now, burning him from the inside. It would consume him if he did not consume something else, anything. His search for some kind of sustenance grew frantic, but he had nothing.

'Help me, son,' he croaked, not sure which of his boys he meant. 'I need –'

He blacked out for a second and came to with Jack kneeling over him.

'Dad? Dad?'

Toby stood a few feet away, his face a frightened mask.

'I need food,' said Dave. 'Anything. I need –'

He faded out again and when he came to he coughed. Choked. Both boys were kneeling by him. Jack held a water bottle to Dave's lips, the warm water running down his chin as much as his throat. Dave coughed again more violently. The storm of gunfire had been joined by something else, a thumping series of dull concussive thuds followed by the distant roar of explosions. He could make sense of none of it. He was too far gone. He almost shouted at Jack that water wouldn't help, but it did. A little. Just enough to clear his mind for a second and show him what he had to do. There was food aplenty here. Meat for the taking.

All it would need was one bite. Just one. That first forbidden taste.

'Dad?' said Toby. 'What is it?'

'Are you all right?' Jack asked.

Dave blinked and this time his eyes were crusted with blood and daemon ichor. He could still see clearly though. The bright eyes of his children. The delicate curves of their cheeks and necks. Their slender arms.

Just one bite.

He pushed them away, reached a fist into the shattered skull of the Sliveen warrior and scooped out a handful of blue-green pulp. It was still hot and seemed to shiver in his hand. Before he could stop himself he shovelled the lump of daemon offal into his mouth and swallowed, forcing it down past the gag reflex.

'Oh gross!' cried Jack.

Toby just shuddered with deep revulsion. Dave's own body shuddered too, partly with revulsion, but partly with revelation and the strength of redemptive healing.

'Yeah, let's not tell Mom about that, okay?' he grunted as something hot and powerful coursed through him. He reached for the broken skull of the Sliveen again, but caught himself at the last moment. Or perhaps he just caught the expression of shock and disgust on the faces of his children.

Either way, he stayed his hand. He did not need to eat again. The hunger was gone, even as his body burned with the heat of healing, the pangs which had crippled and threatened to end him dissipated as thoroughly as morning mist on a summer's day.

That was when he knew they were doomed.

* * *

Threshy knew what was wrong. Those fucking meathead SEALs. Igor the giant fag, and Allen the corn-fed cunt. His Threshrendum had taken out Hooper's warp drive, but the SEALs and the Russian woman had put out such a withering volume of fire that the first wave of Hunn dominants had been cut down, or tripped up by the fallen, burning bodies of their nest mates. And now Gaddis was putting out his own personal artillery barrage with that jeep-mounted grenade launcher.

Cowering behind a granite outcropping, cringing at every bomb burst, Threshy prayed that Gaddis wouldn't raise the muzzle of the launcher and drop a few rounds right on top of him. If the SEAL knew he and Guyuk were out here, he'd target them in a heartbeat.

The lord commander gave every impression of having lost his mind in the maelstrom of fire and high explosive. Until Compt'n ur Threshrend realised Guyuk hadn't cracked up. He was laughing. Roaring with laughter.

Maybe he had cracked up.

'They fight well for cattle,' the lord commander bellowed as long yellow and red streams of tracer fire snapped over his head. 'They slaughter us like vermin, Superiorae. The scrolls will resound with tales of this night.'

'You fucking looney,' muttered Threshy. Or maybe it was Compton. Or maybe Trevor Candly. The empath daemon was so messed up with fear and shock he might even have reverted to thresh version 1.0.

The stupid old fuck was actually enjoying this. He was blowing his wad as the cattle blew the shit out of his thrall. Threshy dared not even raise an eyestalk for fear of having it shot off his head, but he didn't need to. He could see perfectly well what was happening through the eyestalks of the veteran Threshrendum Majorae who observed the battle from all the points of the compass, and stopped Hooper from orbing – from *warping* – out here and killing them all. Threshy dug himself deeper into the damp sandy soil, watching the slaughter from six different vantage points, as though through the eyes of an insect.

The first wave of Hunn dominants who had led the charge had been broken by savage automatic weapons fire and expertly placed volleys of grenades. It seemed that both SEALs and the Russian were equipped with underslung twenty- or even thirty-millimetre launchers, and the popping *shunk-shunk-shunk* of their fat, high explosive rounds leaving the barrels preceded another storm of detonations amongst the Hunn, who still hadn't learned not to bunch up under fire.

Not like the Grymm, he thought sourly.

Through the eyes of the Threshrendum he could see them fanning out, dispersing, sacrificing the power of the massed charge, but blunting the impact of the fiery hammer blows landing amongst the thrall.

He had seen one Sliveen scout make it through the intersecting fields of fire and even gain entry to the upper floor of the cottage, but there had been no falling away in the murderous barrage of armour-piercing and tracer fire. The scout was probably toast.

Guyuk's laughter was threatening to drive him mad, before the gunfire wiped him out, and Threshy started to cast around looking for one of the portals maintained by the Masters of the Ways. It never hurt to have an exit plan.

* * *

'Come with me,' Dave said. 'Quickly, and keep low. Try not to show your heads above the window sills.'

Toby and Jack did as they were told. They closed up behind Dave and followed him down the stairs. He paused, just the briefest of moments, at the top step, where he could see through a window looking out over the driveway that Igor was crouched in the back of the Growler. The thumping and thudding detonations were explained by the weapon he fired. The grenade launcher.

The giant SEAL laid down a sweeping arc of fire and destruction in front of the cottage, holding back the charge of the Dread Company. Zach stood beside him, raking the killing zone with the heavy machine gun. Between them, and Karen and Pat picking off flankers, they had broken the first assault.

But Dave knew there would be more.

Dave knew everything the Sliveen knew.

As he hurried down the stairs – 'Careful on these bottom steps, boys, I think I broke them' – he knew the forces arrayed against them were too great. He knew the Horde could absorb all of the firepower currently holding them at bay. Absorb it, survive it, and wait it out. Dawn was still too far away. They would wait until the calflings had exhausted their magicks and then they would simply overrun them. Hundreds of Hunn and Grymm and Sliveen pouring in through the doors and windows, hacking and slashing, stabbing and biting and tearing until they were done. And there was nothing Dave or Karen could do in return. Six ancient and powerful Threshrendum ringed the cottage, ensuring the champions could not warp, all of them answering to Compt'n ur Threshrend who sat safely some distance away, enjoying the spectacle in the company of Lord Guyuk ur Grymm.

'*Karen*,' Dave called out over the cacophony of battle.

She turned away from her firing post and as soon as she saw him she knew.

'Oh gross! You didn't! You ate its brains?'

'He totally did!' Jack cried out. 'And that's what I said.'

'It was awesome but,' Toby said from where he crouched hidden behind Dave's legs. 'Dad went UFC on that Bigfoot.'

'Sounds more like your Dad went KFC on him,' said Annie as she scrabbled across the floor, never raising her head above knee level. 'Toby, Jack, to me,' she said in a high voice. 'I'm going to get them out the back on Dad's boat.'

'No you're not,' both Dave and O'Halloran said at once. Pat had taken up position near the window where Igor had been standing before he'd run out to the Growler. Immediately after speaking he lifted his shotgun in a smooth, unhurried motion, and fired off a round with a dull roar.

'You won't get ten yards,' Dave said. 'Archers will cut you down.'

But he had a thought.

'Haul them down into the root cellar. It's better than up here.'

As if to emphasise the point a flurry of iron bolts poured in through the window, provoking an answering hail of fire from Karen.

'Go. Go on now,' Dave said. 'We'll hold them off up here.' Knowing he was lying to them as he said it.

Well, it wasn't like that was the first time.

He shielded the boys with his own body, ushering them into the kitchen which ran off the lounge. Annie crawled through after them. The root cellar was an old damp dugout carved from the granite of the rocky headland. Pat used to tell stories about bootleggers having used it, and Annie's old man had indeed kept a few crates of booze down there. The kitchen windows looked out on the waters of greater Penobscot Bay and for a second Dave considered whether Annie might be right and they could escape over water. But he dismissed the idea for the same reason he'd rejected it before. A Sliveen archer could put a war shaft through them hundreds of yards out into the bay. At its leisure.

They were much less exposed to *arrakh* fire in here. Dave hauled up the heavy trapdoor, and he was about to jump down into the dark hole and check it out for them when Karen called to him.

'Hooper. Better get out here now.'

'Get in,' he said to Annie, no time to argue.

The boys, who were forever sneaking into the cellar to play, needed no invitation. Annie hesitated.

'Is it going to be all right, Dave? Are we going to get through this?'

'Yeah,' he lied. 'Just get down out of sight and stay there. Don't come out until I come to get you. No matter what you hear.'

'Hooper. Hurry the fuck up.'

'Coming,' he yelled back at Karen. 'Go on,' he said. 'Everything will be fine.'

Annie looked back out the door toward the lounge room, where things were obviously not fine.

'I don't blame you,' she said, turning her eyes on his. 'I don't blame you for this. You came back for them.'

'And for you,' he said. It seemed the right thing to say.

'Now I know you're lying.'

She followed their boys down into the cellar and he closed the trapdoor behind them, wishing he had time to find them some candles or a torch.

'HOOPER!'

'Coming. Fuck. This is *just* like being home.'

He ran back through to the lounge. Something was missing. The big guns had stopped firing.

They were about to be overrun.

33

'Now, Superiorae! Up, up and into the fight. We will hack them down.'

The Lieutenants Grymm who had prevented Lord Guyuk from charging pointlessly into the teeth of the human fire now flanked him, ready to charge alongside their commander. The entire thrall, what survived of it, was moving as one.

The terrible fires of the human warriors had sputtered, and although they had not died away completely they no longer cut through the ranks of the Dread Company like the hot breath of *dar Drakon*. Individual Hunn and Grymm still fell to aimed fire, but their loss only meant greater glory for those who remained.

'Have at them, Threshrend,' roared Guyuk. 'We have exhausted their magicks, broken their defences and now we shall crush them under our dead if the need of it be so.'

He plucked the tiny daemon from where it hid behind the cover of a rocky spur, and thrust it into the charge, not judging the little creature for its cowardice, for he too had wisely sheltered from the worst of the firestorm. Instead, Lord Guyuk ur Grymm felt sincerely grateful to the mutant empath, the daemonum and the host of calfling souls it had consumed.

Its plan seemed to be working.

They had the Dave trapped and at their mercy.

He roared with good-natured laughter at that. The mercy of the Horde. Compt'n ur Threshrend squeaked something like a protest but Guyuk was having none of it.

'Stiffen those eyestalks, Threshrend! Summon up the ichor. Set your fang tracks a-blur and stretch wide your jaws to feast upon *DAR IENAMIC*.'

'Dar ienamic!' roared the Lieutenants Grymm, and within moments Guyuk's entire thrall had taken up the chant to honour the foe it was about to devour.

'Yeah yeah, the fucking enemas,' cried Compt'n ur Threshrend. 'We all love the fucking enemas.'

'That's the spirit,' Lord Guyuk shouted over the din and crash and mad shrieking tumult of war and murder.

He started at a run through the thin forest, toward the little barracks house where the Dave and his thrall were entrapped. It was pricked and feathered with the shafts of arrakh-mi and arrakh-du. The path forward was beset with the fallen bodies of Grymm warriors and Hunn dominants, some of them burning fiercely with the eldritch flames that consumed those touched by Drakon fire. But Guyuk knew there was no magick to this. Just the human magick of 'science' which had fashioned the tiniest of the calflings' *arrakh* munitions and locked within them the secret of fire. Even now, a long sinuous line of yellow calfling fire licked out of a port in the stone redoubt and took the head off one of his own Lieutenants Grymm, spraying hot steaming skull meats over the lord commander's face.

'It is good,' he roared at the Threshrend he half-carried, half-dragged along beside him. 'It is meat for the Horde, Threshrend.'

* * *

'Where the hell have you been?' Karen shouted at Dave.

She tossed something through the air and he caught it without thinking.

Lucille.

The return of the strength and spirit he'd felt upon choking down the brains of his slain *ienamic* redoubled as the hardwood shaft slapped into his palm. Lucille's battle song swelled with the power of a massed choir in Dave's head. He felt her strength, her will, her killing soul flow in to him. And he saw that it was still useless.

They were all going to die.

The night moved toward them.

A dark, unbroken line of Horde warriors charged across the short distance between the cleared forest and Pat O'Halloran's perfectly maintained front lawn. Or at least it had been perfectly maintained until Zach had parked a jeep on it and he and Igor had raked the free-fire zone with bullets and bombs. It was the dark hour before dawn. Not the gloaming pre-dawn in which the promise of sun is present in the creeping grey light where shadows take on form. No. It was the darkest of hours and monsters moved through it.

'Don't bother,' Karen warned him, sensing his instinctual reaction to warp out there and start swinging. 'Threshers.'

Having exhausted the big, jeep-mounted guns, the SEALs had retreated inside again. Zach stood in cover by the same window he'd first guarded. He fired two short bursts from his machine gun, and threw a hand grenade out into the night. It exploded a few seconds later. Igor fired blind, poking the muzzle of his machine gun out of the window while remaining in cover, squeezing the trigger once, twice, three times. He cursed, swapped out the magazine and turned back to the fight, loosing a strangled scream into the chaos when two arrakh-mi, shot from an extreme angle, punched into his shoulder and thigh. The big man went down, his gun dropping to the floor amongst dozens of spent shell casings.

Dave leaped to him, covering the fallen commando with his own body as he swept up the gun and stood in the ruin of the window frame firing into the mass of accelerating Hunn and Grymm berserkers.

'Hunn. Hunn. Hunn ur HORDE.'

The gun bucked in his hand, surprising him. He'd half expected to have to fuck around with the safety, which he doubted he could find in time.

'Hunn ur HORDE. Hunn ur HORDE.'

The mad horror of the monster charge slowed down, but only in his mind, the way everything slows in extreme moments. It wasn't magic, just human neurology. There was magic, however, in the way he was able to size up the shots he took. The lines, angles and calculations of timing and effect he had first experienced in New Orleans were available to him again, like a pull-down menu of enchanted options. He squeezed the trigger and the gun roared. Two armour-piercing rounds and one tracer bullet left the muzzle, travelling straight and true across the fifty yards to the leading dominant, taking the Hunn at the base of his throat and climbing up the fright mask of his face. The monster's head exploded like a fat piece of jungle fruit dropped from a great height and he went down, lifeless arms and legs tripping two more Hunn behind him. Dave killed them with three round bursts, right into the cabbage. The gun, Dave understood, was set to fire three bullets for every trigger pull, and he wished he knew enough about the weapon to quickly set it to single shot. He was certain he could make every shot he took.

But there was no time.

Igor disappeared from beneath him, crying out as Zach dragged him away from the exposed position by the window.

'Get him in the cellar with the others,' Dave yelled as he cut down a Sliveen scout that had cocked a long arm to launch a clutch of throwing stars at him. Multi-tasking like a boss. 'We can retreat there. Hold them off.'

'*HUNN UR HORDE.*'

The chant seemed to grow in volume as more and more of the beasts emerged at a run from the trees, undeterred by the pathetic blatting of O'Halloran's Ruger; the dry cough of Karen's submachine gun clicking on an empty magazine.

'Do it,' she cried at Zach as he struggled to haul Igor out of harm's way.

Dave snorted with laughter at that.

Maybe they'd be out of harm's way in Tasmania.

'Hooper is right. We can hold them at the choke points,' she shouted, and she sounded mad for it.

'You're fucking crazy,' Dave said as she drew the long killing steel of *Ushi to yasashi to.* 'But hot. Crazy hot.'

'No. I am not crazy,' she said, and her voice was different. It was *her* voice, in his head, not his ears. She spoke into him as Ekaterina Varatchevsky, a loyal daughter of the Rodina. 'I am Russian,' she cast into his mind, holding her katana so that it glinted in the moonlight. 'And this is my fate. *Ushi to yasashi to.* Sorrowful and unbearable.'

'*Hunn. Hunn. Hunn ur HORDE.*'

'Help Zach with Igor,' Dave yelled at O'Halloran. The Navy

SEAL had dragged his comrade all the way into the kitchen, a thick blood trail marking his passage. But he was going to have trouble getting him down the ladder into the root cellar. The old seadog slung his shotgun over one shoulder and hurried to lift the trapdoor as Zach manoeuvred the wounded man over the lip and down into the dark. A monstrous face appeared at the kitchen window, then disappeared in a gaudy green and yellow splash as Dave swung the submachine gun around and snapped off a tight burst, threading a bright, neon ribbon of tracers over Zach and Pat as they bent to the task of lowering Igor down.

The machine gun was empty. It might have had a grenade he could have fired off, but there was no time to check and he wasn't sure he'd be able to work the underslung launcher anyway. He tossed the weapon aside and took up Lucille as Igor slipped out of sight and Zach unseated his fighting knife. He too was out of ammo.

Dave heard him reciting the Lord's Prayer as the first of the daemon killers hit the front porch at a run.

'. . . thy Kingdom come, thy will be done, on earth as it is in Heaven . . .'

O'Halloran's Ruger barked fire and thunder and seemed the loudest noise Dave had heard in the confined space all night. A swarm of super-heated wasps flew past his face and punched into the chest, throat and face of the first dominant to reach the house. The Hunn collapsed in a crashing train wreck of armour plate and flopping, flying limbs. The corpse slammed into the window frame, blocking it just a little with its bulk.

'Go!' Dave yelled at the remaining SEAL. 'Get down there with Igor and my family. Take Pat. He keeps trying to shoot me.'

But Zach did not. He bundled the protesting old seadog down the steps and slammed the cellar door shut on top of them.

And the three remaining calflings, champions all, stood into the thunder of the Horde. Dozens of the beasts, hundreds of them, were mere yards away now, moving as fast as big cats. Dave heard glass breaking. Wood cracking and crashing. The charge hit the little red brick cottage like a tsunami made flesh. Rank, profane, corrupt daemon flesh. The entire structure shook and shuddered and unknown tonnages of snarling, seething monster meat piled up outside, trapped for a few, undoubtedly short moments, like a crowd in a theatre piling up at the doors after someone shouts 'Fire!'

Karen's magic blade flashed. Sorrowful and unbearable. Carving meat and cleaving bones.

Zach produced another firearm from somewhere. A handgun, which he fired slowly, methodically, into the pile-up at the doors and windows, picking his targets carefully. He had all the time in the world because his time in the world was surely done. He was building a barricade of dead monster bodies, laying down each huge stone as carefully as a master mason.

In Dave's hands, Lucille did not so much sing as she pealed to the heavens, like the ringing of a great, black cathedral bell, while the ur-Champion swung mightily at the press of unyielding muscle and bone, forcing it to yield to the savage bite of the enchanted weapon's cutting edge. He and Karen fell into a dance, a rapid blurring ballet of slaughter that hacked and smashed at the black wave which crashed on them. The Hunn and their Grymm allies howled and bellowed in rage and pain and the psychotic need to close and kill, but all they did was close and die. At least as long as the champions held.

And then, at last, inevitably, they fell.

Not through fatigue or a failure of will. Not through a want of courage or *gurikh*. It was simple math. Speed and mass. So many daemonum piled on so quickly that first one sword swing missed, and then a hammer blow, and then another, and then the room was full of thrashing claws and blades. Zach's gun fell silent as the last magicks of men petered out.

Hot drool spat and flew as Dave swung Lucille's axehead into the skull of a Sergeant Grymm, hacking off the jaw. Beside him, Zach stabbed a Sliveen MasterScout in the throat as the creature scrabbled to free itself from the seething crush. His knife hand, his whole arm, was dark with daemon ichor. In his other hand he held a single grenade, unable to use it without a clear throw. Karen was no longer slashing, she simply plunged her steel into the mountain of monster flesh, stabbing deeply again and again. Dave smashed at the writhing pile, severing arms, cracking skulls, showering brains and bone and fangs around him. He thought, for one brief shining second, that they might just hold them. And then the dam burst and hell poured through.

Zach Allen screamed as a Sergeant Grymm impaled him on a broken pike and threw the dying SEAL over his massive shoulder, into a ravening horde of teeth and claws.

'NO!' Dave screamed, even louder than Zach. He launched himself after his friend but was thrown back by an explosion. The grenade Zach had been holding. He must have already pulled the pin and been holding the lever in place. It detonated in the savage, roiling tempest of Hunn and Grymm as they tried to tear him apart.

The Horde surged in and over them. Dave lost sight of Karen and lashed out with boot and fist, and in the final moments with fingernails and teeth. The fiends piled on top of him, protecting their prey momentarily as he closed his jaws around the throat of a Grymm warrior, felt the monster's own fangs puncture his shoulder. The world was a cyclonic gyre of madness and violence and loss. He was buried under mountains of writhing, roaring monsters. He had lost contact with Karen. He had lost Zach. Lost Igor. Lost Annie and his boys and soon enough he would lose his life.

He forced his teeth together, his tiny jaw not suited to ripping and tearing like these brutes. The crush of so many foul-smelling creatures muted the uproar around him, but he thought he could hear the howling of the Grymm as its hide tore between his teeth and the thick, acidic daemon ichor flowed into his mouth, choking him. Almost drowning him. The Grymm wailed and flailed and tried to get away from the ridiculous little calfling which had dared to nip at it. Dave saw, or maybe imagined in a blurred shutter-rush of imagery, a giant chunk of A-Grade Dave steak being torn from his torso. Imagined his head being pulled from his body.

The Grymm bayed in horror as Dave refused to unclamp his jaws, instead working them harder, sucking more and more of the monster's blood from its veins. The snarling death throes of the elite warrior increased in volume until Hooper thought he might go deaf before he died. With one snarling bellow of his own he tried to rip another mouthful of hot meat from the Grymm, coughing and all but choking as the head fell away.

He'd bitten it right off.

The twitching corpse rolled away and Dave clawed his way up out of the heavy scrum, laying about him with his fists like a drunk in a car lot brawl, swinging and hitting nothing, because there was nothing to hit. The Hunn. The Grymm. The Horde.

They were dead or dying.

Dave Hooper perceived this only dimly through the red veil that hung over everything. He shook his head, throwing off long ropy strings of daemon offal and ichor. The Grymm he had decapitated was not snarling and he had not bitten its head clean off.

A woman, not Karen, stood in front of him, her face a mask, painted in blood. She was short and thin, birdlike he would have said, dressed in an army uniform of some sort. She wore a strange collar.

A priest's collar, he realised, without being able to accept the truth of it.

And she carried a snarling chainsaw.

Threshy knew something was wrong before the pile-up at the doors and windows of the cottage. He could have told them that would happen. Not that he gave a silver-plated shit. The more of these dumb, bloodthirsty fucks got jammed up between him and Hooper, the better as far as the Superiorae dar Threshrendum ur Grymm was concerned. Unlike Guyuk, he'd be happy with leftovers.

Hell, he'd be happy kicking back watching the movie in his pad with little Polly Farrell riding his monster cock like a pussy cat on a Roomba. That was wrong he knew. He should be thinking about *eating* her – not, you know – eating her. But as he was dragged beside or mostly behind Lord Guyuk ur Grymm, rushing headlong toward the human champions, all he wanted to do was get as far the fuck away from them as possible.

His stomachs knotted and sloshed with acid and anxiety as Guyuk hit the rear of the tightly compressed daemonum multitudes surrounding the cottage. Hopping and stumbling over the corpses of dozens of scarred and tattooed veteran Hunn and Grymm to get there hadn't helped. But as Guyuk elbowed and shouldered his way into the heaving pack, Threshy couldn't help but think about what a tempting target it would make for a gun run by an Apache, or even a flurry of rockets from a Warthog. There were so many of them mounded up in a dense press around the house that for a good pilot it would be like carving a big old hunk of breast meat from the Thanksgiving turkey. And stuck here at the back, his cock would be first on the chopping block.

Suddenly Compt'n ur Threshrend was raking and snarling and muscling his way deeper into the rank and overheated throng of warriors. His only hope; to bury himself in a bunker of armoured daemon-hide.

'Now you have found your *gurikh*, small one,' Guyuk roared happily. 'Have at them, Threshrend. Honour to your nest and proof that She of the Horde did beget you.'

But Threshy was too scared to pay much attention to the murderous old fool. He had not just been eating doughnut-sellers and pointy-headed neckbeards after all. He'd snacked down on some prime special forces grey matter and those dead souls were telling him that his warty little ass was sitting on a big red bullseye. He needed cover. It was all too easy to imagine the ripping snarl of miniguns, the cracking boom of rockets exploding, the protective mass of monster flesh and iron armour disintegrating around him. A shudder seemed to run through the ground, through the very mass of Guyuk's thrall as though Threshy's fears had propagated outward, possibly riding the carrier wave of the Threshrend Majorae. And then he was no longer imagining the industrial jackhammer sound of machine guns. He could hear it. For fucking reals.

The crushing weight of hundreds of enormous daemonum pressed in on him even harder for just a moment and then disappeared entirely. The near total blackness of being caught beneath so many behemoths gave way to the relative darkness of open night, and the terrible man-made lightning of explosive ordnance and high velocity cannon fire.

'By the withered scrotum of A'brctson ur Grymm,' Lord Guyuk thundered.

Human Drakon fire, the eldritch rivers of light which tore through good armour and hard flesh as though they were but insubstantial dreams, ploughed great furrows through his host. The lord commander, old but wise in the ways of war, dived sideways, narrowly avoiding a hot, bright torrent of fire that swept over the ranks immediately in front of him, disintegrating them.

He could hear the fearsome reverberations of human war machines now, the iron Drakon they called 'choppers' – a grimly appropriate appellation as the flying engines hacked gruesome chunks out of his command.

The fog of war was thick upon the world.

He knew not the disposition of his forces, but in a moment of insight he knew that Superiorae Compt'n ur Threshrend would describe them as 'fucked'. Of the empath there was nil to be seen as Guyuk thudded to the wet earth, landing on a sizeable boulder which broke the bone cage of his upper torso in a place or two. The last he had seen of his pro-consul Compt'n had been lost in the blood frenzy, raking and snapping at the tightly packed thrall to have at the Dave and his lieutenants. The brave little urmin squirt had proved his mettle after all. Were he fallen, his fall alone would be enough to do the Sect grave loss. The lord commander would see to it that the scrolls reflected this. But first he must survive the engagement himself.

Guyuk rolled and grunted. The pain was a sweet and familiar balm, bringing him back to himself as he climbed to his aging knees and quickly up on to his hind-claws. The cloak of night still lay across the Above, but the darkness was rent with the fire and lightning of Man.

Guyuk was no fool.

He had known a counter-ambush was always possible and his Grymm at least were drilled in tactical withdrawal under fire. The Hunn were not. It was good. Their sacrifice would cover his departure from the field. He cast about, looking for his Guardian Grymm, the surviving officer at least, but could find no sign of the lieutenant in the chaos. Another swooping attack by a great iron flying machine further reduced the survivors of the first attack and Lord Guyuk ur Grymm turned on his heel.

They had come close.

So close.

The risk had been worth it, but the rewards had proved meagre.

He turned and began a loping run back toward the Way back to the UnderRealms.

The inky blackness of the portal hovered on the breach between the worlds in the thicker woods from which they had emerged. He hoped he might see Compt'n ur Threshrend already in retreat toward the demesne of the Horde, but of the brave little empath and adeptus there was no sign.

'Mr Hooper?' the woman said, not even flinching as two shotgun blasts rang out and another wash of daemon ichor sprayed walls that were already running with it.

Dave spun around, giddy, almost losing his footing in the charnel house. An enormous black woman in a police officer's uniform racked another round into her riot gun – that's what they used to call those things in the olden days, Dave thought, stupid and numb. They called them riot guns. The blast took the head clean off a Sliveen which had been crawling out the front door.

He heard thudding, the sharp-dull thudding of helicopters, and for no reason at all he thought J2 had come to get him from the Longreach. The jackhammer pounding of heavy machine guns cut through the chop of rotor blades. The snarling chainsaw was loud enough to muffle them both.

'Mr Hooper?'

He ran shaking hands over his face and through his hair, which was matted with gore.

He had hair again. That's right.

'Mr Hooper, sir?'

It was the woman. The black lady. Although, he thought dully, you weren't allowed to call people black anymore. Were you? Or ladies. No. You definitely didn't call your modern Ms a lady.

'Where's Karen?' he asked. His voice sounded muffled to him, as though he was talking through a pillow. He put a finger in his ear and it came away crusted in blood.

'Ms Varatchevsky?' the black woman, the sheriff, said. 'She's out front, with the medics and Ms Ashbury.'

'What?' Dave said. 'Emmeline? What? The fuck?'

It was hard to hear himself over the chainsaw and he frowned at the other woman, small and white. He hoped she would understand him, because he understood very little.

'Oh, sorry,' she said. She turned it off. The chain stopped turning, the teeth came to rest. They were strangely shiny. How could that be? The woman and the body of the chainsaw were as badly soaked in blood as him. But those sharp steel teeth gleamed as if they had just been cleaned.

'Hooper.'

'Dave?'

Everyone knew his name but nobody was saying anything. He knew these voices. He tried to turn toward them but his legs were still caught in the thick carpet of monster corpses and he toppled forward. The thin, grey-haired lady with the priest's collar and the magic chainsaw reached out for him with surprising speed. Her free hand clamped securely but gently around his arm.

'Careful,' she said. 'You wouldn't want to get hurt.'

'No,' Dave said. 'Thanks . . . Em? Heath?'

Professor Emmeline Ashbury and Captain Michael Heath stood at the front door, both looking tired. It was still dark outside. They looked like the only people hereabouts who hadn't been swimming in the rendering vats at an abattoir.

'Where's the others?' Dave asked.

'We're looking for them,' Heath said. 'I was hoping to find them in here with you.'

'They're not?' Dave asked.

But that was a stupid question.

Stupid questions were all Dave had.

Emmeline hurried over to him, bearing medicated swabs and protein bars. She had to climb over a raft of bodies, some of them twitching. He thought the obvious digust on her face was down to this and his appearance, but then he remembered that despite his appearance she probably wanted to fuck him as soon as she got within spitting distance. That was probably difficult for her.

'You'd better clean yourself up,' she said, all busy work and stern advice.

'Who . . .?'

He waved a hand numbly at the two women.

'Sheriff Sheila May Robertson,' the black woman said. 'Buttecracke County.'

She pronounced it 'Beyoo-cray'.

'Hi. I'm Pastor Nancy Kemp,' the other woman said, saluting him with the chainsaw. It seemed to weigh nothing in her hands.

Neither of them looked even remotely interested in a taste of ol' Dave's special sauce. They were like Karen, he understood dimly.

Dave pulled one leg out of the monster mash, as though extracting a boot from the sucking mud of a swamp. Emmeline let him lean against her, but she backed away, her face flushed, as soon as he had his balance.

'You guys are . . . you're like me, right? You killed something.'

They both nodded, but Dave stumbled away toward the kitchen. There were fewer bodies in here, none of them human. He wondered if Zach or Igor were back out in the lounge, buried under the dead, like he had been. And then he remembered. Zach was dead.

And Igor?

The trapdoor was closed, just as he had left it. Heath and Ashbury followed him into the kitchen with some difficulty. Heath's artificial leg wasn't made for hiking over bodies.

'I couldn't leave New York until I was sure we had Sheriff Robertson and the padre,' he said. 'They were in transit. We came straight here.'

'Karen said you would . . . do . . . She said there were five of us?'

Dave trailed off. Not sure what he was even trying to say.

Heath frowned but nodded.

'Mr Johnson remains in LA. He is, ah, working with another agency.'

Something about that sounded familiar, but Dave couldn't figure it out and right now he didn't care. Instead he kneeled down at the trapdoor and knocked on the thick wooden boards. Nothing. He pulled at the ring and heaved the door open. It swung and fell to the flagstones with a crash. Dave flinched away at the last moment in case Pat decided to let him have another face full of shot.

'It's me,' he said. 'It's over.'

Another lie. But one he could live with.

His heart felt as though it was slowing, possibly stopping, as he peered into the darkness. Nothing moved down there. No sound reached him from below.

Until he heard Annie.

'Dave? Is that you? Can we come out now?'

Dave's knees gave out and he collapsed to the gore-slicked floor.

Heath appeared beside him and helped Dave back to his feet. Emmeline produced a small torch which she shone down the hole.

'I'm sorry about Zach,' Dave said. 'He died. He's gone.'

Emmeline stiffened for a moment and he saw her working her jaw, biting down hard on the need to say something she probably meant and might even regret. Heath took in the news with a brusque nod, turning down of the corners of his mouth. The first face appeared in the small square of thin light that penetrated down into the root cellar.

O'Halloran, still holding his shotgun, pointing it up into Hooper's face.

'Third time lucky, Pat,' Dave croaked. Annie appeared behind her father, looked worried.

'Your friend, Igor. He's not well,' she said. 'We looked after him as best –'

'Medic!' Heath cried out. 'Medic! Stat!'

Two navy corpsmen bustled past Heath, Em and Hooper, and dropped down the wooden ladder into the cellar. They disappeared into the darkness as Dave's two sons appeared out of it into the light of Emmeline's torch.

'Dad?' said Toby. 'Can we come out now?'

Dave looked around what he could see of the house. It was rotten with death. But there was nothing for it.

'Sure,' he croaked, 'come on up. But just know, it's not pretty.'

Em and Pat helped Annie climb the ladder first. Heath peered down into the hole, anxious for news of Igor. The old man and the boys came up after Annie.

'Oh my god,' she breathed when she could see just a little of what had happened. 'Your friends? Are they all right? Karen and Zach?'

Dave shook his head.

'Zach's dead. Karen . . . I don't know . . .' he trailed off as more medics arrived, hauling a stretcher, and dropped into the cellar.

'I'll live.'

They all turned toward the familiar voice which now sounded different to Dave. Her accent, he thought. Her real accent. She's not pretending anymore. She looked about as bad as he felt.

'*Znal by gde upást*' – *solómki b podstelíl,*' she said and then translated. 'Would I know where I will fall down, I'd lay some straw.'

When they all stared at her she shrugged. 'It's a Russian thing.' And to Heath and Emmeline, 'Your man Allen fought bravely. Mourn him, then finish those who killed him. That's also a Russian thing.'

'Thank you, Colonel,' said Heath. 'We'll do our best.' He sounded as though he didn't think their best would be nearly good enough.

'How did he die?' Emmeline asked. 'Was it...' she trailed off, looking upset.

'He died well,' Karen offered.

'It was quick,' Dave added. 'He took a lot of them with him. And we'll take more. Promise.' He looked to Karen for confirmation.

'We will,' she agreed as she tore the top off a tube of energy gel.

Annie, who had corralled the boys into a corner of the kitchen, now herded them toward the door, saying to her father, 'Dad, I might go sit with Jack and Toby until we're ready to leave. We're still leaving, aren't we?' she asked Dave.

'We are,' he said, without bothering to check whether Heath agreed or not. 'You might want to go wait in Pat's den, I reckon. It's pretty gross in the lounge.'

'And there's a dead monster upstairs, Mom,' said Jack.

'Dad ate its brains,' Toby told everyone, just in case they'd missed the good news.

Pat led his daughter and grandsons out of the crowded kitchen. As he passed Dave he said, 'You did all right.' And that was all. That was about as good as it was ever going to get from Pat O'Halloran.

Annie stopped and wiped some of the daemon ichor from Dave's face, creating a small clean spot which she kissed, chastely.

'You did better than all right. Thank you for coming home.'

'It's not my home,' Dave said, more sad than anything else.

'You can always rebuild a home, Dave. Or make a new one.' She cast a quick glance at Emmeline and whispered. 'She keeps looking at you like, well . . . I think she really likes you.'

'And you don't?' Dave asked, his eyes narrowing.

Annie smiled, a lopsided expression.

'I know you,' she said and then she was gone.

Movement and noise from below signalled the corpsmen were ready to move Igor. They'd removed the *arrakh* bolts and strapped him to the stretcher, but it was going to be difficult lifting the heavy man up.

'I got it,' Dave said. 'Ekaterina? A little help?'

Colonel Varatchevsky quirked an eyebrow at him, questioning the use of her birth name, but she nodded as Dave dropped into the hole. All that Grymm ichor he'd drunk was doing him a powerful amount of good.

'I got this, boys,' he told the medics.

Igor was barely conscious, but his eyelids fluttered and he focused on Dave with a great effort.

'I still say you fight like an idiot,' he whispered.

'And I still say you punch like a girl,' said Dave as he took a firm but careful grip on the stretcher and lifted it gently up to Karen, who took it from him in one smooth, fluid motion.

'Wow,' said one of the medics.

Dave bent a little at the knees and jumped the eight feet up, out of the root cellar. Emmeline was bent down beside Igor fussing over him, but the wounded SEAL was out of it.

'So what now, Captain?' Karen asked Heath as the medics scrambled up from below and carried Igor away.

They followed the stretcher out of the kitchen. It was hard to believe the number of bodies in the wreckage of Pat O'Halloran's living room, but Dave could see even more of them outside. Zach would be out here somewhere. Unless . . . Dave turned away from the thought, and from memories of Urgon chewing through Marty Grbac. He could still hear the occasional gun blast, and every now and then, the snarl of a chainsaw. The good lady reverend going about God's work. The sun was coming up though, and it would do the real work of cleansing the earth for them. This part of it anyway.

'I don't suppose you found a stumpy little Thresher with a neckbeard out there, answers to the name Compt'n?' Dave said.

Heath was not ready to have his mood lifted.

'No,' he said. 'We didn't, but we'll keep looking.'

Emmeline appeared at his other elbow. Tears had cleared tracks down her dirty face.

'Michael,' she said. 'Poor Zach. And Igor. I said they should come up here.'

Dave and Heath spoke at the same time, saying the same thing.

'Bullshit.'

But it was Dave who went on.

'Em, if it was anyone's fault it was mine. Zach was with us right up until the end. I should have made him get in the cellar. But I didn't. I couldn't . . .'

He trailed off, feeling what he always felt around Heath. That he was being judged.

'I'm real sorry about Zach,' he said again, feeling guilty and responsible for the young man's death. He was standing very close to where he'd died. Heath held up one hand.

'Chief Allen was a warrior, Dave. Like your brother.'

Hooper felt a heavy swelling in his chest. It wasn't pride.

'Yep,' he said. 'He was. They were.'

Then he sighed.

'So. What now?'

Heath's eyes narrowed as he surveyed the wanton ugliness of the battlefield.

'I won't lie to you, Dave. It's going to get worse. Much worse. And I can't promise we'll win. But for now? Now we fight.'

ACKNOWLEDGEMENTS

These first three novels of The Dave have been a joy to write and much of that is down to the work of the editors and publishers who've nursed manuscripts and author from conception to delivery. Cate Paterson, Haylee Nash, Deonie Fiford and Lord Alex ur Lloyd in S'dney, and Tricia Narwani in Manhatt'n.

Before Dave ever got to them however, he was given a protein bar, a beer and a hurry along by my research guy, Master Scolari SF Murphy.

And before Murph ever met him, Dave was willed into being by Russ Galen, my agent superiorae who dealt with forces beyond our comprehension.

Writing all three books at once was both a challenge and a gift. One of the unexpected benefits was being able to see reader reactions to the characters and their relationships in *Emergence* while I was still working on the hot drafts of *Resistance*. I made a few tweaks here and there in response to feedback and I'd like to say thanks to everyone who reached out at my blog or online. I do listen and it does help.

Finally, I write these words as my long-suffering family plays without me in the backyard. They don't put up with nearly as many shenanigans as the Hooper clan, but they do have more than their fair share to endure.

My thanks to them and now I'd best get out there. I think the dog has chased something into the pool again.

ABOUT THE AUTHOR

John Birmingham is the author of the cult classic *He Died With a Falafel in His Hand*; the award-winning history *Leviathan*; the Axis of Time series: *Weapons of Choice, Designated Targets* and *Final Impact*, and the *Stalin's Hammer: Rome* ebook; and the Disappearance trilogy: *Without Warning, After America* and *Angels of Vengeance*.

Between writing books he contributes to a wide range of newspapers and magazines on topics as diverse as the future of media and national security. Before becoming a writer he began his working life as a research officer with the Defence Department's Office of Special Clearances and Records.

You can find John at his blog, http://cheeseburgergothic. com and on Twitter @johnbirmingham. You can also buy his books at johnbirmingham.net.

Want to save the world? Join the conversation on Twitter at #TheDave.

For more fantastic fiction, author events, exclusive excerpts, competitions, limited editions and more:

VISIT OUR WEBSITE
titanbooks.com

LIKE US ON FACEBOOK
facebook.com/titanbooks

FOLLOW US ON TWITTER
@TitanBooks

EMAIL US
readerfeedback@titanemail.com